LOST IN TRANSITION

LOST IN TRANSITION

A NOVEL

JAKE WARNER

CourtYard Editions
Berkeley

Lost in Transition is full of real places and events. But the story itself, and those who people it, are entirely fictitious. So if you think you've met one of its characters at Amherst, Puerto Escondido or in the lobby of Tokyo's Imperial Hotel—you didn't.

ISBN: 979-8-218-08300-7
Published by CourtYard Editions
Berkeley, CA
info.courtyardeditions.net

For Toni,
always
stunning

You only lose what you cling to.
BUDDHA

Not all who wander are lost.
J.R.R. TOLKIEN

To get lost is to learn the way.
AFRICAN PROVERB

EARLY SEPTEMBER

WITH HER RIGHT HAND on the extended handle of her roller bag, and an overstuffed Oakland A's knapsack slung over her left shoulder, Tamiko Gashkin stops outside a door with her name on it. Fighting the urge to turn and retreat back along the dormitory hall, she reaches for the knob, only to hesitate. Then, pushing a renegade strand of long caramel-colored hair back over her shoulder, Tamiko knocks. When there is no reply, she knocks again, harder.

"I said come in, so come," a husky voice shouts.

Opening the door, Tamiko sees a small, pleasantly rounded young woman, eyes covered by a yoga-style pillow, lying on her back on one of two single beds, her short legs draped over a red bolster. "Eloise, is that you under there?" Tamiko asks tentatively.

Sitting up so abruptly the tiny pillow flies into the center of the dorm room, the girl's guppy-like mouth breaks into an unexpectedly wide grin as she says, "Tamiko O'Shea Gashkin, I presume."

"You presume correctly," Tamiko says, dragging her bag into the room behind her. Then, seeing that Eloise is off her bed and stacking several books on the floor, Tamiko asks, "What are you doing?"

"Getting ready to hug you."

"Gah! I'm not that tall!"

"But, I'm pretty much that short," Eloise replies, now perched dramatically on top of the textbooks, arms outstretched.

Stepping into the smaller girl's embrace Tamiko is struck by how warm and welcoming her soft round body feels. At a loss for something to say, Tamiko asks, "So how tall are you, anyway?"

"Wearing three pairs of hiking socks, almost five feet. *Et tu?*"

"Five-foot-ten with no socks and a crick in my knees," Tamiko replies, meeting Eloise's round brown eyes with her almond-shaped blue ones, reflecting that she's always drawn to people who make unabashed eye contact.

"Since you weren't here I picked a bed, but I'm happy to switch if you like this one better," Eloise says, nodding toward where she'd been lying.

"I'm good over here," Tamiko says, confirming her choice by slipping the heavy bag off her right shoulder and flopping on the bare mattress with something between a sigh and a groan.

"Tamiko, are you okay? When you texted that you would be a couple of days late because of a boyfriend emergency I imagined…"

"Despite wanting to beat Lec—the boyfriend in question—into small pieces with a stick, I guess I'm more or less okay-ish, or I will be as soon as I eat something. I had an emaciated bagel in Chicago, but nothing else since California ten hours ago."

"Dinner is in an hour and a half, but we can grab something over in town in the meantime."

"Antonio's?" Tamiko asks, hopefully, as she pushes up on her right elbow.

"Mind reader. The truth is that half the reason I enrolled here instead of Yale or Princeton was remembering from my college trip how good Antonio's pizza was," Eloise replies.

"Just curious, but what was the other half?"

"I got wait-listed at Yale, which felt ruder than being some nerd's backup prom date."

"And Princeton?"

"I look like a poisonous toad in orange, which is even worse."

As the mismatched girls walk across the few blocks from Amherst College to the small New England town with the same name, Eloise says, "In case you don't already know, your picture is on the front page of the college newspaper, which someone with a serious imagination deficit a century or two ago named 'The Student.'"

"You have to be kidding, right?" Tamiko asks, in genuine disbelief.

"Nope," Eloise replies matter-of-factly, somehow failing to register her new roommate's obvious discomfort. "You're, like, the pretty face for an article about first-year students who are expected to be hotshot athletes. It goes on and on about your being a high school phenom in two sports. I mean, Tamiko, from one of your emails I gathered you were recruited to pitch for the softball team, but you forgot to mention that before you switched to pitching you were a nationally ranked shortstop," Eloise says, pouting her lips. "And, who knew anything about basketball?" she adds, sticking out her tongue. "It's like, when I went online and saw that you were the point guard for one of California's best high school teams, I got intimidated about being your roommate since I was the klutz who gave coaches heartburn as far back as third grade. So, if you want to petition for a new roommate who doesn't trip over her own tiny feet, I'll get it, I guess."

"I thought when we FaceTimed in July and saw how we made each other laugh, we agreed we'd be friends for life."

"I hope so, but..."

"Count on it. But, hey, about the picture of me? I'm really hoping they didn't grab the one from the *Berkeley Times* where by some trick of the light you have to look twice to be sure I'm wearing a top."

"Bingo! Or maybe, given your body, *Eureka* is a better word."

"*Merde, merde* and triple *merde*," Tamiko says, her fists clenching. "But just so you know, I'm not playing basketball here at Amherst, which is something I've already told the coach so I absolutely don't get why the article even..."

"Really! I mean, why not play if you're so good?"

"Hmm," Tamiko replies with a long sigh as the two girls wait for the light in front of Amherst's red brick firehouse at the corner of Amity and North Pleasant streets. Too tired to come up with a short version of a story that started eleven years before when she was spotted as the best athlete in second grade and continued through her having played on an almost endless list of teams in seven sports, Tamiko says nothing. After waiting a few beats, she asks, "How about we talk about you for now and I'll try to explain how I learned to say *finis* to everything but softball when

I'm not so jet-lagged."

"I warn you, 'me' is my favorite subject, and once I start you'll probably wish you had ear plugs."

"Ha! When we FaceTimed you said you were hoping to get over being a virgin before school started. And then in August, you texted *'Been there, done that'* under a beach pic of this good-looking dude with his arm draped around you."

"Yup, finally! I mean, Tamiko, or do people ever call you Tami, which is beyond cute for sure?"

"I'm in recovery from a lifetime of Tami."

"Say no more, I spent years trying to escape 'Elli' Island. So, like, anyway, I was going to say that my dating history before this summer was almost nonexistent since I went to this tiny private high school in Palm Beach, Florida. To put it tamely, the guy choice was on the anorexic side of skinny. Add the world's most cliché helicopter parents, who hovered no more than ten feet over my head 24/7, and even designed boy-proof summer vacations, and you…"

"But this summer you obviously broke free," Tamiko interrupts, hoping to encourage Eloise to skip to the exciting part of her tale.

"Right, like I told you, my dad was scheduled to have his hip replaced by a hotshot specialist in Boston in early August with our whole family staying in a hotel up there for two or three weeks after the surgery. Fortunately, this prospect made my sister Phoebe, who's a year and a half younger, so overwhelmingly cranky that at the last moment the two of us were airmailed west to stay with Mom's sister Debra in Laguna Beach."

"As in Southern California, right?"

"Definitely. Deb has a house perched on a cliff a couple coves north of town. I mean, like, Tamiko, to get to the beach you walk across a postage-sized patch of lawn, down forty stone steps and *voilà*."

"And if I remember your email, Laguna's where you met Mr. Chill?"

"Yup, the day after we arrived Aunt Deb invited a bunch of neighbors over for drinks so Phoebe and I wouldn't feel like strangers on the beach, which, during the week especially, is kinda like a private club since the public access path at one end is easy to miss. It turned out that the family five houses to the north also had visitors, two cute brothers out from Milwaukee, also without their parents. Caleb, or 'Mr. Chill,' is a junior at the University of Wisconsin in Madison and his younger brother, Ben, is a senior in high school."

"Yo! Who says God is dead? All four of you must have been hanging from the moon," Tamiko says as she makes a fist and taps Eloise's.

"Like, pretty much literally. I mean, Tamiko, at home I was allowed two sips of watered wine on my eighteenth birthday and here, suddenly, my aunt was pouring margaritas from a pitcher."

"For Phoebe too?"

"Phoebe was limited to half of one because she's not eighteen, which Aunt Deb believes is the sensible drinking age. But, as it turned out, a little tequila goes a long way with my minx of a sister."

"What a story," Tamiko says as they reach Antonio's, a narrow pizza take-out on Amherst's main street that displays at least thirty types of pizza behind a long glass counter. As the two girls join a line of seven or eight bantering guys, several wearing Hampshire College T-shirts, which identifies them as attending the smaller of Amherst's two other colleges, Eloise continues, too excited to lower her voice.

"Anyway, as I was draining my second margarita and Caleb was off searching for the pitcher, Aunt Deb leaned over and said in a neutral tone someone might use to point out a left turn lane, 'Just so you know, if you take another sip of that Caleb will have your heels up in the bushes ASAP.'"

When Eloise pauses for effect, Tamiko recognizes her cue and asks in a whisper she hopes will be catching, "Did you? Did he?"

"Well, since it was a moonless night it was plenty dark on the beach so we went down there instead," Eloise brays excitedly. "And..."

Seeing that several of the guys have now turned to listen, Tamiko interrupts, "How about pizza first, then finish the story outside."

Back on North Pleasant Street a minute later, each girl juggling two slices of veggie pizza with sausage added, Tamiko asks, "Okay then, so, what was Phoebe up to while you were experiencing your big moment?"

"She and Ben were already on the beach when Caleb and I crept down the steps," Eloise replies with a laugh. "It's like Phoebe claimed later that her plan had been to stop at third base, but only went the last ninety feet because she heard me, well, er…, 'squealing' with delight," Eloise replies, as she wiggles the first two fingers of each hand to emphasize this was Phoebe's term.

"Ha, 'delighted squealing,' that's funny," Tamiko replies, deliberately ignoring her roommate's air quotes.

"I've never told her that most of my noise was the result of its hurting, especially at the beginning and then, just when I began to get into it, having to deal with the sand, which kinda…"

"Enough said," Tamiko interrupts with a sound halfway between a chuckle and a groan. "But anyway, Phoebe blames you for her going all the way?"

"Not at all. In fact, the next morning she kissed me for the first time since, like, she was ten and said 'Thanks, Sis, you finally came through for both of us.'"

As an only child, Tamiko knows that parsing sister politics is beyond her, so instead asks, "How long were the four of you in Laguna together?"

"A week."

"How did the logistics work? Like, in the daytime, I'm guessing you all were still very much in the mood, right?"

"Deb has a small guest room over her garage—kind of like a garage attic."

"Big enough for all four of you?" Tamiko asks, trying not to sound startled.

"Even über competitive sisters can arrange to take turns, especially when the older one gets first dibs."

"What about birth control?"

"Last winter when I got so horny I thought about propositioning our gay mailman, I snuck over to Planned Parenthood to get pills, which of course I kept hidden from my mom. And Phoebe swore they always used a condom."

"Your aunt was okay with all this?"

"She asked the same question you just did and when I gave her the same answer she replied, 'Enjoy your California beach vacation, but when you get home, remember—*loose lips sink aunties.*'"

. . . . .

Weighed down by a moist blanket of late afternoon heat, Tamiko and Eloise collapse on a shaded maple bench on the Amherst Common, a tree-dotted park that stretches a couple of blocks from town to college. They sit facing the faux-colonial bulk of the Inn on Boltwood. For nearly a century, it had been called The Lord Jeffery Inn after Jeffery Amherst, the general who, in addition to leading British and colonial troops to victory during the French and Indian War, allegedly distributed smallpox-infected blankets to the Indians. "I don't get why they renamed the Inn, but not the College, since they're both named after the same Indian killer," Eloise remarks, as she flicks a hunk of green pepper off her purple shorts.

"The official answer is that Amherst College is named after the town of Amherst, not Lord Jeffery," Tamiko answers, having read a *New York Times* article her mother had pointed out.

"But since the town is also named for Mr. Smallpox dude, doesn't that elevate hypocrisy to at least low earth orbit?," Eloise replies, indignantly.

"Logic isn't part of it," Tamiko says. "Being politically correct was easy when it came to renaming an obscure hotel, so they did. But, because it was far harder to change the name of either a prestigious college, or a prosperous town, they didn't. I mean, you must have noticed that when Americans rename things they much prefer it when they are a thousand miles away, and preferably in the South."

"Let's talk about something more interesting," Eloise says, clearly sorry she's ever raised the subject. "Ever since you told me you've had a real boyfriend for the entire last year I've been super-envious, so it's your turn to…"

"I'm not sure I still have him, or I guess, more accurately, whether he still wants me," Tamiko interrupts, realizing from hearing the edge in her voice that her anger is just beneath the surface.

"Still, if it's okay, can you show me the pics you must have on your phone?" Eloise asks gently.

Shrugging, Tamiko places her remaining pizza slice on the bench, taps the photo icon on her iPhone and hands it over.

"Skiing, surfing, smooching, you two seem to have mastered the three S's," Eloise says as she scrolls through the images. "But can you really surf? Or, are you just, like, posing as the world's most stunning Barbie in that shorty wetsuit?"

"A few years ago Lec, short for Alec, took off eighteen months from Cal Berkeley to travel around the southern hemisphere. To help support himself on beaches from Australia to Argentina to Aruba he gave surf lessons, which meant he knew how to get me standing by the end of the first day. It helped that I've done quite a bit of snowboarding. But, really Eloise, surfing is not that hard once you get the balance part."

"Which is kinda like a heron telling a hedgehog how easy it is to stand on one foot. But Tamiko, it's like, honestly, you two look beyond brilliant together."

"Lec's six-foot-three so that helps."

"Were you two really together for a year, like, every day?" Eloise asks, still obviously impressed by Alec's athletic good looks.

"Four days a week. I mean, still being sixteen, I was officially living at home with Mom, but the rest of the time Lec and I were pretty much inseparable."

"Almost like you were married. I mean Tamiko, you're even wearing that cute little red stone on the serious finger of your left hand."

"Last September, a few weeks after we met, Lec and I made a one-year commitment. We were so zonked on each other it only made sense. But, the year's up in a couple of days and I've already decided to move the ring to my other hand."

"It's only your seventeenth birthday tomorrow, right? So, sorry to be skeptical, but I don't see how you could have pulled all this off with a hot dude who's like, what, twenty-two?"

"Twenty-three now. And Eloise, even after we somehow bridged the age gap, I can't tell you how. I mean, it's like the day I met Lec I was a high school kid who had never been kissed and then a couple of weeks later I had this amazingly beautiful college senior boyfriend, who if he hadn't taken a gap year would have been a grad student. For sure, Mom was horrified at first and it took a lot of really bizarre happenings to even begin to get her on board. But since I hardly slept last night and this heat is making me feel kinda woozy, maybe we can save the long version for later."

"Sure, but what about dinner in an hour? Don't you want to meet people?"

"I might just crash and catch up with the intros later."

"Makes sense. And since the first-year camping trip leaves early tomorrow, you'll have plenty of time."

"Actually, I wriggled out of the three-day trip since I need to meet with this professor over at UMass Tuesday morning to try to get into his stats class."

"You're kidding, right? You seriously plan to stay in the dorm by yourself on your birthday? And anyway, girl, doesn't Amherst have plenty of stats courses?"

"Not grad level. I've already taken a bunch of stats at community college back home so I'm pretty much done with what Amherst offers."

"C'mon, you must be exaggerating."

"Unfortunately, that's exactly what Professor Gupta at UMass says," Tamiko answers as she tries to explain why she's nevertheless determined to use Amherst's five college exchange program to take an advanced course.

"But your birthday?"

"I told you, I need to move my ring, which means I want time alone to be sad and maybe even sniffle a little."

"Okay, let's head back to the dorm, but when are you actually going to tell me about what has you so down? In early July you seemed to be overflowing with happiness. So where is this Lec dude now?"

"On a plane to Japan, or maybe already in Tokyo. He deferred grad school at MIT for a year so he could work for his uncle's international consulting company and learn Japanese."

"Weird, so instead of being in Boston he chose to go six thousand miles away? Oops! Sorry Tamiko, that didn't come out quite right."

"Exactly right, I'm afraid. But, in fairness, Lec's Japan gap year before grad school was in the plan since late last year, the same way I planned to come back here to college. I mean, Eloise, six months ago I was just so damned happy I kinda convinced myself our year together would never end. Then, in late July, with our separation suddenly rushing at me like a runaway locomotive, I freaked and decided I wanted us to stay together no matter what. To accomplish this I proposed ditching Amherst for a year to go with Lec to Japan."

"Obviously he didn't agree, or we wouldn't be having this conversation, right?"

"Right, and Mom and pretty much everyone else I'm close to, agreed with Lec. My going off to college, they all insisted, would be such an exciting rite of passage it would be a serious crime to miss it."

"So how exactly did things come down? Did you and Lec have a big blowup, if that's even the right term?" Eloise asks. Then slipping her card into the reader next to Appleton's lantern-framed black door, she leads Tamiko up the stairs to their second floor room.

"More like a slow motion crash," Tamiko replies. "It began at Lec's uncle's wedding in late July, to Emiko, this amazingly smooth woman he met in Japan. It's a beyond funny, sweet story how those two got together thinking they were on a sex date, but for now, the point is that the wedding was in Nantucket at the same house Charlie had lent Lec and me last year and where, well, I guess you could say we'd had our Laguna Beach moment, minus the sand. Seriously, Eloise, I thought Lec would be delighted when I proposed accompanying him to Japan. So, at first, when he insisted that I should stick with my college plans, I was more surprised than upset."

"I already know you didn't change his mind. So was that it? Or did you see each other again?" Eloise interjects.

"The next day I had to fly off to Bloomington, Indiana to pitch for Chaos, my summer softball team because we'd qualified for the national championships. Then, since Chaos kept winning, I was there for a week which meant that I only saw Lec for a day, when he dropped in for the final game on his way to visit his parents back in New York for two weeks."

"But you guys talked, right?"

"For sure, I called, emailed and texted every day, each time concocting another unassailable argument as to why we couldn't be apart, while Lec mostly tried to avoid the subject and for this past week we were both back in Berkeley and together-ish, I guess you could say."

"What's that supposed to mean?" Eloise asks.

"Since, by then, we both knew nothing was going to change, we agreed to hang out, but not talk about it."

"Was that even possible? I mean, what did you…?"

"Surfing and camping down by Big Sur plus plenty of the one thing that still made words irrelevant," Tamiko replies, now sitting on her bed as she wonders whether she has the energy to put on her sheets before closing her eyes.

Finally, seeming to understand how exhausted Tamiko is, Eloise says, "Okay, for real I'm about to leave you to your nap, but first you have to tell me how things stand now?"

"According to Lec, nothing's changed except that we're going to be apart this year," Tamiko replies, as she again thinks this is bullshit since being so far apart has already changed everything.

"Are you two still, like, an exclusive couple? I mean, are you planning to go out with other dudes?" Eloise asks from the door.

"Oh my god, Eloise, I have no idea. We never really talked about that, or anything about the future, really. So, can we please just give this whole subject a rest?" Tamiko implores, blinking rapidly.

"Got it, but for sure I'm bringing you back a piece of cake so we can celebrate your birthday a few hours early."

"Anything with lots of chocolate. And maybe a shower of salt."

"On top of the frosting? You're kidding, right?"

"Not a bit. I love them both, especially together," Tamiko replies, finally mustering a weak smile.

"Gross."

"That's what Lec always says."

"Then given your mood I'll slather on the sodium chloride."

"Perfect," Tamiko says, stretching out on the bare mattress.

. . . . .

When Alec Burns clears customs at Japan's Narita Airport he's surprised to spot his Uncle Charlie. At 6'2" and wearing dark jeans, a black polo and a faded Red Sox cap, Charles Burns stands out from the crowd of mostly besuited Japanese businessmen like a tuna in a school of anchovies.

"I thought you and Emiko left for New York yesterday," Alec says, giving his uncle a strong hug. "And anyway, aren't I supposed to cope with Japan on my own?"

"There will be plenty of time for that. Since I had to hang on here for one more meeting I thought it would be fun to get you settled in the apartment Emiko found. I have a car waiting so we can talk without my having to concentrate on staying on the wrong side of the road."

"Driving on the left hasn't gotten easier over the years?" Alec asks, as the two men thread their way toward the luggage carousel.

"In Tokyo and Osaka where I am eighty percent of my Japan time, good metro systems mean I never need to drive. And now that I have a Japanese wife who loves Formula One, I've become a permanent passenger wherever we go."

"How's Emiko coping with U.S. roads?"

"Even in New York City, it only took her about twenty minutes to get the hang of it. I count myself lucky she's not driving for Uber in her spare time."

Settled in the back seat of a white Lexus twenty minutes later Alec says, "Charlie, I want to thank you again for July. Being back in Nantucket again with Tamiko for your wedding was special for both of us and that B&B you got us overlooking the harbor, well…"

"With Emiko's family filling our house, I was pretty sure you two would appreciate your own romantic nest, even if I'm guessing you didn't have much time for the view," Charlie interrupts with a chuckle.

"For sure, but I hope you know how excited we were to celebrate with you and Emiko. What a ride you two have had. It was hardly a year ago that you told me you were involved with a sex worker in Tokyo and here you are married to—hmm, how should I describe Emiko now?" Alec adds with a chuckle. "A respectable matron, perhaps?"

"Ha! I'm guessing that no matter how inaccurate it turned out to be, Emiko would join me in preferring your original description. Which, I guess, is another way of saying we count our blessings. But it's not lost on me that we weren't the only ones who had an amazing year."

"Only eleven months, I'm afraid. For Tamiko and me, things started unravelling our last day at Nantucket when, out of the blue, she told me she planned to skip Amherst and come with me to Japan."

"Since she's not sitting next to you, I gather you didn't initial her plan."

"Worse than that I'm afraid, since, at first, I didn't take her seriously. It seemed so obvious to me that she should go to college that I flat missed the fact that she saw my reaction as tantamount to saying I didn't love her. Then, in August, when we should have patched things up, our time together kinda disappeared between her softball tournament in Omaha and my family visit. In short, our rift never got bridged, or for that matter, fully understood by either of us. But Charlie, I still think I was right. I mean, someone as intellectually precocious as Tamiko obviously needed to go on to college like any other bright high school grad, not tag after me."

"Lec, I confess a year ago when you two got together, I was skeptical. Tamiko being barely sixteen was a big part of it, but I also worried that the drama of her mom's crazy ex-lover trying to kill half the family acted as a false catalyst for the two of you bonding. But spending time with both of you several times this last year, I quickly came to see that Tamiko's an amazing young woman, more mature if that's the right word, than half the adults I know. Even my brother, who initially thought you should be busted for statutory rape, told me he was proud of you for making such an inspired choice."

"Dad did fall under Tamiko's spell pretty quickly. And I'm the last one to dispute anything else you just said."

"Hmm, well I also remember that when I was your age I wasn't ready to commit to one person even though there were a couple of lovely prospects. In short, I get it, if this is about your not wanting to give up the fun of being single."

"I don't think that's most of it, anyway. Perhaps it will surprise you, given my lively dating history, but being with Tamiko this last year I barely glanced at other women. Just the same, while we're on the subject, I've been carrying around something I'm a little ashamed of."

"The confessional is open, or not, depending on what you want," Charlie replies, after a long pause.

"My old girlfriend Teri Kim, the Korean summer session student I was going out with in Berkeley when I met Tamiko, contacted me to say she'll be in Tokyo for a week this fall to do research for a big history paper."

"Hmm."

"It's probably not what you think."

"Which is?"

"That I rejected Tamiko's offer to come to Japan because I wanted to see Teri. In fact, I didn't hear from Teri until three weeks ago."

"Still, maybe the prospect of seeing Teri again, or perhaps meeting someone new, wasn't the furthest thing from your mind during August when I gather you continued to say no to Tamiko's entreaties to change your mind. Or, is it something else that's gnawing at you?"

"Even though my summer with Teri last year—just before I met Tamiko—was a lot of fun, I never thought of her in a long-term way. But, well, you must know how some women have a knack for lovemaking that you never quite get out of your head. It's as if..."

"I do know," Charlie interrupts, as he hopes Lec will finally get to the point. "Charlie, the thing is that by the time Teri contacted me, Tamiko was already so disappointed, and I guess, hurt, I decided that mentioning Teri would amount to piling on."

"Got it! But how do you feel about that decision now?"

"Like I said, more than a little guilty. So much so, that it's mostly swamped my fantasy of spending time with Teri. Also, I realize now that Tamiko and I should have discussed dating rules. I mean, with us being half a globe apart, I guess I thought a measure of openness would be assumed, but maybe she doesn't see it…"

"Sorry to interrupt," Charlie says, "but begin to look around to get your bearings since we're entering Tokyo proper. As I said, your apartment is tiny, but it's in an international district so lots of people in your neighborhood will speak at least a smattering of English."

"Cool, but Charlie, you haven't given me your opinion as to whether I should tell Tamiko about Teri, or hold onto the idea that it's kinder to keep my mouth shut."

"You noticed that."

. . . . .

Even at 10:00 a.m., it's already a heavily humid eighty-five degrees, when a sweat-soaked Tamiko heads back toward Amherst College from the campus of the University of Massachusetts on the north side of town. With her long-sleeved white shirt and dark pants sticking Velcro-like to her body she wonders whether she's ever been this miserable, excepting only the time after her dad's death in a traffic accident. It hasn't helped that she has just endured a nasty battle with Professor Gupta who, based primarily on her age, has tried to reject her application to take a grad level course, although, given his frequent use of the term "Missy," being female surely hasn't helped. Indeed, Tamiko would have been sent away empty-handed if she hadn't channeled the angst from her recent disappointments into an angry threat to appeal Professor Gupta's rejection on the grounds of both age and gender discrimination. Nevertheless, even when the round-bellied, tight-lipped little man had reluctantly agreed to give her a qualifying test, which she'd aced in half the allotted time, it had felt like a pyrrhic victory. After all, if at seventeen she could easily handle grad-level work, why had Lec said no to her proposal to defer college to accompany him to Tokyo?

Passing Antonio's Pizza on North Pleasant Street, Tamiko follows the now familiar route across the green expanse of the Amherst Common, where, probably because of the aggressive heat, no one is in sight. Perching on the same shady bench where she and Eloise had sat yesterday, Tamiko schools herself to take a series of deep breaths in an effort to slow her wildly juddering thoughts. It's not lost on her that on the short walk from UMass she's arrived at a dozen angry, often conflicting, judgments including:

- Most male professors are ageist, misogynist or both
- Her mother, Amy, only supports Tamiko's making her own decisions when she agrees with them
- Lec's Uncle Charlie coaxed Lec to Japan in order to interrupt Lec's relationship with her
- Lec's moved six thousand miles away because it made it easier to dump her
- True love is a pathetic fantasy.

Oh no you don't, Tamiko tells her thoughts as they threaten to run down new rabbit holes of angry despair. And when they refuse to listen, she exclaims out loud, "Enough!" And then, in a quieter voice, "Obviously, Tamiko O'Shea Gashkin is losing it." But more to the immediate point, she wonders, does all of my undoubted angst stem from my shock at being rejected by Lec, or is something else involved? Having no answer, Tamiko stretches out on the bench. She tries to keep a grip on the present by counting the branches of the sugar maple, which like the spokes of an overturned umbrella, fan out above. As her usual mood of equanimity slowly returns, Tamiko imagines herself ascending to the furry green canopy far above where she feels almost as if she's being caressed by a friend. Realizing, not for the first time, that when it comes to a sense of well being, people have much to learn from trees, she rolls to her feet and heads toward her dorm feeling better. With most of the first-year students either off on the bonding outing, or not yet back from the summer, she hopes she'll have enough time alone to finish her spirit mending.

Two hours later, after lunch and a jet lag-fighting nap, Tamiko returns from a cold shower to sit on her bed wearing only red bikini panties. Again, nagged by a plethora of awkward thoughts, and with no comforting maple tree in sight, she reaches for her computer and begins to type:

Lec, So here I am sitting on my skinny bed in my small Amherst dorm room trying to move as little as possible in the ninety-degree, impossibly sticky air. My roommate Eloise (who I like a bunch) is off on a get-to-know-you camping trip for a couple of days (Amherst is that kind of place). Yesterday was my birthday and being alone has the advantage of giving me the chance to think things through re you and me. Yes, I do see I have an email from you, but before I read it let me tell you what I've concluded during the couple of angst-filled days since we parted. So, acknowledging that I'm still more than a little confused, here goes my best effort.

First: I love you, all of you. As you well know infatuation instantly slammed both of us a year ago on the Cal campus when our eyes met after you picked up my Brothers K on that path across Memorial Glade. For me, at least, that remains both a life-changing and life-defining moment.

Second: Every fiber of me thanks you for being my soul mate, bed mate, and best friend this last year. I don't mean to sell myself short when I say that it was a miracle dipped in a rainbow for this tomboy teenager with a teddy bear on her backpack to somehow find a beautiful, patient, generous and amazing friend and lover. I think I've done a pretty good job of grabbing your extended hand to pull my kid self up a few pegs (sorry, it's too hot to think beyond clichés), but Lec, it's not lost on me that I'm still auditioning to become an adult.

Three: At the end of July after experiencing the joy at being back on Nantucket—the magical island of our first impossibly passionate days— I made the colossal mistake of blindsiding you with my announcement that I had decided to defer college and accompany you to Japan. Then, I compounded my blunder, by reacting petulantly when you didn't immediately agree. Somehow, the girl who had been given everything could only think of demanding more.

Four: During August when we were mostly separated, we never found a way to make things smooth. Granted, this was never going to be easy given that after a year of nesting our souls together we were facing the trauma of being separated by half the world. Still, since I was the strident one who refused to talk compromise, I take most of the responsibility.

Five: I need to pay attention to the fact that you, Mom, Ed, Ruth, my buddy Jazz, and for that matter, pretty much everyone we both know (except maybe my grandmother Vera who believes in FATE) think I should be here at college, not tagging after you to Japan. Yes, it's possible that this precocious girl has become so used to talking her way into advanced courses, sports teams, and I guess, maybe even my relationship with you (although, as I remember, you said "I love you" first), that she's lost touch with reality.

Six: OK, so enough with the mea culpas. *Lec, here is where I tell you what's truly in my heart, and probably annoy you in the process. When we met—the twenty-two-year-old man of the world and the almost-sixteen-year-old high school kid—the odds of our establishing a mutually chill (not to mention, awesome) relationship was thought by our friends and family to be close to zero (and in my mom's case, 30 degrees below). Very fortunately neither of us believed the naysayers—not for a second. Instead we both knew in our hearts that if we loved each other fiercely enough nothing could stop us. So Lec, here is my big question. Why did you decide to put sensible practicalities before continuing to trust in impossible love?*

Seven: Surely it's polite to wait for your answer. But in the meantime, sitting here sweating on this miserable hot bed instead of being with you in Japan, I have to conclude that for some reason you lost your nerve—or maybe your desire—to defy common sense and go for broke with me.

Eight: So where does that leave us? As soon as I hit send I'll move the dear little ring you gave me exactly a year ago to my right hand. Perhaps, I'd get more immediate satisfaction by tossing it in my sock drawer, but given the luminous year we've spent together I still hope we have a future.

Of course, I love you, Tamiko

Closing her laptop, Tamiko tries to tug the thin gold band with its tiny ruby off the ring finger of her left hand. When it refuses to budge she heads to the bathroom where, after slathering on great gobs of liquid soap she finally frees it. Now, squeezing it onto the ring finger of her right hand, Tamiko's not sure whether she feels liberated, or lost.

. . . . .

Early that evening Tamiko grabs a salad and bagel at Valentine Hall, Amherst's almost deserted dining commons. Back at Appleton in the eerie quiet of the empty dorm, she tries not to feel like the last guest in a condemned hotel. Determined to face up to Lec's message, whatever it may say, she touches the little ruby ring on its unaccustomed finger before tapping his email.

Hiya,

So here I am in the tiny apartment Emiko found me in the Hiroo, Shibuya district of Tokyo. No doubt things will seem brighter tomorrow, but now I'm jet-lagged, disoriented, and given the failure of my stressed brain to come up with a more nuanced word, miserable. A big reason for this is wrapped up with missing you and regretting some things I said, and many I didn't say, in the last few days we spent together (a lot more about all this below). But another part has to do with a subject that's harder to broach. Put simply, for the last three weeks I haven't told you the whole truth. Talking to Charlie a few hours ago in the car coming in from Narita

Airport (he was kind enough to pick me up), I came to see I've not only made a mistake, but one I now see is going to be a lot harder to fix than if I'd been upfront earlier.

In early to mid-August, maybe ten days after Nantucket, my old girlfriend Teri Kim emailed out of the blue to say that, as part of her research for her senior history thesis about the Japanese occupation of Korea, she needed to come to Japan for a week this fall. Teri then asked if I would be glad to see her (for what it's worth she also said she had connected with a cool boyfriend that her dad, more or less, tolerated so this would likely be her last adventure). To my double discomfort now, I not only said yes, but then didn't tell you.

Tamiko, please believe that I had absolutely no clue that Teri would propose coming to Japan when I said no to your proposal to ditch college to accompany me. If you are thinking that this doesn't excuse my failure to be upfront about Teri in August when you were still importuning me to change my mind, you are right. My only defense (and I know it's weak) is that by the time Teri told me about her plans you and I were a few thousand miles apart both physically and emotionally. And by the time we finally got back together this last week, things were already so fraught, I didn't want to make them worse.

Tamiko, my head is almost bursting with things to say to you, with "I love you" being at the top of the list. And, the fact that I miss you desperately, being number two. I also want to say that over these last weeks when I continued to say no to your coming with me to Japan, I was honestly convinced that to be happy together long term we (especially you) needed the chance to spread our (your) wings. The prospect of college, grad school, first jobs, and growing out of our age difference, all seem to shout that we need to experience life on our own before considering whether to commit to being an exclusive, long-term couple. Part of me still believes this, while another desperately hopes I haven't logic-chopped our beautiful relationship into mush.

All my love, Lec

PS: I want to tell you once more how magnificent you were leading Chaos to the National Eighteen and Under Softball Championship. I'm sorry family obligations meant I could only get to Nebraska for the final game, but even given my own experience with world class competition, I've never seen a more brilliantly focused athlete than you were in Chaos's 1-0 victory.

PPS: Now that I'm here in Tokyo I'm looking for something useful to do when I'm not studying. I've asked Charlie if he knows of some volunteer work that might fit my skills. More on this next time.

. . . . .

Lec,

As you well know, on the few occasions when I'm seriously mad I tell myself to say nothing until I go for a run, or do something else to get the stabbing anger out of my system. But, as I said earlier, it's too hot to move and I don't know a soul in this mostly empty place. So, having just read your email, here is what pissed-off me thinks, unfiltered. For starters, let me ask if I'm supposed to congratulate you on deciding to screw your drop dead gorgeous old lover instead of the girl down the hall, or someone from the shop around the corner? And, presumably, I'm supposed to feel better because Teri's cheating on an allegedly serious boyfriend means your tryst is time limited? But, just so you know, I have an overflowing thimble full of doubt that Teri didn't contact you before the end of July when I proposed coming to Japan (people who lie once, etc.).

But, even assuming all your reassurances about the timing and casualness of this re-relationship are true, remind me again why you have such a pressing need for recreational fucking?

OK, after a ten-minute cold shower, I just reread your message. And, yes, I do see and appreciate that you reluctantly recognize the possibility that, just perhaps, my proposal to accompany you to Japan wasn't as daft as you, and everyone else, made it out to be. Just the same, I've now yanked the ring off it's very short new home on my right hand (no soap needed this time).

Before my mind-settling shower I planned to toss it in the nearest river, but being marginally calmer now, I've instead deposited it in my box of erasers.

As you may guess, my brain is churning with lots more to say (much of it even more impolite), but instead I'll take the inimitable Kinky Friedman's advice—"When the horse dies, get off." And, in case you're in any doubt as to what this means, here's your cheat sheet. Starting now, I'm putting my relationship with you, including future communications between us, on the far back burner.

Possibly—but definitely short of probably—I still love you, T.

PS: I pitched over my head at the Nationals because I was so disappointed about your rejecting me, I was determined not to be a loser twice in the same month.

. . . . .

When classes begin Tamiko attempts to pour her considerable energy into learning new things—something that has always given her joy. However, even though Quantitative Methodology Statistics at UMass where her classmates are at least five years older is challenging, her Amherst courses in Economics, American History and a first year seminar on Japanese Design Aesthetics largely disappoint. With so many of her classmates seemingly determined to major in partying, it's hard for her to gain intellectual traction. But it's Ancient Greek, the subject Tamiko is most excited about, that turns out to be the loudest snore. Because she had eagerly inhaled much of the first-year text over the summer, including the Greek alphabet, she sits altogether bored while the other eight students laboriously bang the twenty-four unfamiliar letters into their brains.

But it isn't only her disappointment with academics that has her thinking about transferring to a larger university. With the exception of the ever enthusiastic, and increasingly dear, Eloise, she feels like a misfit, seemingly the only person in the hyper-social environment of her first-year dorm who would prefer to close her door and read a book. Perhaps Tamiko's penchant for going her own way would have gone unnoticed had she been less attractive. But her good looks, plus the notoriety that goes with being a highly recruited athlete, mean half the guys in Appleton literally elbow one other to be first in line to try to bed her. Beer pong, the inevitable college drinking game, encapsulates Tamiko's disgust. Most nights about ten, Sean and Adam, preppie roommates at the end of the hall, lift a salvaged wooden door onto the backs of two chairs to form a table in the middle of the corridor. Six plastic cups half full of beer are placed in a triangle pattern at each end with teams of two taking turns to try to throw, or bounce, ping pong balls the length of the table and into their opponents' cups. When a tossing team succeeds in sinking the ball into the receiving team's cup, a member of that team must drink its contents. And just to add a bit of prurient excitement, should the losing team miss every shot for an entire game, both players are supposed to strip and parade naked around the dorm.

Tamiko, who dislikes beer and is put off by the aggressive, alcohol-fueled flirting that seems to be beer pong's principal point, is nevertheless dragooned into playing a couple of games the first night. But, having resolved to resist future invitations, she tries to remain in her room with her door firmly shut thereafter. However, dear klutzy Eloise, who loves to play, but sensibly fears her lack of coordination will result in a naked run, persists in trying to coax her highly coordinated roommate into partnering. But each time Tamiko gives in, she ends up wanting to scream, "Please God, get me out of here," well before the end of what she inevitably sees as a lewd, loud and stupid evening. Things come to a head at the end of the first week when, after Tamiko makes six shots in a row to single-handedly crush Errol and Sean, two tipsy Choaties, Sean shouts, "In future, bull dykes should be banned."

"Right after alligator shirt assholes, Asshole," Tamiko responds.

"You could maybe try a little harder to fit in," Eloise says timidly, when a few minutes later she returns to their room to find Tamiko sitting on her bed, fists clenched. "I mean, like, Tamiko, I know Sean and a couple of the other guys really are preppie morons but, still, half the dorm is starting to call you 'Ice Queen.'"

Now stretched out on her bed, Tamiko snaps, "I don't mean to embarrass you by being stuck with a social misfit roommate if that's what this is about." Then, as she realizes she's being unkind to her one Amherst friend who undoubtedly means well, Tamiko searches in vain for something mollifying to add.

"I hope you know that isn't it at all," Eloise eventually replies, not trying to disguise the hurt in her voice. "I mean, Tamiko, we're still homies for life, right? I just feel bad that you don't seem interested in having other friends, which would be your business, I guess, except, you don't seem very happy."

"I know this is going to seem uber-pretentious, especially given my age, but this last year I got used to hanging out with Lec's upperclass and grad student friends where the social scene was way different. I mean, Eloise, people were actually interested in things like plant genetics, artificial intelligence, medieval music, romance philology…"

"Whatever that is," Emily interrupts dismissively. "But Tamiko, even believing you aren't trying to put on some kind of weird Einstein act, I can't figure out why you're so overwhelmingly bored by the possibility that acting your age might occasionally be a hoot. I mean, being a pre-med student, I know I'll have to buckle down soon, and once I do, it will be grind, grind, grind for the next four years to try to get into a decent med school where the competition is sure to be even fiercer. And I'm actually good with that since becoming a doctor has pretty much always been my dream. But, Tamiko, every older kid I talked to—even nerds like me—said not to miss the fun of the first college fall, 'cause it ain't never going to happen again."

Not wanting to further offend, Tamiko replies, "The best I can promise is to think about what you just said. But, Eloise, like I told you, being an only child who was always being pushed forward academically, I got disconnected from my age cohort. And then there's my relationship with Mom who after my dad was killed when I was twelve, kinda became my best friend. I mean, I know this sounds impossibly dorky, but I not only had a part-time job at Mom's publishing company, but I'm a member of her book group."

"But you did all those sports with piles of kids, right?"

"Even then, because I'm big and a good athlete, I mostly ended up playing with kids two or three years older. The truth is, Eloise, if I make a list of my true friends, people who absolutely have my back, most of them are older than I am, many by a generation."

"Except me, I'm sure you meant to say. But, okay, even assuming the first-year social scene here at Amherst is not what you hoped for, would it kill you to try to blend in a little? I mean, at beer pong, couldn't you deliberately miss once in a while, drink a beer or two and laugh at yourself? It's, precisely because guys have become so intimidated by you that they've become offensive. But there's zero excuse for what Sean just said, and I wouldn't be surprised if someone reports him for hate speech, or whatever."

"I plan to sidestep the problem by staying late at the library."

"I doubt becoming a hermit is going to make you less sad. I mean, Tamiko, you're not thinking of dropping out, or transferring or something?"

"El, right now I'm trying to make it a day at a time. And, given my disappointment about not being with Lec, I do understand that I'm seeing everything through a glass darkly. In short, I'll try to hang in, and avoid making big decisions."

"That's a relief. But, hey, can we talk about me for a minute?"

"Absolutely," Tamiko replies, hugely relieved that Eloise is done trying to improve her. "And despite being a certified social misfit I still have eyes in my sad head, so I'm guessing this is going to be about Jason Sprague the Fourth, who seems like a sweet dude, despite being a preppie in serious danger of choking on his great grandfather's name."

"We had sex last night. Well, three times if you're counting."

"Hmm. I'm guessing that's somehow connected to that shiny silver thumb ring you've been flashing," Tamiko says, as she can't help glancing at her own empty fingers. But instead of giving in to her feeling of loss, she asks, "But what happened to your rule of 'no intimacy before Thanksgiving'? And, how does this affect your plan to go to Madison in a few weeks to see Laguna boy?"

"Both roadkill, obviously," Eloise replies, dramatically. "And, by coincidence, Caleb canceled on me by text this morning a half an hour before I planned to email him! For about thirty seconds I was teed off about being kicked to the curb without even a call, but then I realized I was about to do the same thing, so…"

"Caleb probably met someone playing beer pong at Wisconsin," Tamiko says, trying to keep a straight face.

"Ha! But listen Tamiko, I need you to be serious for a minute. It's, like, when Jason—I call him Four—told me it was his first time I kinda, sorta pretended I was a virgin, too, so everything about me and Caleb is absolutely on the down-low."

"Eloise, methinks the old fate worse than death plot has long since become a parody."

"Huh?"

"These days dudes don't care if you're a virgin, except maybe to be relieved there will be no blood on the sheets," Tamiko says with a chuckle, as she remembers Lec's pretend threat to wave their sheets from the window after their first time.

"Actually, I don't think he noticed," Eloise says. "We were both pretty tipsy, and at the beginning especially he seemed worried about his own issues—trying to slow down I guess."

"Hopefully, things smoothed out on your second try."

"Much smoother, for sure. But, Tamiko, can I ask you how it was with Lec? I mean, like, did you two have sex every time you were together? And, did you, well, um, always respond, I guess?"

"Yo, El, is nothing private with you?"

"Hmm, the way I see it," Eloise responds calmly, "I've been your good buddy despite your being Ms. Misery two-thirds of the time, so you owe me. Also, if I can't ask you about sex, exactly who am I going to learn from?"

Pausing for a moment to allow her twinge of annoyance to pass, Tamiko realizes that Eloise has a point. Not everyone is as lucky as she was to have had an experienced guide like Lec. "Okay then, like I told you, Lec and I were together maybe four nights a week. And since we couldn't keep our bodies to ourselves we often went for seconds and sometimes more."

"So you're telling me you've had sex hundreds of times, maybe even five hundred, if my math is right?"

"I haven't counted, but I guess."

"Then, like, how many times did you get off, or climax, or whatever I'm supposed to call it?"

"It's funny how much you remind me of my friend Jazz, since neither of you can leave a bodily fluid undiscussed," Tamiko replies, standing and reaching for her bathroom toiletries bag.

"Tamiko, please don't brush me off. The truth is that despite having sex with two guys I haven't had an orgasm, so I'm starting to get freaked," Eloise responds, as she springs up to block Tamiko's path.

Sighing, as she sits back on her bed, Tamiko says, "Okay, then, just about every time Lec and I made love I climaxed and often more than once, since he's a patient dude. And, since he eventually did too, it didn't take our bodies long to figure out how to do it simultaneously. Like I've told you, I have nothing to compare this to, aside from reading novels but, I guess we were seismically lucky in the physical response department. But, remember, unlike Four, Lec knew what he was doing, so I only had to suspend my disbelief and go along for the ride."

"I've had sex maybe fifteen times counting three last night and so far there have been no explosions. Mind you, the screwing has felt great and pretty much all I think about is doing more of it. But Tamiko, I obviously need coaching on how to finish the deal."

"When I was a kid every Little League parent fancied themselves a coach. Unfortunately, it took me way too long to realize that most advice falls someplace between iffy and bad. And, I'm sure one or the other of those terms would sum up anything I might say about orgasm. But assuming you're not going to take no for an answer, I guess I would say don't worry about it, at least for now. If Caleb and Four are typical of the over-hyper young guys I've read about, they've probably had trouble hanging in there long enough to give you a fair chance to respond. That said, it can't hurt to show Four what you do to get yourself off. But what about the ring? Did that have something to do with your saying 'yes'?"

"Not at all, since I'd been trying to encourage him to get past third base for the last ten days," Eloise replies seriously.

"Maybe seeing you wear it was a necessary part of his sprint for home," Tamiko says, kindly. "Is it engraved?"

"With a heart inside and our initials," Eloise answers, slipping the ring off of her thumb and holding it out for Tamiko to examine.

"Chill! Congratulations on catching one of the few sweet dudes in this whole place."

. . . . .

"Tamiko, it's so nice to hear your voice."

"You too, Ruth. And thanks for making time for me so fast. When I emailed you this afternoon I didn't mean to sound desperate, but the truth is maybe I'm trending in that direction. At the very least I'm anxious to get your advice on an epic list of muddles. But, since this is an official consultation, you'll send a bill to Mom, right? She told me you still haven't sent an invoice from when we talked in August, so…"

"That's because I don't plan to."

"C'mon Ruth, ever since my dad was killed, the deal has been that I talk to you when I feel the need and you bill Mom."

"That was then. With your consent I'd like to change our relationship from therapist and client to being friends, and maybe, even to an honorary mom/daughter thing."

"Hasn't it always been sorta like that? I mean, I obviously have a great mom, but you've been like her shadow."

"That warms my heart. And all the more reason to end the professional part, which you don't need anyway. Think of it this way, I already have too many clients, but a big shortage of daughters."

"But you have two chill kids, right?"

"Both boys and a husband of the same persuasion. I love them dearly, but now and then I'd like to chat about something other than who's starting at linebacker for the Forty-Niners."

"Okay then, but Ruth, like I try to tell Mom, if I'm gonna be your kid, even an honorary one, we have to share things both ways."

"Perhaps you didn't notice, but I just did. But for now, why don't we start with your list. I assume you're in Massachusetts and Alec is in Japan, so I guess question one is how's the long distance relationship going?"

"It isn't. Lec barely got to Japan before he confessed that Teri, his Korean girlfriend, the one before me, plans to show up there in Tokyo for a week this fall. I'm actually pretty sure she's not a long-term threat, but still, why do guys…"

"That news obviously smarts," Ruth interrupts, kindly. "Had you two promised to be monogamous?"

"What with the miserable fallout from Lec's refusing my request to accompany him to Japan, we never talked about dating rules. But, when he told me about Teri I immediately tore off the ring he gave me last year. I meant to take a few deep breaths first, but I was too damn mad."

"Sweetie, as a therapist I could lead you through a bunch of textbook questions that might help you clarify your feelings, but as a friend, the truth is I'm probably not the right person to advise you about jealousy. Even after twenty-five years of marriage I turn green if I catch Larry glancing at some busty woman's décolletage."

"Given your figure, I doubt the competition has much chance."

"Spoken like a true friend, even though I've put on twenty pounds since my glory days. But back to you. Let me ask, if this Teri is more annoyance than threat, what are you so upset about? No hurry, take a minute to think."

"As you know, a few years ago, once I pretty much recovered from the shock of Dad's death, I got back to basically feeling happy. Like, I'd mostly get up in the morning with a grin on my face and my day would roll out from there. And that was even before my magical year with Lec, when I often woke up feeling as if I could fly. But here at Amherst I get up sad and stay sad except when I get angry at something stupid, which is way too often. Sorry, Ruth, I know I'm blathering, but if you'll hang in there for a minute I'm not quite done. I mean, it's like I've been here almost three weeks and I fit in about as well as a turtle on a trampoline. Outside of my roommate Eloise, who's a definite sweetie, I've made zero friends, in part because everyone in my dorm seems so immature. I mean, yesterday I saw two dudes competing over who had the trendiest Yeezy sneakers and don't get me started on beer pong. And the academic challenge I've looked forward to for years has pretty much been absent except for the grad level stats course I fought to get into over at UMass. For the rest, I could be learning twice as much in half the time if…"

"Whoa girl, whoa! Do you want to focus on missing Alec, being frustrated with Amherst's social life or your disappointment at its powder puff academics? We'll never get anywhere trying to deal with all three at once."

"I've learned the hard way in the last six weeks that I can't do anything about Lec, so I guess right now it's the lack of academic challenge that's most annoying."

"Having two sons at highly selective schools, my conclusion is that for reasons I don't understand, it's a lot harder to get in, than stay in. Especially in the liberal arts, students somehow seem to get away with demanding inflated grades for mediocre work in an atmosphere where the professors are too intimidated, or maybe just too indifferent, to resist."

"Sounds right, but even a bunch of the STEM people in my dorm seem to be more interested in beer and mating, than studying."

"Ha! I'd surely be leading that band with my tits pushed up if I had another chance to be young and stupid. But, Tamiko, I'm guessing that before long lots of the A-type personalities, of which there must be a gaggle around there, will start to obsess about getting top grades for grad school which should make your classes more interesting."

"Nice to know I guess, but I'm not sure how this helps now."

"Relax dear, I'm just getting started."

"Okay," Tamiko says, letting go of a long, relieved breath as she realizes how badly she needs Ruth's perspective.

"Tamiko, just as you've always done, find a way to push ahead academically until you eventually encounter material that challenges you.

In the short run this may make you more isolated from your first-year cohort, but I gather that's no bad thing, right?"

"For sure, but what do you think about my simply transferring to a bigger school?"

"Not much. Or at least I wouldn't until you give Amherst a real chance. When I checked online I saw that by most measures it's the top-rated small college in the country so I'm sure you can find plenty of challenges right there. Why not start by meeting with your profs to ask for a more rigorous individualized curriculum?"

"Hmm, do you think that will work?"

"Maybe not at a giant school like Cal Berkeley where no one wants to notice you. But at a boutique college like Amherst, where parents fork over the price of a Porsche every year, I'm guessing that if you can handle tougher material you can pretty much write your own ticket, or maybe I should say, thesis."

"I hope so. Professor Spurgeon, my Greek prof, emailed me earlier today to suggest I stop by during his office hours tomorrow so I'll begin with him, even though I think he wants to see me because I've been a borderline brat in class."

"Really? That's not like you."

"He keeps giving quizzes that are about as hard as the DMV written test. I did the last one in five minutes and then sat there for another twenty waiting for the others to finish. When they didn't, I got up and left, which wouldn't have been so impolite if I hadn't maybe groaned on the way out."

"Seems like you've made your point. So, at your meeting, you just need to follow up. I'll be curious, so shoot me a text. Ready to move on to your social life, or lack thereof?"

"You sure this isn't therapy?"

"When you tell me you're positive you're depressed because you're not eating enough kale, I'll send your mom a bill. Until then, we're still firmly in friend mode."

"Got it. Thanks. So, like I said, being surrounded by a dorm full of mostly sex-addled adolescents is annoying, but I know it's not really a huge deal. However, the fact that the student newspaper ran a front page profile about me being a super athlete along with a borderline pin-up type picture, isn't making it easier to blend in."

"Fame never lasts as long as you think, or most people want. More to the point, I think this is another problem with a relatively easy fix. Simply, hang with kids your own age."

"There aren't a lot of seventeen-year-olds around here if that's what you mean, which I'm guessing you don't," Tamiko replies, as she scrunches up on the bed so she's half propped against the wall.

"I'm referring to your emotional age of course. This last year, with the exception of sports, your peer group pretty much consisted of Alec's housemates and friends, right?"

"As well as the folks at Bay Books, and a couple of friends from sports, who, it's true, are also a few years older."

"So, stop judging the people in your dorm, and, more important, stop wasting time judging yourself for judging them, and go find some juniors and seniors to hang out with. Didn't you tell me you met a few when they recruited you for softball?"

"Softball practice doesn't start until after Christmas, but Ruth, as usual, I think you're on to something. Last year I stayed overnight with two juniors, Missy Frank, who plays third base, and her roommate Virginia Pruitt, one of the catchers who has already volunteered to work out with me twice a week starting in October."

"What will happen if you tell one or both of them you are feeling socially disconnected in your first-year dorm and ask to be invited to an upper class kick-it or whatever they call parties these days?"

"Good idea. I'll give it a try. As usual Ruth, you're a lifesaver."

"On my end, let me confess how good it feels to have a college student who actually listens. But hey, I need to run."

"Wait a second. If I'm going to be your honorary daughter, don't I get to give you advice?"

"Absolutely, but if it's going to be now you'll have to be quick, since I'm..."

"When you're finished with your last client today go buy a top with a scary low neckline and then, start hitting a gym every other day. If your husband wants to look at a hot body, it may as well be yours."

"You know, I think you might be right."

MID-SEPTEMBER

ON HIS SECOND WEDNESDAY AFTERNOON in Japan, Alec unlocks the door to the small two-room office suite of Burns, Short and Associates in an unremarkable office building in the Shinjuku Hiyashi section of central Tokyo. Surprised, he stops when he sees a young woman wearing a high-necked long-sleeved black knit top and no makeup sitting at the desk in the outer office where he often studies after class. Since Yuko, Phil's and Charlie's middle-aged assistant, only works mornings, Alec feels annoyed that his usual spot has been appropriated.

Apparently registering Alec's flash of territoriality, the young woman, says in a full-throated contralto, which unaccountably reminds him of Tamiko, "Mr. Burns, I hope someone told you I'm helping out with a couple of research projects." When Alec doesn't respond, she stands, revealing herself to be perhaps a foot shorter than he is. "I'm pretty sure I said that in English," she insists, "but in case you're hard of hearing, I'm Mayumi Yamada, a recent graduate of Tokyo University whom Phil Short hired to…"

"Right, sorry," Alec interrupts. Then, as he tries to shake off his residual irritation, he leans over to shake Mayumi's extended hand as he registers long black bangs over wide set eyes. "Phil did email me that you were preparing background reports for Kibu Financial and another client, whose name I forget."

"Ito."

"Of course. Trying to learn Japanese five hours a day has obviously fried more than a few of my brain synapses," Alec says, even as he realizes that it's more likely that it's the presence of this precocious woman who has him on his back foot. When Mayumi doesn't respond, he adds, "Oops, sorry to go all slang on you. I meant…"

"Mr. Burns, is your brain so fried you haven't noticed that I speak English as fluently as you and might, just possibly, grok a smidge of slanguage? But, no big deal, since I began English when I was two and a half."

"Really, you started learning English when you were in diapers?"

"Hmm, methinks a hint of a compliment may be buried in there," Mayumi responds with a smile that shows off a dimple in her right cheek. "But, Mr. Burns, I can assure you I was nappie-free by my second birthday. More to the point, would you prefer me to use the other office?"

"Stay where you are, I'm not going to be here long. And, as I'm guessing you know, it's Alec."

"Actually, Alec, I'm surprised you're here at all, since Charlie happened to mention in a text that you'd probably be taking a few days off this week to entertain a Korean friend," Mayumi says, so matter-of-factly, only the fleeting reappearance of her dimple tells Alec she's teasing.

His face flushing slightly despite his best efforts to ignore Mayumi's remark, Alec realizes he's annoyed that Charlie discussed his personal life with her. Saving the question of why he could possibly care what this audacious young woman thinks until later, he tries to steer their conversation back to neutral ground by fixing his gaze on the wall behind Mayumi's left shoulder as he asks when the reports will be done.

"Today I'm pulling material from the net. Tomorrow I'll hit our biggest business library. So the answer is that by Monday afternoon, they'll be done, dusted and right here," Mayumi replies, as she taps the desktop. "And if you're still preoccupied with your friend for a few more days they'll still be here," she adds with a grin wide enough to show him she has dimples in both cheeks.

"I'll definitely be here Monday," Alec insists so stridently, he wants to kick himself, as he pushes through the door to the stuffy inner office. Sitting at the steel-framed, glass-topped desk, in a minimalist but impressively ergonomic chair, Alec pulls a list of vocabulary words from his shoulder bag before rubbing his temples in an effort to wipe away the beginnings of a headache. As Charlie predicted he's making good progress with written Japanese, even given its three very different scripts, but speaking the simplest phrases feels like chopping green wood with a dull axe on a cold day. Indeed, he's become so annoyed at hearing his tone deaf-self mangle the pronunciation of basic sounds that he's begun to question his judgment in trying to learn this difficult language. But, today, Alec reflects, Japanese isn't his biggest problem. Teri Kim is scheduled to land at Haneda Airport in two hours. Assuming customs is typically efficient, she'll arrive by cab at his apartment by six o'clock. Given that he readily agreed to her visit only a month ago he wonders why he now feels so conflicted. After all, he tells himself for at least the tenth time, why shouldn't I cope with my Japan blues by hanging out with an old girlfriend for a week, especially one as lovely as Teri. Unfortunately, his answer is always the same. Although it may be logical that a short-term dalliance with Teri shouldn't affect his bond with Tamiko, he now sees that it does. True, he never planned to be a monk for all his time in Japan, just as he's assumed Tamiko wouldn't be celibate at college. Nevertheless, it's obvious that by agreeing to see Teri almost before he's over his jet lag—and then telling Tamiko about it—he's somehow hurt himself as well as her.

But more to the immediate point, Alec thinks, why am I sitting here in Charlie's office when I only stopped by to pick up a file on the way home to tidy my apartment? Sighing as he realizes he'll have to face the frustratingly sassy Mayumi Yamada sooner or later, Alec opens the door to find the outer office empty. A single sheet of paper with a couple of lines written in bold calligraphy lies on top of the desk.

A.—I grew up in a family with older brothers who loved to tease their little sis. Please excuse my bad manners.—M.

. . . . .

Alec's phone pings as he enters his tiny third floor walk-up, shopping bag in hand. Seeing it's a text from Teri, he reads:

Plane down now. When I finish customs I stop by my father's apartment to dump stuff. Can we meet in front of big screen at Alta building in Shinjuku at 7:00?—XOXO

Unsure of what to make of Teri's change of plans, Alec wonders if she is also having second thoughts as he texts back:

Got it. Everything good?

See you soon :) Teri immediately replies, without answering the question.

Deciding no amount of thought will make any of this clearer, Alec changes the sheets and wipes down the postage-stamp-sized bathroom. After a forty-five-minute headache-banishing nap, he sets out to walk the mile from his apartment to the famous department store complex, his guess that Teri is in hesitation mode somehow making him feel more relaxed. Perhaps he can even walk back his promise of intimacy without disappointing her, he thinks as his eye is caught by the improbable peacock colors of a butterfly-shaped kite in a shop window. Pausing for a better look, Alec's mind leaps unbidden to a fantasy of Tamiko joyfully running beneath it on a breezy California beach.

"Do you need help with directions?" A well-dressed, middle-aged man asks in heavily accented English. Marveling at the routine kindness the Japanese exhibit to apparently disoriented strangers, Alec is inordinately pleased to have mastered enough rudimentary Japanese to assure the good samaritan he isn't lost.

When the huge screen of the aggressively triangular Studio Alta building comes into view a few blocks ahead, Alec checks his watch to see he's ten minutes early. Turning aside to examine another shop window, he's surprised to spot Teri barely fifty feet ahead doing the same thing. Perhaps because he's been so conflicted about his parting with Tamiko, he realizes he's forgotten the breathtaking beauty of Teri's heart-shaped face and the sensual grace of her slim body. Surely, it's just plain dumb to let guilt ruin this moment, Alec resolves as he steps forward, arms extended.

"Alec, you are always my big beautiful American dude guy," Teri whispers as she all but collapses into his arms.

"Hungry?" Alec asks after they cling together for what, by Japanese standards, is an indecent amount of time in a public space.

"My stomach is way too jumping," Teri replies. "So maybe we walk little bit first."

"Anyplace in particular?"

"Just walk, so I be able to talk to you," Teri says as she turns and points down the busy sidewalk. After proceeding several blocks along the crowded Shinjuku-dori, Teri half turns to make brief eye contact before taking Alec's hand, "Alec, I decide not to come at least three times every day this week. I even pick up phone to tell you. Pick up, put down, pick up, put down, over and over."

"And now?" asks Alec gently, "are you more in a pick up, or put down, mood?"

"I glad I come, but can't stay long, maybe just for weekend. It not so easy to explain."

"Let's stop here," Alec says, as he squeezes Teri's elbow so as to maneuver them out of the stream of relentless foot traffic. "A couple of months ago in an email you said you were dating a sweet dude your dad might eventually accept. Does that have something to do with your ambivalence?"

"Brian is his Western name. He studied at Columbia in New York to get his PhD. Not big dude that make my heart jump like you, but sweet and good to me."

"I gather Brian's a huge improvement over the guy your dad wanted you to marry last year—the one you joked made you go dry from a hundred feet."

"Ha, my father big idiot in many things, but ever since I get more serious about school and mostly put credit cards in drawer, we better friends. Still, getting him to approve of Brian, who is not rich, or from important family, is, how you say, a work in preparation."

"Progress."

"Yes, and progress start to happen, but still slow. Alec, last month when I ask you if okay to be together for a week I think it easy to have romantic vacation and then, well…"

"Teri, I understand a lot better than you probably think," Alec interrupts. "This summer Tamiko, my girlfriend since you left, suddenly proposed coming to Japan instead of going to college. I told her no, mostly because I thought she needed to learn to live her own life. Although I still think this is true, I've been worried that seeing you without agreeing on new dating rules with Tamiko somehow means I'm breaking her trust even though…"

"This is very young girl you told me about in email?" Teri interrupts.

"Barely seventeen, but in both heart and head probably more mature than I am."

"What about here in Japan? Do you already have girlfriend?"

"No, not at all," Alec replies, surprised when Mayumi Yamada's slightly mocking face pops into his head. "But Teri, the truth is, now that you're here I'm quickly recovering from my guilt attack. Still, if you want to just hang out, I totally get it."

"I stay till Monday and we love each other like Berkeley last year," Teri announces determinedly. "I save guilty feeling until on plane back to Seoul, and when I land I have big smile on my face for Brian."

"But what about your research project?"

"Big history paper is true, but plenty material in Seoul. Mostly I make up Tokyo University part to see you."

"Smooth," Alec says, as he thinks Teri has probably learned more from her tycoon dad than she credits. "Are you hungry yet?"

"Definitely, we need plenty energy for later since I now remember exactly why I come. What about Italian restaurant we pass? I read they're world's best lovers."

An hour later after they both have polished off large bowls of spaghetti and meatballs and combine to inhale a loaf of garlic bread at the Trattoria Bricola, Alec asks, "Do you need anything from your dad's apartment?"

"Toothbrush and sexy-girl clothes in here," Teri replies, swinging her large purple shoulder bag as she exits the restaurant before him with several hip-wiggling steps. "I think I not needing anything to sleep in," she adds as she winks at the two men in business suits who stare, mouths agape.

. . . . .

"Wait here a few seconds, I'll be quick," Alec says at the door to his two-room apartment as he sheds his shoes. Leaving Teri in the dimly lit hall he enters the tiny living room where he quickly lights half a dozen candles before calling, "Okay, c'mon in."

"Oh Alec, it so sweet," Teri gasps as she enters the candlelit room to see a bottle of champagne cooling in an ice bucket next to a chocolate cake with *Happy Birthday Teri* printed on top. Then, as she stands on tiptoe to kiss Alec, she murmurs, "My birthday is three weeks ago, silly."

"Last year in Berkeley when your dad dragged you home to Korea we missed it by a day so…"

"Alec, you always such a beautiful American man who know how to make me happy. But now you open champagne while I change."

"Deal, but I have a present—the one I never had a chance to give you last August," Alec says holding out a flat, book-sized package. Carefully untying the red ribbon and folding back the shiny gold paper, Teri finds a smiling picture of the two of them in a hammered metal frame standing in front of Cal's Sather Gate. "Probably you won't be able to bring it home," Alec says seriously.

"Of course I keep it. Maybe hide for a few years, but always have. And if Brian ever brag about old girlfriend, or especially if I find out about new one, well…. Now, where is bathroom?"

"Through the bedroom," Alec replies, motioning toward a door. "But it's so tiny why don't I just hang here so you can use the bedroom to change. I'll bring the champagne when you give me a shout and we'll save the cake for break time."

"I hope you mean first break time," Teri says, blowing Alec an air kiss as she disappears into the bedroom.

After Alec pops the champagne and fills the flutes, he tosses his shirt on a chair before going to the tiny sink in the kitchen nook where he wets a towel and wipes down his slim torso. Happily registering that the anxiety he has felt all day has given way to good old-fashioned lust, he maneuvers his tight black pants around his erection before dropping them on the floor.

Just as he slips out of his briefs, he hears Teri call, "Alec, you come now."

Not quite yet, but soon I hope, Alec thinks, as he picks up the glasses and follows his hyper-erect cock through the bedroom door. Expecting to find Teri dancing around the small room in her red lace teddy as she had on their last night in Berkeley thirteen months earlier, Alec is surprised to see her in bed, the sheet pulled so far up only her almond-shaped brown eyes are visible. "You okay?" he asks.

"About to be very okay as soon as you put down glasses and come here."

"No dancing? No bubbly?"

"No need, I think," Teri says, kicking back the sheet as she extends her arms.

"You are one gorgeous creature," Alec murmurs as he admires Teri's delicate teacup breasts, her remarkably slim waist and her prominent Brazilian-waxed mound. Now, with his weight on his elbows, Alec extends his body plank-like over Teri's touching only his lips to hers.

As Teri's right hand finds and grips Alec's shaft she pulls her mouth away long enough to murmur, "This be my gorgeous American dude."

"I've been on my own for a few weeks so I wouldn't pull too hard if…"

"Think of sumo wrestling because I want us to last plenty long time," Teri murmurs as, with no further preliminaries, she slips Alec's cock into her wet vagina.

As Alec experiences the age-old male delight of literally plunging into the welcoming center of an alluring woman, he unaccountably thinks of Tamiko, and how instead of waiting for him to act, she would be rising to meet him, her breasts, hips, belly and pelvis full of an eager excitement. But with Tamiko almost seven thousand miles away and Teri now snaking her long legs around his butt, Alec doesn't have to tell himself twice to focus on the present.

As if reading Alec's mind Teri places his large right hand over her left breast as she whispers, "You squeeze, okay." Obediently catching Teri's eraser-pink bud between his thumb and forefinger Alec does as asked. Gasping, Teri murmurs, "Now you do thing like in Berkeley."

Remembering what had given Teri the most pleasure during their summer together in Berkeley, Alec slowly eases his cock out of Teri's vagina so that its head presses the top of her tunnel. Now with only its tip still inside her, he immediately hears her familiar moan as her nails dig into his shoulders. Then, as she lifts her hips so as to further increase the pressure on her magic spot, Teri urgently whispers, "I ready now, you come, you come to me."

Not having to be asked twice, Alec leans into half a dozen quick, deep strokes with the happy result that both surge to simultaneous, juddering climax.

. . . . .

Alec wakes deep into Saturday morning still elated by the animal satisfaction of having repeatedly and gloriously joined with Teri for much of the night. Feeling only a little guilty that as host he's not the one making the breakfast preparation noises in the tiny kitchen he nevertheless pulls a light-blocking T-shirt over his eyes as he rolls over.

"Breakfast in six minutes," Teri almost immediately calls. When Alec doesn't respond, she shouts, "I throw cold water over all of you if you not come for special breakfast I make."

"American style, or a bunch of seaweed and little fish?" Alec yells back.

"Bacon, three eggs, toast and even strawberry jam I go buy down the street," Teri adds, with a laugh.

"After last night, four eggs might be better," Alec replies, when he joins Teri in the kitchen.

"Ha, I take as compliment," Teri says, placing the laden plates on the table, which is hardly big enough to hold them. "But maybe you also mad at me."

"For what?"

"I curious, and maybe even little bit jealous, so I look around for picture of young American girl you tell me about. In desk drawer I find big one with you together on beach looking at each other like first man and first woman in first garden. Also, I see she has Asian-shape eyes, but blue like sapphire."

"Tamiko's mom's half Japanese and half Irish, and her dad's family came from Russia."

"So Alec, why you not with this girl who shines like most beautiful star and who obviously make you happy? You tell me in email you get into good grad school in America, so why you even be here in Japan without her?"

"I ask myself those questions every day."

"So what is answer?"

"I believe it's important to experience life on one's own before committing to a long-term partner. Like I told you, Tamiko's barely seventeen. As for me, I never planned to settle down until I was at least thirty, preferably thirty-five. It's been almost a century since most people paired off in their teens, in large part because life expectancy is so much longer now. And then…"

"Hmph! Alec, those just be words, words and more words," Teri interrupts, clearly unimpressed. "Most people search and search for love like this, but never find. You be sorry if beautiful girl finds another love while you follow silly rules and forget true feeling."

"Probably, but since we're here right now, how about focusing on me and you," Alec replies, determined not to let his ambivalence about having said no to Tamiko's coming to Japan trample the joyful feeling he and Teri created a few hours before.

"I really do need to check one thing at Tokyo University library, so I go there now and let you wash dishes," Teri says, pushing back her chair. Then giving Alec a surprisingly deep kiss, she adds, "I call as soon as I be done, okay?"

. . . . .

At 4:30 Alec's phone begins playing John Coltrane's *Blue Train*. Picking up, he says, "Hope you wrapped everything up. Where can we meet?" When there is no reply he asks, "Teri, are you there?"

"Alec, I be back in Korea."

"What? Why? I thought we…"

"Last night perfect, even better than our last night in Berkeley. When I wake up, I even think for tiny moment our bodies are so beautiful together that despite everything, I can have big love with you. But when I see picture of you and beautiful young girl I know this never be true."

"But, I thought you'd at least stay until Monday."

"Alec, or Lec as Tamiko call you in note on back of picture, I so happy last year in Berkeley when I see myself as exotic Asian beauty in your eyes. But, truth is that here in Seoul, I just one more skinny girl with okay face. This morning I realize I lucky that Brian look at me like you look at Tamiko and I don't want to mess that up hoping for something I can't have."

"Teri, I want you to know that last night was fabulous for me."

"Alec, both things true—very fabulous, and our last night together," Teri says before the line goes dead.

. . . . .

"Take a closer look," the slim, balding, fiftyish professor says with an impish grin, not bothering to disguise the pride in his voice.

"Wow! I love the detail, the tiny people, the donkey carts, and oh my god, there's even a three-legged dog," Tamiko exclaims, as she leans over the diorama, forgetting why she's been summoned to Professor Spurgeon's office.

"It's no easy thing to make a thimble-sized donkey, to say nothing of a spotted dog that's less than half that size," the professor says with the pleased chuckle of someone who has done it.

"Did you construct this whole thing?" Tamiko asks with something approaching awe.

"While it's true I've been at it for fifteen years, I've had a huge amount of help from students, as well as my wife and daughters. Actually, my daughter Andromache is one of several subjects I want to talk about."

"Your daughter? Really?" Tamiko asks, genuinely surprised.

"In the small world department, Andromache was your babysitter when you were four and she was going on fourteen."

"You have to be kidding, right? I mean, it's like, my mom often talks about when we lived here in Amherst, but since I was so young when my dad got his PhD over at UMass and then we moved, I don't remember much. But, wait! Does Andromache have light blond hair? I sometimes have this warm, fuzzy dream of a pretty girl with light hair helping me put on my snow boots."

"She has white blond hair, the next thing to albino."

"Ha! Now I know why I always smile at blondie blondes."

"Actually, my wife and I also casually knew your parents. We only lived five blocks apart, and on rainy days in the winter I'd sometimes drive over to pick up Andromache at your place. One afternoon I was surprised to see you holding a kids book about Rome, you know, the kind with lots of pictures and a few words. Even though I was pretty sure you weren't old enough to read the text I asked you how you liked it."

"Seriously, you remember that," Tamiko says as she sits in the chair Professor Spurgeon points to next to his desk.

"Undoubtedly I wouldn't, if your answer hadn't been so surprising."

"Which was?"

"You asked me to name three Roman generals not counting Caesar or Pompey. I've always had a know-it-all tendency, something I'm afraid you've recently noticed."

"I didn't see it that way then, and I still don't. In my line of work an inquiring mind is the Socrates standard."

"Thank you, but I do want to apologize for being impolite in class."

"Socrates made a living being impolite. But Tamiko, more to the point, in my sixteen years here at Amherst only one other student thought my first-year Ancient Greek class was a snore and she recently got tenure in the Classics Department at Wisconsin."

"How did you cope with her impatience?"

"Created an advanced class that amounted to her simultaneously taking Greek 101 and Greek 202, which is the same plan I'm about to propose to you."

"You mean a one-student class? But is that okay with Amherst?"

"With only fifteen students taking Ancient Greek at all levels, I'm free to organize things as I wish. If you're on board, we'd meet privately until you catch up with some of the more advanced students, at which point you'll join them."

"For sure and thanks, I'm totally psyched about going faster," Tamiko replies. "But can I ask you another question?"

"Of course."

"Is there a way I can somehow work on the diorama? It looks unfinished in a few places and I'm pretty good at crafty projects."

"I thought you'd never ask. My wife Sandy and I host Diorama Night on the first and third Sundays of the month at five p.m. A revolving cast of six to eight folks who love both miniatures and ancient Greece show up. Come hungry because Antonio's pizza is a featured attraction. Also Tamiko, I want to say how saddened Sandy and I were when several years back we heard your dad had been killed. I know you must be exhausted by other people's grief so I won't say any more."

· · · · ·

The Sunday morning after Teri's departure, Alec plans a long walk around Tokyo hoping if he expends enough physical energy his mental knots will begin to loosen. But he barely places a foot on the pavement when he sees that the heavy air, low gray clouds and falling temperature suggest rain is coming. Tempted to ignore, or maybe even welcome the possibility of becoming soaked, Alec reluctantly turns back to get his parka. Even when I'm in a rotten mood, he reflects, it's stupid to be stupid. Back on the street, Alec heads toward the five-kilometer path that circles the Imperial Palace in central Tokyo as he focuses on his most immediate worry—how to word an email to reassure Tamiko that Teri has already come and gone for good, especially given the fact he so insistently claimed that Teri's stay in Japan was no big deal. But no sooner does he compose a couple of bland sentences than his inner voice shouts—bullshit, disingenuous bullshit—hardly more than twenty-four hours ago you were doing your randy best to fuck Teri through the mattress, and you'd still be at it if she hadn't left.

Now on the temple path, Alec picks up his pace as if to out-walk the now heavy rain. Although he is no closer to deciding how, what, and when to communicate to Tamiko, he keeps coming back to the thought that he would surely feel less hangdog if he and Tamiko had mutually agreed on open dating rules for their time apart. As he'd told Charlie, while he may sensibly assume that being half a world apart for an extended period means they are both free to date others, Tamiko may just as reasonably think otherwise. And given her prickly response to his email about Teri coming to Tokyo, she almost surely does.

When ninety minutes of fast walking does little to slow Alec's mental merry-go-round, he remembers that writing down his thoughts can help put them in order. Relieved to have a goal, he heads through the still-heavy rain toward the busy area around Tokyo Station where he knows there's an internet cafe. But he's only gone a few steps when the dark clouds abruptly part and a thin shaft of sun illuminates the last slanting drops.

Stepping into the clear, cool air, Alec feels almost as relieved as when his head finally breaks the surface after a huge wave has given him a long tumble. When a few minutes later Alec reaches the Costoma Cafe near the Yaesu Central entrance to the massive red brick edifice of Tokyo Station, he grins as he does his best to decipher the menu of services. In addition to rental computers there are showers, tiny sleep rooms rented by the half hour, and access to a huge library of manga comics. Only in Japan, Alec thinks for at least the hundredth time since his arrival, when he notices a small boy wearing a Golden State Warriors cap staring up at him. As Alec mimes taking a jump shot, he and the boy both grin. Then, tentatively entering the crowded central area of the cafe, Alec's fast improving mood is reinforced when a bespectacled young clerk, eager to practice his English, takes him by the arm and steers him to a computer.

Faced now by a blank screen, Alec realizes that all the words that have pattered around his head that morning have disappeared with the rain. Small loss, he thinks, as attempting to channel his errant feelings he enters:

T. I'm disappointed by your decision to have a communication break, but I'll try to respect it for the short term (well, mostly, anyway). In the meantime, know that I hold you in my heart and imagine holding you in my arms. Be happy. I love you, L.

PS: Just in case you are wondering, Teri visited Japan for less than twenty-four hours before returning to Korea with plans to marry a nice guy named Brian.

With a finger hovering over the send button, Alec hesitates as he rereads this short message. Caught between the desire to try to say something about what he regards as the inevitable tension between freedom and commitment, he realizes that even were he able to sort out his own conflicted thoughts, communicating them across half the globe is the next thing to hopeless. So instead he inserts *truly* between *I* and *love* and frees his finger to do its work.

. . . . .

Alec's first evening at the Tokyo Support Center threatens to turn into a disaster.

After Charlie's introduction to the organization Burns-Short helps finance, Emi Yoshida, the nonprofit's director, asked him to teach English two nights per week. Even when Alec insists he has no teaching experience, Emi is just as insistent that since English is the one subject that the young, primarily Vietnamese contract workers repeatedly request, he should give it a try. When a surprised Alec asks why young domestic, restaurant and construction workers don't prefer to better their immediate prospects by learning Japanese, Emi's answer is depressingly simple. "Alec, as a result of laws that narrowly restrict the possibility of imported workers ever attaining Japanese citizenship, plus the typically hostile attitudes of the Japanese to immigrants, few have a future here. Add to this the fact that many are recruited from farming and fishing villages with false, or at least exaggerated, promises of good wages and working conditions only to find themselves stuck working long hours for low pay, the truth is that most wouldn't stay even if they could."

Five young female domestics and two only slightly older male dishwashers appear for Alec's first class. All recent arrivals from Vietnam, none speak more than a few words of either Japanese or English. Not understanding any Vietnamese, Alec is at a loss as to how to proceed, especially after his efforts to engage them in a conversation using the simplest English and Japanese words fall flat. Distressed in the face of the disappointment he reads on the faces of his young students, Alec grabs a marker and relying on the knack of drawing he's inherited from his mom, begins to sketch simple shapes on a whiteboard. The sun, moon and stars, a house, a cat, and an elephant standing on a beach ball appear, each one labeled in English. Notebooks in hand, his now grinning students copy the shapes before mimicking Alec to sound out the names. Then, remembering a comic strip he had created for his middle school's newspaper, Alec quickly draws the first half dozen frames of a manga style story featuring two lonely overworked contract workers. With class almost over, he barely has time to label the boy, girl, dog, street and store, as with relief he sees that his students are leaning forward, fascinated.

On his way out after class, Emi Yoshida asks Alec how it went.

"To my surprise, okay-ish. I'm pretty sure I won't be able to turn anyone into an English scholar, but by the end of class folks seemed to be learning a few words and maybe even enjoying themselves."

"Which sadly is really all our little center can hope for," Emi replies with a wry grin. "For good reason, many of these young people are isolated and depressed here in Japan. At the political level members of our group lobby for better rights and protections, but in the here and now, the best we can do is to offer a hopefully hospitable refuge. But since speaking even minimal English really can be a ticket to a better life back in Southeast Asia, I suspect that when word of your class spreads more students will appear."

"Okay, I guess, but I don't see how what little I teach can help anyone."

"I guess we'll see, but in the meantime, if your young students feel better about themselves for ninety minutes twice a week it's already a good thing. Also, Alec, when these kids go back home most will have seen enough of a first-world lifestyle that they won't want to go back to their villages. The best alternative is to try to get a job in the booming tourist business where even a few words of English can increase their chances of landing an intro-level job parking cars, cleaning rooms or being a busboy."

LATE SEPTEMBER

HER CHIN SMUDGED, Amy Gashkin shoulders through the partially open front door of a white clapboard bungalow on Santa Barbara Road a block north of Marin Avenue as she strains to carry a disintegrating carton of books. "Finally, the last one," she grunts, as with two quick steps, and a lunge, she deposits it on the dining room table. "For better, or worse, we are officially moved in."

"Good thing, too, Ms. Filthy Face, since you look like a cross between a disgusted raccoon and a pissed-off skunk," Ed Crane replies.

"Best not repeat that," Amy answers, as she tries to brush a swath of clingy white packing material off the front of her black T-shirt. "Instead, it might be better to reflect that I'm already disgusted at the prospect of spending the evening painting the kitchen and scrubbing mold out of the shower grout. And, that I'm biting my tongue so as not to list all the literally hundreds of hassles involved in selling our comfortable old houses in order to fix up this derelict dump so that it's barely fit to move in."

"Hmm, have you noticed that on occasion you don't mention things pretty loudly?"

"Hmm, have you noticed that it's best not to bait me when I'm already pissed?"

"Are you really angry?"

"Mostly tired, as well as dirty and hungry, and I don't know what else exactly. Maybe also dealing with a mild case of the blues."

"How about a dirty martini accompanied by guacamole and chips served in the hot tub? Which, let me remind you, is half the reason you agreed to buy this not-quite-so-derelict dump."

"But with my parents visiting in a few days I really do want to finish the last of the painting and anyway, the tub is as cold as Iceland. Or is it Greenland that's buried by ice?"

"I took the day off from novel writing and finished the painting."

"Really?" Amy replies, going into the kitchen to look. "But the water is still cold, right?"

"Not anymore."

"Are you putting me on? Aren't you the guy who wants to call the plumber when the toilet is clogged?"

"When I opened the deck hatch next to the tub I spotted a red handle. Before I called Ben at Hustle and Flow, I thought, why not flip it," Ed says, his right hand acting out the motion. "And *voilà*, gurgling ensued."

"But the tub is filled with filthy, cold water and has no bottom drain," Amy says, as if this is surely an insurmountable barrier to a happy soak.

"Thanks to the Ace Hardware guy in Kensington turning me onto something called a sump pump, it's now watering our backyard dandelions. And then, just in case you are wondering, I…"

"Oh my god, Ed, I really do hope you're about to say you scrubbed it, filled it, and flipped the red heat thingy meaning we can go in right now?" Amy interrupts.

"No need since you just said it for me," Ed says, leaning over to kiss his now-grinning partner.

· · · · ·

Sitting in the hot water ten minutes later, gin in hand and munchies within easy reach, Ed says, "I don't mean to annoy you, but I kinda look forward to your occasional grumpy day."

"That's beyond weird, and if you're somehow trying to make a larger point, I don't get it."

"The way I see it, most of the time you're calm, even tempered and, dare I say, phlegmatic, so if once in a while sparks fly, it's a clear signal something is bothering at least your Irish half."

"I hate to admit it, but you're probably right."

"So tell me what's up with you lately?"

"I'm not even sure about a bunch of it and I don't want to bring you down for no reason."

"Moving into a house with a view of both San Francisco and Mount Tamalpais with my one true love has me in such a happy frame of mind I can absorb a lot."

"As you know, ever since the end of July when Tamiko suddenly decided she wanted to scamper off to Japan with Lec instead of going to college, I've been worried about her. This last year, and despite my initial misgivings about her falling for a guy so much older, she'd been happier than any time since her dad was killed. Then, when Lec sensibly said no to Japan, it was as if she tumbled off a cliff marked 'End of the world.' And since then…"

"For what it's worth, I texted her 'How's tricks?' this morning," Ed interrupts.

"And?"

"Wait, I have Tamiko's reply here," Ed says, plucking his phone off the deck.

Hanging as tight as a monkey dangling from a branch by her tail as she reaches for a banana. The banana is still just out of reach, but it's a lot closer than it has been lately unless, of course, my arms are growing.

"Beyond her iffy grammar, I'm not sure what to make of that."

"I wasn't either, so I texted back a couple of question marks to which she replied,"

I've talked to a couple of profs and arranged for more challenging course work, and I think I have a plan to make friends with some people my own age (twenty-one, and up, in case you're counting)! In short, a few things, at least, are looking up. Hope romance burns bright in Berkeley.

"Banana or not, she definitely sounds more cheerful than she did a couple of weeks ago when I thought she might even quit Amherst," Amy replies, as she feels her muscles relax. "I know I need to trust that Tamiko will make good decisions, but still, she's only seventeen and, well…"

"She's also entitled to screw up now and then while you grit your teeth and know she's such an amazing young woman that she'll recover PDQ."

"Still, with the benefit of hindsight, I wonder if I, or maybe we is the better pronoun, since you were definitely involved, were wrong to take such a vehement stand against her proposal to defer college and go to Japan with Lec."

"I can listen to you worry for as long as you like, or I can tell you what I think—your choice."

"Tell me, please."

"First, as close as you and Tamiko are, nothing you said or didn't say, about her going with Lec, made a jot of difference. That decision was up to the two of them, full stop. I mean, Amy, ask yourself, when you were pregnant at eighteen, how much did your parents' opinion count when you and Yuri decided to marry and have the baby? Second, whether anyone was listening or not, I think your advice (and mine too, for that matter) was sound. If Tamiko had gone off with Lec to Japan it might well have worked in the short run, but I doubt their relationship would have prospered long-term. When people meet and fall in love, they fling open their personal suitcases and begin to show each other all their accumulated experiences, interests, loves, hates and so on right down to bad jokes. As long as both lovers know how to refill their bags on the fly, this process can go on forever. But absent this considerable, and usually hard-won life skill, their suitcases will inevitably empty and their relationship will die of boredom."

"I'm only half following you at best," Amy says, using her elbows to lift her slim body up and onto the edge of the tub so only her legs still dangle in the water.

"Bear with me," Ed says as he pulls his eyes up from Amy's small, pert breasts to focus on her deep-set, round eyes, the only feature that clearly signals she's not one hundred percent Asian. "In Japan, Lec is both interested and involved in learning Japanese and working with Charlie. So, to stick with my example, he is actively refilling his suitcase. But were Tamiko with him, and therefore away from school, sports and for that matter even her assistant editor job at Bay Books, her suitcase would continue to empty out. In short, I think Lec was wise to understand that

Tamiko needed to get on with her own life's plan, which, after all, involved her going to one of America's coolest little colleges."

"Despite mostly agreeing with that, it breaks my heart to see both of them so miserable being apart," Amy replies.

"Lec, too? How can you be so sure?" Ed asks.

"I've been meaning to tell you that I had an email from Charlie this morning that's also addressed to you. He's back in Japan with Emiko for a week and wanted to share the exciting news that Emiko is three months pregnant."

"Whoa! Is that wise? Charlie must be in his mid-fifties, right?"

"Apparently he wasn't consulted. And, when he got mad at Emiko for quitting birth control without his knowledge, her response was, 'What you going to do, Mr. Charlie? Divorce your poor pregnant Japanese wife who, by the way, you are madly in love with?'"

"Wow!" Charlie exclaims, "you've got to admire that woman's spunk."

"Charlie obviously does, which means he has no choice but to get behind the idea of becoming an elderly papa. But more to the point, there is also news of Alec, who Charlie reports is dutifully getting on with his studies, but sans Tamiko is a glum young man. But, hey, between the gin and the hot water, I urgently need to get all the way out of here," Amy says, swinging her legs out of the tub and standing in one graceful motion.

"Did anyone ever tell you that you have the most beautiful body on God's green earth?"

"Discounting your woeful cliché, and dismissing the idea of a supreme being, you still know the way straight to a skinny girl's heart," Amy replies with a grin. "And now if you'll towel off and follow me to bed, I may decide you're a man worth showing a good time."

"What about the rest of your angst list?"

"Isn't it the male who's supposed to believe that a good roll in the hay solves all problems?"

· · · · ·

Wanting to look attractive for the first time since she's arrived at college, Tamiko wears tight black pants and a fitted blue tee with a scooped neck as she crosses Amherst's well-lit campus with a spring in her stride. It's 9:30 on a summery Friday evening and she's on her way to Missy Frank's and Virginia Pruitt's upperclass suite in Jenkins Hall. As Tamiko passes graceful red brick buildings sprinkled around expansive lawns seemingly guarded by a legion of tall spreading trees, she quickens her step. I'm actually excited, she thinks with surprise.

The door to the suite Missy and V share with several others is half open when Tamiko tentatively steps into the good-sized common room. "Gorgeous one," V almost shouts as she steps forward to hug Tamiko, a wide smile lighting her round, freckle-dusted redhead's face. "You have no idea how much credit Missy and I give ourselves for talking you into playing ball at our Lilliputian school."

"For a bright girl, my best friend here has a huge knack of putting her cleats up her ass," Missy says, as she too, turns to hug Tamiko. "What I'm sure V meant to say is 'Welcome to our humble digs and we hope our friends will be your friends.' There are only a few folks here now, but the rest of the gang are sure to trickle in. As you must have already learned, the grand city of Amherst doesn't provide much competing weekend entertainment, assuming you don't count the contest to see who is first to put on their PJs."

"I'm not much of a party animal," Tamiko replies seriously. "In fact, I'll do best if I find a quiet corner and peek out now and then," she adds, even as she wonders why, despite spending forty-five minutes on her presentation, she's making herself sound like an uber-nerd. But before she can dwell on it, Missy leads her over to adjacent beanbags where she introduces her to two attractive fair-haired girls and a big, homely, mocha-colored guy. Seeing that the girls are drinking red wine from plastic cups, Tamiko goes over to the corner drinks table and pours herself a glass of club soda. Then, glancing around to be sure no one is going to object that she's underage, she adds just enough red wine for convincing color. Not quite knowing what to do next she claims a chair near the window, which she hopes is close enough to the beanbag threesome to appear sociable, but far enough away not to seem as if she's demanding to be included. When, over the next few minutes, a half dozen more people straggle in, followed quickly by a casually confident gang of five, Tamiko sees she's surrounded by a mostly athletic looking group of juniors and seniors, none of whom she knows, except for her hosts.

"I hope it's okay if I say 'hi' to the Ice Princess," the big dude, whom Tamiko has already nicknamed Au Lait for his skintone, says with a disarming grin as he slides his beanbag closer to her chair.

"Oh my god, does everyone on campus call me that?" Tamiko replies, not attempting to hide her dismay.

"Chill, it's not that dire. My kid sister Clemmie is in your dorm. When I saw your pic in the *Student* I asked her what you were like, and she told me what a bummer it was that half the guys in the dorm were dissing you for refusing to run with their first-year rat pack."

"The truth isn't half that interesting. I'd be happy to fit in if I knew how. But, for one thing, I'm not remotely into the music most people listen to—Drake, Kanye, Cardi B, K-pop or whatever—it mostly sounds like angry noise to me. I have a lousy ear so it's my fault I'm sure, but the truth is I've had to buy ear plugs to survive. If I had the choice, I'd hang in a quiet place with a book, although whatever music is playing now is chill."

"Aretha Franklin singing 'You Make Me Feel Like a Natural Woman' from, like, fifty years ago. Aretha just died a few months ago. But as an unreconstructed loner I can identify with your annoyance with the first-year dorm scene. Over time, the preppie contingent at Amherst is slowly declining. But you'd never know it the first few weeks when by virtue of their experience at being away from home they rule the social roost."

"Is your sister Clementine Fine?"

"Our color gives us away, huh?"

"White, black or tan, there's only one Clementine in Appleton," Tamiko responds as she tentatively makes eye contact, and adds with a grin, "I think I missed your first name, unless of course, it's Clem," she adds with a grin.

"Derrick, thankfully, and I hope your asking means we have a chance to get to know each other."

Unsure whether this is a come-on, a simple offer of friendship, or both, Tamiko extends her long fingers to include everyone in the room as she replies, "You obviously hang with an interesting bunch of people and I can definitely use help developing that skill."

"I play basketball. I'm not a starter, but usually the second or third man off the bench when Coach needs a big body underneath. Combine that with writing the occasional column for the newspaper and lots of people know me. However, since my girlfriend is off to Italy for her junior year, when it comes to social life I probably feel almost as adrift as you. Incidentally, Ericka started at point guard the last two years so you're the one Coach Raines hoped would take her place."

"Honestly Derrick, no matter what Coach Raines implied in that article in the campus paper, I've made it clear from the beginning I wasn't playing basketball here at Amherst. I love pitching so I'm in with softball, but otherwise my desire to run after a ball is rapidly evaporating."

"With Ericka in Europe, and no one on the roster who can come close to filling her shoes, Coach can maybe be forgiven for confusing wishes with fishes." Then, seeing that Tamiko isn't following, he adds, "If wishes were fishes, beggars would eat."

"Ha! Well, I'm not sure a coach who won the NCAA Division Three Championship last year can be called a beggar, but I definitely have experience with coaches so desperate to win they pressure a kid to play even when they may not want to. When I was nine or ten and travel ball coaches began pursuing me to be on their teams, I thought it was all about me. But after playing lacrosse with kids three years older, soccer when I was hurt, and water polo long after I was bored with being wet, I tumbled to the fact that it was mostly about the coach's needs, not mine. More important, I finally learned that the pressure to play wouldn't stop until I said no and stuck to it. But, hey, I guess we have one big thing in common since my boyfriend is also out of the country, except to tell the truth I'm not sure we're still together."

"Where? And for how long? I mean how long has he been your boyfriend, not how long he's been away, although you can tell me that too if you want. Or, if I'm being too personal, let's talk about something else."

"Lec and I met a year ago this last August and were pretty inseparable until a month ago when he left for a year in Japan. Since he was a fifth year senior at Cal, and I was barely sixteen when we got together, I guess you could say it hasn't been your typical high school romance."

"Your parents were okay with that? I mean, your dating a considerably older dude?"

"My dad was killed by a truck when I was twelve. Mom was totally into treating Lec as if his name was Humbert Humbert until he saved her life and then a few days later, mine."

"Whoa! Did he really do that? Or, are you talking metaphorically?"

"To oversimplify a lot, Max, a deranged guy whom Mom briefly crossed paths with in Europe after Dad was killed, showed up in Berkeley with hate in his heart and rape on his mind."

"Sounds like a B movie."

"I can't argue with that, and fortunately it also had an old-fashioned Hollywood ending. Specifically, after terrorizing us, Max, accidentally shot himself dead. At this point Mom concluded that since without Lec's intervention, she and I surely would have been raped, killed, or likely both, fate had decreed that Lec and I have a chance to be together."

"Obviously you two are now half a world apart."

"Lec, which is short for Alec, is in Japan learning the language and business culture and, at least to hear him explain it, giving me the golden opportunity to experience college life on my own."

"And the future?"

"All this last year when we were together I thought that, because we loved each other almost to distraction, life would just somehow continue to roll out like an endless magic carpet. Now that I've woken up to the fact that my carpet has turned into a hunk of cracked linoleum, my focus is on making it through each day."

"Which pretty much describes my situation with Ericka, who

believes that a year in Europe gives her a chance to completely reboot her romantic life. But, in addition to wayward lovers, we have something far more fraught in common. My parents died in a small plane crash when I was eleven, and Clemmie was barely seven."

"Oh my god, I'm so sorry," Tamiko says, her right hand flying up to touch Derrick's shoulder. "Derrick, it's like, as horrible as it was to lose one parent, losing both has to be exponentially worse. Did you two move in with your grandparents?"

"My mother's parents had already passed. My dad's, who had long ago disowned us because Mom was Black, saw no reason to change their mind."

"Yowser! So your dad was white and your mom African American?"

"She hated that term, but yes, something like three hundred years ago many of her ancestors were brought by force from Africa, although her skin was light enough that slave owners undoubtedly made contributions. My dad was an orthodox Jew by birth, but not in practice."

"So what happened to you and Clementine?" Tamiko asks, as she realizes that somewhere along the way she's become comfortable with meeting Derrick's light brown eyes.

"Very fortunately my dad's younger brother Ben took us in. At that point Ben was a thirtyish, single, striving Hollywood screenwriter, nowhere near the successful dude he is today. In short, his agreeing to parent two uber-traumatized kids was an act of true courage."

"Since you're both here at this elite little college, he must have done a good job."

"Ben really is amazing, part buddy, part indulgent uncle and when he needs to be, a no-nonsense dad. However, to make things work while he was off climbing Hollywood's greasy pole, he hired us a mother."

"You're kidding?"

"Well, she was our nanny first, but Mary McCarthy soon became our substitute mom. To find Mary, Ben interviewed something like fifty women. At that point she was in her mid-forties and recovering from the death of her husband from prostate cancer. Her daughters were off in college and I guess Ben thought Mary needed us as much as we needed her. Anyway, bless her heart now and forever, Mary was willing to take us on, which included the whole deal—getting us back and forth from school, supervising homework, coping when we cried our little hearts out and so on. At first she commuted, but after a year, when Ben had his first huge success with *Clothesline* he bought a biggish house in Pacific Palisades and Mary moved in."

"Yo, Derrick, the penny finally dropped. Sorry to be so slow, but your uncle is the big deal director Ben Fine? *Alice in the Air* is all alone at the top of my favorite movie list. But what about Mary? Did her whole life revolve around caring for you and Clementine?"

"Like every third person in SoCal, Mary writes screenplays, which is how Ben knew to interview her in the first place. Even though she's only sold a couple of concepts and a doomed pilot, she believes her pot of gold is only one rainbow away. In short, the idea of having free time to write while we were in school appealed to her. Add in the slightly spacey, but certifiably sweet physical therapist she met four or five years ago, and Mary has a good life."

"But no more job since you two are on your own."

"Not hardly," Derrick replies with a loud laugh. "Now that Clemmie has joined me, Mary has morphed into a cross between Ben's personal assistant and house manager. And like every good mom she is still all over Clemmie and me, never mind we're toilet trained and three thousand miles away. But, listen Tamiko, despite being delighted to meet you I have a paper due at midnight, which I'm interpreting to mean anytime before Professor Wang wakes up tomorrow and checks her email. But, I definitely have to push."

"What's it on?"

"*Far From the Madding Crowd*, a book you've probably never read."

"When Farmer Oaks smiled the corners of his mouth spread till they were within an unimportant distance of his ears, his eyes were reduced to chinks and..."

"Whoa girl, are you Thomas Hardy's great granddaughter or something?"

"I read it two years ago, so I've probably misplaced a few commas."

"You're joking. Sounds like you inhaled it this morning."

"I'm taking Ancient Greek, American History, Economics and a grad stats course over at UMass, plus my first-year seminar on the Japanese Aesthetic, but no nineteenth-century English literature."

"Ugh! Tell me you're not another one of those pesky geniuses with eidetic recall who swarm this campus? But, in case you are, can I bribe you to write my paper?"

"Just because I have a Velcro memory doesn't mean I have deep thoughts."

"Why is it I'm guessing you probably do? But here's a more practical idea. Ben's new movie, *The Battle of Tule Lake*, which focuses on the most ruthless of the World War Two prison camps Japanese Americans were locked up in, opens at the Amherst Cinema tomorrow. Clemmie and I have a date to see the early show and I wonder if you might like to join us and grab a bite after?"

"Definitely. I've been looking forward to seeing it." Then, motioning to her eyes, Tamiko adds, "As you may have guessed, I have genes in the game. My great grandparents were locked up in similar World War Two prison camps, in Rohwer, Arkansas, and Gila River, Arizona."

"I suspect you've seen Scott Hicks's *Snow Falling on Cedars* about the Japanese strawberry farmers on that little island off the coast of Washington State who were incarcerated at the Manzanar prison camp in California?"

"Another of my favorite movies," Tamiko replies, her hands flying up to emphasize her enthusiasm. "I'm still bummed that Ethan Hawke lost both his arm and Youki Kudoh."

"Ha! I've heard Ben use almost the same words and also say he hopes *Tule Lake* is half as good. But now I really am on my horse so how about the three of us meet outside Appleton at five-thirty tomorrow?"

. . . . . .

Tamiko waits for ten minutes to be sure Derrick is well clear of Jenkins. Then, giving Missy a thumbs-up, she mouths *thanks* as she heads for the door. But, before Tamiko can slip out, Missy hurries over.

"You're leaving early. Everything smooth?"

"Definitely, but I'm kinda beat, so…"

"It looked like maybe you made a friend."

"I hope so," Tamiko replies, reddening slightly. "And Missy, thanks for including me. It's, like, tonight was pretty much the first time outside of my Greek class that I've had fun since I got here."

"Sweet! For the next couple of weeks I'll text you where and when weekend stuff is happening. After that you'll be part of the crew if you want to be. And just so you know, Derrick Fine is a good dude."

Back at Appleton at 11:30, Tamiko bounds up the stairs and into her room, which is mercifully free of Eloise and Four. Glancing in the mirror to see a smiling face staring back, she is delighted to realize that the brain fog that has blanketed her since she and Lec separated has finally lifted. Whether or not this has anything to do with the long-faced, big-eared dude she's just met, is not something she wants to think about let alone be quizzed on by Eloise. Flopping on her bed she opens her laptop and rereads Lec's email from the week before. Finally ready to answer, she types:

Thanks for your message. For sure I feel the same way when it comes to the open heart and arms part. As to your PS about Teri being back in Korea, it's nice to know, I guess. But, going forward, when it comes to dating others, let's both adopt a "don't ask, don't tell" policy.

As for the soap opera called TAMIKO RELUCTANTLY GOES TO COLLEGE, things are improving. I've wormed my way into more challenging course work and begun the process of making a few friends. Ruth was a big help when she pointed out that for a variety of reasons (you being the biggest) my social age seems to have settled somewhere north of twenty. As a result I've gotten out of my first-year dorm and begun to hang with an upperclass crew. Baby steps so far, but headed in the right direction.

—Yes, I still love you, T.

. . . . .

At five-twenty Sunday afternoon there's a knock on Tamiko's door. Opening it, she finds a slim tannish girl several inches shorter than herself with arresting gray-green eyes.

"Clementine Fine, I do believe."

"Hey, Tamiko, and it's Clemmie to my friends, and for that matter, to my enemies as well," the smiling girl replies. "We met briefly at one of those get to know you events a few weeks ago, but since we're on different floors I thought I'd say hi before my big brother shows up his usual fifteen minutes late and then, literally gallops us off to the show."

"As long as we get there. I've been amped about seeing *The Battle of Tule Lake* all day. It was nice of Derrick to invite me, and also to watch out for me last night."

Making a face as if she's sucked a lemon, Clementine replies, "Ha, you might think such a nice dude would invite his only sister to a chill, upperclass party now and again. Instead, I'm assured that it's best if I make my own way here at Amherst."

"For the record, I badgered one of the girls on the softball team into inviting me," Tamiko replies, with a laugh. "There's no guarantee I'll fit in."

"Given that my super well-connected brother has sent me three texts asking about you, I kinda doubt that."

"Derrick seems like a chill dude," Tamiko replies, keeping her voice as neutral as possible.

"Definitely. But with his girlfriend Ericka off to study in Italy, my brother has also been nonstop grumpy this fall so it will be a relief if meeting you changes that. And maybe you…"

Not certain what Clementine is about to say, but very sure that having barely gotten to know Derrick, she isn't ready for sisterly intervention, Tamiko interrupts, "Actually, I'm in a similar situation except my boyfriend is in Japan, although honestly, I'm not sure he can still be called that."

Apparently deciding not to pursue this obviously sensitive subject,

Clementine waits a few seconds before saying, "Tamiko, it's not lost on me that a bunch of the guys around the dorm have treated you like crap, so…"

"Maybe I should have lost at beer pong a few times," Tamiko interrupts with a chuckle that she hopes will obviate the need for a long chew over her social standing.

"I hate that game too, and all the beer-swilling and aggressive posturing that goes with it," Clementine responds, blowing right past Tamiko's reticence. "In fact, I pretty much retreated when you did, but since I'm far from the hottest girl in the dorm, no one took it as a mortal insult to their manhood."

"If Ice Princess is the worst thing I'm ever called, I'll have an easy life," Tamiko replies, almost surprised to find that she means it.

"Great attitude, but let's go sit on the steps just in case Big Bro is on time for once." Coming out of Appleton's front door a minute later, Tamiko is surprised to see Derrick Fine leaning against the trunk of a maple as Clementine says, "Yo, Bro, why do I think it's not me that has you here early?"

Detaching himself from the large tree and good-naturedly bumping fists with both girls, Derrick says, "And my little sis wonders why I keep her big mouth away from my friends."

Falling into step on Derrick's right, with Clementine on his other side, Tamiko is happy to listen to them banter. The fact that their good-natured teasing is clearly for her entertainment lets her know she's a valued member of the group, a sweet feeling she's almost forgotten.

After the film the three head to nearby Pasta E Basta, a family style restaurant locally famous among students for its hefty portions. While all three wolf down fettuccine alfredo with sausage and chicken, Clementine asks Tamiko what she thought of *The Battle of Tule Lake*.

Pausing a moment to swallow, Tamiko asks, "Do you want my here and now opinion? Or, based on the extremely shaky foundation that my great grandparents, who I never met, were locked up in the World War Two prison camps, should I attempt to pontificate about its larger historical meaning?"

"Given the fact that my being part Black gives me close to zero insight into what happened with slavery six generations ago, how about you stick to how you liked the movie, unless of course your Japanese grandparent passed on some interesting family lore."

"That would be my grandfather Tosh, who, unaccountably, everyone calls Al. He wasn't born until three years after the war. For sure he must have heard stories about the camps from his parents and aunts and uncles, but Grandpa Al is a man who prefers fishing to talking, so he's told me remarkably little. But I've read a bunch of books on the Japanese incarceration so I've picked up enough to write a paper on the subject every year since second grade."

"Ha, the art of pushing your white teacher's guilt button to get an A-plus," Clementine interrupts. "I did the same thing concerning Derrick's and my slave ancestors somehow surviving both picking cotton in Mississippi plus the vicious apartheid century that followed the Civil War. As long as I had a white teacher, all was golden. But the year I got Mrs. Duperone, a Black woman born in Alabama, I got back 'Missy, this ragtag gaggle of platitudes, stereotypes and hokum is a disgrace to the memory of the real people who suffered the misery and degradation of the real bondage you are obviously so pleased to wallow in.'"

"Gah! Fortunately, I never had a Japanese-American teacher, or probably the same thing would have happened to me. But, back to the film. The truth is, although I thought I knew something about what went down in the camps—I mean, that there was barbed wire, guard towers manned by guys with guns, and in the beginning, the inmates were even housed in horse stalls. Still, what we just saw was beyond shocking. I mean, assuming your uncle didn't exaggerate, Tule Lake with its tanks, machine guns, twenty-eight guard towers and especially, the routine brutality practiced by the guards, was pretty much the same as a German concentration camp, absent the ovens."

"Ben told it pretty straight," Derrick replies seriously. "I was up there at the Tule Lake museum reading first person accounts and it's hard to exaggerate how grim it was. As the movie explains, Tule Lake was the heavy-duty prison for the whole ten-site gulag system—the place where they put the so-called 'No-No Boys,' or, prisoners whose only crime was to say no when asked to pledge absolute loyalty to the U.S."

"But, even if they were only one-sixteenth Japanese, these people had been ripped out of their normal lives and locked up for a couple of years before they were asked those two so-called loyalty questions, right?" Clementine asks, incredulously. "I mean, isn't it like asking a field slave if he'd lay down his life for the country that enslaved him, and if he says no, sentencing him to a chain gang?"

"Good analogy," Derrick replies. "And at Tule Lake, which is way isolated in the sparsely populated northeast corner of California, the military had what amounted to carte blanche. For sure, that scene where the sadistic guards use bright lights and horrendous noise to wake up two hundred and fifty prisoners in the middle of the night and march them before what appeared to be a firing squad of soldiers with machine guns really happened. And, the fact that ultimately the prisoners were threatened, but not killed, excuses nothing."

"I thought one of the most telling parts of the movie was when the 'good ole boy' guards who had no clue how to construct the top security stockade had to literally beg one of the Japanese-American prisoners, who had been a contractor and engineer in Los Angeles before the war, to get the job done," Tamiko says.

"And, coolest of all," Clementine adds, "that dude managed to delay construction month after month by requesting specialized materials he knew the army would have a hard time supplying."

"Derrick, but what about the general strike and big riot? Did all that happen?" Tamiko asks.

"In a word, yes. As shown in the film, after the prisoners protested their rotten food and pitiless treatment, the army moved in seven tanks and jeeps with mounted machine guns. Inmates were gassed and many were removed and beaten. The way Ben sees it, it was the only World War Two military action fought on U.S. soil."

"I wonder what happened to the No-No Boys after the war?"

Clementine muses. "And what about No-No Girls? It's like, if there were any," she adds with a chuckle, "I'm guessing at least they didn't get pregnant."

"Oops! Sorry Tamiko," Derrick interjects quickly. "As you can see, we have a family penchant for making tasteless jokes. But to answer my sister's question, women over seventeen were also asked to sign the so-called loyalty oath and a fair number who refused were sent to Tule Lake. When the war ended and the camps closed, everyone was released no matter how they had answered the two questions. However, several hundred men who had already been sent to prison for resisting the draft, remained there until President Truman issued a general pardon in 1947. A few of the No-No Boys were so bitter they relocated to Japan, but the cultures were so different I don't think many stayed. But here's a bitter sidebar to this already sad story—many of the Japanese Americans who had answered 'yes' to the loyalty questions were so anxious to be seen as loyal Americans, that they discriminated against the No-No Boys and, indeed, everyone sent to Tule Lake, for many years after the war."

"Well, I thought it was a powerful movie," Clementine says. "I mean, maybe the love story between the No-No Boy and the goodie-two-shoes girl whose brother enlisted and died fighting in Italy was a tad contrived, but otherwise, well, I've already texted Ben 'Wow!'"

A hour later as she gets ready for bed, Tamiko hears her phone ping. The text from Derrick says, *R u free to hang at 4 Weds? Maybe take a walk so we have time to get to know each other?*

Counting slowly to sixty, and then, even more slowly, back to zero, Tamiko texts back, *Definitely*.

. . . . .

With Teri Kim back in Korea for good and little else fun to do with the exception of teaching his Support Center class, Alec pours his considerable energy into his studies, determined to make real progress by the time Phil Short arrives for the October meetings. Telling himself he's happy to be on his own Alec nevertheless catches himself being disappointed that Mayumi Yamada is never in the office in the late afternoon when he stops by. Is she actively avoiding me, Alec wonders on the last Thursday afternoon in September, when he again finds the office empty. But, even if she is, why could I possibly care, he asks himself, as he sits at the outer office desk pretending to study.

An hour later, as Alec walks back to his apartment via the noisy, crowded, neon-soaked streets of the Shinjuku district, he finally admits to himself that he's lonely.

Although he's been in Japan almost a month, he's formed only a few superficial relationships. An experienced solo traveler through India, Australia, New Zealand, and much of South and Central America, Alec's used to being on his own, without this feeling of profound aloneness. So his question to himself becomes, does he want to continue his studies for the foreseeable future in a country he finds so bewilderingly strange? Or, is it time to admit his Japanese venture is a well-meaning mistake? After all, joining Charlie's Japan-centered consulting business after finishing grad school only makes sense if he enjoys Japan. Then, as he waits for the light at Takeshita Dori, an upscale street lined with fashionable shops, Alec finally admits to himself that were Tamiko with him, her lively intelligence and overflowing good cheer would surely combine to put him in a much better frame of mind. Which leads him back to the question he's already asked himself many times. Did he blunder in refusing to agree to her accompanying him? Realizing that his mind is once again poised to dive into its all-too-familiar rabbit hole of Tamiko-centered what-ifs and could-have-beens, Alec forces himself to return to the here and now by trying to translate a rainbow-colored sign on a building fifty yards up the block, which says something about a legendary memory foam futon. But as he crosses the street to get a closer look, he recalls Tamiko's recent email about making new friends among upperclass Amherst students and it suddenly dawns on him, Copernicus-like, that he may no longer be at the center of her universe.

Arriving at his apartment after picking up a six-pack of Sapporo Yebisu and some chili-spiced Karamucho potato chips, Alec is grateful to be diverted from his sour mood by seeing that he has an email from Charlie:

Lec,

Anata no kenkyu ga umaku itte iru koto o negate imasu. *No question, if you just read that, the answer is hai.*

Turns out that on October 10th you'll find me, not Phil, on your doorstep. Because my partner has to undergo a minor procedure to scrape several incipient skin cancers off his nose he wants to hide until he's "less splotchy." I'll be in Tokyo for a week of pretty much nonstop meetings. Don't know if you've heard, but Emiko is pregnant (yes, I'm way too old for this, but then I wasn't consulted, was I?). As a result, she feels too nauseous to make the trip, and also (I think) wants me to have a few days to get over being annoyed at her (actually, I've already come around to being pleased, but am not ready to concede the moral high ground quite yet).

I'd like you to sit in on a couple of my more important meetings. Mayumi Yamada tells me she's left you the necessary background reports for Ito and Kibu Financial. In addition, you'll find files full of contracts, minutes, and a jumble of other stuff concerning both corporations in the locked file cabinet in the inner office (combination 1853—the year Commodore Perry sailed into Tokyo Harbor) which should fill in the background you'll need. I'd include you in more meetings, but I don't think it makes sense for you to skip a week of school when you'd likely understand less than a third of what's being said.

Finally, let me go out on a little bit of a limb to say a few words about Mayumi. Since she asked about you, this seems only fair. Also, my belated apology for forgetting to tell you last month that she's helping Burns-Short with research this fall. As you may have gathered, Mayumi's dad is the founder and CEO of Yamada Designs, one of Japan's most innovative and profitable software companies. Her mother, Shoko Shin (she's half Korean) runs a fashionable Tokyo art gallery that specializes in the work of artists who fuse Western and Japanese styles. And of course, you've met Mayumi, so know she's a formidable young woman in her own right.

Yamada Designs has been one of our core clients for over fifteen years and from the first, Tosh and Shoko have been real friends, meaning that I met Mayumi when she was wearing a tutu and trying to twirl on her toes. Over the years both Phil and I have come to see ourselves as her honorary gaijin *godparents. Although, Mayumi has had the equivocal fortune of being the bright youngest child (she has two older brothers) of wealthy, talented and famous parents, she's mostly succeeded in her determination not to become a privileged brat. Mayumi graduated from Tokyo University with high honors a few months ago and has been waiting for a girlfriend to finish up so they can go traveling together in Europe starting in December and lasting all the way through until Mayumi starts journalism grad school in London in September. Mayumi also spent part of her senior year at the University of Iowa with an American guy she became enamored with when he was completing his PhD in Tokyo. Because she abruptly returned to Japan in the middle of the spring semester, her dad hopes (but doesn't know for sure) that their relationship is over. Late this summer when Phil heard that Mayumi was temporarily at loose ends, he hired her to do client research. Although it's always a pleasure to do a favor for the Yamada's, the real reason Mayumi's on our payroll is because she's highly competent.*

OK, enough (too much, probably). I'll send you my itinerary soon. As usual, I'll stay at the Imperial Hotel.

Cheers, Charlie

Feeling unaccountably intrigued by Charlie's message about a young woman he'd found annoying at their one short encounter, Alec starts to pace around his apartment only to be frustrated by its Lilliputian size. So instead, he drops to the floor and does fifty push-ups before grabbing a Sapporo from the mini-fridge. Now sitting at his tiny table, he reaches for his laptop and types.

Emiko: You go girl. I just got the fabulous news from my secretly delighted uncle. I hope you can hear my pleased whoops (in Japanese, of course).

XOXO, Lec

. . . . .

"Ready to boogie?" Derrick asks with a grin when Tamiko meets him on the main quadrangle after her last Wednesday class.

When, by way of answer, Tamiko jumps and taps her running shoes together twice, Derrick continues, "We are only a couple of minutes from the Norwottuck Rail Trail, which follows an abandoned Boston and Maine railroad line. If we go far enough, we can get a nice view of the Connecticut River."

"Right behind you, big guy."

"I'm hoping maybe you'll hang next to me so we can have a real conversation," Derrick says, with a chuckle. Nevertheless, almost ten minutes pass in what Tamiko registers as companionable silence as they wind along a paved path through the autumn-hued woods. Striding briskly to keep pace with Derrick's almost cantering lope she's just beginning to rummage around her brain for something appropriate to say when Derrick beats her to it.

"So Tamiko, here's where I tell you what I'm thinking, but also ask you to interrupt if I'm so far off base I'm making a dummy of myself. All good?" Registering Tamiko's nod Derrick continues, "Okay, then. I'm attracted to you and I choose to assume because you're here, you feel at least somewhat the same toward me. Of course, if you…"

"Yes," Tamiko interrupts too loudly as she kicks at a pebble. Then, turning to look at Derrick's quizzical expression, she adds, in a quieter tone, "To the attraction part, that is."

"Great! But why am I guessing you have more to say?"

"Derrick, it's just that I'm clueless about how to flirt, which I guess is what people are supposed to do in our situation. So, is there any way we can skip it? It's like, since we met Friday I've been attracted to you and would definitely like to get to know you better."

Slowing his pace slightly, Derrick laughs as he says, "So, 'yes' really does mean 'yes,' which of course is music to my ears. I have to grind for the next couple of days, but how about we grab supper Friday over in town and, well..."

"Sounds like a sweet plan, which I hope means we don't have to run all the way to Connecticut," Tamiko interrupts, with a grin.

. . . . .

Having introduced an additional ten panels to the illustrated tale he now calls *The Adventures of Bao and Linh*, Alec deems his second class, which has grown to eleven students, a success. This time he's numbered the key elements of each drawing and handed out a sheet with the corresponding English names. And the fact that Dong, one of the new students, already speaks rudimentary English, also allows Alec to include a conversational element. Specifically, while the class is on a ten-minute break, Alec quickly jots a half dozen common verbal interactions on the whiteboard, including:

"Hello, how are you?" "I'm fine, how are you?"

"How much is that cabbage?" "It is two dollars."

"Are you hungry?" "No, I just ate."

Next to each, Dong then writes the Vietnamese translation. When the students return, Alec divides them into two groups with Group 1 asking each question, and Group 2 answering it. By the time the groups reverse roles a couple of times and everyone begins to feel confident of their pronunciation, enthusiasm soars to the point that Emi Yoshida peeks in to see what all the laughter is about.

Yet the evening ends on an awkward note for Alec when Ca, by far the prettiest of the girls, hovers around him after class, making it clear she's available to hover much closer should he give her half a chance. Momentarily tempted by Ca's flashing eyes, the delicate line of her collarbone, and her perky derriere, Alec immediately realizes that no matter how lonely he is the cavernous power gap between them all but dooms any romantic liaison to end in grief. Not sure how to step aside without hurting Ca's feelings, Alec knows he has to come up with a strategy before the next class.

And so, two nights later near the end of the session, Alec hooks his iPad to the Center's large monitor and displays a number of photos from his personal collection. He starts with a picture of himself standing by Sather Gate on the Cal Berkeley campus. When the students have mastered the relevant English words, he continues by showing photos taken on his various travel adventures. By far, the class favorite is from a backpack trip in the Sierra that shows a bear standing on its hind legs as it tries to reach a bag of food tied to a tree branch. When the laughter fades Alec moves on to a picture of Tamiko and himself standing on a beach holding surfboards. "My girlfriend," he says simply.

. . . . .

Back in her room late Wednesday evening, Tamiko is pleased to see that Eloise is off someplace, probably with Four. The possibility of a romantic friendship with Derrick is still so new she isn't ready to mention it to her voluble roommate. Putting on her pajama bottoms and a clean Oakland A's T-shirt, Tamiko wonders if dating Derrick will make her feel like a traitor to Lec. But hey, wasn't it Lec who insisted she go off to college to gain new experiences? And even though her having a romance with Derrick may not be exactly what Lec had in mind, it's her life isn't it? True, her growing affection for Derrick is nothing like the stunned feeling she'd experienced when her eyes first locked with Lec's that August day thirteen months ago. But, so what? Even if hanging with Derrick doesn't turn out to be a huge deal, the possibility of having sex with him gives her a pleasant head-to-toe buzz. It's been a month since she's been with Lec and she's beginning to understand how addictive lovemaking can be.

. . . . .

In Japanese language school on Friday Alec tells himself half a dozen times that despite wanting to avoid his empty apartment for as long as possible, he definitely won't stop by the Burns-Short office to study that afternoon. But as his class winds down he admits to himself that the real reason for avoiding the office is his fear that Mayumi Yamada won't be there, adding an exclamation point to the fact that he faces another lonely weekend. Ashamed of his own gutlessness, Alec all but forces himself to walk over to Shinjuku Hiyashi and take the elevator to the fourth floor of the now-familiar office building. But when he sees that the door to the Burns-Short office is ajar, a heady rush of excitement blows away his dour mood. Pausing to finger-comb back his shaggy dark hair, Alec pushes through.

"Catch," Mayumi says, as she tosses Alec a silver can of Sapporo Premium beer from where she sits with her feet up on the outer office desk.

Deftly spearing the high throw, Alec says, "*Arigato.*"

"That's my peace offering in case you didn't guess. I was bitchy when we met earlier for no good reason except probably I was a little jealous of your being Charlie's favorite nephew, which of course is no good reason at all."

"Also, his only nephew," Alec says, grinning back at the widely smiling girl who, with both dimples on display, is more attractive than he first thought. Then, realizing he's staring, Alec quickly adds, "But, having read the mini-bio Charlie sent me about you it's obvious you're very special to him."

"I hope so."

"I have a confession," Alec almost blurts, surprised at his own frankness. "I've stopped by a couple of times hoping you'd be here."

"How about I match that with an admission of my own. When I saw that my research papers were gone, I hoped that you were a little curious about the girl who wrote them. Alec, I have to scoot since I was due at my mother's gallery reception ten minutes ago. But later on I'm getting together with University friends at a bar in Shibuya. If you're even a little interested, I'll text you the details."

"Please."

"Okay then, I'll hope to see you later," Mayumi replies, and with three quick steps she's out the door, not looking back.

. . . . .

Alec starts early for the Aldgate British Pub, still not having overcome his dread of becoming lost in the bowels of Tokyo's metro, which mystifyingly weaves together a dozen distinct lines run by at least several different companies. Almost never, he's learned, can one get from point A to point B without changing trains at point C, and probably D, both of which offer fresh chances to get lost. But, perhaps anticipating the muddle he's likely to face, Mayumi's step-by-step directions are so tight Alec arrives at the Shibuya station without a hitch. Since it's now only a short walk to the Aldgate Pub on Udagawacho, he makes his way slowly around several blocks so as not to be embarrassingly early. Finally entering the Aldgate at 9:45, he's surprised to encounter a faithful, if not fawning, copy of a typical London pub complete with dozens of craft beers, fish and chips, and even bacon sandwiches. Several huge wall-mounted TVs show soccer and basketball games with the sound turned down while a band warms up on a soundstage. Pausing to take in the scene, Alec sees Mayumi wave from a long corner table full of eight or nine chattering young people.

As Alec approaches, everyone stops talking and looks up. Feeling thumped by their unabashed scrutiny, Alec slows. Then, thinking, I may as well do my best to provide the drama they're hoping for, he steps around the table to where Mayumi has pushed back her chair to stand. "How do, mate?" he asks, extending his fist.

When, not missing a beat, Mayumi replies, "Brilliant! 'Ow ya going?" as she taps his fist with hers, Alec leans over and kisses her lightly on the cheek.

For a few seconds everyone freezes as Alec kicks himself for having needlessly embarrassed Mayumi in front of her friends. He is about to take the one free seat further along the table when, with a resigned shrug, the tall fellow sitting next to Mayumi slides over so Alec can sit next to her. Still grinning, but also slightly flushed, Mayumi introduces Alec to the others, saying in English, "This is my new work colleague, Alec Burns." Then, turning to him she continues, "Alec, everyone here has been to the U.S. at least once so prepare to be grilled on everything from topless pole dancers in Las Vegas to the depth of the Grand Canyon."

"Believe it or not," Alec replies in awkward Japanese, "I have never been to the Grand Canyon, and I hate Las Vegas." Then, as he struggles to find the words to explain that he lives in Northern California, a moon-faced young woman at the end of the table says, "This all-English night now—no Japanese allowed."

Recognizing this is a polite way to welcome him, Alec bows slightly as he says, "When you guys come to the U.S., we'll only speak Japanese."

During the eighteen months when Alec took a long holiday from UC Berkeley to travel a good chunk of the world, he had often been bored by people who insisted on recounting every granular, and usually predictable, detail of their American visits. But tonight, delighted to be out of his tiny apartment and included in this congenial group, Alec is cheerfully patient as Mayumi's friends share their almost endless photos, including the inevitable King Kong impersonations at the top of the Empire State Building. When Hana, the pretty girl across the table, describes her day at the beach in Malibu including several revealing bikini-clad selfies, Alec is unaccountably pleased, when Mayumi treats Hana to a no-nonsense stare as she inquires as to the whereabouts of her boyfriend.

At 11:15 when everyone says their goodbyes outside the pub, Mayumi volunteers to escort Alec to the Metro to be sure he gets on the right train. After a few steps Alec says, "Thanks for including me, Mayumi. As I'm sure you could tell, I had fun. And, apologies if I embarrassed you there at the beginning. Are those your closest buddies?"

"My university group, for sure, except for Fujiko, who couldn't come because of a family obligation. But, when it comes right down to it, I'm mostly a loner, happy enough with my own company much of the time. A big part of the reason I like this kind of get-together is that nothing is required at a deep level. Oh my god Alec, I'm sorry to bore you with all…"

"I'm the last thing from bored," Alec interrupts, as he stops to face

Mayumi outside the Metro entrance.

Raising her eyes to meet his, Mayumi seems about to continue when, apparently deciding she's already revealed more than enough, she asks neutrally, "Have you been to the Hamarikyu Gardens? It's modeled after a seventeenth-century shogun's garden and you don't have to be a Japanophile to be awed."

"No, but it's near the top of my to-do list," Alec answers, hoping this is a run-up to an invitation, not just a polite tourist tip.

"How about I show it to you Sunday morning?"

"I'd like that, Mayumi. I really would," Alec replies, not trying to modulate his eagerness.

"Can you get there by nine when it opens? That way we'll have an hour before it gets crowded. And Alec, before, when you greeted me, I was happy, not embarrassed."

. . . . .

Late Friday afternoon Tamiko hangs in her room in a tank top and sweatpants, pretending she has a heavy date with her books. But as soon as Eloise bounces out to meet Four, Tamiko pulls her black lace top from the back of her bottom drawer for the first time since she's arrived at Amherst. In front of Eloise's long mirror a few minutes later, she gives the hem of the clingy top a downward tug to display a bit more décolletage. Satisfied, she peeks out her door to be sure no one is in the corridor. Just because I feel pretty doesn't mean I want to advertise it to the dudes around here, she thinks as she almost skips down the stairs and out into the crisp October dusk to find Derrick, already leaning against his now-familiar tree.

"Wow," Derrick says, a wide grin lighting up his long, angular face so that it becomes almost attractive. "You look so damned stunning, words fail me."

"Obviously, a couple leaked out," Tamiko replies, as she shrugs into her jacket trying not to show how pleased she is by Derrick's honest admiration. "And, what can I say, big dude, you look pretty chill yourself.

But, just in case you are in doubt, I want supper before anything threatens to get the better of us."

. . . . .

Early the next morning Tamiko wakes to hear someone knocking on her door. Not having gotten back to her own bed until a few hours before, she reaches up to push her ear plugs more firmly in place. After an evening of awkward, less fulfilling sex, she's determined to block out the need to wake up and think about it. But when the knocking turns into banging loud enough to cause Eloise to groan the groan of the righteously hungover, Tamiko drags herself to the door. Surprised to see Clementine Fine, Tamiko searches for a polite way to explain that it's far too early on a Saturday morning and to come back later. But before Tamiko can find the words Clemmie gives her an enthusiastic hug as she almost shouts, "I have seriously exciting news that won't wait. Throw some clothes on, girl, and let's grab coffee. I'll meet you downstairs in ten."

Wondering whether Clemmie somehow already knows she has spent much of the night in bed with Derrick, Tamiko is unsure what to expect. Then, reminding herself that older brothers typically guard the virtue of their younger sisters, not the other way around, she steps into a pair of jeans, pulls a hoodie over her head, makes a quick bathroom stop, and heads downstairs and out the door. Expecting her friend to immediately hold forth on whatever she's so excited about, Tamiko is surprised when Clemmie says, "One glance at you shouts extra large latte. We'll talk as soon as you've downed the first half."

A few minutes later as Tamiko instead sips her second cup of black coffee and begins to dig into a cheese omelette at Valentine dining hall, Clemmie enlarges a photo on her phone before handing it to Tamiko. Taken outside the movie theater the week before, it shows a laughing Tamiko standing between brother and sister Fine.

"Scroll down," Clementine says.

Tamiko does and finds several more pics, the last showing the three of them mugging for the camera. Somehow, instead of looking like high school sophomores trying to look cooler than they are, Tamiko is impressed at how all three radiate infectious delight. Yet, both puzzled and annoyed that Clementine has rousted her out of bed to show her photos that could have easily been shared via text, Tamiko starts to protest.

"Wait a second, there's more to this than you think," Clemmie interrupts. "As part of my weekly check-in with Ben and Mary I sent along these pics, to kinda reassure them I was fitting in. As it happens— and Tamiko, please believe I'm not making this up—Ben's about to start preproduction on a new film that has a small part for a college girl. She only appears in a few scenes, with several lines in each, but apparently Ben believes she's important to the arc of the story. Anyway, the point is that despite auditioning a legion of pretty faces, he's had trouble finding someone he feels is authentic. Finally, last month, by working with the UCLA Theater School he succeeded, only to have the girl in question fracture her leg in a car crash last Wednesday."

"Interesting, I guess, but I still don't see…"

"C'mon smarty pants, wake up and smell the opportunity," Clementine blurts. "After seeing your picture Ben thinks you might be the perfect replacement."

"Clemmie, you have got to be fucking kidding!" Tamiko replies, incredulously. "And just so you know, that's only the third time I've ever said the F word."

"Nope. Ben famously has hunches, and just as famously acts on them. He often jokes that when his unconscious speaks, the cash register rings. Anyway, he hopes to get you on film, or I guess technically, video to see if his hunch holds up."

"Forget it! I've never even been in a school play and besides, when, and where, would I…"

"Over at Hampshire College where the Film School is their crown jewel. I guess they got some bucks from Ken Burns, who's an alum. Anyway, Ben knows a prof over there who can do the job at four p.m. tomorrow. And, I can come with, if you want." Then, seeing that Tamiko is still skeptical, Clemmie leans forward and raises her voice, "Tamiko, get a grip. It's, like, for even a small speaking part in an A-list film, you could earn enough to pay for a year of grad school. And anyway, this is only a first step—the test may not prove out."

. . . . .

At 8:50 Sunday morning Alec arrives at the entrance to the Hamarikyu Gardens to see Mayumi already waiting on a bench holding two cups of Starbucks coffee. As usual, she's dressed in black except this morning she's also wearing a jaunty wine-red knit cap that looks to be a cross between a beret and a beanie. At rest, Alec again registers that although Mayumi's face is quietly attractive, she's no great beauty. Just the same, when after spotting him she smiles, Alec's heart skips a beat.

Bouncing to her feet Mayumi holds out the containers as she asks, "Black or au lait?"

"Your yen, your choice," Alec replies, surprised that he again has the urge to lean over and kiss the still-grinning young woman.

"I'm good with either."

"Okay, I'll take the *au lait*," Alec says, as he reaches for the left-hand cup.

"Can you pour a little of yours into mine?" Mayumi asks as she looks around to check that they are alone before pouring two fingers of her black coffee behind a bush.

"I thought you were happy with no milk?"

"Being disingenuously polite is a Japanese disease in case you haven't noticed."

"Got it, but I thought Asians were lactose intolerant?"

"Nice try, but I'm not one of them, so please pour," Mayumi replies, still holding out her cup.

After doing as asked, Alec takes a step toward the entrance.

"No food or drinks inside the garden, so let's sit for a minute. And, besides, I have something I want to say."

"Me too, but you start," Alec says, hoping that Mayumi isn't going to make some sort of relationship-killing declaration, before they even have a relationship.

"Okay, I guess I'm worried you may think I'm chasing you," Mayumi says, head down as if she's talking to her shoe. "I…"

Alec's laugh is so hearty that Mayumi stops in mid-sentence. Flushing slightly, she looks up to gauge whether she's being mocked.

"I'm only laughing," Alec says quickly, "because I'm pretty sure chasing isn't the right word when the chasee—namely me—is doing his best to catch the chaser. Or, put differently, Friday night when you suggested meeting here, I was about to ask you on a date."

"Truly?"

"Truly."

"Okay, then," Mayumi says, making and holding eye contact. "I'm ready to see the garden when you are."

"Do you mind if I clear up one other thing first?" Alec asks. "I mean, it's just that in his brief bio about you, Charlie mentioned that you may still have this long-term American boyfriend."

"*Had*, not have. I broke up with Josh in April when I came back from the States. But Charlie gets most of his information from my dad, who doesn't officially know yet."

"Since you've answered my question, and made me happy in the process, I guess I should shut up, but I'm curious as to how come you haven't told your parents."

"From the day he met Josh, Dad dismissed him as a lightweight—a person almost exclusively interested in himself, without the brains to disguise it. And Mom agreed. For almost a year I refused to listen, but eventually had to admit that my parents had Josh pegged far more accurately than I did."

"So you don't want your parents to have the satisfaction of being right?"

"Something like that I guess," Mayumi says with a rueful chuckle, "But I plan to travel to Europe starting in about six weeks with my friend Fujiko, so I'll do my *mea culpas* before I leave. But, anyway, as far as you and me go, I'm free until I leave. However, now that we've gotten to the resume stage, what about you? It was obvious from Charlie's brief bio of you that he admires your young American girlfriend a lot, and Charlie doesn't impress easily."

"There's a lot to like about Tamiko," Alec says simply.

After a long pause during which Alec says nothing more, Mayumi finally asks, "Alec, are you going to say another word, or am I expected to sit mute until I turn into a statue?"

Blowing out a long breath, Alec says, "No doubt I'm tongue-tied because I'm more than a little confused as to where I'm at with Tamiko. We just shared a fabulous year in Berkeley, yet, now, we're not only half a world apart, but somehow never discussed future expectations. I mean, Tamiko's barely seventeen and off to college a year early so...." Then, after another long pause during which Alec only belatedly seems to realize he's trailed off, he adds in a rush, "Mayumi, this may sound weird, two-faced maybe, but right now, this minute, while I know in my heart that Tamiko and I are soulmates, I'm extremely attracted to you."

"Thanks for sharing all that," Mayumi says quietly.

Pretty sure by admitting that he's still bewitched by Tamiko, he's killed his chances with Mayumi, Alec stands. "Maybe it's time to see the famous garden," he says, as he looks around for someplace to toss his cardboard cup.

"This is Japan where we're so afraid of litter we actually believe trash bins encourage it," Mayumi says with a chuckle, as she takes Alec's cup, flattens it and places it in a plastic bag in her purse before leading him through the entrance.

Following the trim young woman across a tufted meadow dotted by large black pines, lovingly sculpted bonsai-like for a century or more, Alec's mood begins to lift. Who can stay grumpy in the face of this much beauty, he thinks as he takes a couple of quick steps to catch up with Mayumi just as she reaches a slender wooden causeway that stretches across a mirror-bright pond. As they approach the green-roofed teahouse perched on pilings near the center of the pond, she stops and points to the reflections of the tall fifty-story buildings that abut the centuries-old garden. "Old and new," she says seriously, "see how they coexist so beautifully."

Hoping he's understood her meaning, Alec turns to meet Mayumi's gaze.

"Alec, as long as you're half as excited about me as I am about you, let's do our best to stay in the present. And, anyway, I'll be leaving with Fujiko in early December to see the world, so, I'm no threat to your long-term possibilities with Tamiko."

. . . . .

On Sunday afternoon Tamiko and Clementine finally stumble breathlessly into the correct room at Hampshire College ten minutes late. They are greeted by a pink-faced, balding man wearing a golf shirt stretched too tight across his soft middle who introduces himself as Professor Mickelson, and a rail-thin, scraggly-bearded grad student who mumbles, "Anders."

"Ms. Gashkin, since I gather you're never been in front of a camera before, my job is to guide you through this," Professor Mickelson says in a long suffering tone as he glances at his watch as if to underline his conviction that he's wasting the rump of his afternoon. "And, since I know you've only had the script a few hours I'll prompt you as we go along."

"No worries, I've got it," Tamiko replies, tapping her head. "But I've rewritten a few lines so I'd like to do my version when I'm done with what Mr. Fine sent."

"How old are you, Missy?"

"Seventeen."

"And your drama experience comes from where? High school plays, perhaps, and maybe a walk-on part in an obscure summer production?" Professor Mickelson inquires in a dismissive voice that makes it clear that he isn't interested in Tamiko's answer.

"I've never acted in anything."

"Are you Ben Fine's niece, or something?"

"We've never met."

"Really," the paunchy man says, drawing out the word to triple its usual length.

Finally curious as to why Tamiko is standing in front of him, he gives her a slow, deliberately impolite once-over. Apparently, concluding she's nothing special, he adds, "As a half pretty kid looking for a big break, I'd keep my mouth shut and stick to the script."

"Like you, Professor Mickelson, I'm guessing, I'd rather not be here," Tamiko responds pleasantly, "especially since I have zero interest in becoming an actress. But the truth is, I thought the script needed changes so I made them."

"As you know, Professor, my uncle particularly asked Tamiko to read," Clementine says. "So can you please video both versions?" Then, as if sensing that her direct approach threatens to make things worse, she adds in a more conciliatory voice, "I mean, I know Ben reached out to you because he respects your work. He told me that if it hadn't been for you, *Tightrope* would have been a mess."

"That was ten years ago and my phone hasn't rung until now," Professor Mickelson replies, staring at Clementine as if to say, 'cut the bullshit.' Then, with a resigned sigh, he points to the studio door as he says, "Tamiko, pretend this is the front door of your mother's Malibu house. Wait outside until I call '*Action*.' Then, holding your imaginary roller bag with one hand, open the door with the other, and take a couple of steps inside as you call, '*Mom, I'm home early*.' But, instead of her reply, pretend you hear raucous laughter coming from the back of the house where you know the bedrooms are located. With no idea as to what's going on you stop, unsure what to do next. Not wanting to feel like an intruder, you call louder, '*Hey, Mom, it's me. I'm home a day early*.' At this point, Clementine, it will help if you grab the script and read Mom's lines as she belatedly comes out of a bedroom, still cinching the belt on her robe. Tamiko, you'll then respond as per the script and the two of you will do your back and forth until I call '*Cut*.' When hopefully we get through all that, we'll move on to the next morning's kitchen scene where Mom tells daughter she's too young to understand what was going on in the bedroom."

"And then we can do it again using Tamiko's rewrite," Clementine says determinedly, as if to underline what she regards as Professor Mickelson's tacit agreement.

. . . . .

The wavelike facade of Mayumi's ultra-modern building near Tokyo University is so realistic Alec is disappointed that there isn't a koi pond in the lobby. Entering her fourth floor apartment a minute later, Alec is met by unadorned white walls, with the furniture consisting of two fuzzy blue beanbags and a low black lacquer table on a vivid red rug. Clearly this is more perch than home, he thinks, as he turns toward Mayumi only to realize she's disappeared into another room. Unsure whether to follow, stand there, or sit on a beanbag, Alec is relieved when Mayumi calls out, "Alec, I thought you were into being the chaser."

As Otis Redding begins singing "Dock of the Bay," Alec enters another very white room to see Mayumi standing near the double bed, her small fingers on the top button of her black blouse. "I'll be delighted to do that," he says, pleased that Mayumi is as ready for next steps as he is.

"I thought you'd never ask," Mayumi says, standing on tiptoe to kiss Alec firmly on the mouth. Then, stepping back she says, "But I want you to take off your shirt first."

"As in right now?" Alec replies, as he grips the hem of his navy polo, but lifts it barely an inch.

"C'mon, no teasing," Mayumi protests. "I'm doing my..."

Whatever she is about to add is interrupted by her pleased chuckle when, in a fluid motion, Alec pulls the shirt over his head to reveal wide shoulders, a tapering torso and a narrow waist.

"You're even more beautiful than I imagined," Mayumi says, simply.

"Is it finally my turn?" Alec asks.

"Beat you to it," Mayumi replies, deftly unbuttoning her top. Still holding it closed she adds, "Alec, I have to warn you, I'm small compared to most American girls."

"You're perfect compared to all girls," Alec says, as he spreads Mayumi's hands, unclasps the front clip of her bra and admires her small, high, full moon breasts. Feeling his fingertips twitch in their eagerness to caress their erect brown nipples, Alec instead undoes his belt, wriggles his hips and with a couple of shuffling steps is clear of his pants. Mayumi, having mirrored his moves is already on the bed, arms spread. With words now superfluous, Alec joins her, losing himself in both the pleasure of his skin on hers, and their eager open-mouthed kiss.

But, he is jolted back to the present when Mayumi insists, "Wait a second, Alec," as she wriggles away to open a drawer in the bedside table. Instead of the package of condoms Alec expects, Mayumi produces a purple cylinder. "I like to have this ready since I absolutely hate it when a guy gets off and I don't," Mayumi says, matter-of-factly.

Deciding this isn't the time for a discussion of orgasm, or the lack thereof, Alec asks, "What about birth control?"

"I have that covered. If you tell me STD's aren't a problem, I'll believe you. If not, I hope you have a condom."

"To get inside you, I'd probably lie more outrageously than Donald Trump on his taxes, but, in truth, I'm almost positive I'm clean."

"Okay then," Mayumi says, scooting over to cuddle her round, firm body next to Alec's long, lanky one. Then, raising her head so that their lips meet in another all-in kiss, she reaches for his hand and places it between her legs. A couple of minutes later, when both his fingers and Mayumi's breathing tell him the time is right, Alec slides on top of her, guiding his cock to, and then through, the plump lips of her very wet vagina. But, instead of the enthusiastic response he expects, Mayumi's reaction is muted. Recalling her plan to call on outside assistance if needed, Alec schools himself to slow way down and concentrate on her pleasure. When, despite his best efforts, he still senses tepid enthusiasm, Alec gently catches one of her erect nipples between his thumb and forefinger as he rotates his pelvis hoping to create more friction with Mayumi's clit.

Finally, hearing a small gasp, Alec begins to relax into his own pleasure only to feel Mayumi squirming under him, apparently in an effort to reach her vibrator.

"Hey, I thought we were all about taking time to find our groove,"

Alec objects, surprised and a little hurt.

"Sorry, for sure I was starting to get into it, but then I got paranoid that you were about to gallop to the finish without me."

"How about we take more time to enjoy each other before you bring your orgasmatron into it," Alec suggests as he rolls off Mayumi, and onto his back. Grabbing the small woman by the hips he easily lifts her on top of him as he adds, "I promise to think of the World Cup Finals if I get too far ahead of you."

"Okay, big guy, let's see what you can do."

"Maybe you mean what we can do," Alec replies as reaching down, he inserts his shaft, slips his long fingers beneath Mayumi's bottom and pulls her so close they feel fused. Surprisingly, it takes but a dozen heartbeats for Mayumi's hands to clasp viselike to Alec's shoulders, and a half dozen more before her nails begin to dig into his skin. Now, as she strains her body against his, Mayumi begins to emit purr-like sounds from deep in her chest. Waiting as Mayumi's cat imitation morphs into a series of deep groans and then quick, high-pitched gasps, Alec is confident that the purple cylinder will not be needed. But, still, he bides his time as he keeps a corner of his mind on France's football strategy that was so key to their 4–2 victory over Croatia. But, when Mayumi erupts with an insistent string of Japanese words that even Alec can translate as "fuck me, fuck me, fuck me harder, Alec, oh my god, so good, so good," he puts football aside, sure there is no longer any need to modulate his response. Raising his pelvis to eagerly thrust upward again and again, Alec feels Mayumi begin to shudder as her body rushes to climax. Quickly rolling them over, Alec holds the keening woman by the shoulders and with several more exquisitely pleasurable thrusts, joins her.

"Alec, as you probably guessed, that was my first guy-induced orgasm," Mayumi says quietly a few minutes later. "Seriously, I don't even know how to describe what I just felt, but euphoric is a start. And, as I'm sure you can also guess, I'm massively relieved, and very grateful." Then, as Mayumi slides out of bed and steps toward the kitchen she adds, "I've always imagined pouring Veuve Clicquot to celebrate this moment, but beer will have to do."

"Sounds good to me," Alec mumbles, pulling a pillow over his eyes to block the light.

When Mayumi returns, still naked, with a tray holding two bottles of Asahi Super Dry and a bowl of *arare*, the rice crackers that have become Alec's go-to Japanese snack, she finds him comatose.

"Sadist!" Alec moans, when Mayumi touches an icy bottle to his right nipple.

Then, as he reluctantly scrunches up against an oversized red pillow, beer now in one hand, and a fistful of crackers in the other, Mayumi says, "Alec, I'm hoping you'll make very short work of the beer so we can get back to dopamine land."

"I hardly need alcohol for that," Alec replies, delighted that Mayumi prefers more lovemaking to a discussion of what just happened. Then, hooking his arm around the small woman, Alec pulls her so close he feels her tight breasts flatten against his chest a moment before her beer-cold tongue finds his.

"Want to see my best imitation of a snake?" Mayumi says with a pleased chuckle as she pulls her head back.

Assuming no answer is required, Alec grins as Mayumi wriggles her way down his long body, kissing and nibbling as she goes. When, a lazy couple of minutes later she places her mouth over his erect cock, he knows he's at least as ready for next steps as he had been forty-five minutes before. And now, with the benefit of knowing the key to Mayumi's pleasure, Alec lifts her up and above him to where she completes their coupling as if she's done it a thousand times before.

"So, tell me how long you've been carting around that electric gizmo?" Alec asks laughingly, after their second round of delight.

"It's a long story, which thanks to you, is now absolutely irrelevant. Suffice it to say, that on a pleasure scale of one to ten, I never got past six with any of the guys I've tried sex with. So the fact that you took me to a place beyond scoring is boggling. I mean, Alec, if I had a week, I don't think I could tell you what a fabulous time I've had today."

"I was there too," Alec replies. "But when it comes to the now-irrelevant long story, I have nothing to do but listen."

"Maybe you should amend that to say, nothing to do for the few minutes we have left during our intermission," Mayumi adds playfully, as she leans over to kiss Alec on the lips. "But, if you're really interested, here is a short version of Mayumi's boring intimate history. In the last couple years of high school I played around a few times, but quickly put sex on hold when I got bored with awkward guys popping off almost before we started. My first year in college I decided to try again with someone more experienced, which I did with a young philosophy professor. Akihiro put a lot of energy into being sophisticated—long hair, wire-rimmed glasses, Italian motor scooter, read Foucault in French and so on. But Alec, is all this a total snore?" Mayumi asks.

"Very far from it," Alec replies, deciding not to add how much it turns him on to listen to Mayumi talk about sex with other guys.

"Okay, then," Mayumi continues. "Although I couldn't hop into bed with Akihiro fast enough, it didn't take long before I had to admit to myself that I was back to counting the cracks in the ceiling. And, since, by that time I had acquired my little purple machine, I had at least some clue as to what I was looking for and it wasn't Akihiro. I met Alec the beginning of third year at University when it had been almost a year since I'd been seriously attracted to anyone, I began thinking about trying girls," Mayumi says seriously. "Since I had enjoyed a pleasant girlfriend tryst in eighth grade, why not really check it out, right?"

"Sure, I guess," Alec reponds only to realize that Mayumi is just getting started.

"But before I could step down that path, I met Josh," she continues. "Like I told you, he's an American who, at that point, was finishing his PhD dissertation and coordinating the journalism workshop I was taking. The good news was that for the first time I was totally, stupidly in love. I don't mean to be too graphic, but the sex part with a person I was over the moon for was initially pretty great. And this continued to be true for quite a while, even though I only almost climaxed. No doubt I would have been content with this, at least for a while, if Josh's ego hadn't gotten into a twist about my failure to get off. In short, as he strained more and more, sex became less and less fun for both of us with the result that we began having less of it. Even so, I was more or less okay with the rest of our relationship, since I liked having a chill American boyfriend. And, it was a plus that my parents, especially my dad, didn't approve."

"You were in rebellion mode?"

"Aren't all university students? Although with me it's always been tough to work up real angst vis-à-vis my parents, since deep down I think they're both pretty evolved and aspire to be like them. But, my parents are another story, so let me finish this one."

"Please."

"So anyway, fast forward to last January when Josh was off to University of Iowa where he'd landed an intro-level teaching job. I'd spent the fall planning to go with him, even arranging to take several intriguing journalism courses at the U of I for the Spring semester. So, even though by then I pretty much knew we didn't have a future, I went. And, initially, it wasn't a bad decision, I mean, Alec, since everything in America was so new and exciting, I hardly cared that Josh and I were having unsatisfactory sex maybe three times a month."

"Really! Things were that captivating in Iowa City?"

"Definitely! I loved the American-style college community with its eclectic mix of interesting people and, of course, the University of Iowa is famous for its world-class programs for writers and poets. And don't get me started on the exciting readings at the Prairie Lights Bookstore and the fabulous greasy cheeseburgers at Short's Burger and Shine. If it hadn't been for having to live with Josh, well…"

"The fraught sex deal spoiled the fun?" Alec interrupts.

"At the very least I wanted us to try to get past it. In our wired world it was easy for me to learn that for many women to achieve orgasm a modicum of male patience and creativity is required. But when I even tried to talk to Josh about my foreplay ideas, he clammed up to the point of being hostile. And, anyway, by that time I'd begun to see Josh as my parents had all along."

"You said your dad didn't like him?"

"Dad was more vocal, but as usual it was Mom who cut to the core when she remarked that Josh worked so hard at being cool, it never occurred to him that cool people don't work at it."

"Ha! So your parents were right from the start."

"They almost always are. But my growing up enough to accept that is part of the other story."

"Back to Iowa, then."

"Right! So even though I'd given up on Josh long term, I wanted to finish my two journalism courses, which were unlike anything available in Japan, so I decided to hang in for the rest of that semester. From Josh's point of view, having, what was by Midwest standards, at least, an exotic Japanese girlfriend made him feel chic enough that he barely noticed he no longer particularly liked me. Anyway, we bumped along for another month until a Friday evening in early April. A dozen of us were drinking at the Fox Head Tavern when predictably someone suggested we play Truth or Dare, which I'd come to understand is one of the main ways American university students give themselves permission to talk about sex. As usual, the game started with questions like:

"How many people have you slept with here at University? And were they male or female?

"In the middle of having sex have you ever called the wrong name?

"Right now, would you rather get naked, or confess today's most prurient thought?

"Anyway, we were all tipsy, giggling and having fun, when it was tall blond Amelia's turn to question Vivian, a grad student in microbiology. After Vivian chose Truth, Amelia asked, 'If you weren't with your partner Adam, who here tonight would you like to have sex with?' As everyone began chanting, 'truth, truth, truth,' I looked around the group and asked myself who I'd prefer to Josh. When I realized my answer was all of the guys and maybe a couple of the girls, I knew Josh and I had to be over. And not over tomorrow, or the next day, but over right then."

"One of those moments when time stops."

"Exactly! I mean, Alec, I know it seems over the top now, but I seriously had to act. So, before Vivian could think of a way to finesse her answer, I blurted out that I had a headache and needed to go home and lie down. Telling Josh to hang with the others, I Ubered back to our apartment, where I bribed the driver to wait while I tossed my stuff in a bag. Ten minutes later we were headed to the Cedar Rapids Airport where I slept sitting up in the lounge. Next morning I was on the first Chicago flight and from there on to Narita International."

"No long goodbye for Josh?"

"I was embarrassed at ghosting him, but the deed was done and the best I could do was to send him a polite '*sayonara*' email when I got to Chicago."

"How did he reply?"

"After I read the first few self-pitying sentences, my guilt at slipping out in the middle of the night evaporated and I erased the rest. But, hey, Alec, time to get dressed, big boy, since I need to get over to my parents for a family meal."

"I thought this was intermission?"

"Sorry, but you insisted on the whole story."

"How about a *sayonara* quickie?"

"Better get started," Mayumi says, glancing at her watch. "You only have two minutes to blast us back past the moon."

Five minutes later, as Mayumi hurriedly slips into her clothes, Alec kicks back the sheets and says, "I have an exam Wednesday morning so I need to study a bunch in the next couple of days plus teach class on Tuesday. So how about we get together Wednesday evening?"

"I'm already looking forward to it," Mayumi says as she fishes under the bed for Alec's pants and tosses them to him. "And in case you are in doubt, I plan to leave my purple friend in the drawer."

"I'll enjoy the challenge."

"Now that you've got me going off like a cheap firecracker I think the challenge part is over. Alec, I know I'm repeating myself, but I'm one happy woman. Reaching climax four times in an afternoon may be no big deal unless you've never done it once, so..."

Embarrassed by Mayumi's effusiveness, Alec changes the subject by asking, "How about we catch a movie before the Wednesday fireworks?"

"Going bang with me isn't enough to fill up your evening?" Mayumi asks, pretending to pout, as she steps into the bathroom to pull a comb through her hair.

"I just thought maybe we can catch a late afternoon show and still have the rest of the night to...."

"Alec, I'm kidding. What do you want to see?"

"I'm ready to negotiate, but my choice is *The Battle of Tule Lake*. It's a story about a U.S. prison camp, or maybe more accurately, a maximum security concentration camp established to lock up Japanese Americans during World War Two. It's by this chill director, Ben Fine, who I..."

"Even here in Japan everyone has seen *Tightrope* and *Alice in the Air*, so I'm already sold," Mayumi replies, handing Alec his shirt. "But Alec, Tamiko, your American girlfriend, obviously has a Japanese name, so was her family locked up at Tule Lake?"

"I thought you were in a hurry to get out of here?"

"Since I'm already late and you've hooked my interest..."

"Tamiko's great grandparents, who died before she was born, were imprisoned for over three years at another, only slightly less dire camp. But her gene pool is more Russian and Irish than Japanese."

"Does that mean she's tall?"

"Five-foot-ten."

"Just one more reason to hate her," Mayumi says with a chuckle as she kisses Alec and pushes him toward the door. "Should I come to your apartment Wednesday?"

"If you can get there by four-ish I'll ice some Veuve Clicquot so we can start the party before the film."

"I love the way you think. But since we're celebrating popping my cork, the champagne is definitely my treat."

. . . . .

Tamiko, Ben Fine here. I tried you earlier with no luck, Tamiko reads when she checks her texts on the way back from a late Monday afternoon workout at the Amherst field house. *Can you please listen to my voicemail and get back to me ASAP?* Glancing at her list of recents Tamiko taps the only unfamiliar number. "Tamiko Gashkin, I presume," a deep voice answers before the phone rings a second time. "Did you listen to my message?"

"Oops! Sorry, Mr. Fine," Tamiko stammers, mentally kicking herself for not curbing her bad habit of ignoring voicemails. "It's, like..."

"No apology needed. I never bother either since the caller is sure to repeat everything, including his name, which in my case is Ben. As you may have guessed I'm calling because I liked your video, or to be more precise, I particularly admired the emotion that came through when you did your version of Jennifer's conversations with her mom."

"I hope it was okay to make the changes. It's just that I thought a Cal student wouldn't speak in quite the way the script was written."

"I believe you. Jack and Naomi Gold, our writers, are great, but since both are barking at forty I'm excited by your fresh vernacular. Also, I like how you sharpened the dramatic edge between Jennifer and her mom, by having Jennifer go ballistic after Virginia keeps repeating, 'You're too young to understand.' But, my larger point is that I saw plenty to know you are an excellent fit for the Jennifer part. As I'm sure Clemmie told you, I want someone the audience will immediately know is the real deal, not an actress pretending to be a university student."

Ignoring this, Tamiko asks, "Do I have permission to make another plot suggestion?" Not waiting for an answer she continues, "It seems odd that a junior at a school like Cal would be quite so freaked by the group sex premise of the film. Even, as a new first year, I've heard rumors that threesomes might be in play around here."

"Okay," Ben says slowly. "Can you be more specific? About *2+2*'s plot, I mean."

"Well, no doubt as the script portrays, Jennifer would be shocked to come home from Cal a day early to find her mom shagging the neighbors, instead of out buying a turkey. But once Jennifer has time to process what's going on, I'm guessing she'd also be a little curious."

"Hmph! I agree that making Jennifer less one-dimensional makes for a more interesting story, so good idea."

"Thanks. But just so you know, I did entry-level editing last year for my mom's publishing company in Berkeley, where I was incorrigible when it came to rewriting things."

"We call that a competitive advantage in my business. I wonder if you have more ideas, especially for later in the script."

"Does a giraffe have a neck?" Tamiko responds with a laugh. "As the script is written, Jennifer barely appears after the morning breakfast spat with her mom. But wouldn't it add depth to the story if Jennifer is also included in the scene where Virginia, and her husband Toby, have their martini-fueled meltdown? For example, the doorbell could interrupt Virginia's and Toby's bitter argument about who's to blame for their foursome being outed. Then, before either has time to react, Jennifer, dressed to party, would appear to open the door. After briefly introducing the two dudes who step in as college buddies, she would link arms with them and leave."

"Interesting! It not only eliminates the need to have Sandy and Toby resolve their fight, but more importantly, it underlines your point that Jennifer is a young woman, not an overgrown girl. The obvious danger is that it could make Jennifer seem too slutty. But there should be ways to let the audience know Jennifer's mocking her mom, not seriously planning to screw both guys in the bushes! So, yes, put it on paper and shoot it to the Golds. Anything else?"

"Well, as the story progresses, maybe Jennifer can become at least tentatively attracted to Chad, Jed Streeter's character. I mean, assuming Jennifer really is deep down annoyed with her mom, mightn't Jennifer be, at least subconsciously, tempted to use her own sexuality to upstage the foursome?"

"Hmm," Ben Fine says after a long pause. "In life, it's at least plausible. But as far as *2+2* goes, it's counterproductive to allow Jennifer to hijack a story that's primarily focused on the relationships between the four mate-swapping protagonists. Remember, movies aren't like reality, where there is plenty of time for a plethora of plots, subplots and irrelevancies. Instead they typically amount to a hundred-minute peek into people's lives, meaning less is almost always more. But, hey, can you make a start on the other changes pronto-ish? We start shooting in less than two months so time is of the essence, squared."

"I have a couple of midterms tomorrow, but by midweek I'll be all over it."

"Perfect! Also, as maybe Derrick or Clemmie has told you, I'll be back in Amherst a week from Friday for Parents Weekend. Hopefully by then you and the Golds can go back and forth a few times and in the process get in a productive groove. In the meantime, I'll call your mom. Amy Gashkin, right?"

"Yes, but I don't…"

"Since legally you're a minor, your mom will need to be involved with your performance contract."

"But wait, I haven't said yes to anything except the writing part. I mean, I don't see how I can possibly get to California to perform and still finish the semester. And, what about the fact that I know minus-*nada* about acting and even that might be an overstatement."

"*2+2* is a small film that will be shot on set, with the exception of a few exterior establishing shots. We'll start at the beginning of December and finish by early January. Including you, there are just five in the principal cast and because the others all have big dollar commitments early next year we will absolutely need to stay on schedule. So, how about asking your dean to help you work out a plan to take your exams early, late, or maybe substitute a paper? Derrick says you're scary smart so this should be no problem. And, as far as the acting goes, I've obviously seen your video so know you'll do fine."

"Okay, I guess I can at least talk to Dean Thomas."

"Great, doubtless the rest will be just a matter of details. Next, you'll need an agent."

"You're kidding—right?" Tamiko asks, not sure what an agent does, but very sure she doesn't want to find out.

"Absolutely not. The script changes you've suggested all but guarantee you'll have a chunky little part, not to mention a writer's credit, which, this being Hollywood, means a second contract."

Thinking that she's not only in water over her head, but so far from a familiar shore it's useless to swim, Tamiko pleads, "Can't you just send me something that's fair and I'll sign it?"

"Tamiko, there is no animal named 'fair' in the movie business. And that's especially true given that you're a minor. For all of our sakes, most especially mine, you need to be represented by someone who knows the ins and outs."

"I don't care that much about money, except maybe for grad school. Is there some way I can get paid later so it doesn't interfere with my scholarship here at Amherst?"

"An excellent example of why you need specialized help. For someone who knows tax law there are plenty of ways to legitimately push income into future years. But Tamiko, that isn't the biggest reason you need a good business person on your side."

"Which is?"

"Anyone who says they don't care about money requires all the help they can get."

. . . . .

Worn out by the thoughts clanging around her head like the signature song of an over-eager heavy metal band, Tamiko crawls into bed in her mercifully roommate-free dorm room at 10:00 p.m. In just a few days she's gotten a new lover, only her second ever, and the beginnings of, dare she even think it, a film career. But, despite feeling queasy every time she thinks about having to perform, it's big, funny, sweet Derrick, who is front and center in her concerns. Derrick, who for all his many charms, has been a disappointment on the physical side.

Or, more likely, she's been the disappointing one, having taken what seemed like forever to finally reach a pale climax. Perhaps, she tells herself, based on her consistently mind-blowing experiences with Lec, she'd unrealistically expected sex to be too perfect, too soon. If so, maybe, things will flow more smoothly next time when she and Derrick should be more comfortable with each other. But, putting aside her own mixed and muddled thoughts, did Derrick even have enough fun to want a next time? And, assuming he's good for another go, how does she feel deep down about giving intimacy another try? Damn, Tamiko realizes, I'm going in circles. So in a conscious effort to reboot her whirling mind, she takes a deep breath as she counts to six. Holding her breath for six more counts, Tamiko releases it slowly. Repeating this mind calming technique her Grandmother Vera taught her, Tamiko finally feels her heart, and then her mind, begin to slow. Why not, she decides, try to clarify my Derrick thoughts by making a mental list of the positives and negatives of continuing to have an intimate relationship with him. First, on the positive side, Derrick is:

A kind, smart, dude with a self-deprecating sense of humor.

A very welcome diversion from sitting around being jealous of Lec.

Hanging with Derrick and his interesting friends on campus has all but erased my feelings of loneliness and alienation, replacing them with a pleasant sense of belonging.

Having a sweet dude like Derrick as my second lover somehow makes me feel more sophisticated and perhaps, even powerful. It was one thing to get past my virgin thing with Lec, but quite another to take this next big step toward becoming a woman. It follows that, whether I have sex with lovers three, four and five in three weeks or three years, is less important than trying to make things smooth with Derrick.

Enough! Tamiko thinks. No doubt there are more positives. But, no matter if I come up with a dozen, can they really change the one big negative that sex with Derrick felt more like calisthenics, than the mind-blowing bliss I experienced with Lec? Wondering if she should try to overcome her shyness and raise her concerns with Derrick, she decides, instead, to keep her mouth shut and give sex with him another chance.

. . . . .

"Gashkin Answering Service," Ed says in a voice barely above a whisper.

"Hey Ed, did Mom leave her phone home again?"

"At five forty-five a.m. and until I just picked it up, it was charging on the kitchen table as usual."

"Oh my god, Ed, I'm so sorry! So much exciting stuff is overflowing my head that I forgot the time difference. But how come you're up so early?"

"Chapter ten of my novel has been in a thorny mood and I'm trying to sneak up on it before it wakes up and pricks me. Do you want me to wake Amy?"

"Maybe fill her in later, but in the meantime give me some advice on a couple of things, pretty big deals, actually."

"Only if I'm your favorite stepdad."

"You'd be the top of the list even if Mom had a dozen lovers, but Ed, I need you to focus. I might be in a film, a real one if you can believe it, with Aphrodite Gomez, Mary Ann McCabe, Matt Ridge and Jed Streeter," Tamiko all but blurts. Then, when Ed doesn't reply for a long moment, she adds, "Really, Ed, I couldn't be more serious."

"Did Meryl Streep say no?"

"C'mon, dude, did you miss the word *serious*? It turns out my new friends here at Amherst are the adopted kids of Ben Fine, the director. You know, who did…"

"*Tightrope* and *Alice in the Air* among others," Ed says, finishing her sentence. "In fact, Amy and I just saw his newest, *The Battle of Tule Lake*. Fine's one of the few Hollywood celebs who is famous for a good reason."

"I saw *Tule Lake* last week, too. Pretty chill, huh? But, anyway, Ed, the bizarre thing that's just come down is that when Clemmie, Clementine Fine that is, who's in my dorm, texted her dad a picture of the two of us along with her brother, Derrick, well, what can I say, but 'bingo.'"

"You aren't kidding about this."

"Ed, I know it sounds borderline crazy, but apparently Ben Fine has had trouble finding a college girl type to play a small part that's nevertheless important to the plot of his new movie, *2+2*. After rejecting a bunch of young actresses as somehow not authentic, he finally signed a drama student from UCLA only to have her break her leg in a car crash a week ago. Since *2+2* starts shooting the first week in December, I guess he was desperate to find a replacement when he saw my picture. Anyway, unlikely as it may seem, Ben sent me a script and asked me to do a trial video over at Hampshire College."

"You must have aced it," Ed says, now genuinely interested.

"It's actually a little more complicated. When I saw that the scripted dialogue was slightly off the way college students talk these days, I…"

"Let me guess," Ed interrupts. "Based on what you did at Bay Books last year, you rejiggered a lot of it."

"Sort of, I guess. And, the most exciting part is Ben thinks some of my changes are positive. Anyway, he wants to sign me to a contract, well, two actually, since under Hollywood rules, writing and acting have to be separate. And if that doesn't sound weird enough, especially at five fifty-eight a.m., Ben's going to call Mom later to talk about me getting an agent. Ben says he can supply a list of reputable ones, but I told him maybe you'd know someone."

"I'm sure Roger Allman, the guy Bay Books uses to try to sell film rights in L.A., will have good suggestions. So how about I talk to Amy at breakfast and then make a few calls?"

"Thanks Ed."

"My pleasure, of course, and I apologize for not taking you seriously at first. But you said you wanted to talk about a couple of big things. Is there more?"

"So, okay Ed, here is where you really earn your stepdad stripes. It's like, when two people start an intimate relationship in a nice friendly way, but nothing super exciting happens, what are the chances it will get, um… well, more intense as it goes along? Or, if it starts in the slow lane, is it likely to stay there, I guess?"

"Hmmm," Ed replies, drawing out the m's, before asking, "have I somehow missed an installment in *'Tamiko Goes to College'*?"

"Okay well, Clemmie's big brother, Derrick, who's a sweet dude, is sort of my new boyfriend. Or I guess I should add an -ish, as in boyfriend-ish, since his real girlfriend is studying in Italy, so…"

"And unless things have changed a lot, your real boyfriend is studying in Japan."

"Maybe. I mean it's true, that in my mind Lec's still my main dude, but I'm not sure where I fit in with him," Tamiko replies, deciding against going into how scared she is that their relationship is on life-support. "It's like, Ed, I've learned the hard way that Lec's and my future, assuming we have one, isn't necessarily up to me. But anyway, you haven't answered my question."

"I'm not sure anything I'm about to say will be helpful, since undoubtedly you're well on your way to figuring out that there is no way to generalize about affairs of the heart. How they start, how they progress, how much physical intensity they generate—there really are no rules. That said, in my experience, relationships that start at a boil are more apt to stay hot longer than those, and I hope I'm quoting you correctly here, that began in a nice, friendly way. But if you don't mind a little more editorializing from my single days, it can also be true that when nothing is on the boil, achieving a solid simmer with a person you like is a lot more fun than sleeping by yourself. More specifically, during times when I was trying to cope with the green-eyed monster it was especially valuable to have a warm, friendly body to hold onto."

"Thanks, that's pretty much what I've decided. And assuming you're still coming back here with Mom for Parents Weekend, I'll introduce you to Derrick. Really, Ed, he's a sweet dude."

"Any chance Ben Fine will be there?"

"Definitely. Like you, he's a great substitute dad."

"It will be a treat to meet the entire Fine family," Ed replies with enthusiasm that lets Tamiko know he's appreciated the compliment. "But before we break off, I should mention that Charlie Burns texted Amy earlier suggesting that the three of us grab a meal next Wednesday when he stops in the Bay Area on his way to Japan."

"Give him a hug, you two are my favorite old dudes."

"No doubt you meant to say 'older.'"

. . . . .

Walking back to Alec's apartment holding hands after the *The Battle of Tule Lake*, Mayumi says, "I'll never understand why over a hundred thousand Japanese Americans allowed themselves to be herded like sheep into prison camps during World War Two, especially when there was absolutely no proof that even one of them was spying for Japan."

"I'm guessing the biggest reason why was that, despite everything, most still had faith that America was a decent place and that the camps wouldn't last forever. Also, like Americans generally, most saw Japan's entry into the war on the side of the Nazis as a colossal blunder, with zero chance of success."

"What does your Tamiko think?"

"You'd have to ask her. But, given that by the time she was old enough to learn about the prison camps, they'd been closed for something like sixty-five years, I doubt she thinks about it much at all. But, she did say once, that her Japanese-American grandfather, who wasn't even born until a couple of years after the war ended and therefore never locked up, believed that a sense of shame was part of the reason his parents' generation complied with the Executive Order. That is, the overwhelming majority of Japanese-Americans felt so deeply ashamed by Japan's aligning itself with Hitler and Mussolini, they had little heart to resist. In fact, a majority of second generation Japanese-American men joined the army at their first opportunity and fought with real distinction in Europe."

"But what about the 'No-No' boys? I thought the movie did a fantastic job portraying what happened to the small percentage of prisoners who refused on principle to sign an oath of loyalty to the U.S."

"No doubt. Shame, or no shame, you have to ask yourself why an

American who had been ripped out of his normal life and had American guns pointed at him for almost two years would pledge absolute loyalty to America? And this is especially true when you realize that it wasn't only able-bodied Japanese Americans who were incarcerated, but also ninety-year-olds and babies. I mean, how awful must it have been for an American citizen from Los Angeles to watch his grandma die in a mass incarceration camp in Arkansas. And, as shown so well in the film, many of these No-No boys, and a few women, continued to refuse to sign the loyalty oath even after it became clear that they would be treated pretty much as if they'd tried to volunteer for Hirohito's army."

"Will you show me a picture of Tamiko?" Mayumi asks quietly, as they turn the corner onto Alec's block.

His chest tightening when he remembers what happened when Teri saw Tamiko's photo, Alec gropes for a polite way to say no. Finding none, he stops walking and turns to face Mayumi. "I'm not sure I get what this is about? She's half a globe away and we're right here so I…"

"Honestly, Alec. This is not a jealousy thing, especially since I'm the one leaving in less than two months. I'm curious, that's all. And, when it comes to the size of the globe, maybe you haven't noticed, but the days when it took a sailing ship six weeks to reach San Francisco are long gone. If you set off to see Tamiko this minute, you'd be standing in front of her in less than twenty-four hours."

Again, Alec says nothing as he leads the way up the narrow stairs to his apartment, unlocks the door and substitutes slippers for his shoes. Then, padding the few steps to his mini desk, he opens the one drawer. Bypassing the large photo of Tamiko and himself with their arms draped over each other's shoulders that so freaked Teri, he hands Mayumi a smaller one. Here Tamiko stands on one foot with the other tucked crane-like against her upper thigh as she extends her arms toward the sky in what yogis sensibly call tree pose. Since the photo was taken in the early morning on Limantour Beach at Point Reyes National Seashore, the rising sun turns Tamiko's thick, honey-colored hair into a fiery halo.

"Of course I assumed you would have good taste, but I can tell at a glance that Tamiko is lovely," Mayumi says quietly.

"Like I told you on Sunday, Tamiko just turned seventeen, which is a big part of the reason that after a year of us being together on an almost daily basis she needs a chance to experience life on her own."

"Why am I guessing that you're surer about that than she is?"

"True enough, but I don't see how you could know it."

"Tamiko's beaming two thousand watts of love at someone. And since I'm pretty sure I know who took the picture, well…"

"Can we maybe change the subject?" Alec asks, after a pause.

"Fine, as soon as you also show me the picture you covered up, which I'm guessing is of the two of you."

Realizing that Mayumi isn't going to be denied, and despite his misgivings, Alec hands it over.

"Thank you," Mayumi says simply. "And, Alec, it's important to me that you know that I'm on Tamiko's side here. That is, while I see myself as your big deal fall girlfriend, long term I'm pretty sure your heart is already taken by this special person with whom I don't plan to compete."

MID-OCTOBER

"THIS IS SWEET," Tamiko says on Friday evening as she leans into Derrick on the now-familiar green beanbag. "Everything but the music, that is, which sounds like a raccoon upending a garbage can."

"I don't like The National either. But Missy's playlist is basically chill so hang in and things are sure to improve. Aside from the music, how are you doing?"

"Definitely okay, compared to a couple of weeks ago," Tamiko replies. Then, thinking that Derrick may be offended by this tepid praise, she nudges her shoulder into his as she adds, "I'm particularly delighted to have made a great friend."

"Your courses are finally going better too, right?"

"Absolutely, especially Greek. I can hardly wait till next year to take Greek and Roman history. I mean, despite denying women a public role, those civilizations had so much figured out. If I was gifted one big wish I'd definitely wake up on the steps of the Parthenon in 425 BCE."

"What about your friend Alec? Would he be there, too?" Derrick asks, seriously.

To give herself time to compose an answer, Tamiko takes a sip of her wine, which she's diluted with so much club soda it's barely pink. "Deep down I'm still mad at him, so I'd like to say no," she finally replies. "But, Derrick, the truth is that even deeper down, I feel so all over fused with Lec, that no matter where, or when, I'd hope he'd be standing next to me."

"You just nailed how I feel about Ericka. Pissed, but still wriggling on the end of her hook."

"I figured, but still it's a relief to get things out in the open, where neither of us has to pretend. But how does that leave things between *moi et tu* when it comes to..."

"*Baiser*, is the French word for screwing I think," Derrick interrupts with a laugh. "Tamiko, I hope I'm not being too blunt but I'm guessing that after our second and third tries at fanning friendship into passion, we both suspect the tinder isn't going to burst into flame."

"Still best buddies, right?" Tamiko asks, draping her arm over Derrick's wide shoulders.

"*Absolument!* And, next weekend I'm looking forward to our families meeting. Are you and Ben any further along with getting your contracts signed?"

"Gah! Derrick, this business stuff still feels weird. But, thanks to Ben and Mom's partner Ed, I have an agent and hopefully the beginnings of a plan to finance grad school. Like I've been saying from the beginning, the acting part seems unreal, or probably, surreal is more accurate. Still, every time I try to back out, Ben repeats that he wants a real college girl, not an actress pretending to be one, so I guess I'm going to bumble my way forward. By contrast, working on the script is exciting since, instead of just focusing on the words, which I'm used to, there is also the camera to think about. I don't pretend to understand even a fraction of the subtleties about space, timing, and a dozen other things, but Jack and Naomi Gold, have welcomed me to their team as a sort of junior associate, so I have great mentors."

"Ben is a genius at getting unlikely people to work together and, far more important, to coax his odd duck combinations into producing exciting results. To even make *2+2* he had to talk four of Hollywood's biggest stars into submerging their considerable egos into what amounts to an ensemble cast. Then, he had to convince them to divide twenty mil by four, when typically they each command that much."

"Why did they all agree?" Tamiko asks, genuinely curious.

"Ben reasoned that since all these folks already have more money than God, he needed to dangle a carrot they would value more."

"The opportunity to work with one another, which is normally impossible since each is so expensive?" Tamiko guesses.

"That's maybe a third of it, but probably not the biggest third."

"Ha! It's sweet to know Amherst accepts people who flunked second grade math," Tamiko says, craning her neck to kiss Derrick lightly on the cheek. "But, c'mon, Einstein, what are the two bigger thirds?"

"*2+2* is the kind of small controversial film that can win the big awards that put a shine on an actor's career. Jed Streeter's reputation doesn't need burnishing. But since Matt Ridge mostly does big budget action flicks that are ignored by serious reviewers, he's intrigued by a film that might convince critics he's more than a hunk. And, Mary Ann McCabe, who has obviously earned her chops in romantic comedies, also needs to branch out before her fans notice she's pushing forty with only one Palme d'Or to her name. Even Aphrodite, who did win an Oscar eight years ago for *Cordoba Weekend*, would love another chance to prove it wasn't a fluke."

"Got it, so what's the last third?"

"Ben plans to shoot the whole thing in L.A. in the month around Christmas when everyone can be free."

"So, as they limo to the set, they can imagine a Golden Globe cradled on their lap."

"Exactly, and they also get to say a bunch of their lines half naked, which, no surprise, is a draw for at least a couple of them."

"Oops, I think you're up to four thirds. But, anyway, Derrick, how do you know so much about *2+2*?"

"Since Ben knows I plan to get an MBA with the idea of working on the business side of the entertainment business, he arranged for me to help out last summer."

"What fun! So, do you think *2+2* will be a success?"

"Even given Ben's huge talent, I've kinda doubted it until recently. Over the years there have been several dreadful movies focused on couples swapping partners, I think in large part because in our puritanical society it's difficult to convincingly explore the many legitimate psychological reasons why people might want to participate. *Bob & Carol & Ted & Alice* from almost fifty years ago is the one partial success, although in the end Paul Mazursky chickened out and settled for directing an engaging piece of fluff with no actual mate-swapping. When it comes to *2+2*, I thought the original script was both too predictable and too pedantic, or maybe preachy is a better word. No doubt, the premise that bored affluent people, who can buy everything they want except the one thing their monkey brains most desire, is interesting, but despite a couple of riveting four-way sex scenes, the story never hooked me."

"But somehow you like it better now?"

"Naomi Gold's recent script change to have both couples live on the same beach in Malibu gives the plot a big lift. Now, it's genuinely hilarious to watch each couple agonize over writing their Tinder-style profile for a partner-swapping website, only to have them hook up with their neighbors.

"For sure the Golds' dialogue is priceless when the couples meet and all four pretend to be a lot cooler about casual sex than they really are. Still, until you got involved and suggested fundamental changes to Jennifer's persona, I saw the second half of the film as being little more than a cliché re-chew of typical middle-class, middle-age sexual anxieties," Derrick continues. "It's like, after all their brave talk about how swinging is the new normal, all four, with the partial exception of Chad, the Jed Streeter character, seriously freak when Jennifer walks in on them. You can almost see each visualize their parents, kids or, god forbid, their boss finding out next."

"But aren't those feelings pretty realistic?"

"No doubt. But, for *2+2* to be interesting, the protagonists, or at least a couple of them, must confront their predictable worries, and get beyond them, in the same way that in the last few decades gay, lesbian and trans folk did. I mean, just a generation ago the idea of a man kissing a man on screen was absolutely a non-starter. Now it's routine, and the fact that it is, has helped lots of people accept that homosexuality is no big deal."

"Okay, I guess, but like, how do you see that tweaking my part helps make *2+2* less boring?"

"I thought you'd never ask. Because from the moment Jennifer insists that she's not a sexually clueless kid, but wants to be recognized as a mature adult doing her best to understand her mom's motivations for swinging, she gives Virginia and, by extension the others, permission to own what they have been doing. That is, to explain having more than one intimate partner as a valid way to deal with middle-age sexual boredom. In other words, to present swinging as one possible alternative to our culture's ubiquitous 'until death do us part' plot line."

"But they never really do. Instead, Virginia continues to treat Jennifer as if she's a vagina-less Barbie, as do the others, except maybe Chad."

"Which I believe is still 2+2's biggest flaw. But the fact that Jennifer cracks open the door to an honest reassessment of swinging is still a big improvement."

"I see your point," Tamiko replies. "But I don't have a big problem with Toby and Melanie backing off once Jennifer's arrival forces things into the open. I mean, both have undisclosed reasons for participating in the foursome, right? That is, Toby's fear of impotence, and Melanie's suppressed lesbian fantasies."

"Yikes girl! So fucking what? Of course people try swinging for all sorts of reasons, including being bi-curious, and having performance fears. Again, why not honestly explore these motivations in 2+2 instead of being embarrassed by them?"

"I just submitted additional script changes that you may like. Do you remember the scene a little later in the film where Jennifer's mom and stepdad rag on each other over martinis, while they wait for Jennifer to appear so they can again insist she's too young to even discuss swinging?" Too excited to wait for Derrick's answer, Tamiko adds, "Anyway, after running my idea past Ben, I've rewritten it so that Jennifer doesn't appear until two attractive guys ring the doorbell, at which point she steps between them and waltzes out."

"I'd love to know from where your libido dredged up that one, but it's a strong idea that further transforms Jennifer from the awkward daughter to the daring female in the room. I'm betting Ben liked it at the same time he worried it could make Jennifer appear too promiscuous. But I think it can work if the audience understands it's a send-up designed to confront Sandy's closed-mindedness and that Jennifer doesn't really plan a threesome."

"Ha! That's almost exactly what Ben said. You two must be in the same family. I also made a couple more suggestions, which Ben nixed. Like you, he was kind enough not to point out that I'm a newbie at all this and most of my ideas are crap."

"Not true, but even if it was, you only need a few great ideas to make a splash in the film business. In fact, I'm beginning to come around to the idea that, at the last possible moment, you, Ben and the Golds may just pull *2+2* together in memorable fashion. Preproduction starts in a month, but except for the naked bits the movie pretty much consists of dialogue, which explains why Ben is still open to changes. Tamiko, all this talk about sex has me wondering if maybe you'd like to give *tu et moi un autre tenter?*"

"I thought we just agreed that we were born to be *amis, non les amoureux?*"

"True enough, but for tonight at least, a little friendly naked bonding could be just the ticket."

"Put like that…"

. . . . .

Relaxing in his seat on the bullet train from Kyoto back to Tokyo, Alec shuts his eyes.

After a sweet Saturday touring half a dozen of Kyoto's seemingly countless Zen Buddhist temples, followed by an even sweeter night during which he and Mayumi spent almost as long touring one another, he's in serious need of a nap.

"Oh no you don't," Mayumi says as she digs her elbow into Alec's rib. "In case you forgot, this is when I prep you for Charlie's meetings."

"C'mon, even I can bow and say, '*Kon'nichiwa anata nia ete ureshi.*' The rest of the time I'll keep my mouth shut as befits the most junior person in the room. Just because you can sleep for three hours and function the next morning doesn't mean I can."

"Yo! Mr. Three-peat, you don't get to turn into Mr. Wimp because the sun is up. So here is my best offer. Correctly answer one simple protocol question and I'll leave you to nap. Flub it and you wake up and pay attention." Taking Alec's almost inaudible grunt to be his assent, Mayumi asks, "How will you bow to all the people you'll meet tomorrow?'

Eyes still resolutely shut, Alec replies, "That's a no-brainer. Since all the Japanese executives will be more important than I am, I'll watch how they bow and go a little lower. I mean, that's how a hierarchical society works, right?"

"Follow that approach and you'll have lint in your nose, assuming your hamstrings don't pop first," Mayumi replies disdainfully. "Because Charlie is a very important man in Japan and you're his nephew and assistant, at least half the executives will insist on bowing lower than you, and if you compete, will only go lower. And since, on average, they are seven or eight inches shorter than you, it's not hard to know how that contest will end."

"Okay, then, what should I do, Sensei?" Alec asks, as he draws out the Japanese word for teacher to make it clear he's still not convinced. When Mayumi doesn't reply, he opens his eyes and adds, "Fine, I hereby apologize for being a brat and certify that I'm paying attention."

"Follow Charlie's example," Mayumi replies seriously.

"Which is?" Alec asks, now genuinely interested to learn what Mayumi is trying to teach him.

"Smile, incline your head and bow very slightly to each person you greet."

"Really? But if I treat everyone the same, don't I insult the more important executives?"

"The Japanese understand that, at least in theory, Americans believe in being egalitarian, and therefore, it's not done in the U.S. to overtly emphasize class or wealth differences. Of course, deference to social rank is deeply embedded in both cultures, and America has a far larger gap between rich and poor, but let's leave comparative sociology to another day. For now, all you need to know is that instead of offering to shake hands Charlie finesses both traditions by making the same small bow to everyone."

Impressed despite himself, Alec inclines his head and gives Mayumi a quick kiss on the cheek before asking, "So, okay, what else do I need to know before you let me have my nap?"

"I thought you'd never ask," Mayumi replies with just enough sarcasm to let Alec know she's enjoying herself. "As it happens," she adds, as she taps her phone, "I've made a list of the ten things people are most likely to say to you before and after the meetings Monday and Tuesday."

"Since my Japanese is obviously still primitive, my first task will be to figure out what's being said."

"In a word, no. Not only will the Japanese executives compete to show off their English, but he, or far less likely, she, will genuinely want to be courteous."

"But I know how to respond in English," Alec replies, the long suffering tone beginning to creep back into his voice.

"Hmm, well, let's see," Mayumi replies with the pleased grin of the hunter whose prey has just put a foot into a carefully laid snare, "Suppose someone asks, 'Mr. Burns, how are you enjoying your Japanese studies'?"

"I guess I'd respond something like this—'I like my classes and I hope I'm making progress, but I'm having trouble with my Japanese accent, and also trying to grasp the multiple meanings of many kanji characters. It's as if....'"

"Alec, Alec, where to even begin? The person asking the question is being polite, and expects you to do the same, not channel Wikipedia. Think of it this way, for the Japanese executive, your responding with granular details of your studies is a little like an American answering the question, 'How are you?' by reciting the entire trajectory of a recent bout with constipation, including how it's inflamed his hemorrhoids."

"Okay, then how should I respond?" Alec asks, again realizing Mayumi is telling him things he needs to know.

"The simplest might be, 'Japanese is a beautiful language. It is my honor to learn it.'"

"Sweet," Alec replies. "So let's go through the rest of your list."

. . . . .

Late Sunday afternoon after a long nap and a quick review of Mayumi's list of likely questions and suggested responses, Alec walks the couple of miles to the Imperial Hotel to meet Charlie and Mayumi for an early supper. Entering the expansive lobby with its shiny marble surfaces and glistening chandeliers, Alec spots Charlie and Mayumi on a small couch in the cocktail lounge, their heads close together. As he takes the empty chair on the opposite side of the postage stamp–sized table, Alec extends his fist to bump his uncle's.

"What about me?" Mayumi says, as she extends her small fist.

"What about you?" Alec replies, as, ignoring her hand, he leans across the table to lightly kiss her lips.

After only a brief delay, Charlie smiles and says, "Of course, I wish you both the best."

"Alec, I already explained about you and me being together this fall, but also that I'm not trying to replace Tamiko in either of your affections."

Pausing to let Alec order an Asahi Black from the hovering waiter, Charlie says, "Having my favorite nephew involved with both of my favorite young women may take some getting used to, but I'll do my best."

"For what it's worth, the odds of Mayumi and me meeting would have been infinitesimal if you and Phil hadn't tossed us together," Alec replies, dryly.

"That was ninety percent Phil, who sometimes lacks imagination when it comes to affairs of the heart. When he told me he'd hired Mayumi I kind of suspected what might happen, but decided it would be a mistake to try to deflect fate."

"*Arigato* for that, Charlie," Mayumi says seriously. "Just so you know, meeting Alec has changed how I look at the male half of the planet. And since Alec's American friend will soon be enmeshed in making a film, and I'm only in Japan until early December, hopefully all will end well."

"Yo! Did I miss something?" Alec asks, transparently surprised.

"When I was at a meeting at U.C. Berkeley last week I had dinner with Amy and Ed so got caught up with their family news, which I have to say, could be ripped from the pages of *People* magazine."

"News about Tamiko and a film?" Alec asks, as neutrally as possible.

"Charlie just told me Tamiko has been cast in a movie," Mayumi replies. "And not in some low-budget indie deal, but with Aphrodite Gomez, Matt Ridge, Mary Ann McCabe and, if you can believe it, Jed Streeter."

"C'mon, you have to be kidding. How could…"

"No joke, the contracts are signed," Charlie interrupts. "Mayumi tells me that you two just saw *The Battle of Tule Lake* so you know who Ben Fine is."

"Sure."

"It turns out that Fine's adopted kids go to Amherst. And somewhere along the line they buddied up with Tamiko with the result that when Ben Fine's daughter, Clementine, sent her dad a bunch of routine campus photos, one of them included Tamiko. For whatever reason, Fine then asked Tamiko to do a video audition. Apparently, she not only aced it but suggested script edits he liked."

"Is Tamiko dropping out of Amherst to do all this?" Alec asks, leaning forward and squeezing his beer glass so tightly his fingers hurt.

"Not at all," Charlie answers, reassuringly. "Because the principal actors have other commitments, the entire film, will be shot on set in L.A. in December. But hold on," Charlie adds as he hand his phone to Alec. "Amy forwarded me this pic, which apparently is the one that got it all started."

As Alec sees a grinning Tamiko standing between two young people, he can't help notice she's standing a couple of inches closer to the large, smiling, long-faced dude. Taking a quick sip of his beer to cover his surprise that Tamiko, too, may have a new romantic interest, he asks, "What's this movie about?"

"Some kind of sex farce," Charlie replies. "Or perhaps 'farce' is the wrong word. Fine seems to be trying to deal seriously with two couples having a romantic relationship."

"You mean a swinger foursome?" Alec asks, trying not to sound shocked. "But how can Tamiko possibly fit in with that?"

"Awkwardly, by design, it would seem," Charlie replies. "Her character, Jennifer, arrives home from college a day early to literally walk in on her mom playing horizontal bumper games with the neighbors."

Sensing Alec's growing discomfort, Mayumi says, "Charlie, how about we talk about your meetings this week. I gather you want both of us to be present for Kibu Financial tomorrow morning, Ito on Wednesday and also for the the wind-up dinner Thursday evening."

"Right, there will be close to twenty people for tomorrow's Kibu Financial meeting and only a few less Wednesday, with the Ito group. Although Burns-Short is involved because both companies are considering significant new ventures, these meetings will be largely ceremonial with the principal goal making sure no senior executive feels disrespected. Major decisions will be made later by a much smaller group that you two won't be part of. But, since in Japan the ceremonial element of decision making is vital, I don't think you'll be disappointed. As junior members of my team you won't be expected to say anything beyond polite greetings and goodbyes. Alec, Mayumi tells me you two have been practicing ritual small talk so you should be fine. Some of the discussions will be in English because both companies are pushing, if not shoving, their key people in that direction, but the older men particularly will revert to Japanese whenever they can. Alec, at this point you may not understand much so put your tongue on the roof of your mouth and pretend to be wise."

When the three finish their light supper Alec is the first to say his goodbyes.

Lingering for a moment in the lobby, Mayumi turns to Charlie as she says, "I think Alec was stunned by your news about Tamiko."

"I don't doubt it. With Alec being six years older and light years more experienced than Tamiko, who was barely sixteen when they got together, I'm guessing he's unconsciously assumed their relationship revolves around him. Learning that with her brains and beauty Tamiko is a hot commodity in her own right may take him some getting used to. It's no secret that lots of relationships founder when power shifts from one partner to the other, but the good ones adjust and are the better for it."

"Sounds like a lesson from Charlie Burns's *Book of Wit & Wisdom*," Mayumi replies with a laugh. "I'm tempted to ask how you learned that one, but, I'm even more curious as to whether you think it was a mistake for Alec to come to Japan without Tamiko."

"Not a bit. After the year they spent together almost as conjoined twins, I thought a period apart is an excellent way for both to get back in touch with themselves. A relationship that's meant to last should survive a short separation including any detours that may arise."

"As you know, Alec's a sweet guy and I hope it's obvious that I care for him," Mayumi replies stiffly, offended to be labeled as a detour.

Pausing for a couple of beats to gather his thoughts, Charlie replies, "Mayumi, I'm rooting for both you and Alec to make the very most of your time together as long as that may be. And were Tamiko here I'd say exactly the same thing to her."

"Thanks Charlie, you're the best," Mayumi replies, as she stands on tiptoe and pecks him on the cheek before turning toward the door.

"Whoa! Hold on a minute. Your parents will be at the client dinner Thursday and I need to know if you've told them about…"

"My having a second American lover?" Mayumi chuckles, as she hijacks Charlie's sentence.

"Yes. And more to the point, since Alec is my nephew, how they…"

"Everything seemed smooth when I explained about Alec this afternoon and confirmed that I'm leaving in December for my gap travel year with my friend Fujiko," Mayumi interrupts. "Dad, particularly, was so transparently relieved to learn that Josh really is history, he would probably celebrate my being with a little green guy from the planet Zeon. But, Charlie, when I explained that Alec's your nephew, he grinned."

"Haruki and Shoko aren't worried about the possibility you'll follow Alec back to the U.S. at some point?"

"I assured them that after nine months of travel and another two years getting my masters in London, I plan to come home and ask them to arrange my marriage."

"Ha! A joke, no doubt, but you could doubtless do worse."

"For sure! Which is why my tongue was only halfway in my cheek."

. . . . .

Walking back to his apartment from the Imperial Hotel, Alec's thoughts are in a tangle. One minute he finds himself contemplating FaceTiming Tamiko to pledge his undying affection. The next he wonders if it's too late to take a cab to Mayumi's apartment. Far too self-absorbed to tumble to the fact that by falling for two lovely women he's volunteered to make himself both jubilant and miserable, Alec quickens his step as if somehow he can outpace his confusion.

LATE OCTOBER

ON THE PLANE FROM OAKLAND TO CHICAGO where they will connect to a second flight to Bradley Airport in northern Connecticut, Amy Gashkin nudges Ed Crane. When he doesn't respond, she pokes him with her elbow. "Stop faking, I can tell from your breathing you're wide awake."

"I am now, anyway, but just so you know, partner harassment is an ugly thing."

"Be serious, I want to talk to you," Amy says.

"You've hardly said a word for a week, but maybe that was because I wasn't trying to nap."

"Not funny. In fact, I've been processing what I want to say—just making sure I have it right."

"Okay, eyes wide open," Ed says, swiveling his head toward Amy.

"I know I've been a tad difficult, bitchy even, at times this fall," Amy says, confessionally.

"Not enough to bother me," Ed replies. Then, after a long pause as he waits for Amy to get to her point, he adds, "but you've obviously been annoying yourself, so out with it."

"Remember six weeks ago when we were moving into our new place and I got into one of my 'life is passing me by' moods?" Amy asks.

"Of course, but as I've said many times, since you've never had an opportunity to be single, your doubts about nesting again so soon are reasonable. After all, you were pregnant with Tamiko when you were eighteen, a wife all through your twenties and then, *kaboom*, a grieving widow and single mom at thirty-one."

"Just so you know, I'm over them—my doubts about us, that is."

"Did it help that I arranged for us to go to Burning Man next year and am fine with your plan to travel with your buddy Gretchen whenever you two want your Girls' Month Out?"

"I'm not sure, maybe. My point is, I'm over wanting a life any different than the one I have."

"Nice to hear," Ed replies, noncommittally. "You're not taking me seriously."

"Amy, when Yuri was killed five years ago you two were so bonded it almost finished you as well. If it hadn't been for your responsibility to raise Tamiko I'm guessing you might have evaporated on the spot."

"True enough, but for the life of me I don't know what that has…"

"I'm saying that it's deep in your nature to be all in when you fall in love," Ed interrupts. "And since I'm now the guy who has the honor of being the object of your affection, I'm betting that you're here for the duration despite your occasional fantasy of signing up with Tinder. But, come to that, don't you think it's at least a little funny—or is ironic the better word—that it's your seventeen-year-old daughter who is the one out in the wide world exploring her sexuality?"

"In her film, you mean."

"Hmm. You didn't notice how close she was standing to Derrick Fine in the already legendary discovery pic?"

"Really! Do you think Tamiko might be involved with him?"

"When a highly desirable young woman feels abandoned by her lover, how do you guess she's likely to respond when the next cool guy comes along?"

. . . . .

"That really was fun, wasn't it?" Ed says, on the way to the Amherst Inn following their Friday evening dinner with Tamiko and the Fine clan at Bistro Les Gras in Northampton.

"Definitely. Ben Fine is charming, and Mary McCarthy, a force of her own. To be hired as a nanny and then a few years later find yourself trail boss of the whole family, you'd have to be. But one thing is obvious, between them they raised two exceptional young people. For Tami, losing one parent at a young age was traumatic, but nothing like it must have been for Derrick and Clementine."

"Speaking of Tamiko, she looked radiant tonight," Ed says. "Even though it's mid-October, her hair is still golden from being out in the sun so much last summer. Do you think her relationship with Derrick is serious?"

"I doubt it," Amy responds so skeptically she could just as well have said, "not a chance." "They obviously like each other, and you may be right that they've shared a moment. But, if anything romantic happened, I suspect it's over," Amy adds, raising her voice to be heard over Ed's iPhone, which is insisting that they continue straight for the next half mile.

"Sure you're not just a mom in denial that her only daughter is a sexual creature?" Ed asks in surprise.

"C'mon, that pony left the barn last year when she got together with Lec and began what was obviously a passionate relationship, which, as you know, I eventually became supportive of. But tonight, Tamiko never touched Derrick once, nor he her. With Lec, no matter how many people were around, Tamiko would constantly lean against him, bump him or play footsie. And if she took even a mini break, Lec would grab her hand, drape his arm around her, or lean over and kiss her on the ear."

"The famous ear kiss, how could I forget."

"I rest my case," Amy says, reaching over to turn on the radio.

. . . . .

Propped on her tummy as she memorizes Greek grammar late Sunday afternoon, Tamiko doesn't look up when Eloise enters their dorm room. As usual, ignoring her roommate's signal, she prefers not to be interrupted, Eloise says, "Roll over Beethoven and tell Plato goodbye, cause I gotta hear about your exciting weekend!"

"I like Ben Fine, and we got all of the contracts signed," Tamiko replies, reluctantly closing her book. "I also got to hang out with my mom and Ed and enjoyed meeting your mom, dad and Phoebe..."

"Yo, dummy, enough with the CNN news summary. What about your movie? Are Aphrodite Gomez and Jed Streeter and the others really going to be in it? And what happened with…"

"Mary Ann McCabe, Jed Streeter, Aphrodite Gomez, Matt Ridge and yours truly really are in *2+2*. But, Eloise, half the papers I signed were nondisclosure agreements that say if I talk about the movie anytime, to anyone, I'll be kicked out of it."

"I love you dearly, but I'm so envious I could scream."

"Let's scream together a few times before I get back to my Greek and you start your Sunday battle with Organic Chem. After the last three days of being too polite to too many people, I'm all in."

"Just tell me what's up with you and Derrick Fine and I'll shut up. You haven't signed any nondisclosure agreements with him."

"Nothing to tell you don't already know. We gave romance another try but I've brought my spare toothbrush back here for good."

"He's sweet, chill and smart and you've been abandoned by your former prince, so I honestly don't get it."

"Hmm, how can I put this to rest for good? Making love with Lec is, or I guess I should say, was, like being picked up by a category five typhoon. By contrast, being with Derrick is more like floating along on a light summer breeze. I mean, Eloise, who doesn't like summer, so I might actually be okay with that for a while, if I thought Derrick was remotely satisfied. But since I know he's counting the days until he can get back together with Ericka, there is no joy in continuing to be his interim disappointment."

"So you're in the market for someone stormier?" Eloise asks, her exaggerated laugh making it clear she's teasing.

"I got an email from Lec earlier," Tamiko replies, seriously.

"Whoa! Are you going to share?"

"I haven't read it. The truth is, I'm so drained right now, I'm going to stick to the old Greek guys until tomorrow afternoon after class when hopefully I'll feel centered enough to cope with whatever he has to say."

"Just so you know, I think it's sick, and not in a good way, when you procrastinate like this," Eloise replies with her trademark pouty grin that tells Tamiko she's shared enough to be back in her friend's good graces.

. . . . .

Thanks to Mayumi's coaching, Alec's participation in the Kibu Financial and Ito meetings goes surprisingly well. But as Thursday dawns he begins to worry about meeting Haruki and Shoko Yamada, Mayumi's larger-than-life parents at Charlie's dinner. He hopes they'll understand that he honestly cares for their extraordinary daughter, but since his and Mayumi's plans don't extend beyond getting naked with each other as often as possible for the next six weeks, he fears an awkward evening. Instead, Alec is warmly welcomed by this attractive couple in their late forties, who seem to easily accept his and Mayumi's friendship. And although Alec has no opportunity to exchange more than a few words with either parent, he guesses that Haruki's toast, 'Friends, may your days together be full of joy' is calculated to include him. Later, back at Mayumi's apartment, she shrugs when he asks her what she thinks. Then raising a make-believe glass she says, "Good friend, my joy is having you stop obsessing about my parents. My great joy is having you take off your clothes and put your arms around me. And, my ultimate joy? Well, Alec, I'm gonna trust you to figure that one out."

"Sorry, but it's not going to happen until you take me seriously. I care about you and so, by extension, what's going down with your parents."

"Well, then, I hope it eases your worries enough to know Mom followed me into the bathroom, gave me a hug and said, 'Enjoy every minute with Alec, he's obviously a sweet guy,'" Mayumi says as she takes off her top and unclasps her bra.

"What about your dad?"

"Yikes, Alec, will I never get your attention?" Mayumi asks as she extends both forefingers to lightly tweak her erect nipples. "But just so you know, Mom wouldn't have volunteered that if Dad didn't agree. When one of them announces a position, it's always by consensus. So, I'm sure they dissected my romantic history, what they know of it anyway, and at the very least decided that you're Mr. Right for Right Now. Although honestly Alec, if you keep on about this I'm going to start having my doubts."

"Aren't they worried you might end up with an American in the long run?" Alec persists.

"I'm not a mind-reader, but possibly, a little. Like most parents they probably believe my life will be easier if I settle here with a guy from a similar background. And I'm sure they hope that their grandchildren will grow up close by. But they both have friends all over the world and know good people come in all sizes, shapes and colors. So, if I eventually say 'I do' to a *hakujin* whose name isn't Josh, I'm sure they'll climb on board. Alec, what's all this about? It's as if you're competing to be my long-term partner when, in fact, you don't want the role. And, anyway, as I've told you, I'm not remotely ready to settle down with anyone until I see the world, finish grad school and am well on my way to starting my media empire. But, enough already! I'm giving you just this one last chance to ask yourself how long your lover is going to sit here getting goose bumps on her tiny titties before she pulls out her purple friend."

"Is this more like it?" Alec asks, as he drops his pants, pulls his shirt over his head, and covers Mayumi's naked body with his.

"It's nice to see that even a slow learner can arrive at the right answer eventually," Mayumi murmurs as she wraps her legs tightly around his butt.

. . . . .

When her last class wraps up Monday afternoon Tamiko crosses Amherst's main quad, barely registering the crowning glory of the many multihued trees. Having peeked at Alec's long email, she's relieved she has a full hour to cope with it before her pitching workout with V at 4:30. Claiming a corner seat of the nearly empty Frost Cafe, Tamiko reads:

Dearest Tamiko: I hope it's OK that I'm breaking our deafening silence to actually send you one of the many hundreds (make that thousands) of messages I've composed in my head. As I'm guessing you know, Charlie has been here with all sorts of exciting news. Yo! Huge congratulations on getting to write for, and even appear in, a Ben Fine film. With anyone else I'd think the news was exaggerated, but with you, I know anything, and everything, is possible.

But I confess I don't know how to completely digest the fact that you are soon to be an actor. At the same time I'm excited, I'm also a little worried (for both of us, if I'm honest). However, the fact that you're also getting a chance to help write the script is seriously cool. OK, then, so why am I anxious? Certainly making a film, while meeting all sorts of fascinating people, will be an amazing ride (maybe also stressful, but you thrive on challenges—so that's all good). No question, it will also be lovely to have a pile of loot available to pay for grad school. So, again, I ask myself, what's not to like?

Maybe, that in the process of putting yourself (the image of yourself, or whatever) out into the wide, wide world, you risk losing something of your lovely, unaffected essence.

And I don't mean just your privacy, although for a semi-loner like you, that's not to be sneezed at. No, I'm concerned about something I can't quite explain. The best I can do is suggest that many so-called big stars who make their living trading on their pretty faces and bodies, including a couple in your movie, seem pretty hollow.

Feeling a surge of annoyance, Tamiko picks up her ceramic to-go mug, stalks out of the cafe and makes her way to a nearby bench. Like the clear, chill air that has blown away the muggy Indian summer and turned the leaves to flame, she gives Lec's sweet first paragraph an A. But his second patronizing one makes her want to kick something. Yet, with neither can, nor clod, at hand she instead flings the dregs of her coffee onto a pile of leaves. Who gave Lec permission to drop all these judgments on me based on a tiny part in one film, she thinks, as she stares right through the tall, red-headed girl from her history class as if she hadn't said hi.

Now slamming her boots through the carpet of crinkly brown leaves toward the white columns of Johnson Chapel, Tamiko is tempted to shout "Lec Burns, I don't give a damn what you think," loud enough to be heard in Tokyo. Suddenly, chagrined that she's allowed Lec to so thoroughly hijack her afternoon, she collapses on the Chapel's front steps and rereads the offending paragraph. This time the corners of her lips twitch up as she wonders whether, underneath Lec's exasperating paternalism, he may even be a little envious, or, praise be, jealous. And, in fairness to his larger point, hasn't she had some of the same concerns about the corrosive effects of celebrity? Even assuming the world is ready to embrace a 5'10" tomboy, a notion she still decidedly doubts, does she really want to be that girl? Then, crossing her fingers, Tamiko takes a deep breath as she scrolls down to where she hopes Lec will finally get around to talking about his feelings for her.

But before I go on to explain what's up with me in the here and now, let me briefly fill you in on the weeks we've been out of touch. When I got to Japan I was, to say the least, disoriented by my lack of the language, but also by a culture that does so many ordinary things so very differently than we do (often better, sometimes worse, occasionally weird, but, for a newcomer, almost always disconcertingly different). I was also surprised at how stunned I was by not being with you. It was as if during our year together you became so much a part of me that I was lost without my soul-mate. No doubt, I'm explaining this awkwardly, but since I'm guessing you experienced similar feelings of separation anxiety, and perhaps also disorientation at Amherst, I'll plunge on. By late September, although my studies were more or less going OK, I was depressed. (Yes, seeing Teri for an evening was good fun, but little relief to my feelings of isolation and something, incidentally, I'm sorry I troubled you with since I see now that, while my confession may have somewhat assuaged my guilt, it caused you needless pain). Of course, I've been on my own plenty of times in my travels and have occasionally been lonely, but this went beyond that to a feeling I can only describe as enveloping alienation. (I don't fit in here, never will, and don't even want to.) Again, perhaps you experienced similar feelings when you arrived at your little college, but remember that while a world where rich preppies call the social shots may seem alien, it doesn't have a patch on a place where they eat eel for breakfast. Mercifully, my feelings of being a misfit in a strange land began to dissipate when I volunteered to teach English to young Vietnamese workers (indentured servants, really) who have come to Japan as low-wage workers (domestics, dishwashers, hotel cleaners). What do I know about teaching anything you may ask? Fortunately, the fact that the answer is pretty much nada *turns out to make little difference to my students at the nonprofit support center who are desperate for any, and all, help. I'll tell you more about all this another time, but for now suffice it to say by struggling to help people who are light years more lost than I'll ever be (I teach a two-hour class two nights per week to fifteen students), I began to find my own emotional footing.*

So OK, let me start this next part by saying that as always I hold you next to my heart and that my feelings for you are just as warm and loving as ever.

Oops! Tamiko thinks, as the sentence's disclaimer-like language causes her heart to sink faster than a half dollar tossed into quicksand. Pretty sure she doesn't want to know what comes next, she nevertheless continues.

But I also need to tell you that a couple weeks ago I made a good friend named Mayumi Yamada. Mayumi is a twenty-two-year-old recent graduate of Tokyo University who is doing contract research work for Charlie and Phil. In December she plans to leave Japan with a girlfriend for a gap year of European travel before settling in London for two years to get a Masters in journalism. I tell you this biographical stuff up front, so you'll know from the start that our friendship is effectively time limited—something that, for both of us, surely smoothed its formation. I hope it isn't necessary, but to be absolutely clear, my relationship with Mayumi hasn't diminished my love for you by a scintilla.

Please fill me in on what's going on at Amherst and with the prospect of your exciting new film career. Also, if you're ready to share, I'd love to know how you currently think about you and me, and our big abiding love for one another. And, just in case you are in any doubt, I also hope to wrap you in my arms before long.

I love you, Lec PS: I've told Mayumi all about you and she's seen the photos of the two of us. It's actually her idea that somehow that you and she can be friends. Honestly, I'm not sure what I think of that, but I promised to pass her thought along. Also, since she's seen your picture, it's only fair for you to see hers. But only if you want to, of course (let me know).

. . . . .

On her walk to the gym to meet V, Tamiko feels so hot she pulls off her purple sweatshirt, complete with Amherst's woolly mammoth mascot, that Derrick gave her. Although it's a tangible reminder that she too has had a fling, tying it around her waist does nothing to assuage the sting of Lec's news. True, Tamiko admits to herself, if sex with Derrick had achieved lift-off, I might not feel so bereft. But then, wasn't it the purity of my love for Lec that prevented a new bond? Bullshit, a still-rational corner of her mind calls out. If Derrick and I had clicked romantically, wouldn't I be saying pretty much the same thing as Lec?

Forty minutes later, she pumps four seam fastballs so hard that V raises her stinging hand and begs Tamiko to mix in some changeups. After practice Tamiko strides back to Appleton and fires up her email.

OK then, send me Mayumi's picture—just her, not with you. I'll think about her idea of us being friends but, just so you know, I'm way beyond doubtful. Of course I have loads to tell you, but before I focus on that, I need time to let things settle. In the meantime, I'm more than a little annoyed to admit that I still love you.

PS: I can't help but notice you always point out that whoever you're shagging at the moment is about to disappear, as if somehow this will make me feel better. Sorry, it doesn't. And, hey, what happened to don't ask, don't tell?

EARLY NOVEMBER

"HEY VERA, STEPAN—OVER HERE," Tamiko calls, waving excitedly as she steps off Amtrak's *Vermonter* at Stamford, Connecticut.

"How come no American train ever here when supposed to be?" Vera asks, giving Tamiko a long, firm hug as she adds, "Soviet Union was better."

"How quick she forgets," Stepan says with a grin as he, too, steps forward to wrap Tamiko in his long arms.

Relieved that the reliability of trains is a subject she isn't expected to have an opinion about, Tamiko steps between her grandparents and links arms, knowing it will be an insult to his Russian male sense of propriety, if she doesn't let Stepan pull her bag with his free hand. On the way back to their house in Greenwich, Tamiko is in the middle of describing her small role in *2+2* when she suddenly stops. "Okay, then, what's up with you two? It's, like, I can tell by your loud silence that something is bothering you."

"Being big celebrity, especially in America, is not all grand," Stepan says kindly. "We have done this, so we know of what we say."

"What Stepan means, we are excited for you, but also worried, little bit," Vera adds.

"But, I have a tiny part in a movie with a Milky Way full of stars. It's not like I'm going to be the world's most famous dancers like you two."

"We only that because of defecting," Vera says quietly.

"I was mostly celebrity because of defecting. You were brilliant ballerina because God kissed you," Stepan corrects.

"Anyway, none of this is point," Vera exclaims, impatiently. "*Milaya moya*, they pick you for film because your youth and beauty will steal show."

"C'mon, Vera, you're way exaggerating. My role consists of being the awkward college kid who stumbles into the middle of a tryst between four of the world's most beautiful people."

"Why you think there so many very young ballerinas?" Stepan asks, as if this isn't a non sequitur.

"Hmm, I've never thought about it. Maybe because they're brilliant dancers like I'm sure you and Vera were when you were sixteen," Tamiko replies.

"*Nyet*," Stepan says contemptuously. "The principal dancers who are usually ten or fifteen years older always far better."

"So why, then?"

"Because beautiful adolescent girls so lovely," Stepan answers, placing a hand over his heart.

"Like bud turning to flower on spring morning, the audience adore to watch girls just as they become woman," Vera says simply. Then after a long pause, she adds, "We worry that especially because your mind so full of real things, you do not see effect your fresh beauty has on people. Perhaps yours is not usual pretty face, but few so stunning. And as far as the rest of you, I only have to watch men look at you, then look again, then forget to look away."

"This fall, trying to fend off what seemed like half the dudes in my first-year class, I've glimpsed a little of that," Tamiko says quietly.

"Ah, finally, you begin to see why we worry," Vera says as she nudges Stepan's arm and points to an old man and his spotted three-legged dog stepping off the curb. As the car slows to let the pair slowly cross, she continues, "Instead of a few overgrown boys at little college in Massachusetts, suppose fifty, or even one hundred millions of people all over world get crush on you."

"But…"

"No buts," Stepan says, authoritatively. "Not only can happen, but your smarty pants director picks you because he hope it will happen. You will better understand when you get to California and the two older actresses immediately hate you. Left to themselves they never sure who is most dazzling—but with you in room, answer is obvious."

"C'mon," Tamiko interrupts, her face now as flushed as her light tan complexion will permit.

Apparently not noticing her reaction, Stepan continues, "And you especially likely to be noticed in movie with beautiful people who have become bored with their own beauty."

"Enough, you two. What is this really about? Are you proposing I quit the movie?"

"*Nyet*," Vera replies, as Stepan nods in agreement. "Somehow God, who does of course exist, no matter what you may believe, has gifted you true beauty plus something, which for lack of other name, I call grace," Vera continues seriously. "There can be no hiding all this. We only say prayer you somehow find wisdom and humility to survive this Hollywood place where so many people forget what is truth."

. . . . .

Saturday after lunch, Tamiko takes an uncharacteristic, but much needed nap.

Padding into the high-ceilinged white kitchen midafternoon, she finds Vera sitting behind her iPad in the breakfast nook. Thanks to a floor-to-ceiling window overlooking a patch of still-green grass that rolls downhill toward a stand of birch trees, Tamiko is momentarily mesmerized as the last leaves flutter like tiny yellow flags. Then turning to Vera, she asks, "Are you trying to stump me by searching out a quote by some extra obscure Russian?"

Ignoring this Vera says, "Who writes—*Of two friends, one is always the slave to the other, though often neither will admit it*—?"

"My god, Vera, how did you guess what I came here to talk to you about?"

"First, play our game. What is answer?"

"Hmm, Gorky, maybe. No, wait, I'm actually thinking it's Lermentov."

"With all the fuss of last few months I'm glad to see your mind still has its Velcro."

"Read it, remember it, regurgitate it—that's me. Understand what's been read? That might be someone else."

"Nonsense! And, *milaya moya*, just so you know, false modesty always boomerang for bright people. But, more to point now, how come you stay in Massachusetts more than two months before you visit?"

"As maybe Mom explained, when I first got to Amherst, I was kind of a mess—disoriented, lonely, mad at school, mad at myself. And that's only part of the list. Anyway, I wanted to fix as much of this as I could—to grow up a little, I guess—before visiting."

"And have you? I mean besides somehow getting involved with this film."

"Well, at the very least, I feel better—still confused about some stuff, but basically okay. For one thing, I've wiggled my way into more challenging classes, especially the Ancient Greek language, which I love. And, following Ruth Marcus's suggestion, I've begun hanging with older kids who are more like what I was used to with Lec and his friends. Also, along the way I've tried to relearn how to be happy on my own, without being glued to Lec, like last year."

"Amy also say you find nice friend—or maybe boyfriend—who is the son of movie director."

"For sure, Derrick Fine has become a buddy, and his sister Clementine, too. But the romance part of the deal kinda rolled in to town on one bus and out on the next."

"That was quick."

"What can I say but that being with Derrick was sweet, but nothing like the...well," Tamiko trails off. "I mean, like, maybe if I'd met Derrick first, things might have been different, but..."

"Sweetie, I may be old, but not yet quite dead. I think what you mean to say is that in bed with Alec it was like Mars crashed into Venus, but with new boy planets didn't move, which, I might add, can sometimes be relief."

"Given yours and Stepan's relationship, you probably don't mean that."

"I probably don't. But, *milaya moya*, how is it I can help you?"

"Read this," Tamiko replies, handing over her iPad open to Lec's last email.

After carefully studying it, Vera asks, "Has he sent girl's picture?"

Taking the tablet from Vera and opening a second email, Tamiko turns the screen back toward her grandmother.

"Attractive, but not one of those impossibly beautiful Japanese faces," Vera says, neutrally.

"Vera, why do you think she wants to be friends with me? It's like, at first the idea seemed mega-weird, but then I remembered your telling me that when you were sixteen and had just started at the Bolshoi, you and Clara, this other young dancer, became lifetime buddies over being with the same guy."

"Ha! That only happen after he dump both of us, which I think is much easier than what this Mayumi propose."

"Do you think it's possible for two women who share a man to be friends?"

"In this not so wonderful new world, when people live long and many don't want to choose mate till older, her idea might even be good sense," Vera replies, tentatively.

"Interesting, but it doesn't answer my question."

"Answer probably in DNA, not here, or even here," Vera says, as she places one hand on her head and the other over her heart. "At most deep level, woman need seed of man for making her babies and then need good man to help protect these babies, not other woman's babies. So, while so many things in world change, I doubt our genes keep up."

"But what if neither woman wants to have babies? Or at least doesn't want them for many years? And suppose neither plans for their shared lover to be the father? And, anyway, can't women group together to take care of their babies on their own?"

"Ha! So many questions, but maybe right one is, do their genes know any of this? However, *milaya moya*, since Stepan is one who remember the Lermentov quote, maybe we wait till he back from golf before we discuss more."

"Vera, do you think it's a little funny that one of the twentieth century's best Russian ballet dancers should take up golf?"

"Certainly, but Stepan also want me to learn, which can be much bigger laugh. He say first time I sink long putt to beat him, I will begin to dance. But for now, I'm off for walk. Will you like to come?"

"Of course."

"In those sandals?"

"You sound like Mom. But, just a sec, I have some runners in my bag."

A few minutes later, Tamiko is pleased to find that, even with her long stride, it is no easy task to keep up with her grandmother's graceful lope along the wide dirt trail that, given the number of walkers and joggers, is clearly a community treasure. Vera, it seems, is built to last. Cresting a steep hill at the end of mile three, Tamiko puts her hand on her grandmother's arm as she says, "I want to talk about something even more important than Lec."

Clearly surprised, Vera stops and turns to face Tamiko. However, her reply is drowned out by a flurry of wild yips floating up from the bottom of the hill. When the dogs finally stop, Vera grins as she says, "Just old friends saying hi. So now tell me, what possibly can be half as important as your all-consuming passion for Alec Burns?"

"I've been starting to forget Dad and it scares me. Like, the other day I was thinking about this picnic Dad, Mom and I had the week before he was killed and all I could remember was the photo we took, not really Dad at all. I mean, Vera, do you get what I'm saying?"

"Very well."

"I'm frightened that one day I'll wake up and Dad will be entirely gone."

"Not to worry! Since you are half him, this can never happen," Vera replies reassuringly.

"By biology, sure, but still, sometimes when I try to figure out what Dad would think about something, or what he would tell me to do, he starts to slip away."

"You just describe biggest paradox of memory. But tell me, *milaya moya*, last spring when you ask me to recommend a book I love, and I say *In Search of Lost Time* by Marcel Proust, did you read it?"

"I did."

"Do you remember scene when Marcel eats little cookie dipped in tea?"

"Of course, that's when all sorts of long-forgotten memories come flooding back. But Vera, I doubt you're suggesting I eat more madeleines," Tamiko says with a chuckle, relying on humor to cover the fact she doesn't grasp her grandmother's point.

"I suggest only that many times in life something ordinary, a color, a song, a broken red bicycle or even, possibly, a little cookie, will trigger bright memory of your dad. And when this happens, be ready to stop what you do, or think, to be there with him. Commit to this and you will lose fear of your dad disappearing, because he will always come back when you need him most."

. . . . .

Showered and scrubbed two hours later, Tamiko enters the kitchen to find her grandfather sitting at the kitchen table drinking a glass of Old Rasputin beer from the bottle while Vera fusses with something on the stove containing onions, garlic and cumin. "Smells delicious," Tamiko says. "Hopefully that's your famous Russian chicken and rice pilaf?"

"Yes, very Russian and you lucky to taste my secret recipe," Vera replies as she licks a wooden spoon.

"Dad made it pretty often, so I guess I grew up lucky," Tamiko replies, matter-of-factly.

"Not so lucky as tonight," Stepan says, with a sly laugh. "Since it well known Vera never tell anyone—not even children—secret ingredient."

Turning to her grandmother with her brightest smile, Tamiko says, "But Vera, since you're a kind and generous person you'll make an exception to the no-tell rule for your favorite granddaughter."

"Russians not believe in flattery," Vera snaps, turning toward the stove to hide her smile.

"I hope you don't mind if I change subject, but Vera shows me your iPad with message from Alec," Stepan says, suddenly serious.

"So, how do you suggest I reply?" Tamiko asks, just as seriously.

"What do you think about Lermentov quote?"

"Provocative, but like so many of Lermentov's over-the-top statements I assume he was exaggerating the master/slave analogy to make a point."

"And when it comes to you and Alec…"

"I've never thought of myself as anyone's slave, but I guess your point is that last year Lec was more in charge of our relationship than I was. I mean, how could it have been any other way given how much older and more experienced he was?"

"All true," Stepan says kindly. "And surely it was big help that you had your own busy life, doing sports, going to school and working. But important question, of course, is not about all that, but what kind of relationship you want for future?"

"Oh my god, this is going to sound feeble, but, when Lec and I parted in August it felt as if my house had literally caught fire. All I could think of was how to avoid being incinerated, not what color to paint it next year. But, I think I understand what you mean. Going forward I need to consider how the power in our relationship can be distributed more equally."

"You always quick learner," Vera says, still standing by the stove, but now waving the wooden spoon for emphasis.

"Do you want a beer?" Stepan asks Tamiko.

"Not really. Despite, or maybe because my college is drowning in it, I haven't developed the taste. But a finger and a half of Vera's red wine would be smooth."

As Stepan moves to the counter to pour out a short glass of cabernet, he observes, "Fortunately you now have great chance to gather this new strength of yours."

"I don't quite see…"

"Let this old Russian explain. When Alec last saw you, you were basically lovesick kid, off to college with sad face. On his way to Japan he can almost be forgiven if he thinks your arms wide open whenever he decide to come back. And, if traveling to Massachusetts too much trouble, one whistle and you on next plane to Japan. But, now, maybe for first time, Alec not quite so confident. Not only do you have contract to appear in A-list film, but also to help with writing it. Add interesting new boyfriend and maybe Alec begins to worry he is no longer sun at center of your solar system."

"But as I told Vera earlier, Derrick was barely my boyfriend and isn't anymore and I'm almost sorry I got involved with *2+2*."

"Does Alec know any of this?" Vera asks, kindly.

"Well, no, but I…"

"So, of course, Stepan's point that you very silly to tell him," Vera continues as if Tamiko hasn't interrupted.

"So, you're both telling me to let him fret for awhile," Tamiko says with an impish grin.

"Finally, penny fall," Stepan says, as he absently peels off the label with Rasputin's picture on it from his beer bottle.

"Do I have ten minutes before we eat to compose something that I can run by you after dinner?" Tamiko asks, already pushing back her chair.

"Fifteen, even," Vera says with a conspiratorial grin.

. . . . .

An hour later, after the pilaf and delightfully yeasty apple-stuffed pirozhky have been gratefully consumed, Tamiko picks up her iPad and says, "Okay, here's what I came up with."

Lec,

Sweet to hear from you, and thanks for your sensible advice about looking twice before diving headlong into La-La Land. For what it's worth, Vera and Stepan echo your concerns about the perils of celebrity. But I do love the screenwriting part, so it may be harder to pry me off that pony.

As to what's going on with me. After a slow start at my self-important little college, I'm beginning to find my way, especially enjoying being able to learn two years of Ancient Greek in one. Helping construct the diorama of Athens circa 450 BCE that my prof has been building for over a decade is the cream on top of my baklava. I'm also taking grad-level stats over at UMass, which opens my eyes to the larger opportunities that the five-college course exchange program offers. In addition, I've finally made some new friends. Don't know that I'll want to swim in this tiny pond for four years, but for now, color me a cheerful trout.

No question, Mayumi looks lovely and it's not hard to see why you are attracted to her. And her idea that she and I can be friends is, at least, intriguing. But for now, I think I'll stick to wishing you (both of you) well, while I do my best to continue to live an interesting life here.

Love always, T.

When Tamiko finishes, Vera and Stepan begin to clap. "Perfect!" Stepan exclaims, "You write cheerful, vague words, which do not give Alec one clue about any of things he probably worry about. And no matter how conflicted you may feel, to be gracious about this new girl is also wise."

"If I was Alec, I wonder whether you are too busy with fascinating new things to be jealous of his Japanese friend," Vera adds with a wide grin on her face.

. . . . . .

"Hey good-looking," Amy says as she pops up from a ratty metal chair in front of the Jazz Cafe on Addison Street to give Ed a solid kiss on his lips. "Since you're five minutes late, I peeked to see that the special is eggplant parmigiana."

"And the soup?"

"Split pea with bacon."

"Not as good as bacon with bacon, but still, I might get that," Ed says, as he follows Amy down a short flight of stairs into the low-ceilinged cafe that occupies part of the basement of the Berkeley Jazz School next to the Aurora Theater. Seeing that there's only one empty table he adds, "Grab that one while I line up. Do you want the eggplant?"

"Need you ask?"

"My friend Gretchen called this morning to propose we leave on our girls-only adventure in three weeks," Amy blurts as soon as Ed rejoins her, an Arnold Palmer in each hand.

"Why the hurry? You two have been talking about going off to dazzle the world since before you and I got together eighteen months ago."

"Gretchen says if we don't leave soon, I'll never go."

"I'm not sure I follow."

"She's my best friend after you and Tami, so of course we talk. Lately I've been telling her that I seem to have fallen for you even harder."

Pausing for a second to try and decipher whether he's more annoyed, or pleased by this revelation, Ed finally replies, "Maybe I'm being too thin-skinned, but I didn't realize your affection was so shallow before."

"Never the physical part, for sure. But, as you know, I worried I was being too quick to make a long-term commitment."

"Didn't you tell me on the plane back East a few weeks ago that you were done fretting," Ed replies, as he waves at a server holding what looks to be their food.

"Absolutely, but I didn't have a good opportunity to share the news with Gretchen until last week."

"Actually, Gretchen's timing may not be bad," Ed replies, thoughtfully. "To have a hope of meeting my March deadline, I need to work on my novel every minute I'm not teaching up at Cal."

"If I do go with Gretchen, it's just for the travel adventure. I won't be looking for, umm, you know, well...other kinds of adventure, I guess," Amy says, touching Ed's hand as she meets his soft brown eyes.

"But what if you meet that Dos Equis guy—you know, the most interesting man in the world?" Ed asks, trying to keep his tone lighter than his feelings.

"That dude is old enough to be my grandpa."

"His son then? After all, you'll be traveling with a woman whose favorite website is BeNaughty."

"You're exaggerating, but it's true since her divorce two years ago, Gretchen has been enjoying a slightly slutty phase. Which means I'm concerned that, socially at least, we won't be on the same page. But, Ed, I also worry that you may compensate for my absence by hanging with one of your former lady friends or, maybe, more than one."

"No projecting please. I'm committed to going steady with my novel."

"Okay, then, I guess I'll tell Gretchen a sort of reluctant yes, assuming I can ask you for a huge favor. I'm still anxious that this whole Hollywood thing will be too heavy a lift for Tamiko, no matter how mature she thinks she is. So, do you think you could check on her? I mean, actually fly down to L.A. for a couple of days in December to be sure she's coping?"

"Of course, no problem, but after meeting Ben Fine and Mary McCarthy at Parents Weekend and seeing the great job they've done with Derrick and Clementine, I wouldn't be too worried. Isn't Tamiko going to stay with Mary in Ben's guesthouse until Derrick and Clementine arrive for their Christmas holiday?"

"Still."

"Worry not, Mom. I was about to turn down an invitation to speak on Publishing Politics, whatever that is, at a writers' conference in Santa Monica on December tenth. Instead, I'll tell them yes and get a free trip plus a decent fee. And since I'm hoping Ben can be cajoled into letting me hang out on the set of *2+2* for an afternoon, maybe I can even catch one of Tamiko's scenes."

"Oh my god, Ed, that sounds like too much fun. So much, in fact, that I think I just changed my mind about going on my trip."

Starting to reply, Ed turns it into a cough, afraid he'll say something that might cause Amy to again reverse course.

"What?" Amy demands.

"My lips are sealed, but my heart is happy."

"Mine too, actually," Amy says, leaning over to give Ed a quick kiss. "The truth is that in an effort not to break my word to Gretchen, I was in denial about how sad I was at the idea of being parted from you and Tami over the holidays. Now, I have to run. Will I see you at Yoga later?"

"Unless you want to blow it off and meet in our hot tub."

"Sure, and then maybe a tantric pose or two…"

. . . . .

When they meet late on Halloween afternoon, Mayumi, wearing cat's ears and whiskers, moves forward with three quick steps, to jump into Alec's arms.

"Wolf chasing you?" Alec asks, pretending to check out the street in front of Shibuya Station.

"No, but I seriously need a huge hug, or, I guess maybe we both do."

"Never a problem, but hey, why am I concerned all of a sudden?"

"I can't go to Mt. Koya with you this weekend because my mom insists I go to America," Mayumi blurts, keeping her eyes resolutely on the sidewalk.

"Really! The U.S.? Does this mean she's trying to pry you away from me?" Alec asks in alarm, as he puts a finger under Mayumi's chin to lift it until their eyes meet.

"Not at all. In fact, she's sincerely apologetic since she knows I'm off on my adventure with Fujiko soon and want to spend as much of my remaining time in Japan with you as possible. But, remember I told you that last week she toppled off a ladder at the gallery and twisted her ankle. Well, X-rays show a real mess that they want to fix immediately with some kind of fusion procedure."

"Ouch! No fun there I'm guessing," Alec interjects.

"True, but I'm afraid that's not the point as far as Mom and I go. It seems that two important American dealers she works with on consignment, one in San Francisco and one in Boston, have become upset. So angry, in fact, that one is refusing to pay for a long list of things they've already sold, and the other won't return a valuable antique Buddha. Apparently, this all stems from the fact that an assistant in Mom's warehouse shipped them counterfeit woodblock prints before making off with the originals. Since the high-end international art business floats on trust and reputation, Mom needs this problem to be fixed before it goes public. She's done her best electronically, but apparently can't bow low enough on Zoom."

"But what do you know about the business side of the gallery?"

"Quite a lot actually, since I pretty much grew up there, and then in college worked for Mom several summers. But that's not the point. With Mom unable to make a fence-mending trip, both dealers, who are Japanese by birth, will see a visit by her only daughter (aka me) both as a show of respect, and an acknowledgement of family shame, or *Haji*, in case your vocabulary is slipping. As maybe you've begun to figure out, we Japanese make amends for our bad actions by demonstrating shame, rather than internalizing them as guilt, as you do in the West. I could also…"

Too rattled to focus on a lesson in comparative sociology, Alec blurts, "Since you and Fujiko are leaving in a month, this means you'll be gone for a good chunk of the little time we have left."

"Now you know why I'm upset and also why I'll try to do the whole trip in five days."

"When do you leave?"

"Day after tomorrow. Alec, is there a chance you might come along? Charlie tells me he's gifted you almost unlimited miles and Mom's paying for the hotels, so…"

"Thanks for asking, but in addition to my teaching gig I have big-deal exams next week. Who knows if I'll ever learn enough Japanese to be of value to Charlie's business, or if I'll want to join Burns-Short after grad school, but for now I have to respect the process. And also, well, what can I say, but it's not a good time for me to be in Boston, with you."

"Too close to Tamiko?"

"In a word, yes! I'm doing my best to treat both of you well and I know that wouldn't be cool with her."

"Or you?"

"Or me. Having you two be six thousand miles apart is one thing— my going all the way to her backyard with you is very different. For the record, I wouldn't host Tamiko here in Japan. I just wish your mom could wait to do her penance after her ankle heals."

"I couldn't agree more. So do you want to stand here and sulk, or grab some take-out noodles and go back to my place and try to get over it?"

"Even a dumb *gaijin* knows the answer to that."

. . . . .

"Are you coming to dinner?" Eloise asks.

Tamiko, who is lying on her bed with her eyes shut, replies, "An email from Lec just pinged into my inbox and I'm trying to take your advice and grab the courage to read it sooner, rather than later. So, you go on ahead."

"Yo dummy, I'm glad to know you actually listen to me now and then. But, whether good, bad or indifferent, the news is not going to change by your refusing to eat a plate of pasta with me. What's up with your endlessly fraught emails? Don't you two know how to FaceTime?"

"Sure, but that's not going to happen until, well, things are…"

"Girl, you think too much for three people. I could try to pull you off that bed, but that would just embarrass both of us, so just get your ass into your coat and let's get some fettuccini."

. . . . .

During his second week of teaching Alec gives everyone an English-Vietnamese dictionary. And at each class he continues to update his comic strip *The Unlikely Adventures of Bao and Linh*. The need to introduce new vocabulary means that the story takes outlandish turns, but his students don't seem to mind. Quick quizzes at the beginning of each class show his students' remarkable retention of the five hundred words he's introduced, so much so that this evening he hands out copies of popular American grade school books including *Charlotte's Web*, *Charlie and the Chocolate Factory*, and *Diary of a Wimpy Kid*. Students are told to do their best with the title they receive and to be ready to trade it at the next class before repeating the process until everyone has had a chance to read each story.

. . . . .

Because friends waylay Tamiko about everything from Greek grammar and an American history quiz, to plans for a surprise birthday party for Eloise, dinner takes longer than expected. Finally breaking free, Tamiko is almost at the door of the dining commons when Amy Gottstein literally steps in front of her. Full of ideas on how to redo the Temple to Artemis in Professor Spurgeon's diorama, Amy burbles on and on even as Missy Frank shifts from foot to foot as she waits for her turn to get a word in. Oh my god, I may even be in danger of becoming popular, Tamiko thinks twenty minutes later as she finally dens up in a secluded corner of Frost Library. Having taken high school classes when she was in middle school, and community college classes when her age cohort was in high school, Tamiko is so used to being on her own she hardly knows how to react. Not ready to focus on whether being sought after is a good thing, a weird thing, or just a thing, she pulls up Lec's email.

Tamiko: I love you, all of you, even your slightly crooked right pinky, Tamiko reads as she wonders if her new popularity is a virus that has somehow spread halfway around the globe. Then, fearful that Lec's uncharacteristic hyperbole is somehow a pretty start to a kiss-off letter, she reads on.

I have a load to say, but knowing your zeal to get to the point, I'll start with the most important paragraph.

I miss you and hope we can somehow manage to see each other before long. After dedicating myself to a big study push this next five or six weeks I plan to take a vacation from Japan for a bit (Charlie has laid a bundle of free miles on me). I gather you'll be super busy in December in L.A. so won't propose anything then, but please begin to think about when rubbing noses might be possible. Also, and assuming you're still as interested as I am in making our relationship work for the long term, I think it's past time we make a plan. I, for one, don't want us to accidentally risk losing our special bond.

OK, take a deep breath, since this one will be a bit of a shocker. My friend Mayumi will be in Boston next weekend and proposes that you two meet. Her mother, a prominent art dealer in Tokyo, had a fall and can't travel. As a result, she is sending Mayumi in her place to try and salvage a seriously fraught relationship with a Boston gallery that specializes in Japanese art. Yes, I do remember that you said no to Mayumi's previous friends proposal, but she is determined to try again. What can I say, but that she has it all worked out in her head as to why it makes great sense for the three of us to be long-term supporters of one another, if not buddies. I won't try to repeat all her reasons, so am simply asking you whether it's OK (or not) to give her your contact info, so she can plead her own case?

OK, here is where I confess that while I don't think I'm exactly envious of your upcoming adventure as a celebrity, it does have me a little off balance. For some reason I'm put in mind of the old song that goes something like "How you gonna keep her down on the farm after she's seen gay Paree?" I don't see myself milking a cow, but just saying.

You chided me for downplaying my relationships with Teri and Mayumi, because they were, or are, about to leave town. You're right. If I see other people it's obviously my choice, not some accident of geography or timing. Just the same, I want to reiterate, the fact that Mayumi made it clear from the start that our days together were numbered, has made it easier for me to be with her, while keeping you in my heart.

Wow! Tamiko thinks after rereading Lec's message, which ends humorously with a list of his faux pas trying to use his primitive Japanese in public. What to make of all this, especially Lec's proposal that they get together and plan for the future? Apparently Stepan and Vera are right that her budding film career is causing Lec to take her more seriously. Deciding to think more about all this later, except for Mayumi's request to get together, which she already knows she'll decline, Tamiko heads back to Appleton where she checks her phone and sees that she has a couple of calls from Ben Fine.

. . . . .

"Hi Tamiko, thanks for getting back to me," Ben says, picking up on the first ring. "I want to discuss the changes you propose in your second scene where Jennifer and her mother meet at breakfast the day after she gets home from college and walks in on the foursome. For starters, I'm delighted with Jack Gold's idea to have Jennifer enter the kitchen by the beach-facing door still wearing her wetsuit after an early morning surfing session. I hope I'm not being too personal when I say that having you show off your toned physique is a brilliant way to wordlessly convey that it's Jennifer, not Virginia, who's the new woman. I'd love to include a few shots of you surfing, but I worry this will take us too far from our story."

"If you change your mind and want me up on a board, I'll need a day to practice," Tamiko says. "But Ben, I've been worried I may have exaggerated when I insisted Jennifer wouldn't be that shocked by the idea of swinging because threesomes are a happening thing here at Amherst. The truth is I've only heard a couple of rumors about three-way hookups, but have no idea how common they are."

"I've had the same concern," Ben replies, quickly. "To confidently direct this scene, it will help to know whether, in an effort to annoy her mother, Jennifer is deliberately sensationalizing the college dating scene, or whether she's telling the simple truth."

"Maybe I need to invite a few friends over Friday night to see what happens," Tamiko replies, tongue in cheek. Then, worrying that without seeing her body language Ben might take her seriously, she stammers, "Or I could ask Derrick what he thinks."

"Good idea, talk to Derrick. I know you're busy, but I need an answer ASAP."

"I'm on it," Tamiko replies, as she ends the call.

Shifting her focus back to answering Lec's email, it dawns on Tamiko that by rejecting Mayumi's offer to meet up, she's stepping on an opportunity to explore the very plot line she's supposed to be researching. True, Mayumi isn't proposing the three of them climb into bed together, or, at least, Tamiko doesn't think she is. But isn't Mayumi's proposal that she and Tamiko hang out, and maybe even become friends, at least a step down that path?

Reaching for her laptop before she has a chance to change her mind, Tamiko types:

Lec: It's late here and I have an important stats quiz mañana *so I won't try to respond to the bulk of your email about planning long term, except to say it definitely sounds sweet. For now, let me focus on the fact that I've changed my mind about meeting Mayumi, if for no other reason than I'm curious about what kind of woman turns you on (in case you're wondering, I can't decide whether that's a joke). If I have my dates right, Mayumi is going to be in Boston this weekend, but possibly you're referring to the next one. Either way, give her my email and have her get in touch.*

Not always sure why some days, but YES, I DO LOVE YOU!

Then, before she pulls up her stats notes in preparation for tomorrow's midterm, Tamiko composes a quick text to Derrick and Missy.

U two: Sorry to drop an X-rated bomb on u both, but I urgently need to check on attitudes of upperclass Amherst students to group sex (threesomes and foursomes). Missy, I know this may seem beyond weird, but I'll fill in the background as to why this is important when I see u. Since I've only ever slept with two non-simultaneous guys, I need HELP! HELP! HELP! Can the three of us get together tomorrow to talk? I'm free after 3.

. . . . .

Sure she's aced her stats midterm, Tamiko is tempted to skip back from UMass Tuesday morning. Instead, she rewards herself with a latte and blueberry muffin at ShareCoffee on North Pleasant Street. Turning her back on the bearded guy with glasses staring at her chest as if it's candy, Tamiko checks her messages to see that Derrick and Missy will meet her at the Black Sheep at 3:15.

Perfect, thanks! Tamiko texts back just as a message arrives from Mayumi Yamada. With her heart speeding up, and her fingers suddenly moist, Tamiko opens it.

hi tamiko:

i'm excited at the prospect of meeting the person alec (lec to u, I know) cares most for in this wide world. since i'm hoping maybe i'm second on his list, i'll be pleased if u and i can open our hearts wide enough to also build a special bond. as alec has maybe told u, i plan to travel and study in europe for the next two or three years (and definitely will be open to new adventures), but also hope alec and i can (and hopefully u 2) remain friends long-term. (for sure, in my 23 years i've never met anyone quite so, well...hmmm, since i can't come up with the perfect word, i'll assume you already know it). but i also realize you may be ambivalent about meeting me at all, so will do my best to respect your boundaries.

i arrive in boston this thursday evening and have meetings friday and maybe even saturday morning (as alec may have told u the japanese take forever to decide anything and everything). maybe it will be convenient for u to come to boston to hang out? i've seen the duck boats in movies and have always thought anything that silly must be fun. but maybe getting to boston on short notice isn't possible for u. if so, tell me how to get to amherst. i've driven in america, but only in smaller places without much traffic where i've had time to remember to be on the right side of the road. so i'm thinking i'll be happier with a train or bus, assuming either is available.

please let me know which plan is best for u. i arrive in san francisco tomorrow where i'll grab a sim card and text u my number. also, by way of introduction, i'm adding a short bio. if u're anything like me, u've probably been trying to connect the few data points u know about me to come up with a picture. possibly it's 2 personal, but i'm going to hit send before i chicken out.

mayumi

attachment:

mayumi's mini bio

as the youngest child of affluent parents (i have two older brothers) i was made much of as a child. no doubt, like lots of little girls, i was cute and precocious but, even at the time i knew i was being admired beyond my merits. to justify even a little of this i worked hard at bilingual school (japanese & english since age 2), and was usually at, or near, the top of my class. because it was the socially accepted thing to do in my last two years at high school, i had a few unremarkable lovers. my first year at university i hoped to have a much deeper relationship with an attractive grad student, but again it was more fizzle than fun. it wasn't until the start of my junior year when i met josh, an american phd student who was coordinating my journalism seminar, that i felt real interest in the boy-girl thing.

josh is tall, blond, blue-eyed and very full of his own ideas. when we met, he was twenty-five to my twenty, and i thought of him as this impossibly hunky man of the world. to capture josh i had to almost literally elbow half a dozen other girls out of the way. (in my social circles, dating a good-looking american teacher is uber-chill.) I won't bore you with the detailed chronology of our relationship, but will skip to last january when I followed josh to iowa city where he was beginning a teaching job at the u of i. even though i'd begun to doubt my long-term commitment to him, the next three months were a rude awakening. to oversimplify, on his home turf, the dude who had seemed so endlessly knowledgeable and charming in tokyo, somehow morphed into an opinionated know-it-all. anyway, by april josh and i were history and i was back in japan scrambling to catch up with my course work so as to graduate with my class. not only was I mildly depressed, but also ashamed of my poor judgment, especially given that my parents and even my close friend, fujiko, had warned that there was less to josh than met my eye.

by late summer things were looking up. my loose university friendship circle tightened as we all realized that we were about to go our separate ways. fujiko and i committed to our gap year travel plan starting this december in spain, and i got accepted to an exciting graduate journalism program in london starting next september. (oops! i should probably tell u i like journalism because i was born curious, and modern art, because well, i just do, and eventually hope to fuse them into a career.) also, in august i was pleased when phil short offered me a fall research gig doing corporate background reports for burns-short. this not only allowed me to get research and writing experience, but also to earn enough so as not to have to beg my parents for travel money (well, less anyway).

in early september i ran into alec at the burns-short office and immediately felt my jaw clench. i guess my resentment at josh was still fresh enough that i saw all tall, good-looking americans as superficial jerks. still, tamiko, here's the odd thing. despite being very sure i had no use for alec (i even avoided coming to the office when i thought he might be there), i caught myself repeatedly thinking about how charlie had mentioned that alec's korean girlfriend was coming to tokyo for a visit. why, i had to ask myself, do i give a damn about the love life of a guy i don't like? to find out, i hung around burns-short a couple of afternoons until alec finally showed up. then, before my conscious mind even knew what i was doing, i found myself inviting him to come out that evening to a gathering of my university friends. as i waited for alec to appear i kicked myself, sure that everyone (especially the guys) would conclude that i had what we japanese call white fever (was only hot for white guys). instead, in less than half an hour after alec arrived, everyone at the table, including me, was competing to be his best japanese friend (straight-laced shoko even came back from the restroom with fresh lipstick and the top button of her blouse undone). i'll spare u alec's and my dating history except to say that after years of frustration, he finally taught me what the woman-man thing is all about. like u, i'm guessing, this alone means i'll always treasure him.

. . . . . .

When the three friends meet at the Black Sheep, Tamiko double-swears Missy to secrecy before explaining her involvement in *2+2*. With Derrick's help Tamiko then reviews the film's plot, focusing on the scene that gives rise to her need to learn more about the sexual habits and attitudes of Amherst juniors and seniors. She then asks Missy and Derrick how they think Jennifer, as a typical twenty-year-old junior, might react when her mother insists she's far too young to understand why married adults might want to explore a more open sexual relationship.

"Is there such an animal as a typical twenty-year-old with a typical response?" Missy asks. "I mean, to even make a decent guess wouldn't we need to know a lot about Jennifer's background including, for example, whether she's religious?"

"Point taken," Tamiko replies. "Nevertheless, Ben Fine wants me to research whether, or not, it registers as authentic when Jennifer claims not to be shocked by swinging, at least in part because threesomes are a thing at college and she may even have participated. Also, remember, at this point in the film, we do know Jennifer's age, that she goes to U.C. Berkeley, comes from an upscale SoCal family, surfs and," here Tamiko pauses to bat her eyes, "is attractive."

"Okay, assuming we're here because you've tagged Missy and me as your first two guinea pigs," Derrick says seriously, "I've had two three-ways, but both were in L.A., not here, and both happened at the sloppy end of boozy parties when no one wanted to go home alone. And in case you're curious, although both were fun, neither rocked my planet."

"FMF or MFM?" Missy asks, matter-of-factly.

"One of each."

"Well, I haven't had any," Missy says, "although I somewhat reluctantly agreed to one that never happened."

"Really?" Tamiko interjects, embarrassed that she sounds shocked.

"Two years ago, this guy I had been going out with for a semester put a huge amount of energy into talking my friend and me into trying it," Missy continues, as if Tamiko hasn't spoken. "But, when we finally agreed, he got so excited he downed a shot too many and fell asleep. I know, weird, right?"

"So, Tamiko, how do you propose doing your research?" Derrick asks. "Obviously, Missy and I are not a big enough sample to determine anything. And you can't simply waltz up to a random group of students and ask how many people they screwed last Saturday."

"I was thinking maybe you two could help me by talking to your friends and well, you know…"

Seeing Tamiko's embarrassment, Missy says, "How about I pull a bunch of girls together tomorrow evening after supper? Then, Tamiko, you can ask them yourself. Since you've made it clear that your involvement in the film is still confidential, you can pitch it as a research project and let folks assume it's school related."

"Will your friends talk to me?"

"Why not? You already know most of them and sex is easily the favorite subject here at Amherst. Denial may be an issue, for a few, since it's one thing to get drunk and hook up with a couple of people in the middle of the night, but something pretty different to talk about it the next morning. So, maybe you'll get better information if you start by handing out an anonymous questionnaire."

"Hmm," Derrick muses, "we'll need a different approach with my buddies. Anonymous, or not, having an attractive female question a group of dudes about their sex lives is likely to produce mostly lewd jokes and lies. Probably it's better for me to informally try to get you some answers."

. . . . .

On Tuesday evening Tamiko whips through her American History paper on the Treaty of Ghent. Knowing that it's both short and superficial she tells herself that it's good enough to sum up this justly obscure treaty that ended the pointless little War of 1812. Still needing to put in an hour preparing for tomorrow's Greek grammar review with Professor Spurgeon, she nevertheless accesses Mayumi's email, taps reply and begins:

Dear Mayumi,

I'm on for Boston. To be honest, I'm still conflicted about meeting, but at the very least, I suspect we'll both have a riveting afternoon. I'll meet you at the Duck Boat ticket office outside the Prudential Center at 1:00 p.m. (I see that there are two other launch locations, so don't be fooled.) I was fascinated by your personal story and would like to respond with the same thoughtfulness. But since this week is overflowing with school stuff, as well as research for the film script I'm helping with, I'll limit myself to a few quick words.

See you Saturday, ready to quack. Tamiko

TAMIKO'S BRIEF BIO (unedited)

Fifteen months ago on a sunny August morning I walked across the U.C. Berkeley campus, where I was taking a summer term Physics class. Perhaps you can imagine me wearing baggy jeans, a double X sweatshirt, and still shouldering my kid's backpack with a teddy bear on the flap. I was a few days short of my sixteenth birthday, had never been kissed (or been on a date) and had, as usual, forgotten to comb my lion's mane tangle of hair. True, I had kind of been thinking (or maybe my hormones were thinking for me) that it was time to buy some girl clothes, get a new pack and say yes to a date with the first acceptable college dude who asked (despite my mom's no college boys rule). But, instead of bumbling my clueless adolescent self into that awkward future, I dropped a book. And, glory be to Tyche, goddess of good fortune, Lec (I, too, like it that we call him by different names) picked it up. It's probably little surprise to you that when I looked into his eyes I was immediately clobbered with a wave of feelings I'd never experienced. What can I say but when the same thing happened to him, I resolved never again to doubt the existence of magic. However, based on our admittedly wide age and experience gap, my mom shouted "No, No, No!" But that was before, Max, this bad dude from Mom's past improbably (but very tangibly) appeared out of nowhere and tried to kidnap, rape and presumably kill both of us. Something Max would likely have accomplished if Lec hadn't risked his life to intervene (perhaps he has shared some of the wild details). Anyway, the happy result of this mega-scary five days was that in Mom's eyes Lec morphed from Dirty Old Man to Brave True Hearted Prince who had earned the right to hang with the Innocent Young Virgin (aka, me). Newly sixteen and now equipped with a new hairbrush and wardrobe, I was, of course, delighted to get over all three descriptors (or, at least two of them—since I'm stuck with the young part).

And then, to my happy amazement, for the next eleven months Lec and I lived happily ever after. Sadly, this was followed by our August from hell when I unilaterally announced I was quitting my college plans to accompany my prince to Japan. When, not surprisingly, the unconsulted prince said no, I retreated into an epic pout. Finally, after a September of hating myself and everything about college, I began to confront my feelings of entitlement, rejection and loneliness, with the result that before long I was back on the path to being myself. Happily this resulted in my making new friends and beginning to enjoy my studies. Then, astonishingly, I was asked to play a small part in a big deal film. Having zero interest in performing, I tried to refuse, but was seduced into saying yes when I was also given the opportunity to edit, and even write, a few lines of the script. Like you, I love words.

. . . . .

On a chilly Thursday afternoon Tamiko meets Derrick at his dorm room to hear the report of his conversations with his friends. "I talked to my mom earlier and it's seventy-six degrees in Berkeley," she says as she shrugs off her black fleece jacket.

"Shush, keep your voice down," Derrick mock-whispers. "We don't want the poor fools who plan to spend the rest of their lives back here in the New England slush to move west to make our Promised Land even more crowded. Hey, before we get to Ben's question, I want to be sure everything is smooth between us. I think we mutually agreed that even though you and I didn't catch fire romantically, we're still buddies for life. Right?"

"Definitely," Tamiko replies, as she flops down on a green beanbag, unable to find the right words to tell Derrick how important her friendship with him is.

Apparently sensing Tamiko has something to add, Derrick pauses before saying, "I'm guessing both of us have loads more to unpack, but perhaps it's better to wait until…"

"Derrick," Tamiko interrupts, "I'm trying to get over being shy about asking you for a mega-favor. It's like, when it comes to the you and me thing, is it okay if we still fake being together, at least until I go to L.A.? Ever since I've been hanging with you, it's been this huge relief that other dudes have mostly stopped hitting on me and that even my Ice Princess rep has begun to fade. Of course, if you have something else going on, that's…"

"Your plan suits me perfectly," Derrick interrupts. "Until we began spending time together, a couple of girls I'm not interested in were in my face competing to replace Ericka. So how about we call our new relationship the Tamiko and Derrick Mutual Protection Racket."

"Sweet!" Tamiko says, reaching over to tap her fist against Derrick's. "So, okay, tell me what happened when you asked your friends about threesomes and foursomes?"

"Like I told you, I decided to pull guys together in twos and threes to avoid as much locker room banter as possible and increase my chances of receiving truthful answers."

"Why would anyone fib?"

"When guys get together at least some are sure to brag about their conquests, real or imagined. And especially if they get into a face-off as to who has screwed more women, their imaginations may dictate their answers."

"I'm probably not the first female to say that understanding quantum mechanics is easy compared to figuring out how the male mind works."

"Please note that in the interest of saving an hour, I'll reserve my views as to which sex is wackier. But, to get back to what you and Ben want to know, as I suspected, out of the nine dudes (ten including me) I caught up with, four claimed to be riveted by the fantasy of having a three-way with two girls; and another four (I'll put myself in this group) reported that they would be interested under the right circumstances. Only one dude said an MFM encounter was appealing. Yet, I think you'll find this interesting, just two dudes besides me said they had participated in any type of group sex, no matter the initials. But, perhaps, just as relevant to what Ben wants to know, no one was shocked by the idea."

"What about the two dudes who weren't interested?"

"One is a Jesus freak, or, to stay clear of the campus thought police, I guess I should say committed Christian who assured me the Bible calls for sex between one man and one woman. I literally had to bite my tongue to stop myself asking if he'd ever read the Old Testament. The other is a quiet guy I don't know very well except that he's been with the same girl for the last couple of years."

"Maybe he's just a devoted guy."

"Maybe. But, Tamiko, when we were at the Black Sheep you also wondered if the perceived attractiveness (or lack thereof) of the female involved made a significant difference to male attitudes when it comes to their trying for a threesome with two women. Sparing you several obnoxious comments about female physiognomy, the consensus seems to be no. Or, as one guy, who actually thought he was putting it tastefully, observed 'when it comes to bedding two chicks, faces aren't the relevant body part.'"

"Gah!"

"I don't disagree. But, hey, I know how slammed you are right now, so, if you want I can relay the gist to Ben, including the fact that no one seems to have fantasized much about a foursome, except maybe one dude who said he might do it if the other dude's girlfriend was a lot hotter than his."

"Double gah! And seriously, Derrick, it will be awesome if you can put Ben in the picture. I appreciate you having my back on this and, well, everything else."

"What are running buddies for?"

. . . . .

Dear Ben,

Since Tamiko is overwhelmed by a dozen things I volunteered to help answer your question by conducting a quick and dirty survey of upper division male attitudes to participating in group sex. But, before I report my results, let me guess that, based on how thorough you always are, you've already done your own online research and have probably also talked to contacts at USC and UCLA. In short, you already know that three-ways—or at least fantasies about them are part of the college scene. Since I've rarely known you to ask a frivolous question, I've been trying to work out why you wanted Tamiko to spend time looking into this. My conclusion is that you're engaged in a method-acting ploy designed to have Tamiko convince herself (honestly believe) that Jennifer's assertive sexual banter with her mom in 2+2 is based on fact, not just something a precocious kid would say to send up her mom. Anyway, I dutifully surveyed ten guys including me (doubtless an unrepresentative group since I polled guys I know). Eight were either very, or somewhat, interested in a three-way with two women, but just three had participated. Foursomes were not top, or even bottom, of mind for anyone.

Talk soon—Derrick

. . . . .

Because Tamiko has been hanging with Missy, V, and their roommates for the last month, she already knows all but two of the nine girls gathered at their Jenkins suite. With her usual take-charge approach Missy thanks everyone for coming and, without mentioning *2+2*, explains what Tamiko needs to know for her research project. Tamiko then hands out a brief questionnaire about threesomes and foursomes emphasizing that the answers are entirely anonymous. "Anyone," she adds, "who still feels that the questions are too intrusive is free not to participate." Expecting questions, or perhaps objections, Tamiko is pleasantly surprised when everyone obligingly grabs a questionnaire and begins checking the boxes.

While Missy and V pass around hot tea in paper cups, Tamiko collates the results, not sure how to interrupt the almost giddy level of chatter that fills the room. With results now in hand, Tamiko glances at Missy who mimes tapping a spoon on her cup. Realizing that the sound of plastic on paper won't get anyone's attention, Tamiko instead claps her hands several times. When a semblance of order is restored she reports that when it comes to an FMF threesome, three respondents checked the very interested box, one the neutral box and five indicated they weren't interested. But, and here Tamiko pauses to double check her arithmetic, four report they have participated in at least one. When it comes to an MFM threesome, only one girl is very interested and another somewhat interested.

No one is tempted by the idea of a foursome.

Surprised that as compared to the guys, more of the girls report they have done a threesome, despite the fact that fewer admit to being interested, Tamiko is bursting with questions. But she bites her tongue when Missy says, "In the interest of time, how about I start a brief discussion by summarizing for Tamiko what I think about all this. Then, whoever wants to can chime in." Looking around the room to see she has general assent, Missy continues, "As I've already told Tamiko, last year this dude who majors in romance languages I was seeing made a big deal of wanting a three-way." Then, making air quotes, Missy deepens her voice as she says with a mock French accent, *"Mon cherie, tout ce que je veux pour mon anniversaire est* to fuck *toi et ton ami ensemble."*

Barely waiting for the laughter to subside, Missy continues, "In case anyone is curious, I eventually agreed, but as was typical with this dude, he blew his big chance by drinking so much his pecker forgot how to peck. Despite being a little curious about being naked in bed with another woman, I'm glad it didn't happen, mostly because he's a blabbermouth. It's like, in theory, why would I care if he told half the soccer team he'd tag-teamed me and my friend, but in the real world of this tiny place, well, you already know what I'm going to say about the double standard."

"Oh my god, being hostage to the male view is so annoying," V interrupts. "I mean, lots of guys think it's cool to brag they've slept with twice the number of women they really have, while we're under pressure to say the opposite."

"What do you mean?" Tamiko asks, genuinely confused.

"What do you say if a dude asks you how many other dudes you've been with?"

"It's never happened," Tamiko replies, "but, I guess if I liked the guy well enough to answer, I'd tell the truth and say two, although maybe I'd be a a little embarrassed by my inexperience."

"What if it was a dozen, or maybe a few more?" a small blond girl named Julie asks. "Maybe, like some of us, you'd cut it in half."

"Are you also saying that social pressure could be a reason to say no to a threesome you might otherwise think could be fun?" Tamiko asks.

"No doubt, but sometimes also a reason to say yes," Amber, the only Black girl present remarks. "If your boyfriend hounds you often enough you're going to be tempted to give in, or at least I did, if for no other reason than to shut him up. I mean, you're screwing exactly the same dude, right, so it's hardly a big deal for another woman to be there unless you see her as a long-term threat. And, like Missy, I was curious about touching a female body without going down the whole lesbian road." Then, glancing around the room, she quickly adds, "Not that that's a bad thing, of course."

"I think there's a lot in that," a robust, olive-skinned girl named Althea interjects. "I mean, straight dudes seem to be born afraid of other dudes' bodies, but many women, even unambiguous heterosexual types, aren't that uptight about being naked with other women."

"All this is fascinating," Tamiko says, "but on the basis of an admittedly tiny parallel survey of a group of junior and senior dudes, a smaller percentage of them have actually participated in a threesome."

"You're still missing the point," Missy says impatiently. "Of course it's no surprise more of us have participated, because it's guys who aggressively and repeatedly demand three-ways, and if their girlfriend won't go along, threaten to find joy elsewhere. I'm not saying women aren't sexually curious, but if men weren't driving the bus, I doubt we'd be having this discussion."

"Interesting," interrupts Chloe, the tall, red-haired girl in the corner who Tamiko knows is the star of the volleyball team. "But I'm a pre-med major so I look at this from a science-based point of view, which tells us that the one essential job of all species—including ours—is to reproduce. To this end, the data I've seen suggests that men are only slightly more promiscuous than women, but that our promiscuity takes a very different form."

"Is this going to be a long lecture?" a chubby brunette named Tandy asks, glancing at her watch. "It's like, I'm not interested in sitting with a bunch of hens clucking about sex on a Friday evening when I…"

"It's going to be the most interesting thing you've heard this evening if you give me half a chance," Chloe interrupts in a voice that makes clear she's going to have her say.

"Maybe you can jump to the last paragraph," Tandy replies, "since I have a paper to slam through, before meeting my boyfriend later for what I'm very sure is going to be a night of just him and me."

"If a Type-A male asks for a twosome, threesome, foursome, or whatever-some, lots of females, even pretty traditional ones, will be tempted to say yes because deep down their genes are crying, *fertilize me!*" Chloe continues, unperturbed. "But, when an unattractive guy makes the same offer, most women will mostly say no, because their bodies are messaging them not to waste an egg on a toad. Males on the other hand, with their unlimited sperm, are genetically programmed to spread it far and wide, which means they care a lot less about the perceived attractiveness of any particular female. If you doubt any of this I can point you to a number of gene-based studies that conclude that substantially half of the males who have ever lived have fathered all of the children."

"And all this connects to Tamiko's question exactly how?" Missy asks.

"Were you not paying attention?" Chloe responds acerbically. "Even allowing for historical periods where dominant men could and did, exert physical control over whole harems of women, it's obvious that if they get half a chance women will do what it takes to mate with supermen. And, to bring all this back to Tamiko's questionnaire, it's also obvious that a woman is likely to say yes or no to a threesome depending on her subconscious assessment of the quality of the sperm of the guy doing the asking. So, it follows that if her hot boyfriend is begging for the threesome she may agree, and even help him set it up, if she concludes that this will help her keep access to his sperm long-term. When it comes to an MFM threesome, the same reasoning about the relative attraction of the males involved applies, but as was mentioned earlier, the woman would have to overcome far stronger cultural and perhaps religious norms telling her to say no."

"Actually, Chloe, although I'm sure you're on to something, at least for me, other issues are also at play," Lynn, a slim Asian girl with a pretty face and hair long enough to sit on, says. "I mean, as a few of you know, I didn't get over my Christian, virgin-until-married programming, until last spring, so I have limited experience. Still, I'd be interested in an MFM threesome if I thought that maybe, just maybe, putting the two guys together might result in at least one of them lasting long enough for me to join the fun."

As the burst of laughter finally subsides, V says, "The truth is that if Jed Streeter and Matt Ridge propositioned me, I could probably overcome any scruples."

"Not if I get there first," Julie, the small blonde interrupts, with a grin.

Stung by the realization that Missy has apparently broken her promise and gossiped about the 2+2 stars, Tamiko bites off her indignant reply when she belatedly remembers she never told Missy who's in the film. When it comes to creating a multi-mate fantasy, Ben Fine, Tamiko realizes, has his finger firmly on the libido of the Young American Female.

As everyone now begins to gather their things, Tamiko says, "Wait a second. What about foursomes? How come no one is even a little interested?"

"College boys never push for foursomes," Chloe responds. "I could maybe explain why, from a biological point of view, but…"

"Isn't it obvious foursomes are designed by and for bored married couples with kids, houses and settled jobs?" Missy interrupts, determined to forestall another lecture. "Since, if one partner has an affair it can be an existential threat to the relationship, jointly opting for a consensual foursome is their safest way to walk on the wild side. But for single women in our age group, when a lover is past his pull date, we can simply toss him into the recycling bin and hopefully find someone else to go dancing with that Saturday night."

"Trading one doofus for another is no problem, but given the pool of available dudes around here, trading up is easier said than done," Amber adds, as everyone nods their heads.

. . . . .

Outside, a moment later, Tamiko pulls Chloe aside. "When you mentioned the study about half of the males fathering the world's children, was one of your points that before effective birth control and DNA tests, lots of women who got pregnant with an unattainable guy, pawned the child off on the first dude who would say yes?"

"Exactly! Which explains why so many people who use gene-based tools to research their family trees, find out the man they always believed was their grandpa no longer fits."

A few minutes later, back in her dorm room, Tamiko emails Ben Fine.

By now Derrick has filled you in on the results of his talk with his circle of friends about their attitude to having sex with more than one partner. The nine upperclass women in my similarly quick and dirty scan, are less interested in the prospect of taking part in a threesome (although several are), but a higher percentage have actually done it. I can share the numbers if you wish, but the point is that threesomes (or, at least, the idea of participating in one) are definitely in the conversation around here. So much so, that in the kitchen scene after Virginia insists that her daughter Jennifer is too young to understand why adults might want to have group sex, Jennifer could go all in by replying, "Just so you know, I've had an MFM mash-up." From there the conversation might go like this—

Virginia: "What? I don't know what you are…" Then, as it belatedly dawns on her what the initials stand for, Virginia almost shouts, "Rubbish, you're just making that up to annoy me. I don't believe for a hot minute that you've had sex with two guys."

Jennifer: "You have. And I'm betting it lasted a lot longer than a minute."

Virginia: "That's completely different."

Jennifer (over her shoulder as she slams out of the room): "Like mother, like daughter."

What do you think, is this too much? Or, can we use part of it to light a fire under the scene? How about I work on this with Jack and Naomi in the next few days to see what we can come up with?

. . . . .

On Friday morning Tamiko heads to UMass for her stats lecture. In the hall after class, she explains to Professor Gupta that she'll be in California for a job on the date of the final and asks if she can take it before she leaves, or in January. "Absolutely not," the little man insists, "the exam can't possibly be ready by December first. And there's no way you can take it later because," and here he puffs out his chest like a plump pigeon, "the integrity of the entire exam process would be compromised even by the possibility that you could obtain the questions from another student." Not dignifying this with a response, Tamiko turns and walks away as Professor Gupta tells her back that "none of this would have been a problem if you hadn't forced yourself into an inappropriate graduate level course in the first place." Starting to turn around to point out that she's gotten perfect scores on all five quizzes, Tamiko realizes that arguing with an idiot only makes you a bigger one, and so contents herself with banging out the door.

"Tamiko, come in," Dean Thomas says with evident pleasure as Tamiko pokes her head around the frame of the Associate Dean's door. "My daughter, Libby, was just talking about you at breakfast and begging me to ask for another pitching lesson. Of course I pointed out that it's forty-five degrees and raining today, but when a twelve-year-old is excited, fact-based reasoning is about as effective as telling the neighbor's dog not to poop on your lawn, which, as you may have guessed, was another of this morning's small dramas."

"Maybe we can use a corner of LeFrak Gym Sunday afternoon. I'll check to see if anything's scheduled later that day."

"That would be great, but Tamiko, you don't have to…"

"It's a pleasure, really. Lily's a sweetie and working with her reminds me of hanging with my dad when I was a kid. But also, the favor I'm here to ask of you is a lot bigger."

"I get paid to help you, so no need to trade. Tell me what's up, or maybe sideways, with you today?"

"I doubt you'll need three guesses about the sideways part."

"Professor Gupta over at UMass again?"

"Bingo. Because, as you know, I need to be in L.A. for the film in early December, I've followed your suggestion and talked to all my profs about taking my exams early, or late, or in the case of American History, doing a paper instead of an exam."

"Why am I guessing Professor Gupta is the only one who won't cooperate?"

"Obviously this seventeen-year-old know-it-all rubs him the wrong way," Tamiko answers with a smile. "I mean, if I have to I can fly back here to take the exam and then go right back to L.A., but…"

"There has to be a lower-carbon solution. And I do have an idea. A good friend from when we both taught at Wesleyan ten years ago is now in the Economics department at UCLA. Let me call Barbara to see if she'll proctor your exam so you can take it at exactly the same time as if you were back here. When is that exactly?"

"Ten a.m. on December sixteenth."

"Which is seven a.m. in L.A. so fingers crossed that Barbara is an early riser. Tamiko, have you begun to put your friends in the picture about your movie? I ask not only because I've never been able to resist a bad pun, but also because I wonder if there isn't a better way to get the word out than to have the campus gossip mill go into overdrive. After all, given *2+2*'s controversial content and big personalities, there is plenty to chatter about."

"Ben Fine asked me to stay mum until my contract was signed, but that's done now. So far, in addition to Clementine and Derrick Fine, only Missy Frank and my roommate know even the bare bones and they've been double-sworn to secrecy."

"A secret this juicy is like a Mexican jumping bean, it's not going to stay put for long. When I looked online last night I saw that several prominent Hollywood bloggers have very good guestimates about the plot of what they refer to as Ben Fine's swinger sex farce, including naming the four stars."

"They don't mention me, do they?" Tamiko asks anxiously, as she feels her body tense.

"No, but how long do you think that will last in a business where apparently everything is for sale? So how about you contact Ben Fine to suggest that someone at his end come up with a short, bland statement about your modest participation in *2+2*? In the meantime, I'll schedule a press briefing for Wednesday. Reporters from the five colleges will probably show, plus maybe one or two from local papers."

"Okay, but is this going to turn into a media circus?"

Laughing, the thin, brown-skinned, fortyish dean replies, "Tamiko, for a girl as smart as you, I'm amazed you haven't already figured out that in this little academic pond, a first-year student appearing in a film with four of the earth's most famous people could be anything less."

. . . . .

With classes over for the week, Tamiko heads to the Frost Library early on Friday afternoon. As part of assigning her a paper in lieu of the final exam, Tamiko's American History prof has asked to approve a detailed outline. Fascinated by the sudden formation of literally hundreds of utopian organizations from the 1820s to the 1840s, Tamiko hopes to explore the social context that allowed them to flourish. Three hours later, as she struggles to wrap her head around enough of the zeitgeist of Jacksonian America to pull this off, she texts Missy and Derrick that she'll miss the usual Friday gathering so as to put in more hours. By 10:00 p.m., having finally accepted that she can't learn enough, fast enough, to pretend to explain why so many quixotic groups sprang into being in such a short time, Tamiko decides to instead focus on four of the larger communal organizations, New Harmony, Brook Farm, The Oneida Community and the Shakers, even though this last group was founded in the previous century.

Starting with a brief history of each, she proposes to analyze their most significant differences and commonalities. Hoping this will pass muster with Professor Tigner, she gathers up her belongings and heads to Appleton, where she flops on her bed and texts Ruth Marcus in Berkeley.

Yo Ruth, are you in the middle of din-din? Can we maybe chat when you're done?

Ruth promptly texts back.

Michael and the boys are off to a Warriors game, which means we can talk right now. It's just me and two bowls here at home—ramen and popcorn, if you're curious.

Wedging her pillow to form a passable backrest, Tamiko worms her long body up and against it as she taps Ruth's number.

"What a treat," Ruth says, by way of answer.

"Me too. Hey, how come your family left you home? I mean, Steph Curry may be setting a franchise record as we speak."

"I'm guessing that the fact I nodded off a couple of times at a playoff game last spring has something to do with it."

"Seriously, you fell asleep during the playoffs? That's so beyond feeble you deserve to be abandoned."

"Maybe I planned it that way so I wouldn't have to live through another year pretending to be a basketball fan. But, enough of that, tell me what's up with you?"

"I'm meeting Lee's Japanese girlfriend, Mayumi, in Boston tomorrow."

"Really? You're kidding, right?" Ruth blurts. Then, after a pause, she says more calmly, "I'm sure you have a good reason."

"It's like, Lec apparently told Mayumi about me from when they first got together, which, I gather, was about a month ago. Later, when she saw a picture of Lec and me at his apartment, Mayumi wriggled out the rest of our back story. She then asked Lec if he would check to see if it would be okay for her to message me to propose that the two of us attempt to be friends."

"Hmph, that's weird," Ruth says, surprised.

"Exactly, which is why I told Lec no, but did admit that I was curious about what Mayumi looked like. I mean Ruth, I know this probably sounds feeble but since I knew I'd stay awake imagining Lec screwing his new lover, I thought I might as well know what she looks like. I was imagining someone like Teri, his old Korean girlfriend—you know, the gorgeous heart-faced one with a waist about the size of a softball. Instead, Mayumi's attractive enough, but certainly nothing out of the ordinary. I mean, she's probably way smart and charismatic and maybe Lec picked a less flattering pic so as to not make me feel threatened, but…"

"Whoa Nelly, slow down, as my grandfather liked to say. How does any of this connect to your agreeing to meet up with this Mayumi tomorrow? Did I miss something? Or didn't you just tell me you said no?" Ruth asks in a voice she's used a thousand times in an effort to focus rambling clients.

"On Monday Lec emailed again to say Mayumi would be in Boston this week. Apparently, her mother, who's an international art dealer based in Tokyo, is sending Mayumi to cover for her at some kind of fraught business meeting."

"Got it, so let me guess, this call is about your change of mind, and, more importantly, how you feel about it now. Oops! I apologize, that sounded more like a therapist than a friend, didn't it?"

"No worries, and for sure I called because I'm in a muddle. It's like I was about to say no to Mayumi for a second time when it dawned on me that I'm helping write a film script about unconventional relationships. True, the main plot is about two couples swinging, but the idea of threesomes is definitely part of the mix at least as far as, Jennifer, my character is concerned."

"Really?" Ruth inquires, letting the word hang there. "You're telling me you agreed to meet Alec's other lover, who you just said keeps you awake at night, as part of a research project?" Ruth asks, incredulously.

"I mean, Ruth, wouldn't I be a hypocrite to appear in a film about unorthodox relationships at the same time that I reject even the possibility of forming a non-sexual friendship with Lec's other lover?"

"Before you try to tell me more about that, let me point out that you're taking on a huge unnecessary load, especially since…"

"I'm barely seventeen, I know, I know," Tamiko interrupts, annoyed that Ruth is stooping to play the age card.

"Those are your words not mine," Ruth interrupts right back. "If you'll give me a chance, my point is that, were I in your shoes, I'd find it flat out impossible to hang out with my big love's other girlfriend."

"In three weeks Mayumi's going off to travel around Europe with a girlfriend for eight months ending in London, where she'll start grad school for two years."

"Give me a second to try to process why that's important to you. Are you thinking that because Mayumi will be far away she'll be less of a threat to your relationship with Lec? And maybe also that you'll score points with both of them by being open-minded?"

"Honestly Ruth, I don't know. I guess I'm mostly hoping that Mayumi is a good person who genuinely identifies with me as being the one who is currently left out, and wants me know she's not trying to replace me long term."

"Hmm, maybe we're both saying pretty much the same thing," Ruth replies, thoughtfully.

"I lost you."

"If Mayumi makes it clear that she's not trying to replace you now, the quid pro quo could be that you'll be supportive of her staying in Lec's life later, assuming of course, you and Lec get back together. But listen dear, all of this is so wildly speculative I doubt I'm being of much help, especially since my experience tells me that the concept of sharing lovers is too utopian to fly."

"Funny you came up with the 'U' word since I'm in the middle of writing a paper about nineteenth-century utopian communities, at least one of which, the Oneida Community, was based on plural marriage, and lasted for generations. But, Ruth, thanks for listening. And, despite your doubts, do you have any practical advice for when I meet Mayumi tomorrow? For starters we plan to take a duck boat tour of Boston Harbor."

"Hmm, let me think. How about you propose that the two of you enjoy the afternoon, while staying off the subject of Lec, at least for a while. Hopefully, if you connect about mundane things, folding him into your conversation later will be less strained. And, if for any reason, you don't enjoy Mayumi's company, you can plead the need to study and hop back on the bus to Amherst, without ever dealing with relationship issues."

"Sounds sensible. Thanks. But hey, what about you? Remember, since I'm now your friend slash honorary daughter, and no longer your client, patient or whatever, it's your turn to share."

"Remember last month when I told you I was worried about Michael's starting to take me for granted, and that he might even, well..."

"Go astray was the picturesque way you put it," Tamiko says with a chuckle. "I also recall that you were open to my idea of putting more effort into your physical presentation. But hey, didn't you text me a pic of you working out on a big shiny exercise machine under the caption 'Going steady'?"

"Yup, if you can believe it, I'm at the gym four days a week and even enjoying it. And, like your mom a couple of years ago, I got a trendy haircut, some new tops with almost racy necklines and, dare I admit it, shiny black Prada boots."

"Sweet. So, how's progress on the home front?"

"Michael thought I was having an affair!"

"Seriously?" Tamiko asks, failing to suppress a burst of laughter.

"Hilarious, right? But the best part is that it kicked our physical relationship up a gear."

"Dare I ask if he was cheating on you?"

"No, he was simply in danger of forgetting how much fun sex can be."

"I'm delighted you two have got your joie de vivre back. But, if you have another moment, I also want to ask if you have any insights about swinging—you know, sex between two couples? And just in case you're worried, this is about my working on the *2+2* script, not me personally. I mean, you counsel loads of people so maybe…"

"Apparently I see a pretty staid group with one exception."

"Can you leave out the names and tell me the gist?"

"A woman client, let's call her Zoe, in her mid-thirties who graduated from a top drawer college and grad school, and then quit a prestigious consulting job to marry and have two kids, came to see me. In a nutshell, Zoe was experiencing fairly severe identity issues accompanied by anxiety, depression, and loss of self esteem. Here in Berkeley this is a fairly common presentation for successful, ambitious women who step off the fast track to become full-time moms and, unfortunately, one that typically takes time to resolve. So, I was surprised when after a few months of halting progress Zoe called to cancel her future appointments saying she suddenly felt much better and no longer needed therapy. Indeed, her turnaround was so abrupt, I asked if we could do an exit session at no charge."

"And?"

"Predictably, a big part of her lift in mood could be traced to her decision to go back to work part time, something we'd talked about for several months. But, in addition, Zoe reported that after almost a year with little, if any, desire for sex, she was again interested, excited and active."

"Zoe was having an affair?"

"Nope! Partially out of desperation, I guess, she and her husband signed up with an online dating site that caters to couples. Somehow their several swapping experiences with other couples bumped her libido from park back into what she delighted in calling, 'high happiness gear.' And once Zoe got her groove back she and her husband no longer needed others to enjoy life, although I gather they plan to occasionally include them so as to, and I quote, 'get down, dirty and just a little bit jealous.'"

"So what happened next?"

"We haven't spoken, so I have no idea."

. . . . .

Saturday morning Tamiko climbs on a green Peter Pan bus at Amherst Center hugging two books on America's nineteenth-century utopian movements, plus a history of Jacksonian America. She begins with *Without Sin: The Life and Death of the Oneida Community* by Spencer Klaw, which tracks a thirty-five-year experiment in group marriage. Under the guidance of its founder, John Humphrey Noyes and a coterie of mostly older woman overseers, at any given time hundreds of people who lived communally at Oneida, New York, shared sexual partners. Twenty minutes east of Worcester Tamiko moves on to *The Shaker Experience* in America, a story of another long-lasting religious sect, where no one had sex at all. With fifteen minutes left of her three-and-a-half-hour journey, Tamiko closes her books to stare out at the gray, chilly day. Why, she wonders for at least the dozenth time, has she agreed to spend half her Saturday on a bus to meet her rival for Lec's affections? Then, pulling a banana and cranberry muffin from her black book bag, she takes a bite of each as she tells herself—well, at the very least, I've always wanted to ride a duck boat.

. . . . .

Despite frequently reminding herself how much she hates being early, Mayumi Yamada, bundled in a navy blue peacoat, stands at the windy corner of Huntington Avenue and Ring Street almost fifteen minutes before her scheduled meet-up with Tamiko Gashkin. Suddenly worried that her version of a nautical outfit will seem over the top to Tamiko, Mayumi pulls her white cap over her ears as she looks in vain for a less conspicuous place to perch. When, before long, a tall woman dressed all in black strides toward her on Ring Street, Mayumi looks for a flyaway mane of light hair.

Seeing none, and also concluding that this woman is far too effortlessly confident to be seventeen, she looks away. Then, thinking again, Mayumi looks back to Ring Street to see that the woman, who is now just twenty feet away, has pulled back her long hair, so the bulk of it disappears down her back.

"Tamiko, could it possibly be you?"

"*C'est moi*," Tamiko replies, as she removes her right hand from her pocket so tentatively Mayumi realizes Tamiko is unsure whether to extend it. Stepping forward, Mayumi spreads her arms and says brightly, "Opposites attract, right?"

. . . . .

When Tamiko spots a small Asian girl all but swallowed up by a double-breasted navy blue coat standing on the corner fifty feet from a line of goofy-looking amphibious vehicles, she immediately knows two things: this must be Mayumi, and if anything, the photo Lec sent made this girl look more attractive than she really is. Adjusting her angle of approach, Tamiko wonders how to greet her, when the young woman looks away, apparently uninterested. Again, slammed by the feeling she should never have agreed to this meet-up, Tamiko glances around to see if, perhaps, a prettier young Asian could also be waiting. Spotting no one else, and somehow reassured by the young woman's perky white hat, Tamiko continues forward, her boots beating a tattoo on the pavement. Then, as the small Japanese woman looks back at her and smiles, Tamiko thinks, oh my god, Mayumi's one of those people like Mom, who transform from ordinary to beautiful with a grin.

"I have the tickets, but I wonder if you're hungry," Mayumi says as both girls step quickly back from their awkward mini-embrace. Then, as she nods in the direction of a Starbucks, Mayumi adds, "We have fifteen minutes and although the last thing I need is more sugar, it's a special day so maybe a muffin might be allowed."

"Hungry may as well be my middle name, and it's definitely my treat since you got the tickets," Tamiko replies. Then, with a wide grin she adds, "and you'll need plenty of energy since in that outfit they'll expect you to drive the boat."

A few minutes later, scenes in hand, the two mismatched young women line up beside a World War II-type wheeled landing craft, its wide, square prow looking just enough like a duck's bill to justify its name. "So Tamiko, tell me about your movie?" Mayumi asks. "Charlie reports that it's basically Jed Streeter, Matt Ridge, Aphrodite Gomez, Mary Ann McCabe, and you."

"Gah! Isn't it funny how things can get exaggerated with a few repetitions? While it's true that the movie is all about those four, it's also true I'm pretty much a walk-on."

"How many lines do you have?" Mayumi asks, dabbing her lips with a napkin.

"Maybe eleven when I first saw the script, but the director, Ben Fine, encouraged me to dabble in the editing process so I guess it's double that now, or maybe a few more."

"For pretty much a walk-on, it sounds like you're going to talk-on quite a bit," Mayumi says as she tries not to grin at her own labored joke.

"Ha! One thing is sure, I now have enough lines that I'm seriously intimidated by the acting part. Also, I have to take early exams and finish a couple of papers before I go to L.A. None of it's that hard, but suddenly I have to climb a mountain of stuff in a short time," Tamiko says, as the girls follow twenty others onto the bright red, wheeled contraption, whose name *Tub of the Hub* so accurately sums up its look and feel.

"I get it. Last January when I tagged along with my boyfriend Josh to Iowa only to retreat back to Japan a few months later in the middle of the semester, I literally had to cram ten hours a day to catch up and graduate with my classmates."

"But you did, right?" Tamiko asks, as she forgets about looking into the middle distance and turns to face Mayumi.

"They kindly gave me my diploma with everyone else, even though I didn't finish my senior project until halfway through August."

Sitting near the back of the duck boat's long, low cabin, the girls try to continue their carefully polite conversation as they roll past many of Boston's historic sites. But long before the awkward vehicle finally coasts down a ramp to float around Boston Harbor, they quit trying to shout over the young wannabe comedian whose bad jokes relentlessly boom over the P.A. system, and sit back to enjoy the eighty-minute ride.

When their feet are finally back on the Boston pavement, Tamiko remarks, "You and my mom have similar haircuts. I don't mean this to be weird, but you two even look a little like each other. Probably Lec told you that ethnically, Mom's half Japanese."

"I hope you like your mom," Mayumi replies with a grin as she turns to face Tamiko.

"Definitely! But, although you two aren't twins, or anything, it does seem kinda strange that you look more like my mother than I do. Part of it is that you both look serious most of the time, but can turn beautiful on demand. I mean, I've watched Mom play wallflower in the corner of a party and then chuckle at something and in an instant attract half the men in the room."

"What about the other half?"

"You mean the ones with bad taste," Tamiko teasingly replies.

"Your mom, she's still pretty young, right?"

"Thirty-six, and although, maybe, a daughter shouldn't notice, kinda hot."

"Well, one thing is for sure, you'll never be mistaken for my mom's daughter," Mayumi replies. "Not even in her wildest fantasy could she produce a six-foot movie star with blue eyes and Lauren Bacall hair. Oops! In case you don't watch old movies, she was in…"

"*The Big Sleep, Key Largo* and a bunch more, mostly with her husband Humphrey Bogart. Like you, I'm guessing, I've seen all the Bogey-Bacall movies. And just for the record, I'm five-foot-ten, the boots add a little."

"I love those harness boots," Mayumi says, seriously.

"We can hit a Frye store and pick you up some," Tamiko says, thinking this might be a fun diversion for both of them.

"I only wish, but when you're short like me, you need to avoid boots that chop up your vertical line," Mayumi replies, seriously.

"So, how about we walk around a little and maybe get some coffee or soup or something?" Tamiko asks. "I have an hour and a half before I have to grab the bus back to Amherst."

"I'm flying out in the morning, but I have an upscale hotel room for tonight that my mom's paying for, so you're welcome to sleep over."

"Another time for sure, but like I said, I'm slammed with school stuff, plus a pitching lesson I'm giving a twelve-year-old buddy early tomorrow."

"Makes sense, but Tamiko, can I ask you a favor?"

Surprised by this question, Tamiko nods noncommittally, not ready to agree to anything so open-ended.

"Can you slow down a little?"

Feeling a jolt of relief, Tamiko immediately cuts her stride in half, as she replies, "My roommate, who's about your height, asks me the same thing on a daily basis. It's just that when I'm energized, or anxious, or both, I sort of bolt."

Turning in unison onto Boylston Street toward Boston Common as if they have planned their route, Mayumi asks, "On that note, do we want to talk about the elephant in the room, or I guess I maybe should say, the city?"

"Not really, or at least not yet, if that's okay. I'd rather hear about your life, your upcoming trip, your plans to study in London, or whatever."

"Just you and me hanging out?" Mayumi asks.

"I hope so. But I guess I should say that I've been coming around to your way of thinking about the elephant. It really will be chill if we can have each other's backs. I mean, I'm actually not sure what that even means except that…"

"We do our best to watch out for each other, not just ourselves," Mayumi interrupts. "Maybe it will prove too difficult, but I'm here because I'd like to try."

"Me too. I mean, Mayumi, I never expected to say this, but assuming the elephant and I ever get our trunks back together, I'll do my best."

. . . . .

Ninety minutes later, as she walks back to the downtown Hilton from Copely Square where she's seen Tamiko onto her bus, Mayumi realizes jet lag has caught up with her. Yet, in addition to enveloping exhaustion, she feels a glow of accomplishment.

Yesterday, she'd successfully smoothed out her mother's business problem by explaining that the warehouse employee who perpetrated the fraud is long gone, controls were put in place to ensure that nothing similar can occur and the client's account balance has been appropriately adjusted. And this afternoon, she's not only met Tamiko, but enjoyed their time together.

After a near-scalding bath, Mayumi is warm and cozy under a puffy white duvet, as she drifts into a shallow doze. But in the dream that ensues, her feeling of well-being disappears as she finds her small body is, literally, scrunched to the edge of a giant bed by Tamiko's and Alec's much longer ones now entwined in the middle. Straining for an escape from what increasingly feels like a nightmare, Mayumi is surprised to realize that the others, who have somehow turned to face her, are reaching out. Cocooned now, by her friends' reassuring warmth, she experiences a sense of profound relief as she falls into a deep sleep.

. . . . .

On the 4:15 bus back to Amherst, Tamiko opens Harry Watson's *Liberty and Power: The Politics of Jacksonian America*. But, realizing her mind is too jumpy to concentrate, she closes both the book and her eyes. What to make of her afternoon with Mayumi?

And, more pressing, how to answer Lec, whose last email stated his hope that they get together soon? As a cascade of words flows through her careening thoughts, Tamiko realizes she won't sleep until she puts them on paper even though doing this now will mean copying them into an email when she reconnects with her laptop. Pulling a lined notebook from her pack, she begins:

Lec:

I hope you'll be glad to know Mayumi and I spent a fun afternoon riding the fire engine red Tub of the Hub past the sights of historical Boston and eventually puttering around its harbor (Mayumi has pics). Of course, I immediately liked Mayumi and can easily see why you do. It seems best to keep the details of our conversation private, but I can tell you that, assuming you and I can sync up our futures, I see no reason to ask you to give up your close friendship with Mayumi (especially if she's living on the next continent). And I think you'll find that she'll be equally supportive of me.

In your email you raised interesting questions and ideas about our future. As I ride the bus back to Amherst badly needing a nap, I'll focus on the most important one. Yes, Lec Burns, your soul is still imprinted on my soul and I very much want you to continue in my life long-term. But, sorry, more than that I can't deal with just now. As I think I told you, I compensated for being lonely and miserable back in September by signing up for nearly double the normal amount of coursework (papers and exams loom). Then, out of the blue, came the film, whose script I'm still daily kibitzing (Ben Fine is both a collaborator and a perfectionist, meaning no hyphen is too tiny to escape his full-court press). Then, on December 1, I'm off to L.A. to enter an intimidating new world I obviously know less than nada about. Yes, I'm excited. But I'm also realistic about the steep learning curve I'll have to immediately climb.

So, as much as I'd like to make a plan to see you soon (were that even possible on your end), I first need to deal with all this on my own.

Love always (I hope), T

P.S. Thanks for saying you regret not taking seriously my proposal to come to Japan with you. For sure, it is nice to no longer feel altogether dismissed. But, on balance, I think of the two of us, I was the more unreasonable, and your calling me out on it was mostly legit. Going to college did make sense and still does. But one thing is sure, dating other people while holding tight to the one you love is easier imagined than done.

MID-NOVEMBER

"SWEETIE, I FINALLY CAUGHT YOU. I planned to strap on wings and fly back there if I got your 'leave a message' thingy one more time."

"C'mon Mom, look who's talking? I've returned plenty of your calls, but you never pick up. So anyway, what's up?"

"Not a lot, except me worrying about my only blue-eyed daughter."

"No need. It's true that trying to get the rest of the term's work done in the next two weeks is a tall ladder to climb, but honestly Mom, I'm more than halfway up, so…"

"You're never stumped by anything academic. I'm more concerned about the prospect of my undoubtedly mature, but nevertheless seventeen-year-old daughter, performing in a film about spouse-swapping with four half-naked A-list movie stars…"

"It's only for December. And with Mary McCarthy acting as mother hen, I'm sure you know my clothes are staying in place. Hopefully by January I'll be home for the rest of Amherst's winter break, which, remember, lasts until the third week in January."

"But what about your social life there? When Ed and I were back two weeks ago we weren't sure if you and Derrick were, um, well…"

"Together?"

"Yes. I hate to be nosey, but we used to talk about important relationship things like…"

"Yo! Mom! To be clear, when you say 'we,' you actually mean I used to talk to you. You've never shared three words about your intimate life. And when it comes to your hating being a nosey parent, I call bull excrement. But anyway, as I'm pretty sure you guessed, when it comes to Derrick, there's nothing to talk about since the romance part of our relationship was over almost before it started. And, Mom, that's nothing to worry about, since our step back was mutual and I know we'll be tight buds forever. So much so, that here on campus, we still pretend we're a couple, which is a definite plus for me."

"I don't quite understand why you would pretend unless your plan is to fend off others."

"That's a part of it, but we also like hanging out. In addition, being with Derrick has helped me to break out of Amherst's first-year bubble. Mom, maybe it's outside your experience, but although I badly needed a lover this fall, I'm not all that disappointed that Derrick and I turned out to be no big deal. It's like, I'm not even sure I'm making sense to myself, but trust me, things really are fine here. True…"

"Dare I suggest that your failure to fully bond with Derrick might have more than a little to do with your ongoing feelings for Lec," Amy interrupts. "I mean, it still seems awkward and unresolved the way things ended with you two last August."

"I hope 'paused' turns out to be the operative word. But, Mom, on the breaking news front, I just met up with Lec's friend Mayumi in Boston."

"Really! Did I hear that right? You actually got together with Lec's Japanese girlfriend? I mean, right here in the U.S.?"

"Well, I haven't been to Tokyo, have I? Remember, I told you last time we talked, that I said 'no way' when Mayumi first proposed contacting me. But then, well, it suddenly turned out she was going to be in Boston for her mom's business, and as you know, my film is all about shared relationships so when she asked again I didn't want to chicken out."

"Good grief, Tami, this gets more and more bizarre. I mean, you really are barely seventeen."

"Mom, even though I love your shoutout to Charlie Brown, I can't believe you've regressed to birthday-mongering and name-infantilizing in the same sentence."

"Fine, TA-MI-KO," Amy responds, enunciating every syllable of her daughter's name. "As a very competent young woman I only worry that you are trying to deal with a huge mountain of stuff that would be tough to cope with at any age."

"Will it help if I agree you aren't all wrong, which is why I just told Lec I can't deal with future plans or commitments until I put *2+2* behind me."

"But you haven't given up on him?"

"I'm not sure that's the right question since it implies that I'm in control of my feelings instead of it being the other way around. As I think you know, with Lec, it's always been more like gravity squared—his pull on me is inescapable, no matter what I logically think."

"Ed says you two are trying to live your lives out of order—you should have met when you were both ten years older, when staying together would have made sense."

"Ha! Tell Ed he's right, as usual, but also that I haven't given up on the possibility that with enough stubbornness, timing isn't everything."

"Do you want to tell me about this Mayumi? It's okay to say no if this isn't a good time."

"Mom, here's a funny thing. Mayumi looks and even acts a little like you—five-two, self-contained and serious, but goes all gorgeous when she smiles. I mean, her hair is even cut in an A-line bob if you can believe it. If she was your kid, everyone would say, 'It's amazing how the apple doesn't fall far from the tree.'"

"That must be a little weird. But, again, why did you really agree to meet up with her? Sorry, but your involvement with a film about forty-year-old swingers doesn't convince me."

"Mom, chill. We only spent a few hours together. And instead of talking about heavy stuff, we took a duck boat ride in the Boston Harbor, laughed about both of us loving coffee mixed with chocolate and just kinda got down. I guess I wanted to know if Lec cared for a good person. But really, Mom, for the next few years at least, with Mayumi traveling and studying in Europe we'll be thousands of miles apart so the idea of sharing Lec a little—assuming he's even good with that—doesn't seem nuts. But whatever happens, one thing is now clear, Mayumi's cool and I think you'll like her if you ever meet. And, c'mon, are you really so freaked at the idea of a threesome?"

After waiting a few seconds during which Amy doesn't reply, Tamiko wonders if the call has dropped. "Mom, are you still there? I think maybe…"

"No, I'm here, I was just taking a second to…"

"Oh my god, Mom, it's like you've done a threesome, or whatever-some, haven't you?"

"Tamiko, I'm absolutely not getting into any of that, especially not on the phone, so I'm pleading my Fifth Amendment right to be quiet."

"As I'm sure you know, the Fifth Amendment has nothing to do with silence and everything to do with a person's right not to incriminate themselves, which, as far as I'm concerned, you've just done. Unless, of course, you think that having sex with more than one person can be okay, which would get you off the incrimination hook."

"Sweetie, in exchange for my not trying to edit those barely coherent sentences, how about you give me time to think about what I want to say about my intimate life."

"No problem, as long as you remember you're only nineteen years older than I am. I mean, isn't it going to be weird if when you're sixty and I'm forty-one we're still having the same one-sided conversations about our personal issues?"

"Even if you're right, we have a lot of years to make the transition. For now, I'd like to hold onto being your mom. And for the record, I can't imagine asking my mother anything about her sex life. But, enough, when do you fly to L.A.?"

"December first, like I just told you. And I've already had three messages from Mary about what to stock in the cottage fridge, so I really am in good hands. But hey, I have an idea—why don't you call Mary? That way you two can worry about me together and I can get back to studying."

"Good thought," Amy replies with a laugh. "She may not know you love old-fashioned chocolate donut holes."

"Also, please clue her in that I hate coconut, and liver and am the only person from Berkeley who gags on goat cheese."

"Got it, and since Ed and I will be down for a publishing conference on December tenth and eleventh you'll also be in for some quality Mom hugs."

"Sweet! And that should give you plenty of time to think about our adult conversation."

. . . . .

Mayumi slips out of bed with the first spark of dawn. Cocooned in a long gray coat she picks her way down the bumpy dirt path to the beach where she traces the tide line north. It's the first morning of her three-day holiday with Alec on the Izu Peninsula and she doesn't want to miss a minute. With Alec still curled under his quilt, she also craves private time to sort out her feelings. Just a week ago she'd been in Boston hanging out with Tamiko Gashkin in an effort to establish some sort of…what is the right word?

Friendship? Alliance? Accommodation? All three? Then, unexpectedly, she felt genuinely attracted to Tamiko. Not erotically, or at least not overtly, but still, there must have been a degree of physical appeal since she can't seem to get Tamiko's electric blue eyes or deep-throated laugh out of her head. Does Tamiko feel even a little of the same draw, and assuming she does, what will it mean going forward? More to the immediate point, why is she fretting about any of this now? Mayumi asks herself, as she hops over a weathered board with *Alabama* printed on it in faded green letters. After all, I'm here in Izu with Alec for a three day holiday, and especially given our first ecstatic night together, delighted to have him to myself. Or, might it also be okay, or possibly even more than okay, if Tamiko was here? I mean, how will I feel if I spin around right now and see both of them following me down the beach?

"Hey you in the mummy coat, are you running away from home?" Alec's shout shatters Mayumi's fantasy. Turning to see Alec, clad in sweatpants and a hoodie, jogging toward her, Mayumi isn't sure whether to be glad, or disappointed, that he's alone.

"You good?" Alec asks as he puffs up next to her.

Standing on tiptoe to kiss him, Mayumi says, "I couldn't sleep and you could and also, I guess I needed a moment."

"Ready to go back and cook breakfast with me and then maybe curl up…"

"Not quite."

"That's not much of an endorsement of early morning romance."

"Sorry Alec, I'm trying to sort out a bit of a muddle."

"Which is?"

"At the same time I've never been this happy in my whole life, I'm the one who's flying off in ten days for who knows how long. And, then there's Tamiko, who I'm determined to treat as a friend. In short, I've been trying to work out how to…"

"What happened to your proposal that we stay strictly in the present for the next couple of days, not spoil them by obsessing about the future?"

"How about this?" Mayumi replies, bending down to scratch the ears of the small black-and-white dog that has somehow joined them. "You go back and make me a huge American breakfast, and by the time it's on my plate I'll be there chanting *Be Here Now.*"

As Alec walks back to Mayumi's Uncle Tash's rustic cabin he feels unreasonably pleased. Here on the edge of the sea with this delightful young woman, he reflects that somehow Mayumi has managed to double down on her charm by joining him in thinking about Tamiko.

"This place was literally a falling-down fisherman's cottage built at the end of the nineteenth century when my uncle bought it twenty-five years ago," Mayumi chirps, as she comes through the door fifteen minutes later. "Uncle Tash added electricity, decent plumbing, and replaced a bunch of moldy timber, but otherwise let it be. We Japanese have a term, *wabi-sabi*, for things that are simple, rustic, austere and imperfect like this."

"It's a Buddhist concept originally, right?" Alec asks, as the sun touches the kitchen window and turns it gold.

"I guess, but it's become a sort of romantic icon of Japanese culture which lusts for the future at the same time it fetishizes the past. Talking about cultural history, didn't you tell me you'd brought along some of your favorite American poems?"

"*Leaves of Grass* by Walt Whitman, a small collection by Emily Dickinson and a few poems by Robert Frost and Wallace Stevens. Do you know any of them?"

"Not nearly as well as I will when you read them to me during breaks between entertaining me in as many other ways as you can devise."

"Methinks you're talking about games it takes two to play."

"Methinks I am."

"How about we eat piles of eggs, toast, and sausages followed by a couple of erotic Emily Dickinson poems, and an extended session under the quilt," Alec proposes.

"I like the sound of the word, 'extended.'"

. . . . .

Walking barefoot with Mayumi after lunch on the still-deserted beach beneath a jagged line of clouds marching obelisk-like toward the horizon, Alec resolves not to let the darkening day shroud his mood. Hearing a yip, he looks to see that Mayumi has pulled a bit of toast from her pocket and has tossed it to this morning's spotted dog, who now sports a jaunty red bandana. A moment later as the three detour around the tangle of driftwood blocking their path along the water's edge, Alec says, "I'm all about staying in the here and now as much as possible, but I do need to talk about a few big picture things. I mean, lots of stuff has been happening fast for both of us so…"

"No doubt. And since I'm hoping we're only taking a short break from poetry, petting, and passion, let's hear what you're concerned about."

"The truth is that my mind has been flapping around so fast I'm not sure of exactly what I want to say. So, if it's okay, let me start with a couple things I'm sure of. For one, the truth is that before you and I got together I'd pretty much decided that Japan and I were a bad fit. But now that I've begun to see it through your eyes, I'm getting a crush on this place."

"Does that mean you'll continue your language studies and join Burns-Short after grad school?"

"Certainly I'm a lot more open to it than I was six or eight weeks ago.

But, studying medical technology at MIT for a couple of years is sure to unlock a load of possibilities, so who knows how I'll see things when I graduate? In the meantime I'll keep studying Japanese so I don't lose all I've gained this fall. Yet, with you off to see the world, I'm beginning to think that after the New Year, I may head to New York and find a Japanese school there."

"Really? You plan to go back to the U.S.?"

"My fall courses wrap up the third week of December, at which point I'd planned to fold myself into my parents' Christmas plans. But, last Sunday Charlie announced he and Emiko will be over in late December for meetings he wants me to be part of. So I'll stay in Tokyo until January and then I'm not sure. It seems that although two women say they love me, neither actually wants to be with me."

"Whoa, dude! Who put you at the center of the universe?" Mayumi protests.

"Sorry, I guess I…" Alec mumbles, trailing off.

"Is that all you're going to say?"

"It is, at least until you level with me about what went on with you and Tamiko in Boston. Ever since you got back Tuesday you've ducked the subject."

"Alec, getting into a fight is the last thing I want, especially today, but as Tamiko has maybe already communicated, we agreed that what transpired between the two of us in Boston stays in Boston. And anyway…"

"I don't usually think of myself as being paranoid," Alec interrupts, "but when the two women I'm closest to buddy up and then go silent, maybe I can be forgiven for obsessing a little."

"Forgiven by who?" Mayumi asks. Then, as if poking fun at herself will take the edge off her accusation, she adds, "Or is it 'whom'? The intricacies of English personal pronouns often elude me. But, Alec, although it may come as a slap to your male ego, your name wasn't mentioned once during the several hours Tamiko and I spent together."

"C'mon, you have to be bullshitting me."

"Nope. When Tamiko and I met early on Saturday afternoon and took a duck boat tour, we agreed to limit our conversation to the two of us. Later we walked around a bit and grabbed a snack before I walked Tamiko back to where she caught her Amherst bus. When you think about it for a minute, I hope you'll see why this made sense. Obviously we wouldn't have been there if we didn't both deeply care for you, but since neither one of us wanted to even inadvertently upset the other, we agreed to stay on neutral ground."

"Do you like Tamiko?"

"Very much, which it may surprise you to know is a big relief."

"You wanted to think well of her?"

"More important, I wanted to think well of you, and I guess by extension, myself."

"I don't quite follow. Unless you mean you'd doubt my judgment if you thought Tamiko was, for lack of another word, lacking?"

"Close enough, but I thought a few minutes ago you said you wanted to talk about you, and your plans, not me, and mine."

"I wanted to talk about both, of course."

"Nothing's changed about my intentions for the next couple of years, or my affection for you. And, as I hope you don't need to be told, falling more and more in love with you only makes leaving tougher. And, as far as Tamiko goes, meeting her and liking her, has caused me to double down on my determination to treat her well."

"And on Tamiko's part?"

"She'll have to speak for herself, of course, but I'm pretty sure she enjoyed the time we spent together."

"Which leaves me exactly where?" Alec asks, more stridently than he intended.

"Being one of the luckiest guys on the planet if you're smart and secure enough to accept what's being offered," Mayumi replies. "Or, in case I'm not being clear, perhaps it will help if you think of it this way. Instead of your being like the proverbial donkey, unhappily positioned equidistant between two piles of equally yummy treats, the treats, in this case, Tamiko and me, are doing their best to relocate next to you."

"But can you two actually pull that off? I mean, normal human jealousy being what it is."

"If Tamiko and I were both living down the block from you, maybe not. But since for the next few years we'll mostly be on different continents, I don't see why the occasional exciting meet-up isn't possible. Assuming, of course, that Tamiko and I can stick with our intention to watch out for each other, and you can get back to being chill enough to keep your heart open to both of us. And, Alec, to be clear, I hope it will help both you and Tamiko, to know that given all the exciting new things on my agenda, I'll be okay being your number-two girlfriend."

"No need to put it that way," Alec says, reaching for Mayumi's hand.

"Alec, shut up and enjoy those gulls, or terns or whatever birds are diving over there. I'm absolutely, completely and unalterably done with talking about anything that isn't right in front of us."

. . . . .

After a supper consisting of a veggie stir-fry with rice cooked on the wood stove, and washed down by a number of thumb-sized cups of hot sake in the cozy, cedar-paneled kitchen, Mayumi asks Alec to find the Emily Dickinson poem she'd liked so much that morning. Reaching for the thin book, Alec moves closer to the light and reads:

Wild Nights—Wild Nights!
Were I with Thee
Wild Nights should be
Our Luxury!
Futile—the Winds—
To a Heart in Port —
Done with the Compass—
Done with the Chart!
Rowing in Eden—
Ah, the Sea!
Might I Moor—Tonight—
In Thee!

"I thought you'd never ask," Mayumi says, flashing her double-dimple grin. "But Captain, I have a request before you wiggle your long boat into my port."

"Your wish is my command, Oh, Harbor Mistress."

"I'll tell you as soon as we hop in and out of the bath."

"You first this time, so that I can add a bunch of cold water before I submerge. Something in Japanese DNA allows you to happily soak in water that boils us Scots."

"Probably because your stinky Braveheart ancestors didn't learn how to take a bath until two thousand years after we did," Mayumi says, sticking her tongue out. "But, okay, I'll go first and then you can dump in twenty liters of cold water, which, in case you're still stuck measuring in American, is something like five gallons. And Mr. Sweaty *Hakujin*, don't forget to scrub off in the shower before you go into the lovely clean tub."

"Even *hakujins* can eventually learn how obsessive the Japanese are about taking a bath before they take a bath. But isn't *gaijin* the correct word to describe me?"

"To oversimplify, *hakujin* means white person and *gaijin*, foreigner, but of course, with you, they overlap. Although most Japanese will publicly insist the two terms are descriptive, in truth, and depending on tone and context both are, at least mildly demeaning, which…"

"Got it," Alec interrupts with a chuckle. "Even this ignorant *hakujin* has worked out that since the Japanese quietly, but firmly, believe they're the world's superior people, it follows that even descriptive terms for foreigners are by definition at least mildly disparaging."

"You're so smart you could almost be Japanese."

· · · · ·

Fifteen minutes later Mayumi enters the bedroom wearing nothing but tatami sandals and a smile. Pausing to appreciate her rounded arms, legs, bum and breasts, Alec says, "Your body doesn't have a hard angle," as he gives silent thanks to the heavens for the gift of this moon-kissed woman.

"Good thing, Mr. Bony Elbows and Knees dude, or we wouldn't fit together so perfectly," Mayumi replies, handing Alec a bottle of warm massage lotion before stretching out on the huge red towel laid out to protect the blue-and-white shibori quilt.

"Are you warm enough?"

"I'm counting on you to make sure I am," Mayumi answers with a chuckle. "If a full body massage doesn't do it, there are other places to explore with your long fingers."

"That's your request? You want me to get you off with my hands?" Alec asks, no longer surprised at how up-front Mayumi can be about her desires.

"Who, if not you? And remember, since I had my first guy-induced orgasm just a month ago, I'm still interested in all the permutations. But I'm also hoping that just as I get ready to pop, you'll channel Emily Dickinson."

After a few minutes loosening Mayumi's shoulder, back and leg muscles with long, strong fingers, Alec says, "Time to roll over and spread your pretty thighs." Then, oiling the first two fingers of his right hand, he lightly places them on either side of Mayumi's pleasure button.

"Nice! But no need to be so delicate. Rub me at least twice as hard while you hold my eyes with yours," Mayumi murmurs. "Let's see if they tell you the exact moment when it's time for your long boat to enter my port." Even as he does as instructed, Alec expects this to take a few minutes. But, as Mayumi murmurs, "Harder, Alec, harder," her pupils begin to dilate. Waiting as they widen, and then widen again, he realizes that the time is now.

LATE NOVEMBER

THE EVENING BEFORE TAMIKO WILL FLY to L.A. to embark on what she hopes will be a very brief career as movie ingenue, she meets Derrick and Clementine for supper at Judie's on North Pleasant Street, Amherst's main drag. At a table under a painting of two presumably gay roosters silhouetted against a red heart bearing the motto, *Show the World the True You,* Tamiko pulls out a list of questions about the world she's about to enter. Before she can begin, Derrick holds up his jumbo-sized right hand and points at the three huge golden popovers the waitress is placing on the table. Realizing she needs to adjust her priorities, Tamiko breaks one in half and slathers it with three pats of butter before opening her mouth as widely as possible.

Barely ninety seconds later with all three plates empty, Derrick skims Tamiko's list and says, "Tamiko, I don't mean to make light of your worries but, when you strip away the hype, making a movie is a lot like making a shirt, or a car, or anything else. It's a predictable process consisting of a number of well-defined steps that produce a finished product, hopefully on time and within budget."

Not sure what to make of this, or even whether she's being teased, Tamiko says nothing.

"One of these routine steps," Derrick continues patiently, "is to plug in new talent. Or perhaps a better way to put it is that Ben, and all the key people involved in *2+2,* have tons of experience on how to get a newbie, in this case you, up to speed."

"And, best of all, you have Mary to hold your hand until we arrive on December nineteenth," Clementine adds cheerfully. "She'll not only be your guide, but also your best bud and substitute mom. Trust Mary and you'll be fine. After all, helping you deal with saying a few lines in a movie is nothing compared to coping with my bro and me after our parents died."

"Okay then, so what else did you want to ask us?" Derrick asks with a laugh.

"You two are so great. I mean, it's like, when I walked over here I was almost mad at you for getting me into this. Now, I'm back to being excited about the prospect of doing something beyond my comfort zone. But Derrick, one thing you said doesn't seem right," Tamiko adds, as she points to herself when the waitress reappears, this time holding a cheeseburger and fries.

"Which is?"

"If Ben really has film making so wired, how come we're still rewriting the script? Am I the only one who thinks it's weird that a seventeen-year-old with no drama experience is helping edit a big deal film that's about to start shooting?"

"Tamiko, you're approaching it backwards," Clementine says patiently. "It's precisely because Ben has every aspect of the shoot planned down to the color of Jed Streeter's socks, that he has the freedom to embrace last minute changes. Ben likes to quote the mid-twentieth-century director, Orson Welles, who apparently believed in what he called 'sacred accidents.' That is, unexpected, sometimes off-the-wall things that happen during the production of a film that, if recognized and included by the director, can take it in a new, and hopefully deeper direction. And, I'm pretty sure Ben believes that discovering a precocious college student at the last moment who can write clever dialogue is one of those accidents."

"Have you ever heard of a French director from way back in the thirties and forties named Jean Renoir?" Derrick asks, as if this is somehow to the point.

"Hmm. Was he maybe the son of Pierre-Auguste Renoir, the avant-garde, nineteenth-century impressionist?"

"Tamiko, you never cease to amaze—which is another way of saying yes," Derrick replies. "Anyway, Jean Renoir made a bunch of ingenious films including *La Grande Illusion* and *Rules of the Game,* which are still studied in film school, in part because he often allowed his actors to modify script language and sometimes even the plot arc as they went along. In this spirit, Ben will occasionally make changes—sometimes even big ones—in the middle of shooting. While he isn't into improv, Ben believes that one way to resist what he sees as the almost inevitable drift toward stilted dialogue and cliché plot solutions, is to embrace the real emotions that occasionally bubble up from members of the cast who, after all, are doing their best to inhabit the story.

"For one example, a couple of summers ago when I was watching the filming of *Alice in the Air*, Brad Prine simply couldn't wrap his tongue around an awkward line. After his fourth failure, Prine angrily muttered, 'This is such rot, Jesus crapped himself.' Overhearing this and realizing this was the most engaged Prine had been all morning, Ben included the Jesus line, which of course was seen by something like fifty million people and helped Prine score an Academy Award for Best Actor."

"Oh my god, I definitely remember that one," Tamiko says excitedly. "It was so dope that for the next month, half the people at Berkeley High repeated it whenever they didn't like a class, a school rule, or just something someone said. But how did Ben get it to fit? I mean the script must have called for Prine to say something different."

"Ben rewrote the scene to fit that line," Clementine says. "One of Ben's many theories is that when you get the emotion right, the words always work, but the reverse is also true."

. . . . .

On the night before she and Fujiko will leave on their big adventure, Alec and Mayumi nest in each other's arms by the door of her apartment. Having again pushed aside Alec's request to accompany her to the airport, Mayumi insists this is goodbye. Her small, soft body pressed fiercely against Alec's chest, she murmurs, "Just so you know, I tried to talk Fujiko into putting off our trip for ten days."

"Sooner or later, you'd be off, or if you weren't, I would," Alec replies resignedly. "It's a big world and as you've always said, we both have many places to fly before we settle onto our long-term perches."

"Just because that's a sappy metaphor doesn't make it less true. But, remember," Mayumi adds, as she pulls back to look into Alec's eyes, "no matter how high or wide we fly, I expect to nest with you again, Mr. Burns."

After reassuring Mayumi that he, too, believes this will happen, Alec seals his promise by adding, "I love you, Mayumi Yamada."

"That's the first time you've used the 'L word,'" Mayumi says quietly, her look of surprise quickly transforming into her trademark double-dimple grin.

"Want me to repeat it?"

"No need. I know how to exit on a high note. Now please get out of here so I can cry myself to sleep and hopefully wake up excited to explore Madrid."

EARLY DECEMBER

ON SATURDAY, DECEMBER 1ST, Tamiko sits by an American Airlines gate at Boston's Logan Airport for her 11:00 a.m. flight to L.A., inordinately pleased Mary McCarthy has booked her in business class. Determined to get her history paper outlined before crossing Kansas, Tamiko first glances at her email to see that the second message in her queue is from Mayumi.

hi again—we did have fun ducking it up didn't we? again, arigato gozaimashita *for coming all that way to meet me at your super busy time! in the days since we were together, here is a quick summary of what i've been thinking. first, when it comes to the elephant i promise to always think of u and not just me, me, me. second, i hope you'll find it in your heart to reciprocate. and third, and just as important, i dream, that in the process of sharing our pachyderm u and I will become amazing friends. When u r ready, please tell me what u think. and, of course, I'm looking forward to lots of details about your filmmaking adventure. love, m.*

ps: tomorrow i leave for europe with my friend fujiko. we start in spain, and a big part of the fun is not knowing where we'll go next. but i'll keep in touch and although u, alec and i may be on different continents, a rendezvous might just be possible before long. charlie has given both alec and me a pile of his surplus air miles and I'm sure he'll be pleased to include u. so, keep an open mind.

Not knowing how to process all this, Tamiko grabs a latte at Starbucks, more for something to do than because she needs more caffeine. In seat 2A a few minutes later, her long legs at luxurious extension, Tamiko tries to concentrate on her paper. But when her mind refuses to settle in the 1830s she opens her email and types:

Mayumi,

I'm literally on the plane flying to L.A. When I read your email half an hour ago, I thought how wise it would be to think carefully before I responded, especially since I have no clue how the elephant thinks about you and me bonding. But, seriously, what's the fun in being cautious. And, perhaps like you, when I think about the three of us being in the same place my blood starts racing. Mayumi, however the future unwinds, I do promise to do my best to care for you.

Love, Tamiko

. . . . .

As Tamiko steps past security in L.A. she sees Mary McCarthy holding a sign saying, *Tamiko's Coach, Mom & Chaperone.* Delighted to step into the comfortably attractive fifty-ish woman's welcoming hug, Tamiko says, "I know I need a coach. And based on Clem's and Derrick's raves, I'm pleased to be your honorary daughter, but, Mary, do I really need a chaperone?"

"Let's grab your bags and I'll explain in the car. I brought a snack bag if you're hungry."

"Always. Cookies and fruit I hope?"

"And vanilla yogurt and a chocolate croissant."

"You read my stomach."

"I talked to Amy. Did you pack almost everything you own, like I asked?"

"Pretty much, although I had to borrow a second extra-large wheelie bag to schlep it all."

"Good, because tomorrow morning Donell Rooney, *2+2*'s costume guy, will have you try on everything while he takes notes and measurements. Then, Monday while he goes shopping, you'll be at the salon."

"Really!" Tamiko exclaims, her hand flying to her head as she tries not to sound as stung as she feels. "I mean, Mary, I know there is a lot of it, but I think my hair looks pretty okay the way it is," Tamiko adds, tossing her head so all but a few errant wisps of her wavy mane ripple over her shoulders and halfway down her back. "And when it comes to new clothes, I thought Ben wanted me pretty much like I am—the authentic college student look, I guess."

"Welcome to Movieland, where nothing is authentic, but everything pretends to be. Our job is to start with how you look now and then reimagine it into how every college girl in at least half the world wants to look next year."

"Okay, I get that my clothes are maybe a tad frumpy, but my hair?" Tamiko again insists, as if maybe Mary hasn't appreciated how nice it looks.

"Sweetie, no judgment, but like your clothes, in an expert's hands, and without changing your overall presentation, your hair really can, and will, look an order of magnitude better. But let's talk about more important stuff. I think I told you Ben has a warm pool so I hope you packed a bathing suit."

"Definitely. And maybe I can even swim laps in my old Speedo without it's needing to be reimagined."

"Ha! I'm delighted to see you also packed your sense of humor."

. . . . .

In the car on the way to Ben's house in the upscale Pacific Palisades section of L.A., Tamiko munches a croissant as she tries not to drop crumbs all over the black leather seats of Mary's new red Tesla.

"You'll find your schedule for the week in the glove box, although I should alert you that like everything else you'll encounter in this town, it's sure to change." When Tamiko tries, but fails, to locate the compartment's latch, Mary pops it open by tapping an icon on the Tesla's TV-sized screen. "And, Tamiko," she adds, "it's always wise to expect the unexpected."

As Tamiko runs her eyes down the baker's dozen of entries on her itinerary, she smiles as she remembers Derrick describing how she'd be efficiently plugged into the entertainment factory. Pleased to note that she's included in script conferences on Tuesday and Friday, Tamiko is brought up short by the schedule's last item. "Mary, what does it mean here on Wednesday where it says 'Tamiko Walk Through'?"

"Aphrodite Gomez is delayed on another film until next week so Ben will extend preproduction for a week and use some of the extra time to help you get up to speed. The best way to do this is to have you run through all your scenes using stand-ins for the other actors. Everything will be done as if it's real, but you'll know that if you forget a line, or miss a mark, it's no big deal."

"Okay, I guess," Tamiko says in a voice so tentative it all but shouts that she's far from convinced. "But, Mary, for sure I'll appreciate every bit of help you can give me. For starters, I have no idea what a mark is."

"A spot on the floor of the set, or other location, often marked with a piece of tape where a performer steps to deliver her lines. The camera and lights will have been pre-positioned using stand-ins for the actors during what's called the blocking process. And, as for my help, I'm afraid you'll have it, whether you want it or not since, with very few exceptions other than the bathroom, I go where you go."

"That's the chaperone part of your job I guess. But, really, being the only child of a working mom, I'm pretty comfortable on my own. So, away from the set I can…"

"Tamiko, I have a hunch we'll be good friends but the truth is, my first job is to protect Ben and *2+2*."

"I don't quite follow. Is there something I'm not understanding?"

"For starters, we need to be very conscious that you're a minor working on a movie that half the country will probably see as porn with a plot. To forestall obvious issues, legal recommended that Ben hire a twenty-one-year old to play Jennifer, or at a minimum, an actor who is eighteen. But he stubbornly insisted on you. So, at the very least, you need to be far away from the set when the simulated sex scenes are shooting. But your conduct in public also has to be one hundred percent age appropriate—which means no alcohol, no drugs, no smoking anything, and so on."

"That's easy, I don't do any of that except maybe at a party to hold a glass of club soda colored by a dollop of red wine that I barely sip from."

"Good to know, which means axing the splash of vino will be easy. But Tamiko, because *2+2*'s premise is controversial and the cast is loaded with heavyweights, a gaggle of reporters, photographers and hangers-on are sure to be omnipresent. And with only five people in the principal cast, it won't take long before they're all over you like yellowjackets at a Fourth of July picnic."

"I can keep my mouth shut."

"Suppose someone seemingly innocuous, like a waiter or parking lot attendant, asks you how it feels to be in a film with Jed Streeter. In an effort to be polite you answer, 'Amazing, Jed Streeter's always been one of my absolute idols,' or something similar."

"Sorry to be dense, but again I'm not following."

"Believe me, you will when 'my absolute idol' appears in a gossip mag over a picture of you and Jed that makes it look like the two of you are a half step from the couch that's been photoshopped into the background."

"Everything is for sale in Tinsel Town."

"Pretty much. So, again, it's my job to steer you around obvious pot-holes such as giving the appearance that you're enamored by a much older guy. But Tamiko, I won't birddog you when I don't need to. For example, if you want to hang with your Berkeley High buddies who go to one of the universities in SoCal, that's your business, as long as you keep it private and respect the nondisclosure agreement you signed not to talk about *2+2*."

. . . . .

When they pass through Ben Fine's iron gate, Tamiko is initially underwhelmed.

Tucked into the hillside behind a tall adobe wall, the house appears to be just another unremarkable upscale Spanish-style rancher. It is only when Mary gives her a quick tour that Tamiko realizes that, because much of the spacious main house plus the guest cottage, pool and manicured garden are stepped downhill, this is an elegant villa.

"You'll share the cottage with me," Mary says, "at least until Clemmie and Derrick show up. As you'll see in a minute, it's a good-sized duplex so you'll have your own bedroom, sitting room, bath and deck. We share the kitchen and hopefully the occasional meal, but otherwise you're on your own. My boyfriend Abel will stop by later, but no one else will be around until Ben returns tomorrow evening. It's four o'clock now so let's roll your bags down and then you'll have a couple of hours to swim, sleep, use the gym which is in the basement of the big house, or whatever. At six o'clock, how about we cook spaghetti, make a salad and go over my first draft of your profile? Also, at some point, please take a look at the digest of movie set jargon I left on the desk. The cameramen and other techies love to toss it around and if you don't know the difference between a grip, a gaffer and a best boy, they're sure to make you squirm."

"So my job will be to toss it right back?"

"Precisely, but always with a smile. One of the golden rules of the movie biz is things go far easier for talent when the crew likes them."

· · · · ·

When Tamiko opens the kitchen door at exactly 6:00, she's delighted to smell garlic simmering in olive oil. "I got a head start on dinner," Mary says. "I hope you like *ajo* because the pasta is about to be slathered in it. What do you want to drink?"

"Water is fine," Tamiko answers as she sits on one of the tall chairs by the black granite kitchen island.

"I'm having red wine and since it's just us two, you're welcome to join me."

"That's okay, the truth is I like water better."

A couple of minutes later Mary breaks off a second piece of baguette and glances at Tamiko's plate to see that it's empty. "I thought Derrick ate fast, but you may have just set the house record. There's plenty more on the stove so help yourself."

As Tamiko refills her plate she says, "It's nine-thirty p.m. East Coast time, so despite your yummy snacks, maybe I have an excuse for pigging out. But the truth is I'm always hungry."

"Are you also ready to edit your media profile?"

"Sure," Tamiko says, taking the two printed pages from Mary's extended hand. "Go back to your living room where you'll find a mechanical pencil and fat white eraser on the desk. Scribble whatever notes or changes you want while I clean up here and join you in fifteen."

"I can help with the dishes," Tamiko says, pushing back her chair.

"Which would be fine if Abel wasn't coming over at eight o'clock. But, since he's never learned how to be fashionably late, things will go faster if I clean while you edit."

Reading through her profile, which includes a brief version of her sports biography, her love of everything about Ancient Greece, and even the gold medals she won on the National Latin Exam, Tamiko is amazed at how spot-on it is. Making a note here and there, she's finished when Mary appears.

"How did you pull all this together?" Tamiko asks. "It's like a lot of it isn't even online."

"I have my sources," Mary says with a chuckle, as she pulls a chair next to Tamiko.

"But Derrick and Clemmie don't know half of this. Even my mom doesn't know all…"

"You do."

"Oh my god, Mary, really? When we chatted on Parents Weekend you were interviewing me?"

"Ben doesn't pay me so generously to waste time, although as a new best buddy of both of my kids I was genuinely interested in getting to know you."

"Mary, I don't mean to speak out of turn, but I think it's sweet that Derrick and Clemmie call you 'Mom,' and Ben 'Dad,'" Tamiko says, turning to make eye contact with the older woman.

"We're far from the only unconventional family these days. But, no doubt, the last twelve years since the drunk driver killed their parents have been a big stretch for all of us. At that point I was a forty-four-year-old widow with a daughter just off to college, trying to make it as a screenwriter. I was also, maybe, six months away from having to wait tables to pay the rent so it was a big deal when Ben hired me as a nanny. In short, I was highly motivated to make a success of what turned out to be my new family. But time's moving on, so let's focus on you. I did my best to summarize the sports stuff I pulled off the internet so it may not be perfect."

"I've dusted it. But what about the paragraph about how at the very moment Ben was looking to cast an authentic college girl for a small part in *2+2*, he spotted me in a photo Clemmie sent home?"

"All true, isn't it?"

"There's no mention of Derrick, who I actually met before I…"

"Does there need to be?" Mary interrupts. "Tamiko, I don't mean to airbrush anything that's important to you. But I also think it will be easier for all involved if the press doesn't shout that you got the part because you were dating Ben's son, especially since I gather you and Derrick have moved on from the romance phase of your friendship."

Annoyed that her life is being so casually dissected and edited, Tamiko says nothing. Apparently sensing Tamiko's annoyance, Mary says, "Let's wrap it for tonight. Because the media believes you're little more than a walk-on, no one is likely to dig deeper as long as the headlines check out. And since the *2+2* set will be tightly closed we're hoping no one in the media will realize your bit part has morphed into you being a supporting actor, until you're safely out of town."

"A supporting actor? Really?" Tamiko asks, astonished.

"Based on the number of lines you now have, and your character's importance to the arc of the story, Ben says so. He's asked his lawyer to contact your agent to work out an amended contract."

. . . . .

Feeling forlorn on the evening after Mayumi flies off, Alec nurses a beer in the tiny nine-stool bar a few doors down from his apartment. Although he knows he'll continue to acutely miss Mayumi, he also knows he needs to find something positive about being on his own. But, like someone trying to find a path through thick fog with a failing flashlight, he doesn't get far. Downing most of his second beer, the best he can resolve is to start by trying to figure out what's going on in his own head. And with two weeks before Charlie and Emiko arrive he also decides to keep busy by exploring Tokyo, something that nesting with Mayumi has substantially interrupted.

"Where is cutie-pie girl you so happy to be with?" Tosh, the owner of the izakaya asks in heavily accented English when Alec orders a third Sapporo.

"Gone off to see the world," Alec replies in serviceable Japanese as he raises and lowers his arms to mime flying.

"Leave you behind, very sad," Tosh says, again in English.

"Mayumi's headed for Spain, and then maybe Italy and Greece before going to school in London," Alec doggedly continues in Japanese. Again he realizes that one of his biggest difficulties in learning Japanese is that the majority of people he encounters are so anxious to try out their English.

"See world, but lose nice *gaijin* boyfriend. So sad for her also, I think."

Trying not to show how pleased he is by Tosh's compliment, Alec nevertheless bows his head slightly as he reflects on how nice it is to have made a friend. Hearing his phone ping, Alec sees he has a text from Mayumi's friend Aki asking if he'll be able to make the group gathering at the Aldgate British pub on Friday evening.

I might be catching something, so will skip this week, Alec texts back, regretting his small lie, but determined to hang by himself for a few days.

· · · · ·

To: *Charlie, Clemmie, Derrick, Ed, Eloise, Emiko, Jazz, Lec, Mayumi, Missy, Mom, Professor Spurgeon, Ruth, Stepan, Dean Thomas, V & Vera*

Subject: *Lost in La-La Land (my besties' eyes only—since everything about 2+2 is already being chewed over in the media, I'm hereby bending the terms of my nondisclosure agreement. But no passing this on.)*

It's Wednesday evening and since I arrived last Saturday I've been tucked into Ben Fine's sweet backyard cottage (light gray with white trim with a pool in front) in a section of L.A. called Pacific Palisades, which I gather is near the ocean, although I've been so slammed I haven't seen it. Since it's been another long day and I'm beat, I'm copying you all with this one long email and hoping you will forgive me for not communicating individually.

Thanks to my mentor and new friend Mary McCarthy, things have been moving forward at a canter (you were right Derrick, they do know how to plug a newbie into their entertainment factory). In short order, and despite my kvetching, my hair has been nipped, tucked and shined, my "dowdyish" college girl wardrobe has been replaced by a slicker, better fitting version (no more peek-a-boo bra straps), my bio has been written and polished (who is this girl?) and literally gazillions of studio photos have been taken (they must pay the photographer by the pic). Yesterday I spent much of the very fun day in a conference with Naomi and Jack Gold, 2+2's real scriptwriters, at which Ben Fine occasionally dropped in.

Surprisingly (at least to me), the plot, which everyone who's read an industry gossip mag in the last month knows, focuses on a spouse-swapping foursome, is still being tweaked. As part of this process, my character's role has grown. Instead of simply being the nuisance daughter who comes home from college a day too soon, Jennifer now becomes something of a wild card catalyst (truth-teller) for the whole story. I don't know enough to guess whether this will turn out to be a good idea. But I hope that, at the very least, because the drama now involves an uneven number of people (five, instead of four) it will be inherently more interesting.

You'll laugh when I tell you about today. Because the four big actors won't start trickling in until tomorrow (Aphrodite Gomez won't be on set until Monday), this was my opportunity to do a practice run through of all my scenes using stand-ins for the other actors. With the pressure mostly off, I blasted through them without botching a line.

Given that I'm a clueless novice, I wasn't surprised when Ben gave me a bunch of tips about timing, facial expression, tone of voice, etc. before asking me to redo the whole thing, some lines so many times I lost count. Then, about 4:00 p.m., after my tenth (or was it twelfth?) redo of the breakfast scene where I appear from the beach (the house is at Malibu) wearing a wetsuit and my mom Sandy (Mary Ann McCabe) and I squabble, Ben clapped his hands. "Congratulations Tamiko, you did great, that's a wrap," he said. "And since we're finished now, you're free to head back to Amherst in the morning." Picking up on Ben's cue, everyone on set politely applauded before lining up to shake my hand and say goodbye. Of course, it was all a gag (Ben stages these now and then to keep everyone loose). But there was also a bit of truth hiding in the joke since it turns out Ben plans to use some of my dialogue in the final version (called the final print, from the olden days when they still made movies using film).

Anyway, by this time, I was seriously drained so I just kinda collapsed into a canvas chair (yes, they really use director's chairs) to watch a series of establishing shots (for example, a living room before anyone enters it). At some point a tall guy flops into the chair next to me. Because as a naive newbie I'm so fascinated by what's going on in front of me, I don't look around, assuming it's Diego Leja, one of the second assistant directors who Ben has charged with keeping me up to speed on what's going on. This time, however, Diego's whispered patter is uncharacteristically funny and I'm already chuckling when he makes a stupid pun that's so hilarious I burst out laughing (loud).

When Bonnie Yarnow, the senior assistant director yells "Quiet on the set!" I turn to give Diego a dirty look, only to see Jed Streeter grinning back at me (believe it or not, Jazz, in person he looks even cuter than he did in Romancing Mrs. Jeffries*). Anyway, when Bonnie calls "Cut!" to give the set decorator time to rearrange some furniture, Jed needlessly introduces himself and we start chatting. I put on my best straight face to tell him I hate all his films, and he replies deadpan, "Since I kinda do too, I guess we'll* *be buddies." At this point as we both break up, I look up to see Ben motoring over and fully expect to be chewed out for fraternizing with my elders, or whatever. But, instead he says, "Since you two seem to be getting along, Jed, I hope you'll mentor Tamiko these next couple of weeks when things start moving so fast I won't have the time."*

We'll see, I guess. Tomorrow is another mystery day on the set, at least for a newbie like me who hasn't begun to figure out how the preproduction process works. Friday I get the day off to go the UCLA library to do some last research for my history paper (in lieu of the final exam) before, hopefully, knocking it out in the afternoon. Saturday there is a cast and crew party here at Ben's house. Who knew?

. . . . .

Alec spends the first week of December focusing on his daily language classes before meeting up with his informal conversation group in the late afternoon. This consists of three tech workers—Jaleh, a forty-ish Iranian woman with three kids and a day-brightening smile and two serious Indian men, Amir and Kiran. Although far from fluent, Alec can now puzzle out newspaper articles and much of the technical material Charlie has been steadily emailing. On Friday evening, December 8, Alec is delighted to be warmly welcomed by Mayumi's cohort at the Aldgate. Now, able to catch a fair amount of the Japanese tossed back and forth between the dozen friends, he only occasionally asks for a translation.

The evening's only odd note occurs when glancing toward the other end of the table, Alec sees Mayumi's socially awkward friend Aki, staring at him. At 10:30, having finished half of his second Sapporo, Alec stands and says good night. Leaving a few minutes early, he reasons, will free him from having to deal with any possible flirtation coming from pretty, seductive Hana, whose elbow has bumped his a few too many times that evening. But as he reaches the street and strides toward the metro he hears someone call, "Alec, wait, wait a minute." Chiding himself for being too slow, Alec turns expecting to see Hana, or possibly even pale, elegant, Shoko. Instead, it's spaghetti-thin Aki, who, coat in hand runs to catch up, seemingly oblivious to the chilly evening.

"Please, Alec, I've been wanting to ask if we can get together this weekend," Aki asks breathlessly in excellent English. "Mayumi says it will be good if I can assist you with your Japanese. Since I study linguistics, I know I can help you fix your worst pronunciation issues."

Hesitating, as he reaches for a diplomatic way to dodge this awkward young woman's proposal, Alec finally replies, "Tomorrow I plan to visit the Edo-Tokyo Museum, so maybe another day would..."

"Brilliant idea," Aki interrupts. "You'll be impressed when you cross a full-sized replica of the beautiful cypress Nihonbashi Bridge, which served as an entrance to the city in the early sixteen hundreds. And I can also show you many life-sized exhibits of how people used to live. The museum opens at nine-thirty, so meet me outside the ticket office a few minutes before so we can get ahead of the crowd."

. . . . .

Sure enough, the three hours Alec spends with Aki Saturday morning, are a revelation. The expansive concrete museum, designed by Kiyonori Kikutake to evoke a traditional rice storehouse, but looking to Alec more like something from *Star Wars*, focuses on the two and half centuries of the Edo period, which ended in 1868 under pressure from the West. It tells a fascinating story of a time when, with a few minor exceptions for Portuguese and Dutch traders, Japan determinedly isolated itself from the rest of the world. And with Aki's help Alec can fully understand the many exhibits painting a vivid picture of a prosperous, sophisticated, albeit rigidly hierarchical society with fascinating parallels to the feudal system the West had largely discarded a century or two before. As they exit the museum, Alec thanks Aki for her generous patience and invites her to lunch at a nearby six-table soba shop. Fully expecting the intense young woman to order for both of them, Alec is surprised when Aki sits quietly with her hands folded on her lap. Perhaps as host it's up to me to order, Alec thinks as he motions to the waitress and points at the little picture next to one of the listings.

"No, no, we don't want cold buckwheat noodles on a chilly day," Aki loudly insists, as she screws up her small nose in distaste.

"*Arigato*, Aki, of course you're right," Alec agrees in a tone that sounds patronizing, even to himself.

"No need to humor me," Aki says acerbically. "If you don't want my help, say so."

Momentarily pleased that he is being given the opportunity to back away from this strident young woman, Alec quickly realizes that Aki is precisely the no-nonsense Japanese teacher he needs. "Okay, let's start again so that with your help this ignorant *gaijin* learns how to order hot soba. And then we can go over the rest of the menu."

"Fine," Aki mumbles, grimacing slightly in an effort to disguise her pleasure that Alec has fully committed to working with her.

. . . . .

Having finished her paper, Tamiko returns to the cottage on Friday afternoon planning a long mind-clearing swim only to find Mary sitting in their shared kitchen in front of a white teapot and a plate of pastries that all but shout expensive French bakery. "Sorry to step on the rest of your day, but we have work to do," Mary says, as she pours Tamiko a cup and nods at the two long black garment bags dangling from the back of the door. With no idea what Mary is talking about, but having a strong premonition she isn't going to like it, Tamiko nibbles a pain au chocolat and says nothing. "They're your dresses for the party tomorrow night," Mary continues cheerfully. "Don't you remember me telling you Ben is having a cast and crew celebration?"

"Sure, but I plan to wear black pants and my nice lace top. I mean, like, Mary, I'm halfway to being buds with most of the crew by now, right?"

"Ah, Hollywood euphemisms," Mary replies with a chuckle. "While it's true that half-a-dozen of 2+2's senior production people are invited to Ben's so-called cast and crew celebration, most of the hundred or so guests will be Hollywood A-listers, including a gaggle of the deep pocket types Ben relies on to help fund his films. More important, for what you and I are concerned about now, the men will be in black tie, while the younger women, at least, will be dressed as if for the red carpet on Oscar night."

"Yowzer!" Tamiko exclaims, as she screws up her nose. Then, reaching for her cup she adds, "I hope this is hemlock."

"Not to worry, I have you covered," Mary says cheerfully, as she stands, unzips one of the bags and removes a stretchy black satin shift with a deeply scooped neck that Tamiko can see is designed to mold to her body like snakeskin. "Start by trying on this one, including the mini-bra and panties that go with it."

Returning to the kitchen a couple of minutes later, Tamiko stammers, "Mary, I can't possibly wear this, I just can't. When I breathe my belly button shows."

"Did you stand in front of the long mirror?"

"Just a peek. I mean, I barely recognized myself. It's like, aren't I supposed to be your typical college kid, not James Bond's Pussy Galore?"

"Tamiko, not a woman in fifty has the figure needed to pull off this dress, but on you it's stunning."

Gah! Double gah! Better make that quadruple gah!, Tamiko thinks as she wonders whether she can even sit down. "But what about the other one? Maybe it won't make me feel quite so intimidated."

"You'll never be that dear, but sure, try it on."

A few minutes later Tamiko is back in the kitchen, this time wearing a comparatively demure midnight blue dress and a big smile. Princess cut, with sturdy straps to secure the clinging top, it has a floating, knee-length skirt studded by a thousand silver dots that sparkle like the Milky Way in a moonless sky. Seeing Mary's grin of approval, Tamiko raises her hands high and twirls, hopeful now that maybe, just maybe, she'll survive Saturday night.

"I guess you've made your choice," Mary says. "Even barefoot with your hair yanked up in that poodle puff you look like you're ready to levitate. With your golden mane rippling down your back, you'll surely be the belle of the ball. But, remember, even Cinderella wore shoes at the start of the evening," Mary adds with a chuckle, as she holds out a pair of matching blue high-heel pumps.

"Mary, it's like, you have got to be kidding, right?" Tamiko asks slowly, with emphases on 'got' and 'kidding.' "I have no clue how to stand up in those things."

"These heels are two and one-half inches, not the usual three or four inches," Mary says dismissively. Then, as if belatedly registering the panicked look on Tamiko's face, she adds more kindly, "Dear, if you can surf a ten-foot wave, surely you can totter around a living room on lowish heels for a couple of hours. And by the end of the party you may even be ready to graduate to the slinky black dress and four-inch heels."

"But aren't you going to return that one?" Tamiko asks hopefully. "Even though it's as thin as a butterfly's wing and cut so low it barely covers my nipples, it must have cost as much as a small car."

"The contract you signed contained sixty pages so I don't blame you for not reading every clause. But, if you had, you would know that when *2+2* is released, clause twenty-eight obligates you to appear at publicity events, some of which will be formal. In short, this won't be your last chance to wear it," Mary says, nudging a chocolate biscotti in Tamiko's direction.

. . . . .

"Do you need help putting yourself together?" Mary calls, as she knocks on Tamiko's connecting door at 9:20 Saturday evening.

"I mostly need help hiding," Tamiko responds as she nevertheless opens the door. "But, Mary, I'm guessing you're not here to assist me with that."

"No one who looks as brilliant as you do in that dress is ever going to be able to hide in Tinsel Town," Mary answers, admiringly. Then, as she reaches up to pat down a flyaway strand of Tamiko's hair, she adds, "But I do have a few tips to help you navigate the next few hours."

"Tip away, *por favor*."

"As part of what Ben calls 'Media Management' he asks a few tame-ish reporters to these events. William Wold and Frank Zin are old school entertainment industry columnists who can be trusted to enjoy the expensive food and drink and write pleasant things. But Julietta Semplé is much younger and still very much on the make. So be warned, if Julietta sniffs blood, she'll go white shark in an instant."

"Why does Ben include someone like that? I mean, Julietta Semplé, really," Tamiko adds, drawing out the French é so it sounds like an *a* on steroids.

"Rumor has it she was born Judy Simple, but in a town where half the people have changed their names, no one is going to remind her of that, especially now that she's the acknowledged queen of the Hollywood blogosphere. Given Julietta's huge Twitter following of millennials and gen Zers, the truth is that Ben needs her connection to the tens of millions of people who've never bought a newspaper."

"So, wise mentor, how do I avoid Julietta's pearly whites?"

"By being as boring as possible. As *2+2*'s mystery girl, and the first of the cast to appear, Julietta is almost sure to swim right over. In addition to trying to dig up something titillating in your back story, she'll attempt to sweet-talk you into revealing a few lurid details about the wife-swapping antics on set."

"'Julietta, I'd love to answer all your questions but I've signed a non-disclosure agreement that very clearly says my tongue will be cut out if I say a word.'"

"Good start, but how will you respond when Julietta says something like, 'NDAs, really my dear, no one takes that legal mumbo-jumbo seriously.'"

"Perhaps you're right, Julietta, but since no one has offered me a course on what a newbie seventeen-year-old should, or shouldn't, take seriously, I'm going to follow the Girl Scout oath."

"Nice one, but out of curiosity, what does it say? The oath, that is."

"Since I quit Brownies to play soccer in first grade I haven't a clue, but given your description of Julietta, I'm betting she wasn't a Girl Scout either."

"Ha! But it's time to get moving. Your first test for the evening is going to be to totter around to the front door in those shoes," Mary says, taking Tamiko by the elbow and guiding her out the door and along the well-lit flagstone path.

"Okay, but, aside from watching out for shark woman, when are you going to tell me what's expected?" Tamiko asks.

"Aphrodite and Mary Alice will compete, or surely connive is a better word, to see who can make the last and grandest entrance. This means that...oops, wait a second Tamiko, I need to grab this," Mary interrupts herself, as she pulls her ringing phone from the small green clutch that matches her floor-length velvet dress. After listening for a moment she replies, "Yup, we're halfway around the house now, so let the fun begin."

As Tamiko totters up Ben's three front steps, a woman in a dark uniform opens the door to reveal Ben himself wearing a slim tux and a wide smile. Taking Tamiko's right arm, he says, "Follow my lead, keep smiling and before you know it, you'll be having fun."

Before Tamiko can think of a reply, she finds herself standing on a landing overlooking an expansive sunken living room crowded with a hundred or so overdressed, mostly middle-aged people. Unaccountably recalling the panicked feeling she'd experienced at age seven when her dad talked her into walking out on the high diving board for the first time, Tamiko's eyes dart left and right looking for an escape, any escape. When Mary taps a bronze bell a few hundred eyes swivel toward Tamiko, much as had occurred ten years ago when her dad yelled, "Go for it!" Sensing Tamiko's rising alarm, Ben tightens his grip on her elbow as he says, "Friends, it's my great pleasure to introduce Tamiko Gashkin, *2+2*'s hugely talented supporting actress and assistant screenwriter. Although this is Tamiko's first film, many of you are old enough to remember her grandparents, the legendary ballet dancers, Vera and Stepan Gashkin. Please make Tamiko welcome."

As enthusiastic applause rolls over her, Tamiko feels even more like a cornered possum. Then, remembering that all those years ago, her diving board panic only ended when she screwed up the courage to jump off, Tamiko grabs a big breath, gives Ben an I'm okay grin, and starts down the steps. Even before she reaches the last one, a tall, thirtyish woman with vivid red curls appears, hand outstretched, "I'm Julietta Semplé, I wonder if we can have a quick word before the party swallows you."

"Be gentle my dear," Ben says, kissing Julietta on her very white cheek, his smile not quite dispelling the steel in his voice.

Even before minimum pleasantries are exchanged Julietta locks her eyes on Tamiko's as she asks, "Tamiko, I don't mean to be impolite, but can you help me understand how an underage student at an obscure New England college, with no previous contact with the film industry managed to land a role in one of this year's most talked-about films?"

"Just lucky, I guess," Tamiko replies with a grin.

Waiting a few fruitless beats for Tamiko to elaborate, Julietta purses her lips as she says, "Lucky, indeed, but if you don't mind, I'd like to hear how it really happened."

Informed by Julietta's skeptical tone that she's pretty sure the press release version isn't the whole story, Tamiko begins to explain in excruciating detail how her friendship with her dorm mate Clementine Fine led to Clemmie taking several casual photos of the two of them hanging out. And thanks to Clemmie's weekly email home, Ben Fine saw them at just the moment he was looking for someone to play the college girl in *2+2*.

"All well and good," Julietta interrupts, "but what about Ben's son Derrick? When I called a few people at Amherst, the word around campus was that you two are dating and that…"

"Ha! You probably shouldn't tell that to Derrick's girlfriend, Ericka," Tamiko interrupts dismissively, as she reassures herself this is only half a fib, and a pale one at that.

Then, before Julietta can return to offense, Tamiko rushes into a wordy explanation that she's only an accidental actress with a tiny part who hopes to get back to learning Ancient Greek as soon as possible. As she rolls into an extended soliloquy about her love of the Greek language and the Golden Age of Athens, Julietta interrupts with a question about full frontal nudity in *2+2*'s bedroom scenes. As Tamiko raises her hand to her ear to feign an inability to hear over the roar of the party, she is vastly relieved when Mary McCarthy appears to insist it's time to circulate.

"Well done," Mary says, as she adroitly steers Tamiko through the throng.

"You couldn't hear, so how do you know?"

"Julietta had the frown of a disappointed predator on her face throughout."

Half an hour and few dozen introductions later, as Tamiko wonders how much longer she can stand in her heels with a smile on her face, the gong sounds. This time Aphrodite Gomez stands with Ben at the top of the stairs wearing a floor-length maroon dress whose voluminous skirt only serves to emphasize its plunging décolletage. As the assembled men do their best not to lick their lips while the women search inquiringly for the secret that keeps Aphrodite's world-famous breasts from falling all the way out, Tamiko slips out the patio door, pulling off her heels as she goes. She's barely collapsed into a rattan deck chair and begun to massage her angry toes against a chilly flagstone when a familiar voice says, "Escaping from jail is the easy part, but if you want to avoid immediate recapture you'll want to slide over here into the shadows."

Seeing that Jed Streeter is right, Tamiko edges her chair closer to where she can now make out that the lanky film star is sitting in the near dark. "If Aphrodite hadn't shown up right then I'd have screamed for sure. I mean, Jed, I had no idea that by agreeing to a small part in *2+2*, I'd be paraded about like a prize sow on stilts."

"Welcome to Lotus Land, where beautiful women have always been treated like gilded offerings to the male imagination. But rebellion, of course, is well underway, and if you stick around you can be part of it."

"But doesn't Ben, I mean, um, well…"

"Know better? Of course he does, and for the most part he lives comfortably in the post 'Me Too' world. But, especially with Mary Ann and Aphrodite, who love to channel the old sex on the half-shell days, he's under no pressure to do better. I'm guessing that including you in tonight's gong show was an afterthought, which only came to fruition when a couple of things changed."

"Which were?"

"First, due to your clever writing combined with Ben's unique ability to spot talent, you became a full member of the cast."

"And, second?"

"When Ben looked at the dailies, he agreed with me, that you are the most stunning woman in the film."

"Stop it. I thought you were my…"

"I will, definitely," Jed interrupts, "if you'll answer one question. Why do you think Mary Ann is so determined to appear last?"

"Mary told me it was to somehow upstage Aphrodite."

"Part of it, surely. But the bigger reason is that she didn't want to immediately follow you. But, enough! I suspect it will be a relief to both of us if I change the subject to something I'll value your advice on. I'm worried about my seventeen-year-old daughter, Allison. And since I don't know many people your age, I'm hoping you can give me some good advice. In a nutshell, this fall at the beginning of her senior year in high school, Allison, who is a smart kid, categorically refused to apply to college, any college. In addition, her grades began to slip."

"I assume you asked Allison what's up?"

"Of course, many times, and so has her mom, Carol, whom she lives with in Arizona. Allison's only response is to mumble something along the lines of 'you can't force me to learn a bunch of crap I could care less about'."

"Makes sense."

"C'mon Tamiko, that's not remotely what I want to hear," Jed snaps.

"If that's how you talk to Allison it's not hard to see why she mumbles," Tamiko replies, just as acerbically. "Maybe instead of being upset, you should try being proud of her. Loads of kids salute and follow their parents' plan for them to go to college, sometimes even allowing them to choose the school. Then, after a year or two, the kid drops out because they are completely uninterested in whatever their parents think they should be learning. But, Jed, is Allison okay otherwise? Like with drugs, alcohol or…"

"No problem with any of that, I'm sure," Jed interrupts. "Carol, my ex, is both an involved parent and nobody's fool, meaning she'd know if Allison is out of bounds."

"Okay then, if your daughter isn't interested in college, what does she care about?" Tamiko asks, more kindly. "I mean, everyone is interested in something, right?"

"In a word, horses. Allison has loved horses since I lifted her onto Patches, a neighbor's spotted pony, when she was three. This includes riding them, jumping them and currying them. Allison even sings happy songs to her mare as she mucks out her stall. When she was thirteen and her filly, Diamond, was seriously ill, Allison slept on a cot in Diamond's stall for a week."

"So, Jed, have you asked Allison if she'd be interested in a college with a horse focus? Or I guess I should say, an equine major?"

"Are you serious?"

"Absolutely! I mean, it's like these days colleges have programs in every field that involves money, right? Taking care of sick pets, making fine wine, learning to dance on your toes, and, for all I know, growing more robust ganja plants. Combine horse racing, riding, betting and whatever else, and horses are a good-sized business. It follows that there must be a number of colleges that teach kids the basics."

"Hmm, I never thought of that. But here comes Mary McCarthy," Jed says, pointing to the patio door, "so, I'm afraid it's back to the salt mine for both of us."

"I'll look online tomorrow for schools with equine majors," Tamiko says. "In the meantime you can sound out Allison's interest."

. . . . .

Early on the Sunday morning of December 9th, Alec watches the cold rain bead his small living room window as he rereads Tamiko's group email about her Hollywood adventures. By way of reply, he outlines his plan to relocate to New York City early in the new year where he hopes the two of them can promptly get together. Then, after gulping the last of his cold black coffee, he hits delete. Given that he's the one who said no to Tamiko's coming to Japan, and that she well knows Mayumi only recently left on her trip, it seems beyond pathetic to try to crawl back into Tamiko's life just when she's embarked on her exciting new film adventure. Still, as he makes a second coffee Alec realizes that if, for no other reason than to try to cope with his own loneliness, he needs to say something. So, again reaching for his laptop, he enters:

Hey You,

I seriously enjoyed your email describing your La-La Land adventures. Given your endless creativity it's no wonder you've earned a writing credit. Who knows, before long you may be hanging from the Hollywood sign with one hand while writing a screenplay for a film about ancient Athens with the other. It's rainy, raw and grim here, so no doubt you have the weather advantage (changes in latitudes, changes in attitudes, as Jimmy Buffet sings). I'm doubling down on my Japanese including doing a study group after class and working with a linguist friend of Mayumi's on the weekends. But it's cold/flu season in Japan, meaning every third person wears a mask, so things are not getting easier for a lip-reader like me. (Masks make sense in a society that prioritizes the welfare of the group over the convenience of the individual.)

Charlie and Emiko will be here at the end of next week. E is at the end of her fifth month, so this is the last time she'll travel for a while. When Charlie was over in October I could barely understand a word of the Japanese at the several business meetings I attended. Fingers crossed that I'll do considerably better this time.

I'm off to the Samurai Museum this morning where I can have fun trying to read the exhibit notes and maybe even understand bits and pieces of the explanatory film that I very much doubt will be half as good as Akira Kurosawa's Seven Samurai.

Unfortunately, in public places it can be tough to practice my spoken Japanese since, as a too-tall gaijin, I'm a large target for Japanese folks anxious to practice their English.

Enough!

Each day I think of you early, late and often and hope to see you soon.

XOXO, Lec

. . . . .

Sunday morning Tamiko starts to pour boiling water through a paper filter filled with Mary's favorite Guatemalan roast, when Amy calls. Picking up with one hand as she continues to pour with the other, Tamiko says, "Mom, I was just waiting until I thought your sleepyhead boyfriend might be awake to fill you two in about Ben's fancy party last night."

"There's truth in the first part of that sentence, at least," Amy replies with a laugh. "Without you around to make French toast Sunday morning, Ed pretty much refuses to roll over before lunch."

"For sure, I'm delighted you'll both be here in a few days. Mary's been doing a great job mothering me, but I still miss my real one. Did you get the pics I sent you of me trying to balance on heels?"

"Sweetie, I had tears in my eyes seeing you look so stunning in that spectacular dress. But, since there is nothing I can do about your lifetime habit of looking and acting five years older than your actual age, let's talk about this week. Ben Fine called yesterday to invite us to watch the filming Wednesday afternoon."

"Yo, Mom, that's mega-chill since outsiders have been banned from the set, with no exceptions. But like, can you both really come? I thought you had to speak at your conference thingy."

"We're on a six a.m. flight and I'm done with my two panels before lunch. Ed has a talk in the morning and a panel in the afternoon, so I'm afraid he'll miss his favorite actress, or is actor the politically correct term for both sexes these days?"

"The editor in me prefers actor, since that's what I do. And I'm not sure what an actress should be up to except maybe combing her hair. But since Hollywood fetishizes the past and fears the future, the older folk around here still say actress. You'll know real progress is being made when the Academy Awards switch to Best Actor-Male and Best Actor-Female. Thursday morning I have to go to USC to take my proctored stats exam, but I have the rest of the day off. I mean, if you can hang that long, it would be sick to hang out at the Getty Roman Villa."

"Sick or not, it's a date," Amy replies with a laugh. "So now tell me about the party."

. . . . .

By the time Alec finishes his email to Tamiko he's running late for his 10:30 meet-up with Aki at the Samurai Museum. In a hurry to make up a few minutes, he gets turned around in the metro, and takes a train to the JR lines Shinjuku Station, instead of Seibu Shinjuku, which is a few blocks closer to the museum. By the time Alec is up on the busy street and pointed in the right direction it's already 10:28. With several long blocks still to cover, he dodges people and puddles as he runs past the shuttered bars and nightclubs of Tokyo's red light district. When Alec finally reaches the corner museum's entrance ten minutes late, no one is waiting save a skinny teenage boy wearing a seriously oversized parka and ski cap pulled low. Assuming Aki is already inside, Alec heads toward the door, only to be brought up short when he hears his name.

Aki, of course, I should have known, Alec thinks as he turns, bows slightly and says in Japanese, "I'm so sorry, Aki, please accept my apologies for keeping you waiting. I…"

"You didn't want to come, did you?" Aki interrupts in English, sounding more disappointed than upset.

"Aki, I've been looking forward to today, but let's get out of the cold." A minute later, having insisted on buying both tickets, Alec guides Aki to a lobby bench.

Before he can shrug out of his wet coat Aki says, in English, "Mayumi asked me to teach you, but if you don't want my help I'll…"

"Aki, chill," Alec interrupts, opening his hands in an effort to calm the obviously agitated young woman. "I thought we agreed at lunch yesterday that I need and want your help. The only reason I'm late is that my Japanese is still so crap that I got on the wrong subway. But I'm here now and I'm excited to explore the exhibits with you."

Removing her cap so that, as usual, the bangs of her shaggy 1960s Beatles-style mop fall to her eyes, Aki flips them back as she grabs Alec's hand and says, "Come with me, we have incredible things to see."

Incredible, indeed, Alec thinks a few minutes later as he immerses himself in the history of the Samurai military caste, which he sees is remarkably analogous to the role knights played in feudal Europe. But, because Japan's superior metallurgy resulted in Samurai swords being far lighter and sharper than the heavy, awkward, iron blades of European warriors, the Samurai were considerably more lethal in the centuries before efficient firearms.

A few hours later after lunch and a repeat of yesterday's pronunciation lesson, Aki says, "I need to go to my grandparents, but tomorrow I'll meet you outside your school when you finish at four o'clock."

"Hmm, Aki, that's very generous, but that's when I get together with my study group, the four of us grab a beer and practice conversation for an hour or two."

"Fine, then I'll help all of you."

. . . . .

With the big four finally on set Monday, December 10th, Ben begins filming *2+2*'s table setting scene in which the two couples meet for the first time at a wine bar in Santa Monica. Initially, shy and awkward, the four gradually relax as they begin talking about what motivated them to subscribe to an online swingers site. When it turns out that casual sex with strangers is mostly the fantasy of the men, and that both women have been cajoled, if not dragooned, into participating, Virginia and Melanie bond around the idea that neither is going to take off so much as a scarf unless both freely consent. And this seems likely unlikely until Virginia wonders out loud whether she's seen Melanie and Chad on Malibu's Zuma beach. When the answer is yes, and it also turns out that the couples live in similar upscale houses only a dozen blocks apart, they enjoy the evening's first hearty laugh. Now, with their fear of getting involved with the socially unacceptable dissipated, all four agree to continue the evening at Virginia's and Toby's.

"Tamiko, if you've seen *Tom Jones*, a film directed by Tony Richardson from way back in the nineteen-sixties, you'll realize that Ben is echoing the sensuality of its famous dinner scene," Mary whispers, as she and Tamiko watch the four beautiful costars lounge on pillows around a low table loaded with food and alcohol. "Ben believes that if he can tempt the audience to want to lean forward to reach for the goodies, they will also begin to root for Virginia and Melanie to overcome their inhibitions and say 'yes' to the foursome."

Tamiko, who has long since memorized the script, has no major quarrel with Mary's analysis, but nonetheless thinks that *2+2*'s prospects for success turn more on how the women handle their solidarity, or lack thereof. Specifically, where does it leave Virginia, when Melanie, fueled by margaritas and chocolate cake, returns from the bathroom with the buttons of her pale pink sweater undone far enough to show the tops of her estimable breasts? Not only must viewers be titillated when Melanie laughs at Toby's suggestive jokes, Tamiko thinks, but they must not simultaneously resent her for being the tramp who sells out Virginia, the sexually conflicted everywoman. And as the film's dramatic focus now inexorably shifts, the key question becomes, will Virginia go along with the other three, who it is now clear, are ready to shed both clothes and inhibitions?

Or, will she stay true to her name's root and conclude that swinging offends her sense of propriety? Finally, and even more critical to the success of the film, Tamiko believes, when Virginia tentatively places a hand on Chad's knee, will the majority of viewers cheer her on?

. . . . .

When the lunch break is called, Tamiko nips back to her dressing room. Emerging a minute later she hands a sheaf of papers to Jed as she says, "It turns out there are a gaggle of colleges with equine programs. Some are small schools I've never heard of, but Florida State, Colorado State and, surprise, surprise, the University of Kentucky, are on the list. I've printed out information on half a dozen. Assuming Allison is interested, I'd have a name-dropping assistant call a few of them ASAP to request that they overnight their catalogs. Although all that glossy paper may seem old-fashioned, I loved it when I was looking at colleges last year. And, Jed, since the application deadline for many schools is January first, if Allison is really interested she'll need to get on her horse."

Grinning more widely than Tamiko's weak joke deserves, Jed steps forward to give her a quick thank-you hug. But their shoulders barely touch before Mary McCarthy pushes between them saying with a mock formality that does little to belie her message, "Mr. Streeter, in case you've forgotten, adults don't touch minors on this set. And Tamiko, it's also time for you to vamoose since the set is obviously off-limits to you this afternoon for the first bedroom scene. But you have ninety minutes before your writers' meeting with Jack and Naomi back at our office, so let's grab a bite."

"Hey! Ms. Field Marshal, please give me a minute to catch Tamiko up on my daughter's college thoughts," Jed says, as he extends a palm facing Mary. Turning to Tamiko, he continues, "When I called yesterday to propose your equine major idea, Allison was enthusiastic, or, in her words, 'Tight, Dad, no one gets me like you do!' However, she's afraid it's too late to get applications completed for this year. But Allison's mom and I will talk later today to see what's possible."

. . . . .

Tucked into a tiny table at Nic's on Beverly twenty minutes later, Tamiko says, "As I hope was obvious, Jed's side hug was to thank me for helping with his daughter Allison's college plans, not his putting a move on me.

I gather Allison was in a 'forget about it' mood concerning the whole college thing until I suggested Jed raise the possibility of her applying to equine programs."

"Tamiko, honey, I don't mean to go all jaded old biddy on you, but, as the mama bunny said to her baby bunny, 'You can't be too careful since it's always the snare you don't see that puts you in the middle of Farmer Brown's dinner table.'" Then, after a pause she adds, "And I know you are plenty smart enough to realize that a table is not the piece of furniture I'm worried about."

Recognizing that Mary may have a point, Tamiko says, "Mary, I may be seventeen, but I hope I'm a seventeen-year-old with her eyes open."

"I don't mean to be overprotective. Especially now that you're beginning to get a clearheaded idea of how to survive out here, I'll step back a little."

"Please don't. Without your help I'd already have taken a half-a-dozen tumbles. I mean, really Mary, I haven't half begun to figure out this place."

"Thanks, I appreciate that. But to prove I trust you to cope on your own, Abel and I are planning an overnight in Laguna Beach next weekend."

. . . . .

By Wednesday, with Aki now firmly in charge, Alec's study group settles into a new routine. Aki not only suggests the subject for discussion, but quickly and efficiently corrects errant grammar and pronunciation, sometimes even insisting that all four repeat a difficult phrase a dozen times. Although she keeps them at it for over two hours, no one complains since it's obvious that everyone is so rapidly improving.

Finally back in his apartment a little before eight, Alec boils water, dumps in a package of ramen noodles and pops the top off a Sapporo. Waiting an hour, he calls Charlie in New York where it's 7:00 a.m. the previous day. "Lec," his uncle answers, "I was just composing an email to tell you that Emiko and I will arrive on Friday, December twenty-first and stay until the first few days of January. How goes it?"

"Fine, but, I'm calling because I've decided to relocate to New York

City by way of a surfing holiday in Mexico when our meetings are done and was worried about giving notice on the apartment lease. Charlie, it's not that I don't like Japan. In truth, just the opposite. But I think I'm over the worst of the new language hump and have several things I need to sort out back in…"

"Would one of those things be named Tamiko Gashkin?"

"The most important one, definitely. But, Charlie, I'm not giving up on my Japanese. My thought is to take classes half a day and then, assuming it's possible, work for you and Phil the other half. That's until I start MIT in the fall."

"No worries about the apartment. The lease runs out at the end of January. I'm only sorry I'm keeping you in Japan through the holidays, when probably you'd prefer to go to L.A."

"Not an issue, since Tamiko's made it clear she wants to handle her movie adventure on her own. And, with my hanging with Mayumi until a few weeks ago, I have zero standing to ask her to change her mind."

"Permission to speak very briefly about your private life and then forever keep my peace?"

"Of course," Alec replies, bracing for his uncle's disapproval.

"Until a couple of days ago I planned a drop-by at H.F.D. in Menlo Park next week on the way to Japan. To include a bit of fun Emiko and I invited Ed and Amy to meet us for supper at Boulevard in San Francisco where we could also enjoy the famous Bay Bridge light show. When I called Amy to cancel based on our new plan to fly direct from JFK to Narita, we chatted."

"Okay, I guess, but…"

"Alec, I hope I'm not talking out of turn by telling you that in Amy's view, Tamiko's biggest achievement this fall has been to make a success of her time at Amherst despite feeling bereft and abandoned. But, through it all, she's just as gobsmacked over you as on the day you two met."

"Truly? Amy said that?" Alec asks, as he feels the muscles in his shoulders unclench.

"Truly, and Lec, here is where I apologize for more or less suggesting that you 'fess up to Tamiko about your Korean friend Teri's visit last September. I should have kept my opinion to myself and let you decide whether it was consequential enough to mention."

"I don't follow."

"As it turned out, Teri apparently came and went with hardly a ripple. But your telling Tamiko about it when she was already upset made her needlessly miserable. As I said, she landed on her feet, but still…"

"And then I met Mayumi," Alec interrupts.

"Something that was obviously a lovely interlude for both of you—which, in case you're wondering, is absolutely all I have to say on the subject. Lec, I was astonished when I heard Mayumi and Tamiko had gotten together. I mean, I've never met two young women I've liked nearly as much, but still."

"Probably not half as astonished, and frankly annoyed, as I was, until I gradually wrapped my head around the idea that their making friends was an open-hearted act on both their parts—not only generous to each other, but also to me. Charlie, I want you to know that despite all my beautiful times with Mayumi this fall, Tamiko is always in my heart. Last summer when she proposed coming along to Japan, I acted as if she was too naive to make a good choice. For sure, I'll never make that mistake again. Her coming with me may or may not have been a wise idea long-term, but I now need to accept that Tamiko is fully capable of knowing her own mind. And when I read the other day that it's a truism that young lovers typically screw up and lose each other only to regret it for the rest of their lives, I understood that to avoid this happening to Tamiko and me, I need to up my level of commitment."

"As I'm sure you've noticed, New York City is only about a three-hour drive from Amherst, Mass, so you'll have the opportunity."

"Right, but I worry I may be too late."

"I don't see…"

"Charlie, sorry to interrupt, but did you look at the email Tamiko just sent describing what's going on with *2+2*?"

"I read the first paragraph a few minutes ago, but since I knew Emi will be all over dissecting it at breakfast, I skimmed the rest."

"If you're near a screen, pull it up and scroll down to the attached photos."

"I see a bunch of folks presumably on the *2+2* set. I recognize Aphrodite Gomez for sure, and I gather the efficient-looking fiftyish woman is Tamiko's chaperone, if that's the right word."

"Scroll to the last three."

"All I see is Tamiko chatting, and then laughing, with an attractive guy who, I must say, looks familiar," Charlie replies, tentatively.

"Jed Streeter. He's one of the Big Four as Tamiko calls them. For the past few years he's monopolized the top spot at the box office."

"Sorry to be slow, but I still don't get your point."

"Tamiko undoubtedly took all the shots except the last three for which she must have recruited someone, so she could be in the pictures with Streeter."

"Lec, is the green-eyed monster making you paranoid?" Charlie asks in a tone that makes it clear he's already decided that the answer is yes.

"Possibly, but if you read her email you'll see that Streeter is mentioned more often than the other three stars put together."

. . . . .

With the set still closed to her on Tuesday, Tamiko studies for her Friday stats exam. Although she knows she'll do well without a full court press, she's determined to annoy Professor Gupta by getting the top grade in the class. Done with her review in time to swim her usual fifty laps, Tamiko wraps up in a huge white towel with a logo from the Beverly Hills Beach Club. Back in the cottage a moment later, she's surprised to see she has a text from Jed.

Hi there:

Without doubt, Allison is truly buzzed about your horse college idea. To thank you for your help and pick your brain a little more, how about I cook you dinner at my place, 6:30-ish? All can be arranged so the paparazzi have no clue. And, to be clear, no one named Harvey Weinstein lives anywhere near here.

Now chilly in her wet bathing suit Tamiko shivers as she imagines Mary's voice warning about the fate of unwary rabbits. Stepping into a scalding shower, Tamiko contemplates several polite ways to decline Jed's invitation. A few minutes later, the collar of her thick red robe turned up to keep her mane of damp hair off her neck, she picks up her iPad intending to tell Jed she needs an early night. However, when she sees she has a new email from Mayumi addressed to both her and Lec, she can't resist opening it.

hi u two. i don't usually send x-rated messages, but this is the juicy exception, designed, i hope, to put both your minds at ease about keeping me as your dear friend.

so here's the story. on our second night in seville, fujiko and i met a couple of good-looking dudes at 1987 bar (did you know that clubs in spain don't even open until 11:00 p.m?—i mean we had to take a warm-up nap). anyway, francisco, my dude, claimed to be single and a grad student, but by the mark on his calloused ring finger, i guessed he was a married construction worker. no matter. the point is, on this crazy, more than slightly inebriated night, I hit the big O three times (really!). for sure, they were not nearly as milky way shattering as those delivered with burns panache, but still plenty starry. yikes!

why risk embarrassing myself by revealing all this? because tamiko, as i think i explained, before i met alec my intimate life had been sub-humdrum. and even though i've tried not to dwell on it, i've worried that alec alone possesses the magic key to fully open my libido. free at last! finally i know for sure that this girl is built to fly. and alec, although i'll be annoyed if u didn't feel a prick of jealousy, i hope you also see this is as liberating for both of us.

and so, fujiko and i are heading to granada tomorrow where i'll happily revert to being a sightseeing nun. but italy looms in ten days and i wonder if there are still dudes wandering around florence who look like michelangelo's david? wish me luck.

xxoo, m

ps tamiko, i love your emails. what fun you're having!

pps jed streeter is an a+ cutie! well, ok, +++ is more like it.

Rereading Mayumi's message Tamiko realizes that the warm feeling that envelops her is not just from the hot shower. Reaching for her phone she texts Jed, *Color me hungry. What's the plan?* Then, immediately anxious, she sends a second text. *Since I'm on the set early* mañana, *I need to be back here by 9:30 for absolute sure.*

Still holding the phone as it pings with Jed's reply, she reads:

Be out front at 6:15. My landscaper, Juan Perez, will pick you up in a white Ford F-150. It's less than a twenty-minute ride to my place in Topanga Canyon and I'll have the grill hot. Do you eat things that moo? Or, only those that lie there in the dirt? Oops, Did I just reveal my love of filet mignon?

Steak is great! And even better when it comes with a big potato slathered with butter and sour cream (bacon bits are optional, but appreciated), Tamiko texts back, as she heads to the bathroom to dry her hair and do her best to pull a comb through it. Then, after slipping into jeans and a black turtleneck, she finds a notepad and scribbles: *Mary dear, Out for din-din. Back before you know it. Worry not—this bunny has her eyes wide open.*

. . . . .

From the first evening, Alec has been surprised and pleased at how well his Support Center English class has progressed. Despite having a newbie teacher with zero knowledge of Vietnamese, his students' ardent desire to learn has produced amazing results. Now at his twelfth class Alec is delighted when Hau, the young woman tasked with kicking off the conversation segment screws up her face and says, "All boys are stupid." "Girls are even dumber," one of the young men replies a few seconds before another student insists, "It's stupid to call people stupid."

Bingo! Alec thinks. Albeit at a second-grade level, a real conversation has just taken place. To celebrate he invites everyone for a beer after class. Seeing several glance worriedly at their watches and guessing they're scared their employers will give them flak for being late, Alec says, "C'mon people, you only live once." Then realizing that his slang expression has flown over most heads, he is again delighted when Ma translates it into Vietnamese.

Squeezed around a too-small table at a nearby izakaya popular with half inebriated salarymen, the plainly delighted students sip their beer as they laughingly parrot favorite English sayings with little regard to meaning or context. As Alec looks around to be sure everyone is comfortable, he is struck by both the superficial parallels, and fundamental differences, between this group and Mayumi's Tokyo University crew. Although both are made up of bright young people, the upper middle class Japanese cohort can look forward to comfortable lives, while despite their best efforts, these Vietnamese domestic workers will be lucky to escape a life of grinding poverty. Still, Alec hopes, with grit and luck the most able and ambitious can succeed. Two who he believes have a good chance, are Ma, the brainy beauty who had propositioned him, and Bo, the student with the most English whom Alec has recently made assistant teacher. The fact that after just several evenings, Ma had transferred her affections to Bo to form a dynamic duo, only serves to underline this conclusion.

. . . . .

Tamiko is enjoying a relaxed conversation with Juan about his ten-year-old twins, when his laid-back tone turns authoritative. "Tamiko, this is where you put the seat back and slide way down."

"I thought Jed said there are no paparazzi worries," Tamiko replies, as she, nevertheless, does as asked.

"The security cameras showed *nada* when I left, but Jed asked me to be extra careful."

A minute later, after a tall iron gate opens at the push of a button, the pickup climbs a steep fifty-foot drive through a patch of screening vegetation and stops in front of a brightly lit blue door. As Jed emerges from the rambling adobe-style house with a wide smile, he says, "Sorry for the clandestine bullshit, but Mary and Ben aren't wrong, that it's best to keep our friendship on the down-low."

"Maybe I should do a one-eighty and head home," Tamiko replies in a tone so exaggerated both of them know she doesn't mean it.

Jed leads the way into a large black, white and chrome kitchen where he spears two steaks with a long fork. Continuing to a brightly-lit stone patio, he drops them onto a gas grill as he says, "Thanks for agreeing to this last-minute supper. And, just to be absolutely clear, although I see you as an accomplished young woman, I keep firmly in mind that you are the same age as my daughter, whom I still think of as my little girl. And now, while these babies sizzle, can I get you a lemonade, bubbly water, or maybe San Pellegrino soda?"

"San Pellegrino, assuming you have pomegranate," Tamiko answers, as she reminds herself that, although Jed sounds 110% sincere, it's every young bunny's job to be wary. "Jed, I'm curious, before all the sexual harassment claims went viral in the last few years, would you have been so careful when entertaining a minor?"

"My last couple of girlfriends before I married Brook Morrison were in their late twenties and Brook's thirty-four."

"Nice try, but that's not responsive, is it?"

"Okay, then, ten years ago I foolishly chased a very young woman who worked for a production company I had a stake in. It was after *Landfall* set box office records so I was a pretty big name and she was a not-quite-eighteen-year-old makeup assistant."

"Whoa! How did that end?"

"Very fortunately, when our relationship began to wear thin she dumped me for an actor five years older than I was, so there was no embarrassing fallout from my bad judgment. But enough ancient history. How about I flip these babies, we inhale them and then call Allison? As

I said, she's excited, but also worried about the big pile of things that apparently need to happen before the college application deadline on January first."

"There's time enough if she's serious about going for it this year, but let's save that until we talk to her. For now, Mr. Film Star, tell me something about your life I'd never guess."

"Hmm, Tamiko, again you surprise me. I thought people your age only want to talk about themselves."

"I have a smart mom who convinced me that, especially when I'm with older people who have achieved a lot, I'm the least interesting person in the room."

"I hope you can share that insight with Allison, who believes everyone over twenty-one was put on this earth to bore her."

"If I get the chance, I'll suggest that before she tunes out, she ask herself, am I bored? Or am I boring? But back to your life, please."

"When I was at the University of Arizona I pitched for the baseball team."

"Really?"

"Yup. Among my life's highlights is no-hitting Cal and tossing a shutout against UCLA."

"So how come you aren't pitching for the Dodgers?"

"April of my junior year I met Allison's mom, Carol, at a party. From the start it was an all-in deal for both of us. That summer Carol was interning at Tucson's best community theater. To be near her, I hung out over there so often that when a marginal actor flaked out they offered me his tiny part."

"That was it? No more baseball?"

"Well, I pitched my senior year, but it's true that in my heart I'd already exchanged my cleats for a bug, the acting bug. No doubt the fact that my fastball topped out at eighty-seven was also part of it," Jed adds, with the self-deprecating grin that has charmed half the world.

"Two Oscars and three Golden Globes later, I guess you can say it worked out," Tamiko replies, as she follows Jed and the steaks into the kitchen.

"One of each was for a supporting role," Jed replies with a bored voice, as if they don't count. Then turning to face Tamiko, he waits three beats before his crooked grin lets her know he's having her on.

Five minutes later, sitting at the round table in the glassed-in kitchen nook, Tamiko points her fork at the large baked potato slathered in butter and sour cream on her plate as she asks, "I mean, like Jed, seriously, is this pathetic little, bacon-less, spud all I get for coming all the way over here to help with Allison?" Then peeking up to see that, as she hopes, Jed's taking her seriously, Tamiko counts to three before grinning.

"*Touché!* We might make an actor out of you yet," Jed says, delightedly, as he passes the salad. Then, reaching for his laptop, he taps a number.

"Dad, finally, it's like I've been texting you for hours," a young woman's exasperated voice says, as Tamiko looks over to see an earnest girl with a strong chin, a light brown ponytail and Jed's wide-set brown eyes.

"We're eating steak. First things first, right?"

"Just so you know, that's not a little bit funny. I mean, Dad, for once I love one of your ideas, even if you borrowed it. But, I think it's past its pull date for this year. I mean, I have exams starting next week and if I don't super-cram to make up for slacking this fall, I'm not going to any college."

"I have my college application expert right here and in between bites she says it's all doable."

"Really? But, like, where would I even apply? I obviously haven't been to any of the schools with equine programs you mentioned and it's hard to tell that much from websites."

"Hi Allison, Tamiko Gashkin here," Tamiko says, leaning over so she's visible. "I'm far from an expert, but I did the whole college thing last year so I have a few ideas if you're interested."

"Okay, sure, and 'hi' back by the way. And Tamiko, big thanks for getting Dad, Mom and Fred too, to pay attention to what I might want for once."

"Just so we don't have to repeat a bunch, I wonder if your mom and stepdad are available?" Tamiko asks. "It really will take a team effort to get everything done in three weeks."

"Right. It's like they're bingeing on a super-weird Netflix show called *Midnight Diner* in the front room. Give me a second to slide in there."

A minute later, just as Tamiko finishes her last bite, a pretty woman appears with the same strong chin and light brown hair as Allison. Taking off a pair of dark framed glasses, she says, "Hi Tamiko, I'm Carol Buck and this is my husband, Fred Manion. Jed mentioned that you go to college with Ben Fine's kids and are performing in the film he's shooting."

"It's pretty much an undergrad home for the holidays walk-on deal so the word 'performing' is a serious overstatement," Tamiko replies. "But Ben Fine let me rewrite a few lines with current college-speak so that's been tight."

"Allison says you have ideas about how to deal with a last-minute college application which would be great, since we…"

"Right," Tamiko interrupts. "To simplify, Allison, I'd forget about trying to choose a school right now. Far better to use your limited time to apply to the half a dozen that seem most attractive based on their location, websites and the catalogs your dad ordered, which should arrive soon. You'll have plenty of time to tour campuses with your family early next year, or even after you get your acceptances in the spring."

"Cool, like, I guess I didn't think of it that way," Allison replies, obviously impressed by Tamiko's reasoning. "But all those applications. I mean, how am I going to…"

"Given that time really is short, you'll need help, specifically a college coach who knows the drill. If your mom talks to the parents of the kids in your grade who aspire to Ivy League–type schools, I bet she'll find an excellent person with time to help since lots of hyper-achieving kids will have applied for early admission months ago. Then, while you knock yourself out studying for exams, your coach can organize and prioritize everything that needs to be done. And I think you'll find this will be less difficult than you imagine since loads of colleges now use a common application. Your dad says you did well on your college entrance exams so that's a big positive."

"Not super-great, but my scores were in the top twenty-five percent."

"Plenty good enough," Tamiko replies, having done enough research to know that a number of Allison's likely target schools are only medium selective. "Since a key element of all your applications is sure to be your history with horses—training, awards, prizes and so on, maybe Carol, you can pull together a summary over the next few days. Then, Allison, as soon as your exams are over and your coach is on board, you'll need to write the first draft of your essay, which should logically focus on why you're committed to preparing for a horse-centered career. Your coach should give you good advice on this, but I've worked as a junior editor at my mom's publishing company, so feel free to send me an early draft."

"Maybe we won't need a coach if I take all this on," Carol says.

"Permission to speak candidly?" Tamiko asks.

"Of course," Carol and Fred reply almost together.

"There are two things a parent should never attempt. Teaching their kid to drive is definitely number one. Trying to edit, or even worse write, their kid's college essay is a close second."

"Amen to that," Allison says. "I mean, Mom helping me get things organized will be sick, but I absolutely need to make my own decisions. Hey, Dad—Tamiko, I need to go bang the books so, thanks a million and…"

"Hold on a second Allison, which subject are you weakest in?"

"Math, for sure. I'm taking Pre-Calculus, but have pretty much zoned it out all fall so I don't know if…"

"Carol. If you or Fred can find a tutor for a couple of days' intense work, Allison's chances will go way up."

"I'm on it," Carol replies. And then, looking over her shoulder to be sure Allison has left the room, she whispers, "Tamiko, you are a true miracle worker."

. . . . .

A few minutes later as Jed serves ice cream and hot fudge sauce, he says, "Tamiko, even though you look and act as if you're half a decade older than Allison, I think it's time I drive you home." Without waiting for an answer he reaches for his phone and almost immediately asks, "How's the perimeter looking?" Then, waiting for a few beats for Juan's reply, Jed continues, "Good, so listen, I'll drive Tamiko back so you're free to go read *Harry Potter* to the twins."

Once they pass through the gate and cover a quarter-mile with no one in sight, Tamiko sits back up in her seat as Jed says, "That's the happiest I've seen Allison since she won a big steeplechase event when she was fifteen. In other words, there's no way to tell you how grateful I am."

"Let's save the celebration until she matriculates, but hey, if you don't mind a non sequitur, Carol is stunning. I'm probably being too nosey, but how come you two broke up, especially with a tiny kid?"

"After graduation from the U of A we worked at the community theater for eighteen months. Especially the year Allison was born we were drunk with love. But we were also full of ambition, so like many other kids with stars in their eyes, we headed to L.A. Fortunately, Jim Spaulding, the theater director in Tucson, passed along some live connections which led to me getting a few sitcom parts. When one of these got noticed I landed my first small film role, all in less than a year. In the meantime, Carol was hanging with some young writers Jim also knew and, presto change-o, she began selling things."

"Sounds like a brilliant dream. So how did it turn into a nightmare?"

"As we moved toward, and then into, the fast lane we increasingly began to lose track of each other. Carol had the first affair and then I had two, one to get even and the other, well.... By this time, although we still cared for each other, we'd pretty much forgotten how to exchange two civil sentences. A few weeks before our second Christmas when I was working on location in Oregon, Carol and Allison went home to visit her parents in Tucson. To spare you dozens of anguished phone conversations and a couple of fist-banging visits, she decided to stay, returning to the community theater as an assistant director. I fully planned to move back down there to try and make things right between us, and be a decent dad. But I'd committed to a couple of films and by the time I finally made it in June, Carol had met Fred and that was that. He's a successful surgeon and she's now the creative director of the theater, which has become a big deal in Southern Arizona. In addition to Allison, they have twin boys and a good life, which truth be told, I often envy."

"All that time while your love story was unraveling it sounds as if the two of you still cared for each other and wanted to put things back together," Tamiko says, the concern showing in her voice.

"I'm not sure if that's a question. But if it is, the answer is 'yes.'"

"That's just so sad."

"I agree. But in fairness, it's not all doom and gloom. As I said, things have worked out for Carol and Fred and given my success here in L.A., it would be churlish to kvetch."

"But if you could do it over?" Tamiko insists, fumbling for the door handle of the pickup, which is now stopped in front of Ben's.

"I would never have let Carol get away."

Turning to face Jed in the dim light, Tamiko says, "I'm kinda in that falling apart situation with my friend Lec—the guy I was with last year who is now in Japan. Six months ago I was seriously sure we'd be fused forever. I mean, Jed, in the history of the world, and despite what you said about you and Carol, I don't think any two people can ever have loved each other more. And, now, well, it also seems to be slip-sliding away."

"Maybe it's not too late for you both to figure out how to grab hold," Jed says, kindly, as Tamiko opens the door.

· · · · ·

As Tamiko lies in bed after her long day, she tries to unwind by picturing a happy time with Lec. But, unaccountably, it's Jed's face that floats to the top of her thoughts as, seemingly on its own, her right hand slips between her legs. But, before it can find her pleasure bud, a worried part of her brain begins replaying Mary's kind voice describing what happens to the unwary bunny. Rather than try to rekindle her erotic fantasy, Tamiko rolls over and forces herself to work through a difficult stats problem.

MID-DECEMBER

AS PER THE CALL SHEET'S SHOOTING SCHEDULE, Tamiko is on set early expecting to work on her morning kitchen scene with Mary Ann McCabe playing Virginia, her film mom. But when Ben says he first wants to redo several shots from the day before, she grabs a coffee and a chair to watch and wait. Ninety minutes, and two more lattes later, Tamiko's still waiting. Finally, at 11:30, it's her turn. Since the previous week, when she'd done her walk-through with Effie McPherson standing in for Mary Ann, the scene has been substantially rewritten. While it still takes place at breakfast, Tamiko as Jennifer now enters the kitchen by the beach-facing door fresh from a dawn surfing session. As she watches Virginia make coffee, Jennifer tries to mend fences by again making it clear she's not freaked by having walked in on the foursome the day before, and then apologizing for her part in escalating the angry spat that followed.

But, instead of reaching for Jennifer's extended olive branch, Virginia, wearing a white, floor-grazing robe, pours herself, but not Jennifer, a cup of coffee. Then, turning to face Jennifer, Virginia angrily scolds her for coming home from college a day early without notice. Not allowing Jennifer to get a word in, Virginia goes on to vehemently insist that the subject of what went on with the foursome is absolutely closed. Indeed, Virginia's tone is so shrilly condescending the audience will surely be on Jennifer's side when she steps around her mom to pour herself a coffee. Mug now brimming, Jennifer stalks from the room as she says over her shoulder, "Just so you know Mom, it's not hard to guess why Dad left."

When Ben mutters "Cut" after the fourth take, Tamiko knows the scene has failed to achieve anything close to lift-off. Maybe it's because I'm boiling inside this wetsuit, she thinks, or more likely because I suck as an actor, but either way, it's obvious Ben should have hired someone who has a clue as to what she's doing. No doubt, Tamiko reflects, things haven't been helped by Mary Ann McCabe repeatedly forgetting her lines and at one point turning on Tamiko to say, "Darling, please lower your voice, you're stepping all over my scene." Nevertheless, when the lunch break is finally called, Tamiko grasps two things—somehow she must do better and she doesn't know how. Feeling uncharacteristically drained, she grabs a yogurt, salad and Coke from the lunch table, and retreats to the dressing room she's hardly used. But before she can collapse on the small couch the door opens a crack as Jed Streeter asks, "Can I come in for a minute?" Almost before Tamiko can nod, Jed is across the small room handing her a large glass of water with one hand as he grabs her Coke with the other. "You're already caffeinated to the gills. Chug this and you'll feel calmer. Just don't forget to pee before you go back out there."

"Really? Do you think it's just too much caffeine that's making me so jumpy?" Tamiko asks hopefully.

"Having been overcaffeinated more than once I know the signs. But there's also the inimitable Mary Ann. Especially when there is another attractive female around she has a dozen obnoxious tricks designed to unbalance her rival and remind everyone within a hundred yards who's the star."

"But what can I do about that?"

"Not a thing unless you can magically make yourself twenty years older and turn your deep, sensual voice into a croak. Even more than your looks, I'm pretty sure it's your resonant tone that drives Mary Ann nuts."

"You're kidding, right? I mean, isn't Mary Ann famous for having a voice…"

"Like an angel," Jed interrupts to finish the sentence. "A prominent critic famously said that Mary Ann has the face of a goddess and the voice of a star-touched angel and she's used it in her press packages ever since."

"She does have a sweet, chime-like voice."

"Which, performing next to you unexpectedly turns out to be one more disadvantage. Tamiko, if I wasn't determined to keep our friendship in G-rated territory, I'd explain exactly why a throaty, husky voice like Scarlett Johansson's, Angelina Jolie's and yours turns a lot more male heads than a whole chorus of angels, star-touched or not. But no worries, since Ben will figure out how to use Mary Ann's angst to his advantage. Also, I talked to wardrobe about getting you a shorty wetsuit, which I guarantee will make you feel cooler and look hotter."

"Thanks. I was working up my courage to ask if that was possible. It's like, Jed, I totally appreciate your watching out for me."

"Good news since I'm just getting started. Do you remember last evening when you said something about my Oscars and I got your attention by pretending the two of them hardly counted because they were for supporting roles?"

"Right, you had me fooled for a moment."

"Not long, obviously, since you turned the tables on me by pretending a gargantuan potato slathered with yummy gunk was little more than canary food. But let me ask what you think was the key to making both jokes work?"

"Pausing a few beats," Tamiko replies tentatively.

"Exactly! Timing is everything in acting, like so much else in life."

"You're suggesting I slow down?" Tamiko asks, already realizing this is exactly what's needed.

"In a word, yes, and no doubt Ben will be all over this as well. But, you also need to remember that you're being filmed, which is another way of saying that your physical presentation is at least as important as what you say. At the top of the scene let your body get into the act when you come in from the beach full of fresh air and sunshine cheerfully intent on mending fences with your mom. At this point, maybe it will help if you pretend it's your real mom you're talking to. Later, after Sandy lays into you for coming home early, but doesn't even offer you coffee, let your whole body announce your vexation that she's dismissing you as too much of a kid to be taken seriously. Take plenty of time to let it register before you move on to anger. Then, at the close of the scene when you turn to say, 'Just so you know Mom, it's not hard to guess why Dad left,' you'll want to be so tightly wound every tendon in your body sticks out. Incidentally, one thing that helps me get out of my head and into my body in situations like this is to imagine how I would play the scene in a silent movie."

"Oh my god, Jed, thanks. I'm not sure you know, but the line about Jennifer's dad leaving wasn't even in the script until I suggested adding it this morning in place of the one where Jennifer says she's had a threesome. The Golds approved, but Ben was preoccupied so…"

"I noticed the substitution and told Ben I love it."

"Wow, thanks."

"No need, since Ben doesn't miss much. He said he liked the way you'd more deftly worked the threesome trope into the cocktail scene."

. . . . .

Back on the set twenty minutes later Ben says, "This time we're going to do the kitchen scene in one continuous shot, so please, if you flub a few words, or make an awkward movement, keep going and we'll backfill later. And, please, both of you, let your emotions off the leash. Normally I hate melodrama, but this is an exception. So Mary Ann, when you pour the coffee, let your hand shake enough so you spill some on the counter. And Tamiko, when…"

"*In java veritas,*" Tamiko mumbles, immediately embarrassed when she realizes she's spoken loud enough to interrupt Ben.

After a few seconds, during which the set is eerily silent, Ben says, "Precisely," and the cast and crew join him in a tension-breaking laugh. Seeing that Mary Ann hasn't understood Tamiko's joke, Ben seems about to explain. Then, as if realizing this can only be counterproductive, he claps his hands and says, "Places everyone."

Remarkably, the scene rolls out with easy assurance. Mary Ann, apparently determined to prove she's the pro, produces an enviable level of haughtiness and scorn, emotions Tamiko cattily guesses Mary Ann is all too familiar with on a daily basis. And Tamiko, feeling both more powerful and attractive in her shorty wetsuit, surprises herself by progressing from compassion to pique, to annoyance to anger as if she'd been performing for years. The result is that the moment Tamiko stalks angrily out the door tossing her kiss offline over her shoulder, Ben yells, "Cut and wrap!"

When the crew members, including even the two cynical camera guys, begin to clap, a transparently delighted Mary Ann steps forward to take a bow. "They're clapping for you, but that old ham will never admit it," Jed whispers from where he has silently moved, a step behind Tamiko.

Turning to thank Jed for his coaching, Tamiko sees her mother approaching. "Oh my god, Mom, did you just get here?" Tamiko asks excitedly, as she bends slightly to give Amy a hug.

"I arrived during lunch, but Ben hid me so you'd have one less thing to worry about."

"Smart of Ben, as usual. I already felt far more pressure than I ever have trying to protect a one-run lead with the bases loaded. But hey, Mom, this is Jed Streeter, in case you don't recognize him."

"Or even if you do," Jed says, grinning widely as he extends his hand and frankly examines the trim, quietly attractive woman. "But hey, Amy," he asks in exaggerated concern," what state were you living in when you adopted Tamiko? I mean, don't most require Mom to be at least a teenager?"

"Mr. Streeter, according to the *People* magazine I read the other day while getting my hair cut, you're so charming, you only fib when your mouth moves."

"Except, of course, when I'm talking to a beautiful woman," Jed answers with a wide grin.

"Better quit now, Mom. You'll never get to the bottom of this guy's bullshit," Tamiko says, punching Jed lightly on the shoulder as Mary comes over to snap a picture of the three of them.

. . . . .

Half an hour later in the back seat of a Lyft on the way to Pacific Palisades, Amy says, "Sweetie, you really were good. I only wish your dad could have been here. You told me that your walk-on part had grown, but I had no idea."

"I'm only in a few scenes, but, still, Mom, if I'd had half a clue as to how hard acting is I'd never have left Massachusetts. Now that it's too late to back out, all I can do is salute and follow people who know more than I do."

"Mary and Ben?"

"For sure, but also Jed, since Ben assigned him to coach me. What you saw out there was my doing my best to carry out Jed's instructions. And then there is the fact I don't like Mary Ann so the anger part was real enough."

"Is there some reason why Jed's your mentor, if that's the right word?" Amy asks in a tone so neutral Tamiko knows she's concerned.

"It happened by accident, really. For one thing, we bonded around my helping his high school–age daughter Allison with her college applications. Jed was freaked because Allison was turning her back on the whole idea of college."

"All good, I guess, but the editor in me is tracking back to where you said, 'For one thing'."

"It's also true that we liked each other from the start. And, Ben must see that spark because he plans to rejigger 2+2's ending to allow our characters—Jennifer and Chad—to kind of bond."

"But with all the concerns about adults making improper moves on minors, isn't that potentially dangerous territory, especially given Chad's involvement in the foursome?"

"Well, Jennifer is actually twenty in 2+2 and Ben isn't planning to release it until after my eighteenth birthday. But anyway, since Chad is still hot for Virginia, even with all her flaws, he's not thinking about anything sexually overt, or even suggestive."

"Sweetie, as you well know, eighteen months ago I was deeply worried you would crash and burn when you insisted you could handle an adult relationship. Thankfully, with the help of a lovely guy named Lec Burns, you proved me wrong. So it's probably going to surprise you that I'm not going to lecture about dating older men, especially world-class heartthrobs like Jed Streeter. But just so you know, I'm biting my tongue so hard I worry I'm in danger of boring a hole in it."

"It's like, Mom, chill. No doubt, when Jed is in front of me my mind kinda fixes on him like he's a piece of fudge, but the rest of the time I don't obsess. Also, Jed told me he's been dating his tax accountant, Michelle, who I gather is in her thirties and has a daughter."

"Really? Well, kudos to him. But if he's that committed to her, how come he cooked you dinner?"

"Mary ratted me out, huh? But, seriously, Mom, what happened to biting your tongue?" Then, seeing the pained look on her mother's face, Tamiko adds, "Michelle, the woman Jed has a crush on, is in Louisville, Kentucky helping her mother, who broke her hip. And Mom, just so you can relax, Jed and I spent most of the evening FaceTiming with his daughter Allison, and her mom and stepdad."

"Do you want to talk about Lec?"

"Yes, but how about tomorrow? Now that we're finally back at Ben's I need to flop down for an hour before our dinner at seven o'clock."

"You never nap."

"I never spend the day faking being an actress."

· · · · ·

Mary and her boyfriend Abel join Ben, Tamiko, Amy and Ed for dinner in the high-ceilinged, burnt orange dining room of the main house. Ben, a practiced host, finds something to interest everyone, even himself, when it turns out that he and Ed attended Brown three years apart and even lived in the same dorm.

As the dinner plates are cleared Ben hands Amy a folder and says, "After our conversation on Parents Weekend about the possibility of making Bay Books' *Slide Zone* into a film, I had Jack and Naomi Gold, Tamiko's writing partners for *2+2*, read the book. Then I tasked them with figuring out how we might handle a murder that takes place in the immediate aftermath of a massive Bay Area earthquake without breaking the bank. When you get a chance take a look at their suggestions and let's talk in early March when hopefully *2+2* is well into postproduction and I have a moment to think."

The doorbell chimes just as the group moves to the living room for coffee and dessert under the famous Warhol print showing fifty images of Marilyn Monroe's face. Rising to answer, Mary reappears a moment later, trailed by Jed Streeter.

"Since Jed functioned as my directorial colleague today, I think it's only fair that we feed him a piece of cake," Ben says, as he stands to introduce Jed and Ed. "And apropos of that I want to congratulate Jed on recently landing his first real director's job."

"Wow! You're going to direct for real. Why didn't you tell me?" Tamiko asks excitedly.

"What are you going to direct?" Ed asks, when the ensuing silence extends for a beat too long.

"An Amazon Prime miniseries set here in Hollywood called *First Cut*. On the surface it's a whodunit about a maniac with a straight razor fetish, but the larger point, no surprise, is to wallow in the good, bad and especially the ugly side of ambition and greed in the film business. And, to be honest, I only talked the powers that be into letting me direct by agreeing to appear in several episodes and work cheap."

Half an hour later, after walking Tamiko to her cottage so she can have an early night before her morning stats exam, Amy returns to find the little party breaking up. As she shakes Jed's hand he leans close and says, "Amy, I hope you know I have nothing but honorable intentions toward your remarkable daughter."

"I hope the gentleman doth not protest too much," Amy replies dryly.

. . . . .

Confident that she's aced her morning exam, Tamiko is buoyant when she and Amy grab a Lyft to the Getty Roman Villa near Malibu Thursday afternoon. As they turn from West Channel Road onto the Pacific Coast Highway, Amy asks, "Is it really okay to charge this to Ben's account?"

"Jed jokes my agent should have demanded a limo and driver," Tamiko replies with a laugh. "So, by Hollywood standards, I guess I'm a bargain."

"Out of curiosity what does Jed drive?" Amy asks. "A Ford pickup."

"The more I find out about that guy the better I like him."

"Be careful or I'll rat you out to Ed," Tamiko replies with a chuckle.

. . . . .

Half an hour later as they walk into the white-columned world of a Roman country villa, its pale marble lit by the already descending December sun, Tamiko says, "This is more or less a copy of a real villa at Herculaneum, called Ercolano in Italian. It was destroyed when Mount Vesuvius erupted in the first century of the common era. In addition, they have loads of exhibits of art from all over the ancient world plus…"

"I hate to interrupt my brilliant, well-informed daughter, but can you maybe guess what a professional editor might do before coming down here for the first time?"

"Start with Wikipedia and go from there," Tamiko replies with a laugh. "Sorry, Mom, I get so carried away by Rome, and even more by Ancient Greece, I forget that…"

"Which is why I don't worry all that much about your being captured by movieland," Amy interrupts. Then, pointing to the statue of a drunken satyr at the end of the long turquoise pool, she adds, "Very fortunately, the hedonistic pleasures here in Hollywood will never be as interesting to you as learning more about the ancient world, Dionysian excesses and all."

. . . . .

A few hours later over an early dinner at Tar and Roses in Santa Monica, Amy says, "Since I know you have a writers' meeting tomorrow, I'll head home on the eight a.m. Oakland shuttle. But Sweetie, what about the holidays? Surely Ben can't expect you to work straight through."

"I doubt I can get away long enough to make coming home worthwhile. Because the big four are only committed to *2+2* through the first week in January, Ben is treating every second as precious, even threatening to light the set on Christmas eve. But I'll get home for New Year's for sure."

"This will be our first ever Christmas apart, which makes me…"

"Me too," Tamiko interrupts. Then, seeing Amy is dabbing her eyes with a napkin, Tamiko gives up trying to blink away her own tears.

"So, okay Sweetie, if this is the last time I'll see you for a while, let's finally talk about you and Lec. I hope I don't offend by saying you don't seem to be trying very hard to get him back, assuming that's even what you still hope for now that you've tasted this new life."

"Mom, it's hard to explain. It's like, in August I was so bummed by Lec not wanting me to come to Japan I ruined our parting by acting like a brat. Then I freaked again over Teri's brief visit to Japan, even though deep down I knew it wasn't important. Next, Lec met Mayumi and I got together with Derrick, although on my end it never amounted to more than a friends with benefits kinda deal. And, of course, *2+2* fell on me and I got so…"

"No doubt all that happened, and more. But, Sweetie, I don't see how any of that is relevant to your current feelings about Lec. Maybe I've been reading the tea leaves wrong, but I thought you both wanted to try to rekindle the genuine magic you shared last year. And, if that's true, at least one of you needs to stop equivocating, delaying, or making excuses, and say 'I want to be with you right now.' Oops! Sorry if I'm being too blunt."

"What are moms for, especially when I so clearly need to focus. It's like, even before Mayumi left on her big trip, Lec suggested that the two of us make a commitment going forward."

"And," Amy says, after waiting in vain for Tamiko to say more.

"Oh Mom, I just don't know. I guess deep down I'm still mad and hurt that after our amazing year it felt like he just kinda dismissed me. I mean, I try to get past it but I…"

"This is the perfect time for me to remind you of your dad's favorite parable about the two Buddhist monks on a muddy road," Amy interrupts. Then, seeing Tamiko's look of impatience, Amy's voice becomes more insistent as she adds, "Just hear me, please. Anyway, the monks, who are not only sworn to celibacy, but to not touching, or even deliberately looking at a woman, are walking together on a dirt road after a heavy rain. They come around a bend to see an old woman mired in a bog next to the road with no hope of extricating herself. One monk walks by, eyes averted, but the other, seeing that the woman is in mortal danger, leans over, pulls her out of the mud and sets her safely on the road. As the monks continue on their way for several more hours, it is apparent that the monk who stuck to his vow is furious at the one who saved the woman. Finally he bursts out saying, 'How could you have done that? How could you have ruined a lifetime of right conduct by touching a woman?' The indignant monk continues ranting in this manner for an hour until the helpful monk finally interrupts to say, 'Brother, I picked up the woman and put her down. You're the one who is still carrying her around.'"

"You're right, I seriously needed to hear that," Tamiko says, expelling a long breath. Then, placing her hands in front of her heart as if in prayer, she looks up and mouths, "Thanks, Dad."

. . . . .

The week's persistent chilly rain finally gives way to a cool, clear Friday evening and Alec, who feels increasingly at home in Tokyo, decides to walk the several miles to the group gathering. When he stops in an alley in the Shinjuku district to buy a delicious bowl of pork ramen, he is delighted that the chef understands his compliment. And Alec is even more pleased when, in turn, he understands the chef's lament that most Americans are so dumb they think all ramen noodles are born prepackaged at the supermarket. No doubt, Aki's lessons are helping.

Arriving at the Aldgate fifteen minutes late, Alec spots two empty chairs, one at the near end of the table and the other, next to Aki further down. As he grabs the close one, Alec sees Aki's momentary grimace signal her disappointment and realizes he's been unkind. So, after greeting everyone in his much improved Japanese, he tries to repair the awkward moment by effusively crediting Aki with his progress. "Finally the American boy is sounding less like cement mixer," Shoko says, as everyone laughs except Aki, who still looks annoyed. Letting the conversation flow over and around him like water burbling over stone, Alec is amused at how fascinated everyone is by Mayumi's and Fujiko's emails which apparently hint at their romantic adventures without going into anything like the erotic detail that Alec and Tamiko were treated to. A little before 10:30,

Alec says, "*Mata raishuu*" as he pushes back his chair, bows slightly and heads for the door. This evening no one follows him.

. . . . .

As Tamiko enters Ben's office for Saturday afternoon's writers' conference, Jack Gold says, "Ben wants us to scrub any last hint of romance in your final scene with Jed, so…"

"Free at last," Tamiko interrupts, rising to her toes as she throws her hands over her head with as much dramatic flair as she can manage.

"Not so fast, dear, the scene stays," Naomi says, matter of factly. "Jennifer and Chad still meet by accident outside Virginia's house, where Ben wants them to honestly confront their still-raw emotions."

With a theatrical groan Tamiko removes the lid from her takeout coffee, finding that it's barely lukewarm. As she steps to the microwave in the kitchen nook, she says over her shoulder, "*2+2* is an intense movie about four people's most intimate feelings—lust, anger, disappointment and rejection to mention only a few, so I don't get why Ben wants to wind it up with an awkward conversation between Jennifer and Chad? I mean, is he trying to do a Greek chorus-type thing à la Sophocles?"

"That's a thought," Jack replies, seriously. "But I think it's more that he wants to explore the moment after people come down from a period of intense emotion to emphasize that it's what happens next that really counts. Unlike almost any other current director, Ben likes to remind the viewer that life is open-ended by adding something fresh at the end of his films. Maybe think of it as the opposite approach to having boy and girl ride into the purple haze."

"In addition, I think Ben has fallen for your onscreen charisma and wants to see more of you," Naomi adds with a laugh. "But, Tamiko, while that may be my opinion, there is something I know for sure—that ratty old microwave only works when you push the red button twice."

"C'mon, I totally don't buy the idea that Ben is doing this to see more of me. Compared to the other four, my acting stands out like a skunk at a perfume convention," Tamiko replies, as she finally coaxes the microwave to make an encouraging noise.

"Your acting skills may be a work in progress, but that doesn't change the fact that the camera loves you," Naomi insists. "When you hesitate, it comes across as profound. When you look the wrong way, or miss your mark, it somehow registers as innovative. Even when you fall back on your habit of speaking too quickly while rubbing the side of your nose, the camera somehow gasps."

"If you're trying to romance me into cheering up, it's working," Tamiko says, returning to the table with her now scalded coffee. "So how do we satisfy Ben by pumping at least a little air into Chad's and Jennifer's deflated balloon?"

"How about we take a moment to consider what Jennifer and Chad have likely been thinking during the course of the film, but have never had a chance to say," Jack Gold suggests. "Tamiko, why don't you begin with Jennifer."

"Fine! Although with Jennifer it's not so much what she's left unsaid that's at issue, but what she believes Virginia and the others have been refusing to hear. As a twenty-year-old college student at a top global university Jennifer is convinced, rightly or not, that she's thought as much, or more, about current gender identity and sexual freedom issues, as they have. For example, as we know, the Big Four, as we call them, primarily think about gender in pink and blue terms. For example, when it becomes clear that Melanie participates in the foursome as a way to experience being with someone of the same sex, they immediately label her as a lesbian. My..."

"Right," Jack interrupts, "but sorry I don't see what your point is, or I guess it's Jennifer's point we are interested in."

"Simply that she's the only one of the five who has been exposed to current thought that goes beyond he/she labels to adopt a less binary approach to gender. And, since Chad seems to be the most open-minded of the four, it follows that Jennifer might even hope he would be interested in what she thinks."

"But would he?" Jack asks. "Especially, given the fact that Ben wants this scene wrapped in two minutes. I mean, we already know that his and Melanie's marriage is kaput and that Chad is genuinely attracted to Virginia, so maybe he would be reluctant to engage with Jennifer at all."

"Hmm," Naomi continues. "But isn't it also true that Chad is the only member of the foursome who seems psychologically built to enjoy sex with multiple partners free of debilitating guilt or anxiety? And so, to pick up on Tamiko's point that Jennifer longs for an honest discussion of swinging, isn't he the perfect person to provide it?"

"In a different context, maybe," Jack replies. "But, with Jennifer stalking back to Berkeley a few days before Christmas because she's so mad at her mom, I still think Chad would want to play a calming, if not reassuring role. And, maybe also, propose a way for Jennifer and Virginia to try to get over their spat."

"Enough!" Naomi almost shouts after three hours of exhausting back and forth. "Let's zip our last draft to Ben to see what he thinks. After all, he's the one who insists on ending with a Jennifer and Chad *pas de deux*. Hopefully, in the morning we can get back together to walk the last mile. Tamiko, since my mom is here this weekend to babysit, we're going out with our writer buddies to lift a few, and we'd be pleased to include you."

Reluctant to be the Golds' social obligation, Tamiko tries to beg off.

"Please come," Jack says with surprising intensity. "Stanley Greene, a writer-director colleague has been practically on his knees begging to meet you. Among other things, Stan's created *Air Time* for Netflix, which is now in its fourth season. Before that he did *My Year in Rome* and *Good Morning, Mr. Lincoln*, both of which won a pile of awards."

"But why in the world would he want to meet me?" Tamiko asks, genuinely taken aback.

"Haven't you noticed that Hollywood is full of college girls who have hypnotized Ben Fine into letting them both act and write for his new film?" Jack replies, deadpan.

"And then there is the fact that Stanley recently sold a twelve-part series to Hulu set on a college campus, but doesn't have a clue as to how to put it together," Naomi adds.

"But how can something like that even happen?" Tamiko asks, puzzled.

"In our brave new world where a dozen streaming companies are competing for eyeballs, all it took was a racy concept plus chutzpah and Stanley has plenty of the latter," Jack explains. "But here's the thing Tamiko, because Hollywood runs on relationships, you'll be doing us a favor by coming along."

"Okay, sure," Tamiko replies, knowing she owes the Golds a lot more than a few hours of her time.

"But, Tamiko, be warned," Naomi cautions. "While Stanley isn't a slime ball, he can be a tad slithery. If he tries to pump you for free information, there's no harm in indulging him for a minute or two, but beyond that, give him your best smile and your agent's card. You're one of us now and we don't give away ideas."

"But, oh my god, you two, it's like, I'm seriously not looking for another gig."

"Apparently one may be looking for you," Naomi replies.

. . . . .

An hour later, Tamiko sits with a group of nine successful screenwriters at the Tanino Ristorante Bar, an elegant, old-style Italian restaurant whose antique chandeliers seem to be replicated ad infinitum in its many huge mirrors. Sitting back to enjoy the clever, teasing banter of this verbally precocious group, Tamiko is stunned when she tumbles to the fact that they are playing to her. As Naomi predicted, they all seem amazed that a seventeen-year-old has managed to score a writer's credit on a Ben Fine movie. The fact that she's also performing in the film is of less interest to people who believe that actors are fungible, but writers make Hollywood dance. Finally, Adelia Dare, whose claim to creative fame Tamiko has already forgotten, comes right out and asks, "Tamiko dear, I guess we just don't understand how you jumped from a tiny college directly into the big time?"

"Luck seasoned with a dash of nepotism," Tamiko replies.

As she watches everyone lean forward to hear her elaborate, Tamiko remembers Jed Streeter's lesson about timing and adds nothing but a grin. When anticipation turns to laughter, Naomi Gold interjects, "While it's true that Ben Fine initially saw Tamiko's photo because she's a college buddy of his kids, it's also true that when he asked her to do a quick reading for *2+2*, Tamiko proposed a number of script changes based on how she believed her young character would talk and react. Ben, Jack and I were unanimous in seeing that when it came to a college girl's perspective, Tamiko's sensibility was miles ahead of ours. Or, put another way, Adelia, Tamiko's answer should have been 'Luck, nepotism, charisma and talent,' but not in that order."

A few minutes later when Connie Kumar heads to the bathroom, Stanley Greene slides next to Tamiko and asks, "I wonder what you think of a series set on a brainiac New England college campus that follows a bunch of kids starting as freshmen and continues through graduation? Maybe four boys and four coeds who all meet at a mixer-type dance during orientation week."

"Color me doubtful."

"Really, why?" Greene blurts out, so obviously irked the color of his round pink face threatens to turn purple.

"For starters, Mr. Greene, I wonder how current you are about the college scene. For example, the term 'freshman' is now regarded as borderline sexist at the kind of college you're talking about. Amherst, Williams, and for that matter, Yale, Princeton, and many others have replaced it with 'first-year,' which only makes sense since nationally fifty-six percent of undergrads are female."

"Really? Is that true? My college student nephew didn't tell me that. And please, enough with the Mr. Greene."

"Got it. So, Stanley, where does your nephew go to school?"

"Boise State in Idaho, or at least he did last year."

Resisting the urge to say, "I rest my case," Tamiko says, matter-of-factly, "I'd also recommend you axe the term 'coed,' which kind of reeks of when Eisenhower, if not Truman, was president."

Coloring slightly as everyone at the table laughs, Stanley persists, "So my language is a tad dated, but what about the rest of my concept?"

"Assuming a couple of your first-years are gay, trans or maybe non-binary and there's a diversity of ethnic and cultural backgrounds, it could work, as long as you take time to understand the current college scene. For example, no doubt some students do meet at get-to-know-you type events with music and dancing, but since most dorms are no longer single sex it would be far more common to meet there, perhaps in the hall wearing robes and flip-flops on the way to a gender neutral bathroom."

"Are you saying that even the bathrooms are coed now? That is, gender-neutral or whatever?" Greene asks.

"Many of them, at the kind of college you're talking about," Tamiko replies.

"Okay, but what do you think might happen when an attractive, half-dressed duo of whatever sex meet in the hall?"

"Hold on for a second. I feel something vibrating in my bag," Tamiko replies. "Yup, here it is," she adds as she extracts her agent's business card and hands it to Stanley.

"I told you this young woman is nobody's fool," Naomi says to a chorus of laughter.

"Actually, Tamiko," Stanley Greene asks seriously, "How about reading for the part of the smart, sassy girl whom I see as the leader of the series' female pack? I mean with *2+2* coming out this year, you'd have a big leg up."

"After my very brief career, I'm retiring from acting," Tamiko replies. "But I love writing, so, if you need help with that, why don't you talk to Tom Obanta at Lyman and Weiss?"

. . . . .

Sunday morning Tamiko gets an email from Jack Gold pleading a sick kid as a reason to put off their writers' meeting until the next morning. Delighted for the break Tamiko spends the day doing her laundry, swimming laps and reading by the pool. But instead of being caught up in Elizabeth Strout's *Anything Is Possible*, she lets the book fall to her lap as her head fills, and then overfills, with Lec's smiling face. Damn, she thinks as she unconsciously rubs her ring finger only to feel the familiar pang of regret that she's removed the tiny ruby ring he had given her as a token of their bond.

Maybe Mom's right that it's time to let go of being mad and do everything I can to try to get us back to our happy place. And, to give Lec credit, hasn't he been making exactly that suggestion, albeit waiting a week or two before Mayumi planned to leave Japan to do it. Aware she's in danger of once again plunging down the rabbit hole of relentlessly circular Lec thoughts, Tamiko springs to her feet, takes three quick steps and dives into the sun-dappled water. Yet, it's not so easy to wash away her Lec thoughts and before Tamiko finishes twenty laps, her decision is made. She'll put aside her dented ego and do everything possible to fully reconnect. And assuming all goes well she'll be ready to put Lec's ring back on with the intention of keeping it there through rough and smooth. Full of the eager enthusiasm of the newly committed, Tamiko quickly towels off before grabbing her iPad to check flights to Japan. If somehow Ben doesn't need her for a few days over the holidays, maybe they can even celebrate their reconciliation in Tokyo.

. . . . .

With Ben having suggested only a few edits to the writers' group's draft of the final scene, Monday's writers' meeting goes so smoothly, Tamiko is free by lunch.

Remembering her happy excursion to the La Brea Tar Pits with her dad when she was seven, Tamiko Ubers to the Museum. Spending a nostalgic afternoon recalling her dad's infectious enthusiasm for the saber-toothed tigers and woolly mammoths who stumbled into the oily tar 20,000 years ago, she is back at her cottage a little before 5:00 p.m. Laptop now in hand, Tamiko sees she has half a dozen responses to the second group email she'd sent the previous evening. Grazing a few to see that unsurprisingly they say some version of *What fun! I'd love to hear more about your La-La Land adventures,* Tamiko is brought up short when several messages emphasize how chill she and Jed Streeter look together. But before she can dwell on this, Tamiko also notices she has two messages from Mayumi.

tamiko & alec—so here we are in florence basking in its renaissance treasures at a time of year when this place is as empty of the tourist hordes as it's ever going to be. in addition to eating too much of everything, i'm loving wandering around the effortless magnificence of the chilly streets, which i greatly prefer to the madonna and child paintings that relentlessly wallpaper florence's museums and churches. unfortunately f. and i have been disappointed by the guys on offer here. it turns out that even a cute accent doesn't make up for a jiggling belly and garlic breath. (f. jokes that if things don't improve soon we're going to start looking hot to each other.)

tamiko, I love your la-la land reports. in fact, i've quoted them to f. so often she's out shopping for earplugs. and, seriously, the picture of you and your babe of a mom with jed streeter is an absolute hoot. maybe it's movie-set lighting, but the three of you look pretty much the same age. so I'm thinking that if jed doesn't get anyplace with you, maybe he can tag your mom (that really was a joke—well, mostly).

alec, I'm delighted to hear from aki that you've made enormous progress with both your grammar and pronunciation.

xoxo, m

ps: tomorrow we're off to walk off our pasta tummies around some hill towns! don't know about internet reception, but anyway, it will be fun to enjoy a few "be here now" days!

Glancing at Mayumi's second email, Tamiko see's it's addressed only to Lec. Even as she wonders if she's received it by mistake and should respect Mayumi's and Lec's privacy, she taps it.

alec: aki is delighted to be teaching you. as i'm sure you understand, friendships with cool dudes (any dudes, really), don't come easy to her. aki also told me she's working up her courage to ask you for a huge favor. just so you know, i'll be pleased if you can grant it, but will completely understand if you say no.

love, m

. . . . .

The set is closed to Tamiko Tuesday morning while the Big Four redo their first seduction scene. An hour into her memorizing Greek grammar, a ping alerts Tamiko to a text from her agent Tom Obanta.

Stanley Greene has been in touch to propose that u do a preliminary workup of several story arcs for his college based series. Can u possibly squeeze me in for lunch to talk about it? Obviously this is short notice so if it's easiest I can pick up something and come to wherever u r? Of course if you're too slammed today please suggest an alternate time.

Tamiko texts back, *I'm off today so it's a date, as long as that something is sold at IN-N-OUT Burger. Mary McCarthy, my mentor/den mother over here at Ben's, is a borderline vegetarian so I'm in danger of turning into a kale infused hunk of tofu.*

He replies, *Would 2 double cheese animal-style burgers restore balance?*

She texts, *Add a couple of orders of fries and a chocolate shake and we have a date! I'll text you the address as soon as I walk around to the front door and check the number.*

. . . . .

On his way to school on a chill, bleak, Tuesday morning Alec sees he has two texts.

The first, from Shoko, informs him that because several friends will leave Tokyo tomorrow, the group's holiday get-together has been moved up to this evening at 8:00 p.m. The second, from Aki, cancels her appearance at that afternoon's study session, and says she'll see him at the pub. Because Alec knows Charlie and Emiko plan to arrive at the Imperial Hotel that evening, he is momentarily conflicted. But since this will be his only chance to say goodbye to the group of people who have so kindly welcomed him, he texts Charlie that he'll meet him early the next morning.

. . . . .

When Tom Obanta appears, carrying an encouragingly large IN-N-OUT Burger bag, Tamiko greets a very tall dark-skinned Black man in his thirties. "Although I'm sure I'm not being original, I'm going to guess Nigeria for your background," she says.

"Deep-ish background," Tom replies with a grin, his white teeth lighting up his face. "My parents were born in Lagos, but met at the University of Pennsylvania where both were grad students. I was born in Cambridge, Mass while they were teaching at Tufts. But in the spirit of 'right back at you,' let me guess that your ethnic background is Russian, Japanese and Irish, although it would be easy to miss the Irish."

"You're cheating. No one could spot all that. I don't…"

"There must be thirty articles about your stellar sports career online, several of which mention that your middle name is O'Shea. But let's save the genealogy talk for later and eat these babies before their tantalizing aroma flattens us."

After exchanging the usual polite tidbits, Tom Obanta says, "Tamiko, as I said in my follow-up message, you apparently charmed, and maybe even slightly intimidated Stanley Greene to the point that he not only wants you to consult on his series, but also to test for one of the lead parts. I'm not sure where your magic elixir comes from, but if you can spare a few ounces I'd love to sprinkle it on my other clients."

"They're welcome to the whole bottle. I need to be back at Amherst in a few weeks, where I have an over-full academic load and also plan to pitch for the softball team. And, anyway, I don't plan to read for anything since I'm way beyond uncomfortable with performing."

"Not according to Ben Fine, who told my boss you're a natural."

"Hmm. I'm guessing that's a polite Hollywood way to say I have no clue as to what I'm doing, which, in case you are still in any doubt, I agree with. But, natural or not, I'm just plain not interested in acting."

"Tamiko, thousands of young women in this town would jump off a three-story building into alligator-filled quicksand to have the opportunity Greene is offering you. Of course, you still have to ace the audition, but if you did, you should know that a lead actor in a high-profile series might be paid as much as $75,000 per episode. And if the series is renewed, this could double. And, possibly, even double again if it's re-upped for a third and fourth year as might be likely with a hit college drama. Given your pedagogic talent I surely don't need to point out that in total we could even be talking seven figures."

"Impressive, no doubt! But Tom, it's like I stumbled into the acting business with my eyes closed, but now that they're wide open, I plan to run back out. Believe me, I'm so totally excited about learning a thousand things at a real college, I don't want to miss the experience by being paid too much to be a pretend student at a fake one."

"You can easily transfer to one of the top universities out here and do both."

"I said no," Tamiko replies, raising her voice.

"You did. Sorry to be the cliché agent. Truth be told, as a parent of two young kids, I'm impressed by your, hmm…, for lack of a better word, maturity, I guess. Tamiko, if you don't mind me being nosey, where does all your good sense come from?"

"My grandparents, primarily. It's like several people I'm close to have warned me about the downsides of being a public personality, but it's my dad's parents who really have the street cred to get my attention."

"Tamiko, one advantage people my color have is that you can't see us blush. But if you could, I'd definitely be pink since I have no clue who your grandparents are."

"I'm guessing they retired when you were in elementary school, but through most of two decades, Vera and Stepan Gashkin were probably the world's most famous ballet dancers."

"Of course, the dancers who defected from the Soviet Union and almost caused World War Three. My wife watched a TV special about them a couple of months ago and is still talking about their heart-stopping *pas de deux*. Still, Tamiko, I don't quite grasp your point. To be the world's top ballet dancers, by definition your grandparents had to be famous, right? So, I'd be surprised if they look back and think it would have been better if they'd spent their lives shoveling snow in Saint Petersburg."

"You're missing my point. Since I'm not remotely as passionate about acting as they were about dancing, there is no upside to having half the world recognize my face."

"So let's talk about the scriptwriting part? Since Stanley doesn't want to give up one drop of creative control of Class of twenty-four, he proposes hiring you for fifty hours as a consultant. Your task would be to draft preliminary character sketches and flesh out the college setting. To earn my commission I insisted on $70,000, instead of the $50,000 he proposed, but of course made no commitment."

"If I say yes, when would I have to start?"

"Greene knows you're in L.A. and not working every day. And since, like everyone in town, he's on deadline, he insists you start now."

"I don't know if that's possible since I might be leaving over the holiday. Let me think about it and call you tomorrow."

. . . . .

A few minutes past 8:00 p.m. Alec takes the Hachiko exit from the Shibuya JR station. Finding himself at the now familiar scramble crossing under huge video screens and blazing neon signs, he walks briskly toward the Aldgate. Perhaps a hundred feet from the entrance he hears his name called. Surprised, Alec looks up at the now dimly lit street. When he sees no one, he's about to conclude he's imagining things when Aki steps out from a doorway. "I worried you weren't coming," she says anxiously.

"Since I'll be leaving Japan before the group gets back together in January, I want to say goodbye to everyone."

As Aki leads them through the Aldgate's door, Alec notes with some surprise, that her usual bulky brown jacket with its ratty faux fur collar has been replaced by a slim, calf-length black coat belted at the waist.

Searching for the Japanese words to say how nice it looks, Alec is shocked into holding his tongue when he also sees that Aki's Beatles moptop has been replaced by a stylish pixie. Now taking a long stride to pull level with Aki, Alec again tries to frame an appropriate Japanese compliment, only to be rendered truly speechless when he sees that Aki is wearing both lipstick and eyeliner.

As they now approach the group's table where seven or eight are already gathered, Aki grabs Alec's sleeve to not so subtly maneuver him toward two adjoining vacant seats, the same ones he and Mayumi usually occupied. Feeling pinned by the curious stares of the others, Alec tries to cover his unease by suggesting, "Let's speak only Japanese tonight."

"No possibility way," tall, thin Hideki replies mock seriously, "half the reason we let a hairy *hakujin* like you come is to fix up our English."

"Possible," Alec corrects, even as he realizes that Hideki, who is fluent in English, must be pulling his leg. Recognizing that the prospect of an evening spent butchering two languages will be way more fun than practicing Japanese, Alec proposes a bilingual slang slam. "For example, we go around the table with each person challenged to come up with a sentence that mixes Japanese and English clichés."

Then, before anyone has a chance to demur, Alec says, "*Do shita no,* dudes and dudettes?"

When Shoko enthusiastically responds, "*Domo yo ni sore ga burasa gatte imasu,* big guy?" everyone laughs except Alec who plainly doesn't understand.

"How's it hanging, big guy?" Hideki eventually says, as everyone breaks up.

Twenty minutes later, when Shoko remarks, "Hey Big Mama— *Kanojo wa toranku ni takusan jyunku ga haitte imasu!*" Alec again finds himself struggling with the translation. Taking pity on him Shoko says, "Big Mama has a lot of junk in her trunk, in other words a fat ass."

Alec, now chuckling along with the others says, "I thought I heard trunk and junk in there someplace."

"*Zatsu raito,*" Aki says, "we Japanese are '*majishans*' at adapting English words." Delighted by Aki's cleverness, Alec looks up to see that she has taken off her coat to reveal a clingy white silk top, which, to his surprise, reveals just enough definition to prove she's not a twelve-year-old boy. Finally tumbling to the fact that Aki's makeover is aimed at him, Alec doubles down on his usual strategy of leaving early. Although it's only a few minutes past ten, he explains he has to get some sleep before an early morning trip to Kanazawa. Then, after inviting anyone who visits New York City to contact him, he pulls on his jacket as he all but lopes toward the door. Outside in the chilly evening, he's barely begun congratulating himself on his deft escape when he hears, "Alec, wait for me, please wait." As Aki's hand firmly grasps his arm, she adds, "Please, Alec, it's still early and I want to hang out with you." Ignoring Alec's attempt to politely demur, she continues in a rush, "Please, can we talk in the taxi?" With Shoko now exiting the Aldgate, and looking their way, Alec reluctantly allows himself to be led to the cab. But as soon as the whisper-silent black Toyota is in motion, he turns to Aki to insist this isn't a date only to realize the driver is just a few feet away.

"Aki, please listen," Alec whispers. "Although I appreciate everything you've done for me, I do not want to, well, I don't…" Then, remembering he has a fail-safe excuse he continues, "Mayumi is your best friend, so of course neither of us want to interfere with that."

"Didn't Mayumi send you an email asking you to do me a big favor?" Aki asks quietly.

"She did. But Aki, what does that have to…?" Alec starts to protest. Then, as he finally gets the meaning of Mayumi's request, he breaks off, his heart falling like a lead sinker.

"Alec, I think maybe I only like girls. But this makes me so sad since my parents hope I have a normal life with grandchildren for them, so I want to try again with a man."

Knowing this is not the time to point out that in his view same-sex relationships are as normal as heterosexual ones and children can be adopted, Alec considers how to politely dodge Aki's now obvious intention to bed him. Unable to come up with a persuasive excuse, he plays for time by asking, "What makes you think you're a lesbian?"

"The only happy time with sex for me was with Mayumi when we were thirteen," Aki replies, matter-of-factly.

"You've concluded you don't like sex with men based on the fact you and Mayumi played around a little bit when you were kids?" Alec asks, not even trying to cover his surprise.

"Not so little for me," Aki responds, beginning to sniffle.

"But since then, I mean, you must have had other intimate experiences, right?" Alec asks more gently.

"One guy, one girl, that's all."

"Did you enjoy sex with the woman more?"

"No, both were dreadful."

"So again, Aki, I hope I don't offend you by pointing out you've decided you're a lesbian based on a very small sample."

Then, realizing he's digging himself into a deeper hole, Alec tries to come up with a diplomatic way to dig himself back out, when Aki beats him to it by saying, "That's exactly what Mayumi says. So please, Alec…"

"Oh my god, Aki, did Mayumi cook up this whole idea that we should be together?" Alec interrupts, finding a target for his fast-growing annoyance.

"No, no. In fact, when she brought you to the group two months ago, I asked her what she saw in an such an oversized, ugly *gaijin*, especially after phony Josh. She tried to put me off by making a joke about her being a well-known *hakujin* hunter, which is what we call girls who chase after white guys. Anyway, when I kept pestering, she finally said, 'Aki, in addition to Alec's being a sweet guy, I never came close to grasping what sex is really about until I met him. So you can tease me as much as you want, but it's not going to change how happy I am.' This shocked me so much I asked, 'Really, you just want to be with Alec for sex?' 'Were you not listening,' she replied. 'But even if Alec wasn't a good dude, that would be more than enough. Aki, I hope someday you'll also find out how amazing it is to be so physically blissed out, that every cell in your body sings *Yuki no Hana* in four-part harmony.'"

After waiting in vain for Alec to say something, Aki does her awkward best to lighten the tone by adding, "So, anyway, Alec, since I love this song I thought I should try sex again with someone who would be kind enough to teach me."

"So you decided to trade me language lessons for my teaching you about sex, but never bothered to put me in the picture?" Alec asks, not sure whether to be angry or amused.

"Alec, please don't make this so hard. When Mayumi left I was lonely and depressed and simply wanted to connect with someone, anyone, really. It was only later, when I thought you and I had become friends, that I began to fantasize that I was becoming a little like Mayumi to you. I know this probably sounds crazy, but..."

"Not really," Alec interrupts, kindly. "I was lonely too and looked forward to my next lesson, and of course you've been an amazing teacher and friend."

"Thank you. Anyway, when I sent emails to Mayumi telling her how much progress you were making with your Japanese, I guess it was obvious that I had developed a crush on you. So, that's when she encouraged me to..."

"Proposition me? Really?"

"Not really, or not at first, anyway. She just texted me, *Aki, Alec is your friend now, so don't spoil it by worrying about someone who is ten thousand kilometers away*. Then, last Saturday, after I wrote that now we were working together almost every day she emailed me back to suggest I buy some cute clothes, get a haircut, and go to the department store to arrange for a makeover at the cosmetics counter. And then, well..."

When Aki hesitates, Alec sees his chance to tell her that while he's flattered, this isn't the right time for him. But, before he can get the words out, Aki continues, "Mayumi also said that you are such a sweet, generous person you wouldn't say no."

"I'm sorry Aki, but Mayumi is wrong about that," Alec insists. "You are a good friend and you've helped me in so many ways, but I can't do sex on demand. Plus, even if our getting together might be okay with

Mayumi, I have a girlfriend in America whom I care about very much, and hope to see before long."

"Mayumi told me that you've had sex with many dozens of girls all around the world, sometimes with two or three at once."

"That's an exaggeration, but anyway, it was a few years ago when I was traveling."

"So now you are traveling in Japan. Right?" Aki persists, again gripping Alec's arm as if she's found a hunk of driftwood after a shipwreck. Then, as the cab pulls up at Alec's building, she adds, "Please, at least let me come in. I told my parents I was taking the Shinkansen to Kyoto to visit a girlfriend, so I can't go home."

As Alec lets Aki precede him into the tiny apartment, he is taken aback when she turns and treats him to a bashful, but nevertheless, glowing, smile. Realizing that this is the first time he's seen Aki transcendently happy, Alec feels his determination to say no begin to slip. So, instead of using the overly bright ceiling light, he flips on the desk lamp before turning to Aki whom he fully expects to find sitting on the couch. Instead, she is already in the bedroom. "Alec," she calls, "you wash first and then get into bed. Then, I shower, put on sexy clothes and come next to you."

Reluctantly conceding he's past the point of turning back, Alec plugs his mini-speaker into his iPad before selecting his oldies playlist, which begins with Jimmy Buffet singing "Margaritaville."

"Very nice," Aki says. "Now take your shower."

About to explain that he's washed a few hours earlier, Alec remembers the Japanese fetish for extreme cleanliness and heads to the bathroom, grabbing a robe on the way.

Turning half sideways to fit his shoulders through the tiny shower opening, he uses the mini-wand to more or less rinse all 6'3" of himself. Dry and stretched out on the bed a few minutes later as Aki takes her shower, Alec listens to Rufus Wainwright's version of Leonard Cohen's "Hallelujah" as he worries he'll disappoint her. Having a couple of times tried to have polite sex with women to whom he wasn't fundamentally attracted, he knows how off-putting it can be. As Alec again resolves to do his best to show this painfully shy girl a good time, the bathroom door cracks open. When nothing else happens for thirty slow seconds, Alec pushes up on his elbow to see Aki's small face peeking out. Not sure how best to reassure her, Alec bobs his head and smiles.

Apparently convinced he means well, Aki opens the bathroom door to reveal she's wearing an oversized red Mickey Mouse T-shirt that hangs almost to her knees. Seeing this profoundly unsexy outfit Alec thinks for a moment that Aki has changed her mind about the direction of the evening. This hope is quickly dashed when Aki pulls the shirt over her head to stand in the lamplight wearing nothing but a pair of red bikini panties. Although Aki's tiny, upturned breasts are hardly bigger than wasp stings, Alec is relieved to feel desire's happy lift. Maybe this won't be so difficult after all, he thinks as he pushes back the blanket and motions for Aki to lie down beside him. When she does he spoons his long body around her tiny, slim one, as he murmurs, "Take a deep breath and relax against me for a minute." With physical contact coming as a relief after so many mental gymnastics, Alec now hopes maybe cuddling will be all Aki needs from the evening.

But as she begins to press her buttocks against his groin Alec finally accepts that this determined little woman has more on her mind. As he thinks guiltily of Tamiko, and hopes she'll somehow understand, he nevertheless finds himself pushing back, his tentative erection now coming to full salute. With sex now both inevitable, and if he's honest, something he's begun to desire, Alec reaches a hand between Aki's thighs to find that her remarkably full lips are as open as they are wet. Even though it's an unconventional approach to a first tryst, he lifts Aki's slim top leg and enters her very slowly from behind. When almost immediately she begins to emit short, high-pitched noises, Alec is relieved that things seem to be on a positive path.

A few minutes later with Aki now on top, Alec grabs her ribs with his large hands, allowing his thumbs to extend under her tiny breasts. Lifting his head, Alec then nibbles first one, and then the other of Aki's erect brown nipples. "Oh my god, please Alec, do that harder," Aki murmurs as she leans forward, grabs his upper arms and begins to ride his cock in such a frenzy Alec can only think of the 110-volt electric motor he once plugged into a 220-volt socket. With the thought of trying to slow Aki enough so they can establish a shared rhythm, Alec shifts his grip to her shoulders only to realize to his huge surprise that she has already begun to climax. And not just two gasps and a sigh, but the full throbbing, extended Monty, which quickly works to reawaken Alec's desire. Pounding upwards now in search of his own release, he is on the brink of coming when Aki, finally spent, collapses on his chest. Understanding that the evening's purpose has been achieved, Alec relaxes as he gently cradles her.

Later as Alec drifts off to sleep, Aki kisses him on the lips for the first and only time as she says, "Thank you." In the morning when Alec awakes, Aki's gone. On the coffee table he finds a note:

Alec—I won't even try to put into words the gratitude my heart feels for your kindness. XOXO, Aki

. . . . .

As soon as Tom Obanta leaves, Tamiko calls Mary McCarthy. "I was about to text you," Mary says by way of answering. "If you can keep your lips sealed around Jed and the others, I think Ben is going to okay your request to leave town after Thursday's shoot. He will inevitably want to reshoot bits and pieces of your scenes, but I'm pushing him to schedule that for after Christmas, in which case you'll have five free days before we light back up on Boxing Day. But this isn't quite a done deal, so hold off on your arrangements until I confirm."

"Fabulous. Suppose I want to fly to Japan for a few days. Could I somehow get some of my pay to buy the ticket?" Tamiko asks, in a rush, half-expecting Mary to quiz her.

Instead the older woman replies matter-of-factly, "Since miles won't work a couple of days before Christmas, how about we charge your trip to Ben's business card and leave the reimbursement details until later. But if you don't mind me being a tad personal, the guy you're willing to fly half-way around the world to see better deserve you."

With the set again out-of-bounds to her on Wednesday, Tamiko hangs around the cottage, occasionally swimming a few impatient laps. Just before noon Mary finally texts to confirm that Tamiko won't be needed from late Thursday afternoon until December 26th. Yet, with a sixteen-hour time difference between Los Angeles and Tokyo, Tamiko schools herself to wait to FaceTime Alec, reasoning that he's sure to be up by 8:00 a.m. Tokyo time. After a sixth unanswered ring, she is about to give up when Lec appears saying, "I love you Tamiko O'Shea Gashkin."

"I love you more Lec Burns."

"I was worried you'd hang up," Alec says. "Things tend to get buried here in my tiny apartment and my phone was down in the Pleistocene layer. But, hey, it's just so great to see you! I can't believe we don't do this every day."

"Hopefully this is our new start, since I'm ready to be over everything on my end that has been keeping us at arm's length. And to celebrate, I've planned a huge surprise for you."

"I'm all ears as the elephant said to the giraffe."

"Great. But, before I hop on a plane to spend Christmas in Tokyo, I need to make sure you haven't hooked up with another exotic Asian female," Tamiko says jokingly. Then, seeing Alec's look of awkward surprise, Tamiko's heart is slammed by a locomotive of dread. "Oh my god, Lec, seriously?" she eventually protests when Alec's extended silence becomes its own answer.

Still at a loss to explain what he regards as his "mostly honorable one night tryst," Alec finally stammers, "Tamiko, I really do love you so just give me a minute to explain about Aki..."

"Goddamnit Lec, it will take a lot longer than that," Tamiko replies angrily, as it dawns on her what Mayumi's "favor" request email was about. "I mean, really Lec, was it that goddamn hard for you to go two weeks without screwing someone new? No need to answer since one thing is sure, swallows will fly to Mars before I come to Tokyo."

"Tamiko, will you please listen? It's seriously not what you think,"

Alec asks urgently, even as he sees his screen go blank. Knowing he needs to hustle to meet Charlie at Tokyo Station, he quickly composes an email.

Tamiko—Please, please hold onto two thoughts. I love you truly and true love conquers all. Never doubt either. Also never doubt that we'll be together soon. Since I'm already late to meet Charlie to take a bullet train across Japan (Japanese trains are never late), I don't have time to explain the context and background of what went down with Aki, except to say she's not my girlfriend now, or ever (truly). Because Mayumi really did engineer the whole embarrassing episode I'm asking her to explain as quickly as possible. When she does, I hope you'll understand how and why I was blindsided.

Really, Tamiko, nothing happened with Aki that subtracts even an ounce from my love for you.

XXX, Lec

. . . . .

Immediately after ending her call with Lec, Tamiko sends two texts. The first to Mary McCarthy says,

No Japan after all, but a mega hug for offering to help.

Next Tamiko texts Tom Obanta, *Since it turns out I'll have a bunch of free time over at least the next week, I'm saying yes to the writing/consulting deal with Stanley Greene.*

Now at an angry loss, Tamiko stands at the center of the cottage's living room, not sure whether to cry, smash something or go outside and swim yet more laps. Too mad to cry, and too well brought up to damage Ben's things, she's reaching for her Speedo as the phone sounds. "What?" she shouts, without checking to see who is calling.

"Sweetie, it's me."

"Mom? Sorry, I'm so pissed I…"

"Obviously," Amy interrupts, "I'm calling to be sure you have Christmas plans, but maybe this isn't the right time."

"Oh Mom, I decided you were right about going for it with Lec, so I called him to say I would fly to Tokyo for the holiday. But, almost before I could tell him, I discovered he has still another girlfriend."

"Really? Lec? Already? I don't believe…"

"It's like, when I jokingly asked if he had any new Japanese lovers, he didn't deny it. And then he tried to apologize about his relationship with Aki, this friend of Mayumi's who's tutoring him in Japanese."

"Are you positive? What exactly did Lec say?"

"I ended the call when he was still kind of stuttering. But he did email me a few minutes later more or less admitting he screwed Aki, but also trying to claim she isn't his girlfriend and that Mayumi will somehow explain. But seriously Mom, I thought this would be our big chance to get back together and now…"

"Since you said you weren't coming home I agreed to go to Illinois with Ed to visit his parents. But let me cancel that and we can…"

"No way, Mom. No possible way," Tamiko interrupts. "I'm okay-ish really, and even if that's an exaggeration, I need to do this on my own. When I insisted to be treated like an adult I meant it. Sometimes adults are pissed off, sad or lonely, right? And, besides, Derrick and Clemmie will be back from Amherst tomorrow so I'll have buds to watch my back. And then there's Jed and Mary and…"

"Can I share an opinion you may not like?" Amy interrupts.

"Sure."

"Lec might already be there with you in L.A. if Jed wasn't so literally featured in all your emails."

"Jed isn't my boyfriend, or anything remotely close," Tamiko insists, even as she wonders if her last four words are altogether accurate.

"I guess it could be a crazy coincidence that in your last group email you included a picture of the two of you standing so close a blade of grass couldn't sprout between you. If I were Lec I might…"

"Even if that's true, I don't see that gives him a pass to screw his language tutor. But, listen Mom, have fun in Illinois, or at least as much fun as you can with Ed's parents. And worry not, your favorite daughter will be home for New Year's with a smile on her face."

"Promise?"

"Cross my heart."

. . . . .

Instead of her damp Speedo, Tamiko puts on shorts and runs a couple of miles, occasionally breaking into a sprint as if trying to outrun her feelings of angry disappointment. But as dusk begins to take hold she worries she may lose her way on the Palisades' winding streets, so reverses her steps back to Ben's, where she hops into the pool to pound out thirty laps. At ten to six, finally feeling her agitation begin to ease, Tamiko climbs out of the pool and texts Jed.

Are you done for the day? If the answer is yes, can I maybe come over for another potato, and whatever…

A minute later when her phone sounds, Tamiko answers, "Possibly that was a little forward of me, huh?"

"Forward, or not, dinner will have to wait for another evening. I'm heading out to a charity gala where I promised to say a few words, not to mention the fact that you and I are both filming early tomorrow," Jed replies, in a tone so uncharacteristically flat that Tamiko momentarily forgets her own troubles.

"Everything good? You sound a little down."

"You beat me to the punch with that question, but you're right, I've been feeling a little off all day, and then there's my friend Alicia. Since she hadn't responded to my last two emails I called to say I missed her and looked forward to sharing quality time when she gets back."

"Will that be soon?" Tamiko asks, even as she mentally kicks herself for hoping the answer is no.

"It turns out that Alicia has been trying to work up the courage to tell me she's decided to move to Louisville permanently to be near her mom."

"Things can still work out. I mean, like, you can afford your own plane, right?"

"She also told me she'd reconnected with a guy she'd dated in high school. So, to make a long story short, I've been replaced by a dentist."

"Bummer! Seriously, Jed, I'm sorry," Tamiko says, forgetting her own romantic worries as she identifies with Jed's.

"Yup, it turns out Alicia's decided that dating a celebrity is too high maintenance for a shy, single mom from Kentucky who also, as it turns out, needs a root canal."

"Gallows humor aside, I hope I don't piss you off by saying I understand her point of view."

"If *2+2* is a hit, I'm afraid your celebrity status will be a *fait accompli*, at least for a while. So what's up with you? Or, more to the point, what's happened to cause you to stop worrying about eating spuds with this elderly dude?"

"So, it's like, Jed, I got this crazy idea to fly to Japan for Christmas to try to get back with my boyfriend, Lec. Or, I guess, maybe he really is my ex-boyfriend now. Anyway, when I FaceTimed him with the news, I discovered he's been screwing the girl who's tutoring him in Japanese."

"I hate to sound like an echo, but—bummer! Seriously. So, will you go home to Berkeley for Christmas instead?"

"Mom and Ed are going to Illinois to visit his parents, so I'm thinking maybe I'll hang here. What about you?"

"I'm off to Arizona to see Allison as soon as Ben finishes with me Sunday. But how about I cook you dinner *mañana*? Same deal with Juan picking you up at six-thirty and me driving you back early-ish. Also, I just talked to Allison who has finished the third draft of her essay, but is shy about forwarding it to you."

"Should I reach out?"

"Wait until tomorrow. She promised me she'd email it to you as soon as she knocks out a fourth draft. And, by the way Tamiko, try not to show me up on the set tomorrow."

"Ha."

. . . . .

Half an hour later, as Tamiko tries to cope with her feeling of abandonment and summon enough energy to throw a salad together, she hears a tap on her door. Peeking through the spy hole she almost shouts, "Clemmie, you're here!" as she throws it open. "Oh my god, I really do need the biggest hug. It seems like six months since I've seen you."

"Dad always claims film stars have an unreal concept of time."

"Don't start, but, hey, where's Derrick?"

"Until yesterday he was going to be in the seat next to mine on Southwest. Then, all of a sudden, he grabbed an Alitalia flight in the opposite direction."

"Whoa, based on my own miserable day, I hope Ericka knows he's coming."

"Advance notice, or not, I'm guessing she'll treat him like crap."

"Charitable, aren't we?" Tamiko replies, surprising herself by grinning.

"I only spent an afternoon with Ericka, but the whole time she was haughty, slash bitchy. It's like, Tamiko, when you and my brother started dating I was so damn happy I even fantasized for a second you might be my sister for life."

"Friend isn't good enough?" Tamiko asks with a laugh.

"Friend is plenty good enough for me. It was Derrick I was rooting for."

"Some things aren't meant to be. I know you're on East Coast time, but is there any chance we can go grab a pizza or something? I've had a pathetic day and I badly need to dump."

"Absolutely. My long-anticipated, but nevertheless fraught, reunion with my old boyfriend Chris is on for tomorrow and I've been hoping you'd be free to hang tonight."

. . . . .

As Alec settles into his first class seat on the Hokuriko Shinkansen for the two-and-a-half-hour journey to Kanazawa, Charlie says, "Our flight was delayed which meant we didn't arrive until past midnight, so forgive me if I close my eyes. But, before I do, Emiko wants me to remind you that you're invited to her family party on Sunday. However, since she also knows the prospect of coping with twenty-five of her curious relatives may not be your cup of cha, I'm also to assure you that any excuse is a good excuse."

"Charlie, when you and Claire got together when I was eight, I was positive you married the coolest woman on the planet. And, of course I wasn't wrong. But now, all these years later, with Emiko you've done it again, so, of course I'll be delighted to be folded into your new family for an evening."

"As you know, I barely survived my overwhelming sadness during the years between Claire's death and my bizarrely magical first date with Emiko. But you're right, I've been surpassingly lucky twice. But what about you? If I remember right, there's an old country song that goes, 'Trying to love two women is like a ball and chain. Sometimes the pleasure ain't worth the strain.'"

"Yo cowboy, I didn't know you had a thing for Nashville."

"Years ago when I bought the house on Nantucket Island I took off the summer to work with the three construction guys I hired to pretty much rebuild it. They all loved country music, so I got an earful of the Oak Ridge Boys. I apologize if I've raked up hot coals."

"No need since I've tossed gasoline on the fire in the person of a third woman, although for what it's worth, I tried my damnedest not to."

"My god Lec, aren't Tamiko and Mayumi more than enough?" Charlie splutters.

Then, after a moment of awkward silence, he adds, "Oops! Sorry for the attitude about something that's not my business. But if you want to talk about it, I can keep my eyes open a little longer."

"I hope that one of these days my being entrapped by my language coach may actually seem funny, but in the meantime I'd prefer to talk about something else. For instance, I know we're going to Kanazawa as part of a high-profile, hush-hush business deal having to do with cutting edge medical technology, but of course I'd like to know more."

"I can't reveal details even to you, but in overview, Sato Company has come up with an imaging device that uses an unexpected, but brilliant, technology to see into genes. Suffice it to say, when it comes to imaging DNA, it's enough better than anything on the market that I doubt there's a hospital lab, or medical research institution in the world that won't want one."

"Sounds exciting, not to mention highly profitable, but where does Burns-Short come in?" Alec asks, as he again thinks that after grad school, playing a key role like his uncle's might be an excellent career choice.

"It's no secret that Sato has a huge business decision to make. Manufacture and sell the device worldwide on their own, or license it to others in at least some big markets like China, India and perhaps even North America."

"Assuming Sato controls the patents, why would they want to share profits with others when they're excellent manufacturers themselves?"

"A question a goodly number of Sato executives ask. And it may turn out they'll decide to go it alone."

"From your skeptical tone, I'm guessing you don't think that's the best decision?"

"Whenever a truly unique scientific breakthrough explodes on the scene, you can be sure loads of folks including patent trolls, competing corporations, and sometimes even governments, will claim they invented the underlying technology. The result is that unpredictable patent lawsuits typically sprout like weeds after a spring rain."

"Got it," Alec says, now so interested he forgets his personal worries. "But why would licensing their imaging gizmo help Sato avoid these problems?"

"Suppose a Chinese company with deep government connections sues Sato claiming it invented key aspects of the imaging technology five years ago?"

"Even assuming the Chinese company's claim is bogus, I'm guessing things could get nasty in Chinese courts."

"Exactly. Now assume Sato partnered with one of the largest and best connected medical device outfits in China?"

"The problem either goes away, or becomes a lot less scary with the result that the imaging machine gets to market quickly and profits roll in," Alec guesses. "However, I assume this also means Sato's profits would be substantially reduced by the Chinese partner's share. But would Sato face the same issues in American, or E.U. courts?"

"Maybe not, but since patent trolls are everywhere, and lawsuits often unpredictable, you can't take anything for granted."

"So you think Sato should sign up partners everywhere outside of Japan?"

"In China and India, definitely. In the E.U., U.K. and North America, only if they can negotiate extremely favorable terms, which might even be possible given the value of their unique technology."

"Why not advise Sato…"

"Sorry Alec, I simply can't say more."

. . . . .

Thursday morning when Tamiko encounters Jed on the way to her dressing room she has to school herself not to open her arms to give him a hug. Surprised by her own neediness, she limits herself to a smile and mini-wave. Half an hour later, dressed as Jennifer in a polished version of what Tamiko would have worn on a typical Amherst morning, she joins him on set. Their task is to film *2+2*'s last scene, which kicks off when Jennifer and Chad meet by accident outside of Jennifer's mom's house in Malibu. Location shots of the neighborhood and street will be added later.

From the first things go badly. No sooner have Jennifer and Chad exchanged tentative hellos than Ben calls a halt, saying, "What's up with the coy expectation? As I hope you know, this isn't the runup to a romance." Suspecting Ben is exaggerating to make a point, Tamiko is nonetheless taken aback. Has Ben been reading her fantasies?

"Tamiko, when this scene begins," Ben emphasizes, "please remember that Jennifer's one goal is to hop into an Uber and get to the airport as soon as possible. In this context she sees Chad's appearance on the street as an unwelcome distraction. Also, Tamiko, let me remind you that your cue, which, in case you're in doubt, is printed in parentheses in your script, tells you it's not until line eight that Jennifer relaxes enough to glance up from her shoes to engage the man who, after all, has been screwing her mom. Got it? I hope so. Let's go again."

No sooner do they begin then Ben again yells "*Cut!* TA•MI•KO," he almost shouts, emphasizing each syllable of her name, "Get a grip. When Jed tentatively suggests that you two sit on the steps to talk for a minute, Jennifer's response is to cast her eyes around like a scared mouse cornered by a hungry coyote, not to look coyly enigmatic."

After a third attempt to get the scene right still fails to satisfy, Ben says, "This may be a little unconventional, but I want both of you to go back to your dressing rooms and take a cold shower. And, in case you're in doubt, I mean that literally. No hot water, period. We'll reconvene in twenty minutes. And don't worry if you mess up your makeup, since the more ragged you look, assuming that's possible for either of you, the better."

"Seriously, a cold shower? C'mon, this isn't high school," Jed mutters, his irritation flaring to the point that Tamiko thinks he may refuse.

"Mr. Streeter," Ben says, letting his annoyance match Jed's, "I understand you plan to be a film director. Assuming I'm right, I wonder if you'll appreciate it if your actors, even the big deal ones, occasionally do what you request?"

· · · · ·

Back on the set a few minutes later Tamiko really does feel drained, as if the cold water has knocked the energy out of her. Seeing that Jed also looks enervated, she realizes Ben knows exactly what he's doing.

"Places everyone," Ben says, "Tamiko, please remember, just seventy-two hours have passed since Jennifer burst in on her mom's foursome and that in the meantime she and Virginia have done nothing but pile one angry misunderstanding on top of another. So, when the scene starts, your job is to inhabit the body of an unhappy young woman hoping to escape back to Northern California before her mom shows up to protest. And,

Jed, please remember that Chad, who a few days ago set out to enjoy a recreational screw, now has to cope with the fact that his marriage is likely kaput because his wife Melanie has admitted she prefers women. True, Chad has a crush on Virginia, but she's still married to Toby and even if she leaves him, Chad has no idea if the two of them have a future."

Ninety minutes later, when Ben says, "Cut," he adds, "much better you two. If I had to, I'd print the last take with half a smile. But since I know you both have it in you to make me grin from ear to ear, let's go again from line eight. Tamiko, this is where Jennifer stops examining her sandals to turn slightly toward Chad as it dawns on her that he's a real person who is as muddled as she is. And Jed, this is also the moment when it begins to occur to Chad that Jennifer is more than a self-absorbed college kid whose untimely homecoming interrupted his four-way. Okay, places everyone and stand by."

. . . . .

At 4:00 when Ben finally announces a wrap, Tamiko speeds to her dressing room for a much-needed pee. Then, as she changes into her own clothes, her phone pings with an arriving text.

It was a pleasure to share a bench with you even after a cold shower, but reluctantly I need to cancel dinner since I really do feel crap—the same bug I've been struggling with for the last few days. But nothing keeps me down long so let's try again tomorrow evening.

Having thought that it was his acting skill that had made Jed seem so wan the last few hours, Tamiko quickly responds, *No problema. Feel better. I'm meeting with Stanley Green early-ish* mañana *on the streaming project I told you about so it won't hurt to bang out a few ideas tonight.*

. . . . .

With Clementine off to find out whether her high school boyfriend still glitters, and Mary out with her book group, Tamiko boils spaghetti and slathers it with way too much garlic and butter. Just as she opens her laptop to outline what a college-centered series might look like, her iPhone begins to chirp. "How's your makeover going?" she answers with delight when she sees that it's Ruth calling.

"I'm kind of stuck at the eleven-pound plateau. My goal is to lose nine more, but holidays are a tough time to cancel sugar and butter."

"Holding pattern until New Year's. Then popcorn and grapefruit until MLK Day."

"Ugh!"

"When my mom feels plump she only eats from noon until seven p.m. She swears that if she fasts for the rest of the time she can eat whatever she wants during her magic seven hours."

"Almost any diet can work for people like Amy, who look like they did when they were twenty and freak when they gain eighteen ounces."

"There's that."

"I have an early holiday present for you. It's a flight to Oakland Sunday afternoon, returning on the twenty-sixth. But, it comes with a string attached since I expect you to help me with Christmas dinner."

"Really, Ruth, you don't…"

"Just say yes, or I'll come down and twist your ear."

"No need, I'd love to come, but how did you know I'm…"

"I ran into Amy at Monterey Market," Ruth interrupts. "She told me that your Japan trip went sideways."

"Crashed and splattered like when the Chicxulub asteroid hit the Yucatan and wiped out the dinosaurs."

"That dramatic?" Ruth asks kindly.

"Well, minus the dinosaurs, but pretty much."

"Do you want to talk about it?"

"Let's save it until I see you. I have a dinner date with Jed Streeter tomorrow and I'm determined to put Lec out of my mind in the meantime."

"Is Streeter's grin as devastating up close?"

"Even better, because the closer you get, the easier it is to see that he's a sweet dude."

"Since it would be disingenuous to say 'don't do anything I wouldn't do,' how about 'eyes wide open'?"

"I promise not to blink."

"That's the opposite of what I meant, as I'm sure you know."

· · · · ·

Alec is pleased to find that he understands a surprising amount of Japanese during the ceremonial meet and greet at Sato's ultra-modern Kanazawa headquarters. When Charlie moves on to a private tête-á-tête with top executives, Alec finally has time to email Mayumi. Briefly outlining what went down with Aki, as well as his ill-fated FaceTime conversation with Tamiko, he implores Mayumi to contact Tamiko to explain the context. He concludes with, "So, although I need to take responsibility for my actions, you need to take responsibility for putting me in position to be ambushed."

· · · · ·

On her way to Stanley Greene's house in L.A.'s upscale Holmby Hills Friday morning, Tamiko receives a text from Jed. *Ran five miles this a.m. and feel like I could take on Usain Bolt. If tonight is still good, Juan will pick you up at 6:30.*

Arriving at Greene's large Tudor house, Tamiko is met by a tall, toned Black woman in her mid-thirties who could be the model for a Pilates studio. "I'm Amelia Jackson," she says with a grin, "the lone associate in Stanley Greene and Associates. But since both you and Stan's nephew Mal are on the payroll today, maybe, for once we'll live up to the *s*. For the record, Stan and I used to share a real office in Century City, but dropped it when we realized how much we both gagged at the thought of going there. Now we work from our homes except when we're in production. Since I have twins in fourth grade, I love the flexibility."

After they pass through the house to a professional work space in a small building out back, Greene introduces his nephew and asks Tamiko if she'd like a coffee.

"Better say yes quick," Amelia says, with a chuckle. "Stan attended a seminar on how to treat women in the workplace last week, but I'm guessing he dozed through most of it."

Pretty sure that Greene, who is already leaning back in his chair, expects her to decline, Tamiko instead says, "Coffee with a hint of milk would be great, Stan, and maybe one of those yummy-looking chocolate croissants next to the carafe." Then, seeing from Greene's irritated expression that his offer was indeed for show, Tamiko adds, "Since I'm all for gender reciprocity, next time will be my turn to fetch and carry."

Greene begins the meeting with a broad brush concept for what sounds to Tamiko like a garden variety melodrama set on a college campus in large part so that it can be wallpapered with half-clothed young bodies. When no one comments, she asks, "Stan, would it help us get down to specifics if I show you what I came up with last night?" Then, as Tamiko dovetails her laptop with the conference room's big screen, she adds, "As you see, I created nine principal characters, all of whom are first-year dorm mates with the exception of Eli, the junior student resident whose job is to enforce a measure of order. Beneath the dotted line you'll see that I added several second-tier characters who appear occasionally, but are still part of the core cast—Anna's eventual older boyfriend, the student director of Debra's play, an assistant dean of students and a hot female English professor. Also, since I got tired of leaving a blank every time I came to our college's name, I called it Adams and located it in Abigail, Massachusetts."

"Really Tamiko, you did this all last night?" Amelia asks, as she clicks on Adaora Kaffo's brief bio.

Having just said so, Tamiko sits quietly as the others read. In a kind of staccato shorthand it says,

ADAORA KAFFO: Very Black, very gorgeous, very smart and more than a little pampered. Born in Nigeria, Adaora attended a posh secondary school in London, where her dad is Cultural Attache at the Nigerian embassy. She views herself as a citizen of a post-racial world—African, Asian, Caucasian or whatever, are merely broad ethnic descriptors, since all humans are members of the same race with minor genetic differences. Adaora is less offended by what she regards as America's predictably

*pervasive racism than she is by the microaggression against non-whites
she encounters at supposedly woke Adams. But as hypersensitive as Adaora
occasionally is, she's also charismatic, funny, generous and vulnerable.*

"Wow," Amelia says, "That girl is so alive she almost leaps off the page. This is a fabulous start, isn't it, Stan?"

"Impressive, but listen, while you go over the rest, I need to step out to make a few longish calls and do a Zoom thing," Greene says, getting to his feet and heading to the door. "Amelia, why don't I check in with you for a quick update this afternoon?"

"Since it's Friday, his first call will be the Riviera Country Club to confirm his tee time," Amelia says with a grin. Then, seeing Tamiko's puzzled look, she adds, "Stan is famously bored and twitchy at the start of projects, but when he gets engaged he'll sweat every word and gesture. Based on working with him on three successful series in a row, I can assure you that in addition to often being a royal pain, he really does have the secret sauce. In the meantime, it's my job to move things along."

"Sure," Tamiko replies. "But, it's like, I have no clue whether Stan likes anything I've done so far. I mean, to go forward I need feedback, right?"

"You already have it. If Stan thought Adaora was a bust, he'd be pouring over the rest of your characters to see if there's a smidge of hope. Leaving the details to me at this stage means he's impressed."

"What about me?" Mal asks, stroking the sparse, black beard that Tamiko guesses he's trying to grow in an unsuccessful effort to make his round pink face look less like a fifteen-year-old's.

"I don't get involved in family politics," Amelia abruptly replies. Then, as if she realizes this sounds unkind, she adds more gently, "As Tamiko notes on page two of her presentation, many of your characters and plot ideas seem more suited to a large midwestern university with a Greek social system. Since we are talking about a small brainiac New England college without fraternities or sororities, at the very least you'll need to recast them. But why don't you two compare ideas by the pool for a bit while I review the rest of Tamiko's character profiles?"

. . . . .

"Basically, Uncle Stan thinks I'm a duffs," Mal says, as he slides a white rattan chair from under a blue umbrella to sit next to Tamiko in the intermittent sun of the mid-sixtyish morning. "Letting me help with the series is a favor to my dad, who hopes if I have something to do I won't end up back in rehab. But it's not working since I haven't come up with an idea either he or Amelia has liked."

"What's your approach?"

"I spent a week watching every college movie I could find, going all the way back to *Knute Rockne All-American* in nineteen forty and *The Male Animal* with Henry Fonda and Olivia de Havilland a couple of years later."

"Interesting. I bet you have some good thoughts on how to riff off their most iconic scenes. But what about your own experience?"

"I spent less than two years at a school in Idaho nobody would have heard of save for football. Still, until I got too enthusiastic about Ecstasy, Boise State was an okay fit for me. But it's obviously not a place you would confuse with the Ivy League."

"Who was the most unusual person you met up there?"

"Undoubtedly, Walter W. Walters, this skinny know-it-all who graduated from a tiny high school in Montana with maybe eighty-six students in all four grades. Somehow being valedictorian of his class of nineteen convinced Walter he was the brightest kid at State. To prove it, for the first six weeks his hand was perpetually waving in the air, often before the professor finished her question. But when midterm grades came out, Mr. Motor Mouth never spoke again until he disappeared at the end of the term."

As Mal rattles on about Walter's social ineptitude, Tamiko takes notes on her laptop. "Enough," she finally interrupts. "Since elite, highly selective colleges are dripping with self-impressed windbags, I'm sure we can make Walter work. I particularly like the bit where the one girl who's willing to hook up with him backs off in disgust when he struggles to put on two condoms. And whatever we come up with, you'll get full credit."

"Wow! Thanks Tamiko, and here I'd convinced myself you were going to be the ballbreaker who would finish ruining my life. But seriously, I don't understand why you're helping me?"

"Your uncle is paying me way too much for a fifty-hour sprint, but you have to deal with him for the rest of your life."

. . . . .

With Charlie off at another confidential Sato meeting, Alec works out at the gym Friday morning as he continues to fret that he's heard nothing from Mayumi despite having followed his first urgent email with three more. If she hasn't responded by the time he gets back to Tokyo that evening he'll have to do his best to explain to Tamiko what came down with Aki. In the meantime, Alec's received Tamiko's third group email describing in hilarious detail her long fraught Thursday on set with Jed Streeter, including several photos of the two of them in earnest conversation, which Alec guesses are outtakes from the film. In addition, there is a third, more relaxed shot of Tamiko and Jed laughing, which would be innocent enough except that Tamiko has her hand on Jed's shoulder. Even as Alec tries to tamp down his jealousy, he has to admit they look brilliant together.

. . . . .

Early Friday evening, after the Shinkansen has whisked him and Charlie back from Kanazawa at 180 miles per hour, Alec again checks to see that Mayumi has not replied. Thoroughly annoyed, he attempts to compose an email to Tamiko that explains, but doesn't excuse, how he ended up in bed with Aki. After erasing three drafts, Alec is saved from sweating out a fourth when Charlie texts that he and Emiko will pick him up in fifteen minutes for her family party. With time now too short to possibly get his message right, Alec types, "*T., never doubt that I love you.*" Then, as he tries to frame a few more reassuring words, he is interrupted by the ding of an email.

alec—i'm truly sorry for being such a meddling idiot! and i know that my going hill-walking and ignoring the internet for the last three days has made things worse. What must tamiko think? i'm composing an email to her this instant to do my best to explain my part in encouraging aki to proposition you. will either of you ever forgive me? more as soon as i begin trying to repair things. m.

Relieved that Tamiko will finally hear from Mayumi, Alec decides to save his email for later. Then, putting on the midnight blue kimono he bought in Kanazawa for Emiko's party, he heads downstairs to wait for Charlie.

. . . . .

With Friday afternoon to herself, Tamiko curls up on the couch to sketch ideas for the pilot episode of what she and Amelia now, only half-jokingly, call *Brainy Brats in Heat*. But before Tamiko can open her laptop, Amelia is on the phone saying, "Tamiko, I know I'm repeating myself but, I'm truly impressed by the characters you've invented. I especially love Daphne, the Jesus-freak Korean-American math genius who is convinced she's a nymphomaniac because she got to third base with an anonymous boy in a bathroom on an Amtrak train."

"Religion plus sex equals weirdly fascinating," Tamiko replies with a laugh.

"Don't get me started on my Aunt Lorna. But, I'm calling because I don't understand why you included Nicholas, who is two years older than the rest and only in the dorm because the college is paying him to be a low-level monitor."

"Like a corporal in an army platoon, the student resident is part of the dorm group, but also enough apart to allow for unique interactions. For instance, in the pilot, which I'm outlining as we speak, Nick acts as a social catalyst. That is, after the last clingy parent has finally been chased off, he gathers all thirty first-years in the dorm's common area and initiates one of those embarrassing get-to-know-you games. And, in later episodes, Nick acts as an informal counselor to the needier kids, and dorm policeman when activities like beer pong get out of hand. And I'm also thinking he might eventually become romantically involved with one of the first-years, a serious no-no since if he's busted he'll lose his job, which is tied to his Adams scholarship."

"Got it. Thanks. Since I commuted to UCLA and have barely put my nose in a dorm, I'll definitely trust your instincts. Tell me your ideas for the rest of the pilot."

· · · · ·

At 5:00 Tamiko's phone pings with a text from Jed. *How about Juan picks you up at 6:00 instead of 6:30?*

All good, Tamiko replies, hoping this means Jed is at least half as excited about their evening as she is. Then, as she heads to her closet, her phone sounds again.

Just in case you're wondering, Fridays are cowboy mellow over here.

After slipping into the skinny black jeans she knows flatter her long legs, Tamiko debates between a black cowboy shirt and a clingy green silk top with a scooped neck that Mary liberated from the set when Ben nixed it as too racy for Jennifer. Reasoning that even the mellowest cowgirl likes to show a little flesh on Friday night, she opts for the silk before getting down to the serious work of trying to tame her swimmer's tangle of long hair.

· · · · ·

"For your girls," Tamiko says as she hands Juan a package as she climbs into the Ford at precisely six o'clock. "It's not much, just the kind of pink and purple mouse ears I loved when I was six."

"Really? *Gracias*, I'm sure they'll love them."

"I appreciate your driving me when I know you'd rather be home with your family."

"No thanks needed. Jed treats me generously."

"He's sweet, isn't he? I mean, how special for me to come to L.A.

without a clue and find a mentor in one of the most famous dudes in town."

"Yes, Jed's a good guy and has proven to be a real friend to me and my family," Juan immediately replies. Then, after a long pause he adds, "But, of course you should look out for yourself."

. . . . .

Dressed in jeans, boots and a black cowboy shirt with embroidered red roses and mother-of-pearl snaps that hugs his lean frame, Jed stands in the drive when Juan pulls up. Giving Tamiko a fist bump instead of the hug she expects, he says, "That's it for today, Juan." Then, turning to Tamiko he adds, "I'll drive you back after supper."

Pretty sure returning to Ben's early is not on her preferred agenda, Tamiko nevertheless nods before following Jed through the house and into the now familiar bright kitchen. "I didn't know cowboys drink French champagne?" she says when she sees a bottle of Moët Chandon and two flutes on the kitchen table.

"Or that cowgirls wear slinky silk tops," Jed replies, his poker face giving way to his signature crooked grin. Then, taking a step towards Tamiko he takes both her hands, but holds her at arm's length as he says, "I guess this is where we talk."

"Only if you need to," Tamiko replies, as she steps so close to Jed she knows he'll either have to step back or kiss her.

"An honest conversation is absolutely required," Jed replies as he both drops her hands and moves to the opposite side of the kitchen's black granite island. "Tamiko, as much as I'm attracted to you I need to remind us both that, given our age and experience differences, getting romantically involved isn't likely to produce joy for either of us."

"But hasn't that already happened?" Tamiko asks. "The attraction part, I mean."

"I won't deny that I have a crush on you. But, as I'm sure you know, fantasizing about something and actually doing it, are far different animals."

"Age isn't just chronological," Tamiko replies. "Starting in elementary school I've been promoted out of every grade I've been in to the point that I started taking community college classes when I was in middle school. Even now as a first-year at Amherst, I've been doing a grad stats course at UMass."

"Nice try. But sadly, neither your being precociously brilliant, nor looking like you could be in your twenties, makes you five minutes older."

"I call foul," Tamiko says, genuinely annoyed. "My being ahead of myself both academically and athletically means I've always hung with older kids. True, for years I was kind of an awkwardly precocious freak, but I've learned to fit in. Also last year, when I worked as an apprentice editor at Bay Books, folks accepted me as a peer when they saw I could do the work. And, fortunately, Lec Burns, my last year's boyfriend who was twenty-two when we met, suspended his conviction that I was too young and we had a brilliant year together."

"Whoa, Nelly! If I apologize for treating you like a kid will you quit acting like you're arguing to a jury?"

"Absolutely," Tamiko replies. "On the condition you also answer two simple questions."

"Go for it."

"How many shirts do you own?"

"Quite a few obviously, but I don't..."

"How many are embroidered with red flowers and have mother-of-pearl snaps?" Tamiko interrupts.

"Only this one."

"Jed, is it lost on you that while clothes don't make the man, they can seriously reveal his intentions?"

"I hope I don't hate myself in the morning," Jed says, fingering one of the shiny snaps as he steps around the kitchen island and wraps his long arms loosely around Tamiko's back. After a long minute during which their eyes meet and then do their best to merge, Tamiko clears her throat and says, "I'm gonna guess this is where you're supposed to kiss the cowgirl." Lips still entangled, having somehow negotiated a long hallway,

Tamiko and Jed fall onto his big bed.

Disengaging for an instant, Tamiko says, "Sorry to be so hyper, but I…"

"No need to apologize since I feel the same way. But, I'm pretty sure the next steps will go easier if we slow down long enough to pull off each other's jeans," Jed adds with a chuckle.

"Getting naked break," Tamiko murmurs as she reaches for Jed's silver belt buckle.

With clothing quickly in a wedge on the floor, Jed leans in for a long slow kiss as he simultaneously produces a condom.

"Since I'm on birth control pills, let's skip that," Tamiko says as she pushes Jed's hand away.

"Okay, then since I've been a monk since my last STD scan, how can I make you happy?"

"I'm guessing I'm in an expert's hands," Tamiko replies with a laugh. Then grasping Jed's erect cock she adds, "Like you, obviously, I'm way past the need to be warmed up."

A few seconds later with Jed now extended eagerly inside her, Tamiko feels a surge of intoxicating pleasure as she implores, "C'mon, Cowboy, let's see if we can gallop all the way to Montana."

After Jed leads her on a long, exquisitely sensual journey that finally ends with a shared whoop, Tamiko gradually returns to something like herself. "I sure hope you liked that as much as I did," she murmurs. "My god, Jed, it's like we must have made it all the way to Missoula."

"Or maybe even Bozeman, if I have my Big Sky geography right," Jed replies. "But if you're up for it, I'm hoping we can lope, if not gallop a little further."

"Ready to ride when you are, Big Fella," Tamiko replies as she climbs on top of Jed in her favorite reverse cowgirl posture. Momentarily taken aback when she remembers that the last time she was in this position was with Lec the night before he left for Japan, Tamiko wonders if she should feel guilty. Delighted not to detect even a bit, she reaches down, grabs Jed's cock and guides it home.

Ninety minutes later after a luxurious dip in the Jacuzzi, Tamiko wraps up in a cozy blue robe identical to Jed's. Surely, she reflects, she isn't the first girl to attend one of Jed's Friday night roundups. But, before this insight can dent her euphoric mood, Jed says, "Tamiko, if you're half as blown away at what just happened as I am, then we're in cyclone territory. I just can't begin to tell you how much…"

"No need since I was there too," Tamiko replies, nevertheless delighted to hear him say these words.

"Want to talk about anything?"

"And risk spoiling a perfect moment?"

"More champagne?"

"The truth is I'd prefer pomegranate soda and a lot of food."

"I can fire up the grill and do the whole steak deal. Or we can boil water, drop in some fresh pasta, make a salad and then head back to Montana as pronto-ish as possible. Maybe we can even canter all the way over to the Little Bighorn River for our 'last stand…'"

"As long as you know I firmly believe that Custer had it coming," Tamiko replies with a wink. "How about you do the pasta while I put together a salad? And while we're on a break I want to tell you that I got Allison's essay, which was very decent. Just the same, I called her to make a couple of suggestions, the most important being to hook the reader by opening with her happiest horse moment before following with more mundane biographical details."

"I'm curious, what was it? Her best moment, that is?"

"As it turns out, it wasn't one day, or event. Instead, Allison said she pretty much always feels euphoric when she's mounted on Willow in that last frozen moment before a competition begins. Actually, I can relate since I feel a similar high when I'm standing on the rubber at the start of a softball game, and nothing can happen until I make the first move."

"I know I've told you this a dozen times, but if there is ever anything I can do to thank you for Allison's amazing turnaround, consider it done."

"Well, there's still the Little Bighorn," Tamiko replies with her trademark deep-throated laugh. "But, hey, is that pasta done? If not, I can cheerfully eat it raw."

"Four minutes," Jed replies, glancing at his watch. "In the meantime, I hope you'll tell me a bit more about how you turned into a seventeen-year-old who seems to be going on twenty-five?"

"Somehow it was baked into my DNA, not anything I had much control over. When I was three and a half my dad said that instead of listening to him read my kids' books, I demanded to read to him. He thought I'd memorized them since it was already obvious I had this weird ability to regurgitate almost everything I read, or heard. But when he brought home a new book, *Billy Goat Gruff* and I could read all about the troll under the bridge, he took me to the library. But, what about that pasta. Are you keeping track?"

"Another two minutes, so keep talking."

"The rest is pretty much more of the same. Like I told you, my teachers didn't know what to do with a kid who, by third grade, could read the same books they did. And this was exacerbated by my know-it-all tendencies. My dad, who was both a professor and *Jeopardy* junkie, delighted in having me memorize things like the justices of the Supreme Court, the capitals of every state and the entire list of American presidents. And of course I couldn't resist regurgitating them at school."

"I would have hated to be your teacher."

"A common theme, which is why I kept getting moved up to the point I really did take a community college course when I was in eighth grade. And, because I was big and coordinated, I also got pushed forward in sports. I was mostly okay with this, but sometimes it was awkward, like when I was thirteen and worried about getting my period, but my teammates were obsessed by passing the driver's exam or whether to go all the way with their boyfriends."

"And since I gather you're an only child, I'm guessing your parents treated you like a junior adult at home."

"I suppose, but I also did plenty of kid things until my dad was killed when I was twelve. From then on Mom and I formed a tight bond, which definitely helped us get through the next couple of years."

"When did you turn beautiful?"

"Until I was almost fourteen I was too tall, too boney, and the Asian and Caucasian bits of my face looked like they were at war. Then, to my amazement, my body finally popped out in the right places and my weird face sorted itself into something people started calling exotic."

"And then you met Lec?"

"That was almost two years later. By then, I was mostly doing community college, only taking a couple of courses at Berkeley High so I could stay eligible for sports.

"Surprisingly, although I was six years younger I never felt intimidated around Lec, which I put down mostly to his being a kind dude. My mom was worried about the legal implications of my being a minor and insisted we tell Lec's friends I was nineteen, which pretty soon I came to almost believe. Still, around Lec's housemates, I mostly kept my mouth shut, at least in the beginning."

"No easy task I'm guessing?"

"Don't be a brat. And don't interrupt since I'm about to get to the best part. One evening, Antonia, this way cool twenty-three-year-old genetics grad student from Milan said, 'Tamiko, every time I see you I'm amazed all over again that you're only nineteen. If you said you were five years older, it would be easier to believe.'"

"Ha!" Jed says, as he reaches for a frying pan full of red sauce, intent on dumping it onto a colander of fettuccini.

"It tastes better if you reverse it," Tamiko says, "that is, dump the pasta into the sauce."

"And who did you say is on the Supreme Court these days, Miss Know-it-all?" Jed asks, as he nevertheless does as directed.

. . . . .

First light is barely a glimmer when Tamiko slips out of bed, pads quietly through the house and across the back patio where, with a quick intake of breath, she launches herself into the charcoal gloom. When, seal-like, her head pops up through the black water, she rolls over to float on her back as if somehow last night's otherworldly pleasures have filled her body with helium. But before she can fully embrace her euphoria, Tamiko realizes she's beginning to shiver in the seventy-five-degree water so rolls back over to begin swimming herself warm. Twenty minutes later as she debates whether to go inside to make coffee or knock out another ten laps she hears her name. Looking up, she sees Jed crouching next to the house end of the pool urgently motioning her to swim to him. Not sure what's up, she hesitates. "Tamiko," Jed says insistently, "I'll explain later but for now please do exactly what I say. Swim toward me with your head in the water. When you reach the stairs, wrap the big towel I left on the rail all the way around you as you come out. Don't worry about getting it soaked—just cover up as fast as you can and walk straight into the kitchen keeping your face toward me."

A few minutes later, with Tamiko back in her blue robe, coffee in hand, Jed explains. "Ever since a big Monterey cypress toppled over a year ago, the guy a few hundred yards up the hill can see a good chunk of the pool. Last September, he sold telephoto pictures to a gossip-mongering website showing a couple of well-known women sunbathing topless. Juan's planted a fast-growing tree on the empty spot, but even with regular doses of fertilizer it will take a couple of years to get my privacy back."

"It was still dark when I went out," Tamiko says defensively. "I mean, I'm sorry, but I had…"

"My bad obviously," Jed interrupts, "since you told me you've been pounding out laps at Ben's I should have anticipated that…"

"I had my head in the water while I swam, but I did briefly float face up early on. Since I could still see a couple of stars, it had to be pretty dim. Dawn's only really been happening for, maybe, ten minutes."

"So, even if the bastard was awake and photographing the whole time, chances are he didn't get a good face shot," Jed sums up. "And without that he's got nothing to sell, at least so far."

"So far?" Tamiko asks, pushing a damp strand of hair off her cheek.

"Slimebags often work in packs and split the profits. In short, I'm betting there is already a paparazzi asshole on the way to the front gate. But, more importantly, do you prefer French toast, or a waffle to go with your bacon? I'm good at both, but the waffle topped with fresh raspberries is the house specialty."

"Sold, but like, Jed, what are we going to do?" Tamiko asks anxiously. "If I'm photographed leaving here it won't be hard to put me together with the naked swimmer. And if that happens, the whole world will start calling me Lolita and you Humbert Humbert."

"Take a breath, we're about to have some fun with your extraction. But we'll need help. What's Mary McCarthy's number?"

"Gah! Do you really have to call Mary? I mean, she warned me—both of us—that getting together would…"

"Let me handle her," Jed says, as he takes Tamiko's phone and presses Mary's number. When she answers, he explains their predicament as matter-of-factly as if he was reporting the weather. Ending the call a minute later, he pours batter into a jumbo-sized waffle iron, closes the lid and starts to squeeze oranges.

"I hate being teased, so please, tell me what's going on? And, also, what Mary said?"

"Hold on a second," Jed replies as he answers his vibrating phone. After listening for a minute he says, "Got it, keep me posted if anyone else shows." Then turning to Tamiko he reports, "Juan says there's only one dude in a gray Toyota out front, meaning we should be fine."

"Jed, I'm seriously freaked, so…"

"Freak not. The ever practical Mary will pick up her niece, Diane, who lives in West Hollywood and is about your size, albeit ten years older. But since Diane has dark, short hair, Mary will detour to grab a dark blond wig. A few blocks from here, Diane will crawl under a blanket on the back seat of Mary's Tesla. Twenty minutes after they arrive I'll leave in my pickup with the now bewigged Diane riding shotgun and hopefully Mr. Paparazzi will be on my bumper. Since apparently Diane owns an interior decorating boutique in Santa Monica we'll drop by there to admire fabric swatches. In the meantime, assuming all is clear out front, Juan will give you and Mary a thumbs-up. To be on the safe side, it will be your turn to hide under the blanket. But more to the immediate point, how many pieces of bacon do you want?"

"Six, at a minimum, but, Jed, assuming your plan works, won't it mean that Diane is tagged as your lover?"

"Mary reports she has a devoted husband, two kids, a depraved sense of humor and is always looking for offbeat ways to generate free publicity for her business. But it's unlikely to come to that since no one will pay the paparazzi big bucks for a grainy, indistinct nude photo without a background check. And if they check out Diane they'll find a thirty-five-year-old pillar of the PTA whose body doesn't remotely resemble the one in the picture."

. . . . .

When Mary arrives with her obviously exhilarated niece, Tamiko immediately launches into *mea culpas*. "Tamiko, if you'll just hurry up and turn eighteen, all our lives will be a lot easier," Mary interrupts. "For now, fingers crossed, our little deception goes as planned. And in future if you and Jed want to hang out, please trust me to help you find a much safer location."

"I'm not sure if there will be another time."

"Hmm," Mary says slowly. "From the look on both your faces, please give me leave to doubt that. But, I do hope this is enough of a wake-up call for the two of you to be far more careful. Jed may think he's Mr. Untouchable, but if he's caught *in flagrante delicto* with a minor, he'll find out how wrong he is. And, my dear, if Jed goes down, you'll be tagged as the trashy bimbo who caused his fall."

"No need to exaggerate since I really do get your point," Tamiko replies, her lack of sleep making her sound more irritated than she intends.

"Monica Lewinsky and Bill Clinton happened over twenty years ago."

"Surely, it's not the same."

"You're finally right," Mary snaps, letting her annoyance off its leash. "Jed Streeter is a lot more popular than Bill Clinton ever was, meaning that if he's brought low by an affair with a seventeen-year-old, tens of millions of disappointed women will revile you until the day they die."

. . . . .

The extraction goes so precisely according to Jed's and Mary's plan that Tamiko has time for a much-needed nap before her meeting with Stan and Amelia at 2:00 p.m. To her surprise, Stan has made numerous detailed notes on her character summaries and even invented a compelling new one in the form of a male soccer coach who has trouble keeping his hands off his androgynous goalkeeper. And, the fact that both Stan and Amelia like Walter "Two Condoms" Walters, means that Mal is officially part of the team. Pleased to find that despite Stan's galloping ego, he isn't the buffoon she has taken him for, Tamiko enjoys their creative back and forth.

Late in the afternoon when the four focus on Tamiko's outline for the pilot, Stan says, "Tamiko, your get-to-know-you event at the beginning is a clever way to introduce the key characters. But I don't see how the game you propose achieves lift-off? Apparently, the idea is to have all the new dorm mates stand in a loose circle until one of them kicks things off by making a declarative statement about something they like, or hate. Then the others move closer or farther away depending upon whether or not they agree. Am I right so far?"

"Yes, but of course the point is that after each round the students introduce themselves to whoever they're standing near," Tamiko replies. "For example, I could start things off by saying, 'I love pumpkin spice lattes.' First-years who agree would then move closer to me, while everyone with decent taste would step away."

"Believe it or not, I figured out that much," Stan replies. "My question is why won't this be as boring as the World Championship of Shuffleboard?"

"Even at Boise State we played a version of this," Mal observes, plainly anxious to contribute.

"That's hardly responsive," Stan replies dismissively.

"Stan," Amelia says sharply. "If you'll take a few seconds to read down to round three of Tamiko's outline you'll not only answer your question, but see how far off your shuffleboard comparison is. Because that's when

Jeri, a small red-haired girl says, 'I'm a virgin.' And *bang*, the whole laid-back tenor of the game changes. Is Jeri kidding? Or, is she sincere? No one knows, and more important, at least a third of the first-years are clueless as to how to react. Should they falsely claim to have had sex and join the 'cool' group who immediately slide away from Jeri? Or, by stepping closer to Jeri, should they risk being labeled as nerds forever? And, of course, the longer they hesitate, the more embarrassing their dilemma since everyone understands that when it comes to screwing, 'maybe' doesn't cut it. And the scene only gets more riveting when the deer-in-the-headlights virgins move away from Jeri in a manner that all but shouts they're lying, leaving only plump, pimply Tanner standing next to her. But, just as this scene threatens to turn pathetic, Anna, the leggy beauty from California, joins Jeri and Tanner to cheerfully introduce herself."

"Got it," Stan says. Then, continuing as if he never expressed a doubt, he adds, "Coupled with the shouting match between the Nigerian girl Adaora and Kimberly Lee, her rich southern white roommate rumored to be the great, great grandniece of Robert E., and I think we're off to a good start. Mal, what do you think?"

Stunned that for the first time in his life his uncle has solicited his opinion, Mal appears to be almost as surprised that he has one. "Political squabbles may hook the viewer at first, but they won't be enough to keep Kimberly's and Adaora's relationship interesting over eight or ten episodes. With apologies, Tamiko, it's too much like a *New York Times* profile of political opposites where you're riveted at the start, but turn off the light halfway through. To catch fire, I'd want the audience to pretty quickly pick up on the fact that underneath their surface hostility, the very Black Adaora and the very white Kimberly fantasize about getting their paws on each other. No need to decide now whether this actually happens, just that the audience senses the attraction."

"I love it," Stan says. "But what about the rest of the first-years? To hook the audience at the start, I'm convinced our pilot needs at least a couple of them to get down and dirty. I mean, college kids these days can hardly keep their clothes on, right?"

"Stan, I have no idea whether Tamiko's offended, but you're definitely over the cusp of pissing me off," Amelia snaps. "As you know I don't have a problem with nudity or sex per se, but I'm only working on this project if we treat these kids with a modicum of dignity. And that means they only take their clothes off when, and where, the story honestly demands it, not just when you believe we need to hook male viewers with a dose of soft porn."

Instead of piling on, Tamiko remarks that like for *The Gilmore Girls* a substantial portion of *Class of '24's* audience will be moms and their teenage daughters likely to be offended by too much explicit content. After Amelia nods her agreement and Stan shrugs in what Tamiko guesses is, at best, temporary surrender, Tamiko adds, "But Stan, you might like this idea for a pilot subplot. How about having Daphne, our horny, Jesus-loving Korean American, get up to something farcically embarrassing? For example, she might misinterpret a casual greeting from Matthew, the hunky football star, as a come-on and show up at his dorm room in the middle of the night when Matthew is entertaining Karen, Daphne's roommate. But, more important to the development of our story, we need to put flesh on Anna, the gorgeous Ice Queen every straight guy in the dorm tries for with zero success. If you agree I'll work up these ideas over the next couple of days when I'm in Berkeley and have a draft by Boxing Day."

"Sounds like a possible plan," Stan replies noncommittally. "But, Tamiko, Amelia tells me you've already burned through most of your fifty hours so I wonder if we can double them. Of course this would also mean doubling your compensation."

"Stan, I'm guessing that if I put in a couple more weeks outlining the characters and plot for *Class of '24*, it will be fair for me to get some kind of creative credit. However, since I'm clueless about how that might work, isn't it a good thing I have an agent?"

"Okay, okay, I'll talk to what's his name," Stan says sourly, "but I'm only agreeing to more hours if you'll test for Anna."

"No."

"What do you mean?" Stan demands, his tight lips signaling that he's genuinely taken aback.

"Oops! My apologies, I should have said 'no thank you.'"

"C'mon Tamiko, nobody just starting out in this town turns down a chance at a lead role in a series," Stan says, leaning so far forward Tamiko fears he may fall off his chair. "What are you…"

"Almost nobody," Tamiko interrupts. "But, Stan, since I can't show any skin, you won't want to cast me anyway."

"Are you too prudish to take off your shirt?" Stan demands. Then, after Amelia resonantly clears her throat, he adds, "When the plot absolutely demands it, of course."

"Stan, whether I'm a Puritan, an exhibitionist or halfway in between, is irrelevant since the important thing you need to know is that I'm seventeen and not quite four months."

"You're bullshitting me, right? C'mon, you look at least twenty, probably older. Didn't you say you went to Cal before Amherst?"

"Summer session for two years when I was fifteen and sixteen," Tamiko replies, hoping her revelation that she's a minor will put an end to Stan's fantasy of her being in *Class of '24*.

"But, hang on," Stan says, almost as excitedly as if he's found a gold nugget in the gutter, "if Ben Fine can figure out how to work with you on his borderline X-rated film, I'm sure we can work something out…"

"Stan, give it a rest," Amelia interrupts. "Tamiko said N-O, and let me remind you that, in today's world, that's exactly where the conversation needs to stop."

. . . . .

Back at Ben's a little after six, Tamiko collapses in a comfy chair just as Clemmie barges in on the heels of a perfunctory knock. "Did you forget you're coming out for pizza with my high school homies?"

In a mood to try to walk back her commitment, Tamiko sees the excited look in her friend's eyes and says, "Assuming jeans, a hoodie and my Frye boots work, I'll only need five."

. . . . .

On their way back to Ben's a few hours later, Clemmie breaks into Tamiko's reverie about how pleasant it was to hang with a group of people who don't expect anything of her. "Tamiko, full disclosure, I overheard Mary explaining to Ben what went down with you and Jed Streeter last night. I mean, were you ever going to breathe one word about your night with the world's hunkiest male?" When Tamiko doesn't reply, Clemmie adds, "Really, Tamiko, Jed Streeter has been a friend of Ben's for years and growing up I always had this mini-crush on him. Still, if you don't want to say…"

"Clemmie," Tamiko interrupts, "if I tell you it was one of the most exciting nights of my life, can we leave it there until I've had time to sort out my feelings?"

"Sure," Clemmie replies, not quite disguising her resigned sigh.

"Thanks, you're a real friend."

LATE DECEMBER

A LITTLE AFTER 10:00 A.M. ON SUNDAY, DECEMBER 23RD, Tamiko, shouldering a loaded backpack, leaps over puddles as she sucks in the Bay Area's cool, clear air on her way the few hundred yards from Oakland Airport's Southwest Terminal to BART. Yet, just forty minutes later her buoyant mood begins to leak air on her ride via Lyft, from the North Berkeley BART station to her mom's and Ed's new home on Santa Barbara Road. Since her mom and Ed had sold their old places and moved after Tamiko left for college, this will be both her first night in the new house and her first Christmas alone. And then there are her heart-tugging relationships with Lec and Jed, which are hard to think about, and harder not to. But a few minutes later, her heart again lifts as she steps into the brightly-lit front room complete with a full-sized Christmas tree and a big sign saying, *Welcome Home Tamiko.* Then, as she reaches to touch several of the dear decorations she has bonded with over the years, Tamiko spots a note taped to the top of an electronic gizmo on the table that says, *PUSH MY BUTTON.* When she does, Tamiko is greeted by her mom and Ed singing the first verse of "Home for Christmas," followed by Amy's instruction to *FaceTime us as soon as you hear this.* Half an hour later having sung the first verses of a dozen favorite carols and pledging to FaceTime again on Christmas morning so that the three of them can open gifts together, Tamiko sees she has an email from Mayumi.

tamiko—

mea culpa, mea culpa, mea culpa. *through my pride and arrogance i did u a bad turn, something i hope both of us won't hold against me forever. despite my having fallen for your boyfriend, and then having the nerve to ask for your friendship, i orchestrated events that had the unintended (i promise) result of hurting both u and alec. can the 2 of u possibly forgive me?*

start by understanding that i've been on a 4-day walk with no email so never received alec's urgent emails begging me to explain my part in what happened. now, in my rush i worry the following will be all but incoherent—so please, tamiko, hang in while I do my sincere best to explain how in my determination to help my dear friend aki i somehow lost sight of your needs and feelings. because the first threads that tie me to aki go way back it will take me a moment to even try to explain, so again, please hang tight.

mayumi's hubris: as u know i'm lucky to have been born to prosperous, intellectual and charismatic parents. as the youngest, and only girl, i was doted on, especially by my dad, and encouraged (in truth, required) to learn outgoing social skills. attending an international school and traveling with my parents overseas only baked in these tendencies. the result is that i'm pretty much the opposite of your cliché shy, self-effacing, self-contained japanese young adult. as a result i've often found myself at the center of groups—not necessarily the most popular, but the socially adept one who binds others together.

akiko: i met aki in english language preschool and we have been buddies ever since. to say that she's a different kind of duck (even by japanese standards) is surely an understatement but since she's also my very dear duck i celebrate her eccentricities (i'm attaching a picture of us in first grade and another from this year to give you some idea of our bond). although aki is a brilliant linguistics phd student and talented in so many ways she's also achingly shy, with few friends besides me. because of her androgynous presentation and sometimes prickly personality (at least on the surface) aki's had almost no romantic life beyond (and here i need to trust in both what i hope is still our nascent friendship and your discretion)—playing around with me on a couple of thirteen-year-old sleepovers. apparently the two subsequent times she's tried to have sex with others (one guy, one girl) were cringeworthy fiascos. but aki's inability to connect with lovers is only part of my concern. i worry more that with me being overseas for an extended period and others in our university group going their separate ways aki will become even more socially isolated. and as u may know in japan people who are depressed and lonely are too often tempted to give up on life itself.

the aki/alec connection: despite his hard work at language school (and my best efforts) when i left japan a month ago alec was still having trouble enunciating basic japanese sounds. coupled with his pessimism about "sucking at languages" i feared that he might quit on japanese even though his reading comprehension (ability to master characters) is impressive. so why not, i thought, suggest that alec spend time with aki the brilliant but lonely linguist. so far so good since apparently aki quickly helped alec improve his verbal skills and as a result his attitude to learning japanese at the same time she made a much-needed friend. but tamiko it's here that i made a huge mistake. it happened like this. i received an email from aki moaning that her mother planned to hire a matchmaker to try to find her a husband (yes it still happens in Japan) and also worrying her parents would discover she might be a lesbian. Instead of suggesting that she have a frank talk with her parents (or a therapist), i actually proposed she attempt to discover more about her preferences by coming on to alec (i somehow assumed alec would be kind enough to go along with my aki sex education plan despite his not being physically attracted to her). and to add thoughtlessness to myopia since i didn't consider aki to be a romantic threat (someone to feel jealous over) i never considered how u'd feel.

like jane austen's emma, when her matchmaking plans backfired and hurt her friends i'm mortified by the pain i caused u and alec who i absolutely know was blindsided by aki's advances and innocent of lecherous intent (ok, i'm sure he probably got into it eventually, but would we want a guy who didn't). anyway i'm not sure how i'll make this up to either of u or if u'll give me a chance but I promise I've learned my lesson.

a silver lining: although i gather aki more or less trapped alec into spending the night with her (she can be bossy when trying to overcome her shyness) the result has been little short of miraculous. specifically just this one exciting (to aki) experience has turned her attitude toward sex with men on its head to the point she's even considering her mother's matchmaking proposal. but maybe this won't be necessary since apparently aki's makeover (i attach a picture she sent yesterday) hasn't been lost on hiro (a shy dude who occasionally attends our friday gatherings) who bless his heart has asked her on a date to the zoo (only in japan). but tamiko please understand that although I'm happy things seem to be working out for aki i know this doesn't begin to justify the effect on u of my insensitive and hurtful meddling.

me and u: trying to be true friends (or, at least, not competitors) while loving the same guy was (is) never going to be easy even with me cheerfully occupying the backup role. and now i've obviously made it so much harder. so again tamiko my deepest apologies. even though i don't know how i can make it up to u (and reestablish a measure of trust) i'll do my best. and even should i fail i hope u'll revise your judgment of alec's role in all this.

love, mayumi

p.s. i love ur emails about life in movieland—jed streeter certainly looks like a sweetheart. if it's in the cards for both of u i hope u enjoy a moment before u again open ur heart to mr burns. indeed as i guess u and i have both learned we live in a nuanced world where it seems to be possible to give (or lend) one's heart or at least a sliver of it, to more than one person. no doubt it would have been simpler to have lived 500 years ago when we would have married the farmer next door at fifteen had four kids by twenty, and died toothless at thirty-four. but as i write this from my lovely pensione a few blocks from the arno i kind of don't think i want to go back to that.

. . . . .

Early on Christmas Eve morning, Tamiko goes for a long run up supersteep Marin Avenue and then along Grizzly Peak with its three-bridge views of San Francisco Bay. An hour later, quick-stepping the downhill mile to Saul's Delicatessen on Shattuck Avenue, she arrives just as Ruth pulls into a diagonal space. Giving Ruth a hug as intense as if they hadn't seen each other for a decade, Tamiko blinks rapidly as she finally steps back.

"You good?" Ruth asks, putting a hand on Tamiko's shoulder.

"Sure, fine. I mean, I've only been away since September, but, oh my god Ruth, it's just so great to see you."

"Your life has been on a roller coaster to say the least," Ruth replies, lowering her hand to Tamiko's elbow and steering her through the Jewish delicatessen's door and to a booth under a black-and-white photo of an elderly gentleman perusing the selection of lox at a deli counter.

"For sure there have been some downs, even some upside-downs, but on balance it's been a fun, fast ride. If I can have a wish, it's not to get off, but to slow things down enough that I can better cope with what's whizzing past. Since this is my first experience with a lot of new stuff, I know I'm never going to get things perfect, but still..."

"If you'll forgive me a therapist moment," Ruth interrupts, "it's your life and whenever you need it you have a built-in brake called the power of 'No.' But, tell me what's been going on since we last talked?"

After ordering scrambled eggs with lox and onions plus a double serving of hash browns, Tamiko does just that. Beginning with her discovery of Alec's adventure with Aki, she goes on to describe her exhilarating tryst with Jed followed by her escape from the paparazzi. Winding down, Tamiko glances at the wall clock behind the counter to see that she's been nonstop talking almost forty-five minutes. "Oh my god, Ruth, I'm monopolizing your morning, not to mention boring you witless."

"Not to worry. I have an emergency client with the holiday blues at eleven-thirty, but that still gives us plenty of time. And I assure you any adventure that involves Jed Streeter is never going to put me to sleep. But let's wrap things up here and continue our conversation while we walk around a few blocks."

Ten minutes later, as the two turn left on Vine Street and head east toward the Berkeley hills, Ruth asks, "So Tamiko, what's next?"

"I know my work on *2+2* will end in the next week or ten days, but not exactly when. In the meantime I have plenty to do for *Class of '24*, and..."

"I wasn't asking about work."

Waiting for an elderly Vespa to clatter past, Tamiko replies, "So Ruth, like maybe it was a mistake to get involved with Jed, especially since it wouldn't have happened if I hadn't freaked about Lec being with Aki. But, putting the movie-star hype aside, Jed's a super smooth dude and our night together more than lived up to my most romantic fantasies. After what I guess you could call my erotic disappointment with Derrick this fall, it was chill to discover that Lec isn't the only dude who can, well, who can…"

"Ring your bell?"

"Loud enough they probably heard me on Catalina. But, Ruth, you've been listening to me prattle for long enough, so please tell me what you think? I heard the part about my having the ability to say 'no' when things threaten to fly out of control, but what else?"

Turning left on Walnut Street to head north past its row of settled houses that somehow reminded Tamiko of affluent old widows sunning themselves on a bench, Ruth hesitates as if editing her remarks. "Tamiko," she finally says, "even though we've agreed I'm a friend, not your therapist, I worry that my comments might overinfluence you."

"C'mon, I'm a big girl now," Tamiko replies, as she laughingly points to a miniature schnauzer with a pressing crush on what looks to be a cross between a wolf and a Great Dane. "And as you see, mine isn't even this morning's most riveting romantic drama in North Berkeley."

"From your description, Jed Streeter seems like a decent guy even though he should have far more smarts than to date a minor, even one as mature as you. For your part, I agree that you probably wouldn't have gotten involved with Jed if Lec hadn't disappointed you. But, Tamiko, one thing I've noticed is that whenever you talk about Jed, Alec is almost always in the same sentence. For example, earlier you said, 'Just like Lec, Jed is effortlessly kind and thoughtful.' And a minute before that you told me that 'Jed has the same kind of tall, athletic body as Lec.' I could go on, but…"

"No need," Tamiko interrupts. "What can I say Ruth, but you always read me to the core. But I thought you'd have more to say about my hanging with a much older dude, especially a world-famous one."

"No need, since you're obviously all over that job."

. . . . .

Back at her mom's and Ed's on Santa Barbara Street an hour later, Tamiko finds her laptop and writes:

Lec—

On Christmas morning a year ago I woke up in your skinny bed on Parnassus Street. I have no clue as to how long you'd been waiting for me to open my eyes. But I clearly remember that when our gazes met you began to snuggle against me in a way that invited me to get even closer. When I said, 'let me clean my teeth first' you replied 'are you planning to bite me?' Good point, I thought as I wriggled on top, and slipped you inside me. After an enchanted interval when words flew away, we eventually came back to ourselves. I thought then, as I still do, that I've never had a better gift.

Love, Tamiko

P.S. Of course I have a load of other things to say, but not yet the wisdom to know how to say them. But I did get Mayumi's email, which I see she copied to you, and so better understand what went down with Aki. Just to be clear, none of this means I'm over feeling disappointed. But, Lec, when we FaceTimed, even though my head was spinning with jealous indignation, I should have trusted you enough to have listened to your explanation.

. . . . .

Early that afternoon Tamiko's high school friend, and softball buddy, Jazz, plus two other former Berkeley High teammates, show up with a giant Zachary's deep dish spinach and mushroom pizza and a six-pack.

Excited to catch up with what's been going on with them, and hoping to reminisce about their shared softball exploits, Tamiko is disappointed when they only want to talk about her Hollywood adventures. And no matter how often, and urgently, Tamiko tries to change the subject, it proves impossible to redirect their obsession with *2+2*'s famous foursome, especially Jed Streeter. As soon as she politely can, Tamiko pleads a headache to cut the afternoon short, again resolving to get out of the acting business as soon as possible.

. . . . .

When Alec reads Tamiko's romantically charged Christmas email he's tempted to immediately FaceTime her to propose they meet up as soon as he leaves Japan in a week. However, remembering the evocative pictures of Tamiko and Jed Streeter in Tamiko's third group email, he worries that the time isn't right. It's a fair bet, Alec reasons, that after discovering his relationship with Aki, Tamiko has spent more time with Jed, something that would be consistent with her email reminiscing about times past, but saying nothing about the future. Taking a deep breath, Alec concludes, my task is to be ready to engage when Tamiko is, not to allow my neediness to push her further away. And if this means somehow trying not to listen when my personal green-eyed monster drips poison about Jed Streeter in my ear, so be it. Then, almost as surprised that he's given himself such sound advice, as by his willingness to accept it, Alec types:

Tamiko, my love—

After last year's lovely Christmas morning eye opener we went downstairs to hustle up breakfast. Since my housemates had left for the holidays, it was just the two of us. I can still see you making French toast while I squeezed oranges, fried bacon and asked Margaret's Alexa to play Nina Simone. But, as with all sweet moments time marched on and it was soon time for us to go over to Francisco Street to share jokey gifts with your mom and Ed. I particularly remember us standing in the hall holding our coats, when you said, "How about we pretend we just woke up and have a groundhog day." Who bounded up the steps first hardly signifies, since the other was close behind. But the funniest part of the morning happened when we finally made it to your mom's house an hour-plus later and Ed and Amy were nowhere to be seen. When they eventually peeped out from Amy's bedroom looking sheepish, nobody spoke for a long moment.

Finally Ed said, "I'm not going to ask you two why you're late, but given the glow that's coming off you both I'm gonna guess it's the same reason why Amy and I just... well..."

"Perhaps 'exchanged meaningful gifts' are the words you're searching for," Amy offered with a straight face before we all broke up.

I very much hope that next Christmas you and I will be together and have a chance to add to these special memories. In the meantime, here's my news. As I think you know, Charlie and Emiko (yes, she's both showing it and flaunting it) arrived on the nineteenth and I've been trailing Charlie from meeting to meeting. The good news is that thanks to my classes and Mayumi's and Aki's help I understood a fair amount. When people speak fast in Japanese I sometimes lose the thread, but at social events I do pretty well. I could go on, but suffice it to say that I'm beginning to enjoy Japan and to think that joining Charlie's and Phil's business after MIT might make sense.

You'll laugh at this. For Christmas dinner tonight I'm going with Emiko and Charlie to Emiko's aunt's where there will be about twenty-five relatives (and yes, this being the land of the ritual gift, I've found small presents for everyone—cable car keyrings for the men, S.F.-themed scarves for the women and Batman masks for the kids). Unlike New Year's, Shogatsu (Japan's most important holiday), for which piles of traditional dishes are lovingly prepared, tonight we'll have fried chicken from KFC. No joke! For reasons I can't quite unpack, KFC for Christmas is a massive deal here with literally millions of people getting their orders in months in advance and the KFC people working triple-time to fill them—(an oversized replica of the Colonel dressed as Santa—they already kinda look alike—stands out front to greet people who line up down the block).

After Christmas I have several more days of meetings and then on New Year's Eve I fly to Mexico City on my way to a surfing holiday on the West Coast. Depending on last-minute ocean conditions I plan to hit Puerto Escondido first and then follow the high water. In mid-January I'll head to NYC where I'll keep working for Burns-Short while continuing with Japanese lessons a couple of hours per day. For starters I'll crash with Mom in her new apartment on the Upper West Side until I can find something of my own (Dad is still mostly in our family home in Chappaqua so who knows what's really going on with them).

I hope you are as pleased as I am that NYC is a lot closer to Amherst than Tokyo. And, of course, I very much look forward to seeing you when the Hollywood sign is in your rearview mirror. I have many more things to say, but will wait until we are together.

I love you, Lec

. . . . .

Late in the afternoon Tamiko darts downhill to the overcrowded Monterey Market to pick up fruit and veggies for tomorrow's Christmas dinner. Returning home an hour later she realizes she's muted her phone and flicks it back on to see that she has a voicemail from an Amherst number she doesn't recognize. Tapping it she hears:

"Tamiko—Marcia Raines here. In case you can't immediately place me, I'm the Amherst women's basketball coach. Given our earlier misunderstanding, it's taken me a couple of days to work up the courage to call with the result that I now risk bothering you on Christmas Eve. My apologies. Let me start by saying I respect the fact you decided not to play basketball at Amherst. And, yes, like everyone else in our small pond, I also know you're busy in L.A working on a film. But a desperate coach will make a desperate plea. Assuming you're done with your movie by January one, my proposal is that you consider joining our team for four or five games when we'll have no credible point guard. Here is the background. With last year's starter in Italy for her junior year and you deciding not to play, I worked hard to teach Rosie Wilburn, our most athletic first-year, how to run the offense. Even though Rosie's a natural small forward and never played point in high school, her transition has been a success (our preseason record is seven and two). But, in our last game before break, and one of our losses, Rosie sprained her ankle in the second quarter with the result she won't be back until mid-January. In the meantime, my only backup is a newbie from a tiny high school in Idaho who is, maybe, five-two on tiptoe and not ready to play at this level. During the first ten days of January we have four games, three in our league, of which we need to win at least two to have a shot at qualifying for playoffs. Yet, without Rosie, we'll likely lose them all which would be disappointing since at full strength, our team can be formidable. So, again, how about joining us short term? Even if your answer is a doubtful maybe, please call me day or night."

Yowser! Tamiko thinks. No matter how many times I say no, this woman never quits.

But then, as she fills the egg-shaped Japanese-style sit tub Ed and her mom have installed as the pièce de résistance of the upstairs bathroom, Tamiko finds herself rethinking her position. After all, if her part in *2+2* really does wind up in the next few days, how better to return her life back to a comfortable groove than to chase a ball for the couple of weeks until spring semester begins? Testing the water with her toe, before cranking up the hot, she gratefully sinks into the water, her phone now in her right hand.

"Tell me you and Jed have not been outed by the *National Enquirer* and I'll never ask for another Christmas present," Mary McCarthy says by way of answering Tamiko's call.

"I'm guessing they're too busy paying off President Trump's hookers to get around to us," Tamiko says with a laugh before briefly explaining Coach Raines request. "Mary, I want you and Ben to know I'm fully committed to *2+2*, but if it turns out I'll be finished by the first, I might go back to college early to fill in for the injured point guard."

"As it happens, Ben just walked in for our Christmas Eve dinner with

Clemmie and a few friends. Give me minute to corner him and I'll call you back."

Tamiko is barely out of the bath and downstairs heating up the cheese and broccoli casserole her mom left in the fridge when Ben Fine is on the phone to propose that if she can be on the set early Wednesday, they'll spend the morning reshooting parts of her scenes with Mary Ann. Then on Thursday the 27th, as already scheduled, they'll film exterior shots with her and Jed at Malibu and maybe also redo a few lines of their conversation. The upshot is that if all goes well, Tamiko should be free by Thursday evening, although he'll want her to be available Friday to fix any last-minute hiccups.

Surprised that Ben has all but doubled down on her request to finish early, Tamiko belatedly realizes this means her time with Jed will be over almost before it begins.

Feeling the pique of buyer's remorse, Tamiko asks, "But will Mary Ann agree to work first thing on Boxing Day? I mean, wasn't the set supposed to be dark until Thursday?"

"Tamiko, with all the things you're trying to cope with, how about you leave Mary Ann to me?" Ben replies sharply.

Taken aback by what she takes as Ben's criticism of her relationship with Jed, Tamiko decides not to apologize for something she doesn't regret. "See you bright and early on the twenty-sixth with a smile on my face," she says. "But what about the dialogue changes the Golds propose? Do you still want me to comment?"

"I sent Jack and Naomi my tweaks earlier. I've asked them to react and get the result to you by nine a.m. tomorrow. I know it's Christmas but if you can send us your thoughts by noon, all will be well. Tamiko, if you have a minute I have something to say beyond 'happy holidays.'"

"Of course," Tamiko replies, sure this is where she'll finally be chewed out for getting involved with Jed.

"I want you to know how much I appreciate the way you've handled *everything* thrown at you here in L.A. And I really do mean everything. I hope I'm not being too personal when I say that as far as I can see, you and Jed have handled your friendship well, despite the misgivings of many of those around you. I would offer you both advice about the wisdom of leaving what's happened in L.A. in L.A., but I suspect you don't need it. More importantly," Ben adds with the trademark chuckle that tips Tamiko to the fact that whatever he is about to say, the opposite is more likely to be true, "I'm worried about how you're going to put the basketball in the hoop since you haven't played competitively since last winter."

"You're right—that's definitely a worry," Tamiko says, realizing that Ben isn't teasing. "I've played a few pickup games this fall, but still…"

"How about I see if Mary can find you some quality gym time Wednesday and Thursday afternoons?"

"Fabulous! But can she really do that?"

. . . . .

When Tamiko reaches a drowsy-sounding Coach Raines an hour later, she has to repeat her name before the coach finally wakes up enough to say, "Yikes! Tamiko Gashkin, is this really you? When I sent you that email, I guess I never expected you'd call."

"Sorry to reach out so late, but I thought you'd want to know that my answer is yes."

"Really? You'll come back early to play the four January games until hopefully Rosie can return?"

"My answer is still yes," Tamiko says with a laugh.

"You don't know how beautiful those three letters sound to a coach trying to save her team's season. When can you get here? Oops, sorry, I know you're probably still involved with important things in L.A. so let me put it this way, I'll be delighted to see you whenever you can make it."

"The Wesleyan game is on January third, right? If you'll have the team together I can be there to practice on New Year's day, or January second, if that's more realistic."

"The sooner the better. Possibly not everyone will be back on the first, but more than enough to make a start. Based on what I've seen in your Berkeley High videos, we'll encourage you to speed up our tempo, at the same time I'll simplify the offense since you haven't played with the others."

"Simple, but fast, I love it. But fair warning, I haven't touched a ball since a couple of pickup games in November. When I'm back in L.A. for a few days after Christmas I'll try to get into a gym to shoot, but don't expect too much."

"I'm more concerned about the kind of physical condition you're in. We have plenty of talented shooters, but no realistic backup to direct the offense, so I hope…"

"I've been swimming and/or running every day and I'll step it up this week. In the meantime, it will be a big help if you can send me video of recent games. I'll text you as soon as I confirm my ETA."

. . . . .

Waiting at the almost deserted gate for her Christmas evening flight from Oakland to L.A., Tamiko concludes she's one of the few passengers in a good mood. Her morning FaceTime with her mom and Ed had been a happy hoot, especially when she opened a box to find a dove gray, knee-length down coat, a gift she regards as a kind of karmic exclamation point to her decision to volunteer for a couple of additional winter weeks.

And dinner at Ruth's, moved up two hours to accommodate her flight, was also fun, especially when the turnip haters conceded that her secret butter and lemon-laden recipe qualified for second helpings. Tamiko only feels her equanimity begin to wobble when she realizes she needs to answer Lec's and Mayumi's emails as well as tell Jed what's up with her leaving L.A. early. But before she can pull out her iPad, her phone sounds. Delighted to see it's Jed, Tamiko answers, "Merry Christmas, I loved the pic of you and Allison in Santa hats you sent this morning."

"But you haven't responded to my suggestion that we get together," Jed says, his voice neutral.

"Sorry. The last twenty-four hours have been a blur in part because I've decided to go back to Amherst a week from today to play basketball, which involved trying to arrange things with Ben and then, well…"

"Maybe that's not the only reason you want to leave before *2+2* is in the can?"

"Jed, it's true that after our amazing night together I'm seriously confused about how to think about us, assuming there is an us, which we both know is impossible," Tamiko blurts, even as she realizes she isn't making sense, even to herself. "But the Amherst coach did reach out to me when their point guard got hurt and…"

"I thought we agreed that, for all the reasons we both know, not to let the future become the enemy of the present," Jed interrupts. "Our film hasn't wrapped yet and I hope we haven't either."

When Tamiko doesn't reply, Jed continues, "Tamiko, the way I see it, we still have a few more days to be infatuated with each other and then a lifetime to be good friends."

"But can we really do that?" Tamiko asks in a voice choked by anxiety. When this time Jed says nothing, she continues, "I mean, like, seriously Jed, fall in love and out of love, on schedule?" Then, as if gobsmacked by her own use of the "L" word, she falls silent.

"Tamiko, I can't answer that," Jed replies. "All I can say is that despite my firm resolution to the contrary, you're not the only one who has tumbled in. But, especially now that we've both fessed up to how we feel, I hope we can hold on to our special moment for as long as possible."

"Me too, for sure," Tamiko says in a rush. "It's just that no matter how excited I am about seeing you, I'll need to go back to my own world next week. I never thought I'd be the one to say this, but Jed, no matter how often I insisted you treat me as an adult, I need to remind myself that it's a provisional status, if that makes any sense."

"Absolutely. At the same time I'm over-the-top delighted we connected, I also kick myself for not saying no last Friday night."

"Oh my god, Jed, I'm so glad you didn't. It's, like, in ways I can't fully explain even to myself, I needed that special evening," Tamiko replies, now taking her place in the boarding line. "So, when can we get together?"

"Despite everything I've just said, not until Thursday, which is part of the reason I'm calling. Allison got so excited about touring Colorado State we flew into Denver two hours ago. Since I'm overscheduled for the next couple of months, this is my best chance to participate in the college tour ritual. We're at an airport hotel now and will drive to the campus at Fort Collins early tomorrow. In short, it will be late evening tomorrow by the time I put Allison on her plane to Tucson, and catch the last flight back to LAX."

"You're a good dad and I'm proud of you. So, even though Ben just told me my role in *2+2* probably ends Thursday, we'll still have one night for sure."

. . . . .

Tamiko gets back to Ben Fine's at 10:15 p.m. As she bumps her bag along the flagstone path to the cottage, Mary pokes her nose out to say they need to be rolling at 7:45 a.m. and that she's booked a nearby school gym for Tamiko to shoot hoops late in the afternoon. Too beat to do anything but crash, Tamiko decides to again put off returning Lec's and Mayumi's emails.

. . . . .

After a two-mile run, and a quick bowl of granola with blueberries, Tamiko settles into Mary's car at 7:44 Wednesday morning. "Tamiko, I have a question. If you're as super at basketball as the dozen articles I read on the web portray, how come you're at a division three college, and up until now, not even on the team?"

"That's two questions," Tamiko replies with a chuckle, "but since the answer is basically the same, I'll give you a pass. As the result of the genetic gift of excellent coordination from my ballet dancer grandparents, combined with having always been tall and strong, pretty much every coach I've crossed paths with has wanted me on their team—basketball, volleyball, softball, soccer, water polo, even lacrosse one year. Since I loved sports, all was good until two years ago when I realized that ten years of chasing literally thousands of balls up and down hundreds of courts, fields and pools was enough already. In other words, I started to become bored with everything but pitching."

"But you obviously stuck with basketball through high school."

"My Berkeley High team was simply too brilliant to quit. However, since I wanted college to be about filling up my head, not perfecting my jump shot, I decided that pitching for the softball team was plenty. Yet, now that I'm in danger of being overwhelmed by so many aspects of my life, simple familiar tasks seem newly attractive. So, when Coach Raines asked me to fill in for a couple of weeks, I found myself saying yes. Not having played competitively since last year, I don't know if I'll help the Amherst team all that much, but with their point guard hurt and no real backup, it will be fun to find out if I still have game."

"It's probably not my role to express an opinion, but I'm delighted you're going back to college early."

"Mary, both as my friend, and substitute mom, I appreciate every morsel of your advice, even though when it comes to Jed Streeter, I obviously haven't taken it. But without your hand-holding I'd never have made it through this month."

"Thanks, and, Tamiko, for what it's worth, were I your age, and had the chance, I'd probably have wrapped myself around a guy like Jed even faster than you did."

. . . . .

At the studio an hour later having changed into her Jennifer outfit and had her thick lion's mane semi-tamed, Tamiko joins Ben and Mary Ann McCabe on the set.

"We have a tall hill to climb today," Ben emphasizes. "Hopefully you've both inhaled your new lines for the coming-home-from-college-a-day-early scene. But, it's only going to work if you fully believe them, especially you, Tamiko. Here's where you drop your nice-girl mask and get in touch with your id."

"But didn't you congratulate me when I did this scene two weeks ago, the day I thought we were practicing?" Tamiko protests.

"Sorry to disappoint you Tamiko, but this isn't a small, politically correct college where I'd need to construct a critical sandwich to convince you that pretty good isn't good enough. Especially now that you're working directly with Mary Ann, not a stand-in, I need you to hold your tongue, pay attention, and execute. Start by discarding all thoughts as to how you might deal with a fraught situation like this in your family—or any functional family. Specifically, at the top of the scene, when Jennifer arrives home for the holiday and before she encounters the foursome, remember that she's already deep down pissed at her mother. In Jennifer's view, Sandy has left her marriage to Jennifer's dad for no compelling reason and then compounded her error by marrying Toby, whom Jennifer considers a feckless lightweight. In short, when Jennifer interrupts the foursome, I need you to get a grip on a more angry, cynical Jennifer than you portrayed earlier. As you pointed out more than once, Jennifer, as a sexually mature junior at Cal Berkeley, wouldn't be appalled by discovering three or four people in a bed."

Her face flushed and her mouth suddenly dry, Tamiko feels assaulted by Ben's peremptory attitude. Why, after treating her so kindly all month, is he suddenly acting the tyrant? Even when he made Jed and her take a cold shower, she could understand his motivation. Too disappointed to try to come up with an answer, Tamiko steps to her mark when Ben says, "Places everyone." Two hours and a dozen takes later, Ben shouts, "Enough. Thank you everyone, that's a wrap, although I'll need both of you after lunch for foundation shots."

Choosing a sandwich and a drink from the lunch buffet, Tamiko feels so drained she walks past Mary with barely a nod on the way to her dressing room. "Not now, I'm resting," Tamiko almost shouts a minute later, when she hears a knock on her door.

"Well then, I'll just have to rest with you, won't I?" Mary says as she opens the door and enters. Taking the chair across from where Tamiko is sprawled on a blue couch, Mary asks, "Tamiko, what do you imagine just happened out there?"

"Honestly, I have no clue."

"Has it occurred to you that Ben wanted you to walk into your mother's house with a boulder-sized chip on your shoulder, not just a pretend one?"

"You're saying Ben deliberately tricked me into giving the performance he wanted instead of calmly explaining what he was after?" Tamiko asks. Then, realizing she sounds like a petulant child, she begins tugging at her sandwich wrapper.

"Tamiko, let me put it this way. When you did this scene a couple of weeks ago you were very decent, good even. As a newbie, you exceeded expectations. I'm guessing that part of the reason Ben laid it on so thick with the joke about your being free to go back to school was to help you relax and get over any stage fright. But over the last few weeks when he watched the dailies, Ben realized two things. First, that the scene could pack considerably more punch and second, that you were capable of providing it. Obviously, he was right, since you just delivered a searing performance, one that I frankly didn't know was in you. Tamiko, you may be right that there was a kinder, gentler way to accomplish this, but, given Ben's need to wrap up a thousand details in the rest of the film, it would have been asking a lot."

"Mary, everything you say may be right, but none of it makes me feel less manipulated."

"Welcome to Hollywood, where at bottom, no one cares about anything but results. Also, remember you got here on a magic carpet, not by going to fifty auditions where being polite, or often even civil, is the last thing on anyone's mind. And, frankly, there's also the fact that you're being paid more than enough to take a little abuse."

"Got it," Tamiko replies, before swallowing a big bite of her turkey and cheddar. Immediately feeling revived, she adds, "I guess I'm the one who should apologize for being a brat."

"No need, especially since I'm sure Ben is bummed about laying into one of his favorite young people, even when the result was your giving the performance he'd dreamed of. Just go about your business this afternoon and by tomorrow when, I'm guessing the sharp edges will have begun to smooth out for both of you, it will be time to talk if you still need to."

· · · · ·

At 4:00 p.m., Tamiko and Mary push open the heavy double doors of the Crowther School's gymnasium where they meet Beth Ricketts, the school's whip-thin athletic director. "I have at least an hour and a half of paperwork to catch up on, so this is all yours," Beth says, pointing at the gleaming maple-floored basketball court that occupies about a third of the aircraft hanger-like sports facility.

"Mary, you never cease to amaze. How did you pull this off?" Tamiko asks, as she pulls off her sweats.

"Derrick and Clemmie went to school here. During those years Ben hosted a couple of big-dollar fundraisers that helped build this place. In short, it wasn't hard to pry the door open."

After stretching and five minutes of sprints, Tamiko rolls the ball trolley to the three-point line and begins shooting jump shots. Mary, who, as usual, quickly sees how she can help, removes her shoes and begins retrieving balls. At first, Tamiko mostly clangs shots off the rim or backboard, but after a few minutes her accuracy improves. After half an hour, she switches to attacking the basket with dribble drives with both her left and right hand. Then, as if eluding a defender, she continues her drive under the basket, using her left hand to flick the ball back over her shoulder and into the hoop. Hearing clapping, Tamiko turns to see Beth Ricketts standing next to Mary. "A fat dollop of luck fell on that one," Tamiko says, with a laugh.

"Luck or not," Ricketts says, "I've coached the girls' team here for fifteen years and I've never had anyone who could do that."

· · · · ·

Back in the cottage by 5:45, Tamiko stretches out and immediately falls asleep, not waking until someone pounds on her door ninety minutes later. "Come to pizza with Chris and me and we'll promise not to mention *2+2*," Clementine proposes enthusiastically when Tamiko finally opens the door. Glad of an opportunity to escape her thoughts, Tamiko pulls on a sweatshirt and tags along, not getting back until 8:45. Feeling guilty she's put off answering Mayumi for so long, she grabs her iPad.

Mayumi,

Thanks for the detailed Aki-Alec explanation, which, in its sweet, remorseful, way tells me you do care about my feelings. Really, there is not a lot to forgive except maybe my own jealous nature for overreacting and cancelling my Japan trip without hearing the full story. Really! So, while I can't get behind you encouraging Aki to proposition Lec, it's not hard to see that from her perspective it was important that Lec hasn't lost his magic touch. Also, I know I need to come to terms with the larger truth that in a long life absolute sexual fidelity isn't the end-all and be-all—but let's save that fraught subject for another day.

I'm gonna guess you're wondering what's happened with me and my adventures in Movieland and especially my flirtation with Jed Streeter. To cut to the point, it's no longer a flirtation. That's right, following the Lec/Aki reveal, I pretty literally jumped into Jed's arms. Thankfully, and despite what I know were his gaggle of highly sensible reservations, he caught me. OMG Mayumi, what can I tell you, but that the resulting mashup went neon. You said earlier that your one-nighter with the dirty nails Spanish truck driver dude was important because it proved that Lec wasn't the only guy with whom you could blast off. Ditto squared. What a high! And the drama was magnified by a peeping neighbor spotting me swimming au naturelle at dawn in Jed's pool. Suffice it to say that although I wasn't outed, it was close enough that I can't blame Ben Fine for wanting to wrap up my part in 2+2 so as to get me far away from Jed, scandal-free. And yes, with our twenty-three-year age difference and a load of other barriers including my Velcro-like feelings for you-know-who, Jed and I agree we are enjoying a head-spinning tryst, not an ongoing romance. That said, I'm totally down for our last assignation tomorrow night (at a secret location yet to be announced—LOL).

Next week I plan to return to Amherst early for the Spring semester to play basketball and catch up on my Ancient Greek. And, if the deal comes through, I'll continue to work helping design a college-based Netflix series I've unaccountably been recruited for. To say the least, after my whirlwind life here, I'll be relieved to be back at the sweet little college I've become surprisingly bonded with.

Your friend,

Tamiko

Glancing at her watch to see that it's barely 10:00, Tamiko knows she owes Lec a thoughtful reply. But as she's just explained to Mayumi, her thoughts are too tightly wound around tomorrow night's date with Jed to make this an attractive idea. So after padding to the kitchen to make a cup of Sleepytime tea, she grabs her iPad and enters:

Lec,

Mexico! Sweet! Hope the surf is up and you have a fabulous vacation!

I love you, Tamiko

Then, as she considers whether to add a more forthcoming postscript, Adele begins to sing. Seeing it's a call from Jed, Tamiko answers, "What's up?" as she simultaneously sends Lec's email as is.

"Just getting home as we speak. Earlier I arranged with a friend, who's appearing in a play in NYC, to use his condo in Santa Monica tomorrow night, assuming you're still up for another gallop."

"My boots are next to the door. But Jed, how can the logistics work so we're guaranteed not to get paparazzied?"

"My buddy Fred often rents his place on Airbnb so people come and go without neighbors paying much attention. In addition, it has a semi-private entrance. But to be extra careful, I'll add a beard and hat and slip in a couple of hours before you. Since you're not yet a well-known face,

Mary can drop you off with no need for subterfuge."

"I can take a Lyft."

"Ha! With Mary playing mother hen, I doubt it. Also, just so you know, Ben and I have talked things through enough for me to make clear that what's between you and me is real, and not just an old dude's frivolous dalliance."

"Gah!" Tamiko exclaims with a burst of annoyance. "Really, Jed, has it occurred to either of you middle-aged geniuses that you might be my dalliance?"

"Tamiko, I'm truly sorry. I can see how patronizing what I just said must…"

"Relax, I've made my point and have no intention of getting so annoyed it spoils our last ride across Montana."

. . . . .

Tamiko is stunned by the scene she encounters when she and Mary arrive at the Malibu location shoot on Thursday morning. Not only do barriers block the street for a hundred yards on each side of the house used as Sandy's home, but a small army of uniformed Los Angeles County Sheriff's deputies and private security guards make sure that hundreds of curious onlookers stay behind them. A few minutes later, having used a tiny trailer to change into the same outfit she wore when she returned from college to interrupt the foursome, Tamiko joins Ben and Jed to hear Ben explain what's expected. "Obviously, we've already shot the main part of this scene on set with you two sitting on the steps. Here our goal is to see Jennifer leave her mom's house, almost as if we were running the film of her arrival scene backwards. But instead of Jennifer finding her Uber waiting when she bumps her roller bag down the front steps, she is surprised to encounter Chad jogging past. Then, after you two negotiate your approach/avoidance moment and decide to sit on the steps to talk, I call cut and we're done."

Tamiko is relieved that the shot of Jed jogging along Wildflower Road is up first. Yet her body again tightens as she watches the onlookers strain against the rope lines to get a better view of Jed, who now trots toward her as if he's alone on a deserted street. What did I get myself into, Tamiko thinks for at least the fiftieth time, as she watches a pro in action. As soon as she begins to dwell on her inadequacies, Jed finishes his run and it's her turn. However, before she can take her mark, proceedings are interrupted when Ben decides that the car parked in the driveway should be moved to the curb. Suddenly, Julio Garcia, one of the assistant directors, objects, saying, "In an affluent neighborhood like this, only gardeners and maids park on the street, and even if they won the lottery neither would be caught dead in a Volvo." At first annoyed, Ben quickly grasps Garcia's point and tells a grip to lose the Volvo.

With things finally in order Tamiko steps out of the house and turns to lock the door only to have Ben shout "Cut! Tamiko," he says, "leaving the house to meet a ride may seem like a no-brainer, but, remember we want the audience to flash back to the moment Jennifer arrived. Even though you're wearing the same clothes and pulling the same bag, your experience of the last couple days has not only killed your home-for-the-holidays high but left you feeling as if you are ankle-deep in mud. So, before we try again, let's have makeup rub off a little of your natural shine. And while they're at it I want you to think about slowing everything down. Start by fumbling for the right key as you prepare to lock the door. Also, remember that while you may be a super-athlete who can gracefully negotiate the steps balancing a heavy bag on your head, Jennifer is an ordinary mortal who has to struggle to keep an unwieldy bag with tiny wheels from flipping over."

Even with continued coaching, it takes Tamiko a dozen takes to satisfy Ben, something she accomplishes only when by 12:45 she becomes so hungry she really is shaky. A few minutes later, over sandwiches in the trailer, Ben says, "Although I'm pretty sure we'll use the footage of the Jennifer/Chad conversation that's already in the can, I'd like us to pretend it doesn't exist. In short, Tamiko and Jed, now that you two are finally sitting on the steps, I'd like you to finish the scene."

. . . . .

Tamiko and Mary are finally back in Mary's car by 3:45. As a police officer moves a security barrier back just far enough to let them slowly roll past a large group of onlookers, someone with a camera yells, "It's Tamiko Gashkin! Tamiko, Tamiko, look this way!" When Tamiko does, several people wave and hold out cards and notebooks, apparently hoping Mary will stop so Tamiko can roll down the window and sign. "Oh my god, Mary, I feel like a fraud. I barely know what I'm doing and people are begging for my autograph," Tamiko says as they finally clear the crowd and accelerate toward the Pacific Coast Highway.

Pausing for a moment, Mary replies, "Tamiko, perhaps you didn't notice, but, as we pulled out, Jed was over by the barrier schmoozing with people and signing autographs. He's learned that if you are gracious, most people will return the favor. And, believe it or not, being polite even works with the media much of the time. Seriously dear, this is a lesson you need to learn. As we've discussed, even though your part is relatively small, you're the arresting new face with a role that lots of young people and parents will identify with. So, if *2+2* is a hit, or anything close to it, you'll be the one standing by the rope line."

"Oh my god, Mary, it's like I freak just thinking about it."

"Again, watch Jed, and also Aphrodite, who are masters of poise under pressure. You'll see that while they are both adept at guarding their privacy—that is, avoiding the media when they can, and deflecting personal questions when they can't, neither ever seems to be working at it."

"When I agreed to perform a few lines over at Hampshire College last fall, I never dreamed any of this would happen."

"Which is surely a good thing for Ben and *2+2*, because you might well have said no."

"C'mon, as you just saw, it takes forever to get a marginally decent performance out of me."

"Actually, as I've said and repeated but you refuse to hear, the opposite is closer to the truth. Ben pretty much knows what the others are capable of and he also knows that if he leans too hard they'll revert to prima donna mode and sleepwalk through their performances. But your ability to raise the intensity bar coupled with your willingness to hang in there for as long as it takes has rubbed off on them. I probably shouldn't tell you this, but after yesterday's shoot Ben told me that by trying to keep up with you, Mary Ann is giving her best performance in ten years."

. . . . .

After an hour in the Crowther School gym, Tamiko rummages through Mary's freezer to uncover a pint of Ben & Jerry's Chocolate Peppermint Crunch. Using a serving spoon she begins gobbling it from the carton as she calls Tom Obanta.

"Tamiko, did you read all my texts?" Tom asks, by way of answer.

"I did and I gather the gist of your conversation with Stan Greene is that I only get a full-fledged writer's contract if I agree to test for Anna. But, Tom, I haven't changed my mind. It's like, I'm fresh from a location shoot in a normally quiet residential neighborhood where spectators were lined up five deep behind ropes and barricades. When I arrived no one knew my name, but when I left people were shouting, 'Tamiko, Tamiko' as if we were buddies."

"Easy girl. I'm on your side here. Despite my firm's loss of a sweet commission, you really have convinced me that when it comes to acting, the answer is no. But that doesn't mean Greene is buying it. Even without an Anna commitment he might go for another fifty-hour consulting gig for say, seventy-five thousand dollars. But he'll likely be so pissed he'll double down on his determination to drop you like the plague as soon as he thinks he can. And Tamiko, be warned once the principal characters and story arc are defined, your golden moment will be over. Hollywood is full of aspiring young writers from overpriced New England colleges who will kill for a seat in *Class of 24's* writers' room to refine the dialogue and stick in the 'ha-ha's.'"

. . . . .

At 6:15 p.m. Tamiko texts Jed, *We just turned onto your street, so hope your boots are on.*

He replies, *2712 is the gray cottage with the light on halfway back along the path. Behind the green door is a cowpoke with his arms open and a grin on his face.*

"Enjoy," Mary says simply, as she eases the car to the curb.

A few moments later, as Tamiko cuddles against Jed's lean body she murmurs, "Ready for Montana when you are."

"That would make two of us," Jed replies as he nudges Tamiko far enough back to make eye contact. "Tamiko, even though we both know our time together is measured in hours, I want to say something I hope won't freak you out. Since almost the day we met, and certainly since our amazing Friday night, you've been wrapped around my heart like a warm, fuzzy boa constrictor, which means I've been thinking that..."

"Hmph," Tamiko interrupts, with a laugh, determined to stay in the moment. "As much as I love your fuzzy image, this snake has been looking forward to skin on skin."

"No way I'm going to argue with that," Jed replies as he takes Tamiko's hand and leads her along the hall.

Propped against an oversized red pillow next to Tamiko ninety minutes later, Jed dips a corn chip into a tub of guacamole, as he says, "Shagging you, if you don't mind the Medieval English, is crazily addictive. Hardly any time passes from the time we pull apart until I begin fantasizing about the mind-blowing feeling of climbing back inside you."

"To quote my favorite cowboy, no way I'm going to argue with that," Tamiko replies, as she tosses the chip bag on the floor, slides flat and extends a long arm to pull Jed on top. Half an hour later, just as their repeat is about to morph into a three-peat, the doorbell sounds.

"That will be dinner," Jed says, "but there's no need to interrupt more important things since they'll leave it on the porch in an insulated box."

"Noodles or nookie? That's an easy decision," Tamiko says, scissoring her long legs around Jed's bum and squeezing.

After the two eventually retrieve their Italian dinner and spread it on the coffee table, Jed lights the gas fire. Nesting together on an oversized beanbag, they begin filling their plates with clam linguine, risotto primavera, garlic bread and salad. Waving away Jed's offer of red wine, Tamiko says, "I'm already as high on endorphins as any human has a right to be."

"Tamiko, can we talk just for a moment about how two people who have such a blazing crush on each other can possibly say goodbye forever in a few hours? I respect that you have a long-term boyfriend you hope to get back together with but…"

"Jed, I'm guessing that sometime in your life you've been simultaneously mesmerized, or is transfixed the better word, by two lovers. So, you probably have a good idea what I'm going through. But the weirdest thing is that you and Lec are so much alike that sometimes my heart blurs you. It's as if God created the perfect object of my affection and then cloned him."

"Whoa! That's a knuckleball I didn't see coming."

"Lec, short for Alec, is six-three, one hundred and eighty pounds, lanky, impressively athletic and has an abundance of shaggy dark hair and a strong chin. In addition, he's smart, kind, understated, empathetic and, what can best be described as a gregarious loner." Then, after pausing for a long moment, Tamiko adds, "I don't mean to spoil our evening, but telling you all that is the only way I know to give you half a clue about my confused feelings."

"I doubt I have half of Alec's good qualities, but I get your point. So when does he return from Japan? And after all that's happened to both of you this fall, is it really likely you'll get back in sync?"

"He's in Mexico for a surfing break and I'm heading back to Amherst on New Year's Eve, so we'll have to see."

"Why not find out if the magic is still there by joining him in Mexico?"

"Because I'm not ready to go."

"Because?"

"Of you, of course. Whatever comes down with Lec in the future, this is our moment. After I'm back at Amherst and have time to think, it will be time for next steps."

"That means a lot to me," Jed says, finishing his wine. "And Tamiko, I know this is breaking our rules about what's happened here in L.A., stays in L.A., but, if for any reason you and Lec don't get back together, maybe you and I can see each other now and then?"

"If you keep going down that road I'm going to blubber."

"But you'll be eighteen in the fall so we'd be legal and, well…"

"Damn it Jed, you're supposed to be the sensible adult in the room. There is just no getting around the fact you're twenty-three years older than I am, and the world's most famous film star. And also that I'm still half-woman, half-kid, with a load of growing up to do. But how about we blow off the tiramisu and make the most of the time we have."

· · · · ·

In the Uber back to Ben's three hours later, Tamiko sees she has a text from Tom Obanta. Pleased for any excuse to interrupt her ping-pong thoughts about Jed and Lec, she opens it:

Grudgingly, and only after I rubbed his nose in the Writer's Guild Basic Agreement, Stan Greene has agreed to our offer. In addition to your getting another chunky check, you'll also receive onscreen credit. Since Stan's still determined to show his displeasure about your refusal to do the Anna test, it may be upside down and in Sanskrit, but it will be there. The lawyers will put our understanding into signable form for you and your mom pronto. In the meantime, keep writing.

After responding with a thumbs-up emoji, Tamiko glances at her watch to see it's 1:30 a.m. Texting Amelia, she enters, *Good morning. As you doubtless know, Stan is on board with fifty more hours for me. So if it's good for you we can work together today. But since it's obviously a late night for me how about starting at 10:30?*

Almost immediately Tamiko receives a reply. *Delighted you stood up for yourself. But since I'm also still up (croupy kid), 11:00 sounds a lot more doable.*

. . . . .

Tamiko is finishing a bowl of oatmeal topped by bananas and blueberries at 10:15 Friday morning when Mary puts her head in to ask if she can help by making Tamiko a plane reservation back to Oakland. "I've already booked myself on the nine p.m., which should leave plenty of time to pack after I spend the day with Amelia Jackson."

"You'll want to build in extra time at the airport since in addition to your bags you'll need to check the world's biggest suitcase."

"How come?"

"Our wardrobe people have sequestered everything you wore onscreen in the unlikely event Ben needs you to fly back out here to tweak a scene, but the rejects are all yours."

"Seriously? I mean, that's a pile of dope gear. Is that really smooth?"

"Why not? Those clothes were chosen for you and fit perfectly so who better to wear them? And, as I said, you'll need the evening dresses for the hoopla around 2+2's opening next fall and very possibly after that, since I have a hunch our little film just might receive a nomination or three."

. . . . .

Tamiko disembarks from her Oakland flight a few minutes after ten. Even with three bags to collect and somehow pull in tandem, she'll have plenty of time to make it to the BART station before the system closes at midnight. But as she approaches the baggage carousel, her mom waves.

"I could have done this on my own," Tamiko insists, even as she feels a burst of happiness when she steps into her mother's warm hug.

"I only get to hang out with my illustrious daughter for a day and a half so I thought I'd make the most of it," Amy says. Then, grinning widely, she adds, "Also, Mary called to warn me that in addition to your stuff you'd be pulling a bag the size of a double-wide."

"Oh my god, Mom, it's like they gave me enough clothes to open a store."

"Too bad I'm six inches shorter and twenty pounds lighter, or I could maybe long-term borrow a few things," Amy replies, ruefully.

"Actually, there's a way cool zip-up black hoodie with silver highlights that's too small for me. Of course I could give it to Eloise, but…"

"Who picked you up in the middle of the night?"

. . . . .

In the car a few minutes later, Amy says, "Mary updated me on the part of your privacy iceberg she regards as being more or less above the water. So do you want to talk about Jed? Or maybe Lec, who I gather is surfing in Mexico? Or both of them, for that matter?"

"Not really," Tamiko says, more abruptly than she intends. "I mean, Mom, a big part of the reason I'm going back to school early is to try to quit obsessing about dudes."

"I was as pleased, as I was surprised, when you agreed to play ball, but I doubt that perfecting your dribble drive is going to dent your romantic worries. Maybe you also need to…"

"It's, like, Mom, I'm pretty sure you heard me say I'm letting everything about that subject lay for awhile."

"As sensible as it is to give yourself time to emotionally regroup," Amy continues as if Tamiko hasn't spoken, "sooner or later you'll have to make a choice. Trying to hold onto both Jed and Lec simply isn't going to work."

"Mom, can you seriously think that's escaped me? Anyway, I already did that a year and a half ago when the moment I locked eyes with Lec I felt as if I was at the center of the Big Bang. And despite everything that's happened since, nothing's really changed on my end. But how Lec feels about me is obviously a different deal."

. . . . .

Ed is at the table reading the *Washington Post* on his iPad Saturday morning when Tamiko climbs out of bed and wanders into the kitchen. "Amy's darted down to Bay Books to cope with a kerfuffle over a cover misprint, so I'm the breakfast wallah. How about three eggs, plus a couple of sourdough slices and a pile of bacon that you definitely can't say no to since I just pulled it off the stove. Also there's fresh O.J. and papaya with lemon."

"All my favorites, but really Ed, you don't have to…"

"And miss the double pleasure of hanging with my favorite stepdaughter at the same time I duck the tenth rewrite of the last chapter of my novel?"

"I've missed you too, and the truth is I can use your advice on how to handle something."

"Eat first, explain second. Are four pieces of bacon enough?"

"I could eat six if that leaves any for you."

After inhaling her breakfast almost before it hits the plate, Tamiko explains her work on *Class of '24*, concluding by saying, "I love working with Amelia Jackson, but dealing with Stan Greene is at least two miles past the town of Awkward."

"Where does Greene fit into the industry pecking order?"

"He's had back-to-back-to back Netflix hits, so he's a plenty big deal. But, I'm thinking the streaming world is still a level down from A-list movies."

"It used to be for sure, but with a bunch of iconic media outfits joining Netflix, Amazon, and HBO, to grab more and more eyeballs, Greene may believe he and Ben Fine are playing in the same league."

"He's arrogant enough I guess, but what does that have to do with how I should try to cope with him?"

"You both performed and wrote for Fine, but, assuming I'm up to speed on *Tamiko's Adventures in Tinsel Town*, you've declined to even test for Greene's new series."

"I've explained to Stan over and over that deciding not to act is about my life's plan, not somehow an insult to him. But since writing for *Class of '24* is great fun, and pays like a broken slot machine, I'm definitely down for more of that."

"Hmph!"

After waiting in vain for Ed to add more, Tamiko says, "Seriously Ed, *Hmph!*—that's all the advice I get? C'mon, no need to censor if that's what you're doing."

"I'm hesitating because I fear I'm too far away from the world you've fallen into to have a useful opinion. But, just the same, I'm gonna guess Greene may believe that you aren't sincere about not wanting to act, but only trying to jack him up for more money. Which is why I'd bet my grandfather's gold pocket watch against a drugstore Timex that if you agree to read for Anna things will immediately smooth out."

"Not if he picks me and I back out. Tom Obanta, my agent, finally listened when I insisted no really meant no, but how do I convince Stan Greene?"

"In theory at least, your agent works for you, so has to pretend to respect what you say. But in practice, since Obanta only gets paid when you do, I bet he'll continue to encourage you to rethink your hard no. But for now, let's keep our focus on Greene. There may be nothing you can do to guarantee he'll allow you to be part of the *Class of '24* writers' team long-term without your agreeing to perform, but I have an idea that may keep you employed a little longer."

"Are you still going to tell me even though I'm stealing your bacon?" Tamiko asks, as she reaches over to snag a strip from Ed's plate.

"Obviously, all multi-episode streaming dramas rely on cliffhangers to bring viewers back," Ed replies, as he tips his one remaining piece onto Tamiko's plate. "So how about doubling down on this idea by creating an early dramatic cliff for Anna, who I gather is the most charismatic of your first-years. For example, when you submit your plot sketches at the end of your second fifty hours you might have Anna disappear in a highly dramatic fashion. I'm obviously winging it, but my point is that if Greene wants to find out what happens to Anna, he'll have to extend your deal."

"Stan's been around a lot more Tinsel Town blocks than I have, so he's sure to spot what I'm up to," Tamiko replies, her tone telegraphing her doubt that such a simple ruse can work.

"So what? Even if Greene's so pissed he's tempted to ignore your whole disappearance ploy, I'm betting he'll quickly see that he's the one who gets the huge payday if you manage to bring back Anna in a stunning way."

"Got it. As it happens, I've been playing around with an uber suspenseful episode, which involves Chloe, the racist white girl from Virginia, discovering that Adaora, her Nigerian roommate, is having what appears to be a lesbian moment with a professor. But, sure, let me try to come up with something equally dramatic for Anna and include both in episode five which looks to be the last one I'll have time for."

. . . . .

Alec lands in Mexico City late in the afternoon of December 30th, where he changes to an Aeromexico flight to Puerto Escondido. By the time he arrives in the heart of the small resort city on Mexico's southwest coast, he's so beat he crashes at the first small surfer-friendly hotel he spots. Fifteen minutes later, with a beer in one hand, and a bag of chips in the other, he stretches out on the narrow bed and gives thanks for the warm, velvety air.

. . . . .

On New Year's Eve Tamiko leaves Oakland on the first Southwest flight to Chicago, where she'll board a connecting flight to Bradley International in northern Connecticut. Being home with Amy and Ed for two nights has been a short, but much needed respite from the anxiety that her life is about to skid on black ice. Yesterday, the three of them had put together a traditional Japanese New Year's feast two days early for family and friends, including her Auntie Les, Uncle Dan and their baby, Slugger Ken. It was the kind of fuzzy warm family evening that reminded Tamiko that, whatever the resolution to her immediate dramas, she's part of a community that can be trusted to sustain her.

Having slept most of the way from Oakland to Chicago, Tamiko again closes her eyes when she's back in the air for the Connecticut leg of her journey. Now, lightly dozing, she relives her last night with Jed. Finding herself curled against his long, strong naked body, her sense of vivid pleasure is at least quadrupled when he reaches a long arm around her waist to first find, and then massage, her pleasure spot. At the point of audibly expressing her satisfaction, Tamiko's dream is providentially cut short when she hears the woman next to her ask for a Diet Coke. Even as she hopes the light film of perspiration coating her face doesn't give her away, Tamiko opens her eyes to tell the cabin attendant, "I'll have the same."

Determined now to stay awake, Tamiko opens her laptop to the video compilation of Amherst basketball highlights Coach Raines has sent. No question, Amherst is a polished team, especially in the front court where the two forwards, Margie Prime and Leni Silverstein, have size, quickness and can both shoot reliably from the corners. Miki Nakamura, the sophomore shooting guard, also has game, especially when she's able to penetrate the defense to shoot her jumper from within fifteen feet. And while Rosie Wilburn, the injured first-year point guard Tamiko is replacing, is the most tentative player on the team, she too is a talented athlete who quickly gained confidence and competence as the early season games progressed.

After entering half a dozen notes on her phone, Tamiko is about to close her laptop when she remembers Coach also requested she review several games from last year. With the more experienced, and athletically gifted, Ericka Williams leading the offense, it's easy to see how this faster, more aggressive Amherst team won the Division Three Championship. Not only was Ericka almost always the quickest player on the court, but especially compared to this year's more deliberate pace, her high energy game pushed her teammates into a risk-taking style that often intimidated opponents into a cascade of mistakes. Hoping she'll be able to nudge the team back toward last year's style, Tamiko raises her seat back in preparation for landing.

. . . . .

When Tamiko comes out of the secure area at Bradley International she sees a *Welcome, Tamiko Gashkin* sign. Surprised that Coach Raines has come herself, Tamiko reaches up to smooth down her plane hair as she says, "This is nice, but it's New Year's Eve and I could have…"

"You didn't have to come back to school over three weeks early to try to save our season," the tall, lean, fortyish woman interrupts. "Doing a lunchtime New Year's celebration with my partner in order to save you from the bus is my way of saying thank you."

"Hopefully I'll have enough game to justify your driving a hundred miles roundtrip," Tamiko says seriously. "For sure starting at point guard in a few days for a team I've never played for has me more than a little intimidated."

"I've scheduled three hours of court time tomorrow and Wednesday plus additional hours for chalk talks. Having watched the video of a couple of your high school playoff games, I'm not worried about your skill level, or ability to take charge of a team. I only hope you're fit enough to go forty minutes. You said you've been exercising, but directing an offense for a full game is a lot tougher than jogging a few miles." Then, as the coach wheels her black Mazda 3 out of the short-term parking area she asks, "Have you had a chance to look at the videos I sent?"

"Definitely, and no doubt Amherst has excellent players. As I said, I only hope I can fit in."

"No need for false modesty. In addition to you, your Berkeley High team had two, or maybe even three, D1-level athletes. And more to the point, you ran the offense like you were a cross between Tom Brady and Twyla Tharp, who is…"

"A modern dance choreographer. I grew up watching her company whenever they performed in Berkeley."

"Lucky you, but back to what you saw on the videos."

"Rosie is a solid player, easily the best athlete of your first-years and is improving each game. As you know the rest of the team is strong, but without Ericka's court vision and wizard ball handling, maybe a little too laid-back. A less talented, but more aggressive opponent might even steal a game."

"I'm hoping you'll provide the energy needed to wake them up, and in the process, show Rosie how to play a faster, bolder, style."

"Rosie's outside shot is probably better than mine already."

"From what little video I could find for your Berkeley High team, your perimeter shot is plenty good enough, especially when you get to your favorite spot at four o'clock on the three-point line. And you have the huge advantage of being able to drive to the basket and shoot with either hand."

"Ever since my dad noticed that as a tyke I was pretty close to ambidextrous he challenged me to left-handed-only games."

"Since vanishingly few division three point guards can use both hands equally well, pretty much every outside defender in our league tries to prevent dribble drives to the basket by cheating half a step to the right of the player they're guarding. So, until they figure you out, you'll have fun blowing past them untouched. But Tamiko, I'm curious, is there anything else you noticed in the video I should know about?"

"For whatever reason, Amherst rarely tries to stretch the vertical floor. Perhaps you saw that at BHS almost every time we got possession under our opponent's basket the rebounder flipped the fall to me and I looked for the forty- or fifty-foot downcourt pass to our other guard, who had attempted to sprint behind the defense. Maybe we only caught the defense napping a few times per game, but whenever we pulled it off, it was both two easy points, and a stake through our opponent's heart."

"Excellent! Let's work on that in the next few days. Miki Nakamura is quick and smart and I'm sure she'll love the chance to try to beat her defender down the court."

"Just curious, but how come it's not already part of your game plan, especially since an opponent who has to worry about defending it can't be quite as aggressive on offense?"

"Last year Ericka, for all her great qualities, didn't have your upper-body strength so couldn't whip a ball fifty feet on a line and our two forwards simply weren't accurate enough. This year with Rosie having so much to learn we haven't gotten to it. But Tamiko, since we're almost to Amherst I'd offer to buy you supper, but Dean Thomas texted me she'd have New Year's Eve dinner waiting. Which reminds me to ask whether you wouldn't rather stay on campus. With the school mostly deserted until the next semester starts in a couple of weeks, the athletes on the winter sports teams enjoy hanging together."

"After my month in Movieland I need time to decompress. But, of course, if there's a team event or whatever, I'll be there early and stay late so hopefully no one thinks I'm a prima donna."

"I'm afraid that coming fresh from L.A. you'll be the center of unrelenting curiosity no matter how much you try to hide. But, if you don't mind my asking I'm curious how you've managed to buddy up with an Associate Dean of the college? Obviously, it's none of my business, so it's fine if you…"

"No big secret," Tamiko interrupts. "When I first got here Dean Thomas dealt with a lot of bureaucratic B.S. to get me into a grad course over at UMass. Then, when the film role fell on me, she ran interference with my profs so that it was smooth to skip out three weeks before the semester ended. Now, with her husband off on a month-long research project, it's my chance to repay her kindness by helping with her daughters, the older of whom, Lily, is already a buddy from my giving her pitching lessons."

. . . . .

When Coach Raines's car pulls up in front of Dean Thomas's on Amherst's Lesser Street, Lily and her younger sister Phoebe bounce down the snow-dusted walk. "Tamiko, Tamiko, our very best friend—Happy New Year," they sing in unison, no doubt having practiced half the afternoon.

Giving Tamiko a quick hug just outside the front door, their mother says, "Good thing you weren't half an hour later or they might have burst."

"Thanks for having me, I was delighted when you asked."

"Macaroni and cheese, ribs, and salad in forty-five. Do you want to stretch out?"

Seeing the stricken look cloud Lily's face, Tamiko puts aside her long day as she says, "How about I hang with the girls. But, despite the time change, I want to get to bed early since I asked Coach to open the gym for me at eight-thirty, forty-five minutes before the team arrives. But, um, er…," Tamiko stutters to a stop as she realizes she's clueless as to what to call her hostess.

"Amber, please."

"Really?"

"Amber here at home, but maybe stick to Dean Thomas on campus, unless you mix them up which is absolutely no problem."

"Okay then Amber, if I'm going to hang here for the next couple of weeks I want to do my share of cooking, cleaning, fetching and anything else you need."

"Music to the ears of this barely coping mom. How about you cook two nights, I cook two nights and we do the take-out boogie for the rest. For New Year's tomorrow, I've ordered dinner from my favorite deli so that's covered. As for other tasks, whether you like it or not, yours is primarily going to be girl entertainment. Lily, who just got her first period last month, especially sees you as a role model for everything she wants to be in the next five years. But, for now, the girls have at least half a dozen games laid out for you in the front room so I'll leave you to it."

· · · · ·

When dinner is finished Tamiko is pressed into service to tell the good night story, which just happens to feature the adventures of an intrepid twelve-year-old girl, Sheriff Daisy, and her precocious kid sister, Deputy Missy. After the fictional girls have triumphantly rounded up the Polka Dot Gang, and the real girls have fallen asleep, Amber says, "Tamiko, of course I have at least a dozen questions about what happened in Hollywood since your last email, but perhaps it will come as a relief that I have to prepare for a planning meeting with the president and senior staff, so my priority is to hibernate with my laptop."

"Before I switch off the light, I plan to write the fourth and final *Tamiko's Adventures in La-La Land*. So, I may answer a bunch of your questions before you have a chance to ask them."

Holing up in the second-floor guest room a few minutes later Tamiko fires up her laptop. After detailing last week's Movieland adventures, she again attempts to spell out why she's been put off by her brush with acting. But, when this sounds too much like a trust fund baby whining about the burden of managing her money, Tamiko substitutes a description of how much fun she's having developing plot ideas for *Class of '24*. Now, sitting quietly for a moment, she considers what to say about Jed Streeter, who she guesses is the number one, two and three subjects of interest for most of her friends.

Finally she enters:

A number of special people helped make my unlikely film odyssey both possible and enjoyable (well, mostly). Of course this starts with 2+2's director, Ben Fine, who both selected me, and also pushed me (OK, sometimes shoved me) to do more than I thought possible. And Mary McCarthy, who served as surrogate mom, best buddy, guide and chief extractor when, inevitably, I tumbled into La-La Land quicksand. Jack and Naomi Gold, 2+2's talented writers, have also been a huge source of support and fun.

Remarkably, both put aside any understandable annoyance at Ben's inserting me in their creative process to listen to my often naive script ideas in an effort to find the few grains of wheat amongst the pile of chaff. Finally, Jed Streeter, who extended a guiding hand from my first day on the set, proved to be both mentor and tight friend. There is no way I could have climbed over even half of Movieland's daunting obstacles without Jed's strong arm to lean on. Although I never could have guessed it six weeks ago, I now count Tinsel Town's most famous dude as a true buddy.

Beaming love and good cheer for the New Year to all you dear ones—Tamiko

P.S. I'm back at Amherst a few weeks before spring semester starts filling in on the basketball team. What can I say, but being back in this quiet, winter-draped western Massachusetts town is just the dose of real-world normality that I crave. I mean, really, the moment I step outside and my nose begins to freeze, I pretty much forget about everything else.

EARLY JANUARY

ALEC RISES WITH THE SUN to check out the surf at Zicatela Beach. Although the waves aren't as outrageously vertical as in summer, he knows they're plenty big for a dude who hasn't been in the water in five months. Walking Puerto Escondido's hillside streets he finds a pleasant *cuarto para rentar* in a turquoise house with a view of the ocean. Next, browsing several surf shops he discovers a comfortably broken-in eight-foot board, much like the one he's left in California. Settled in his room an hour later he begins his New Year's phone calls, first reaching out to his mom in Manhattan, and then his dad in the big square colonial house in the leafy suburb where Alec grew up. Already aware that his parents are pointed in opposite directions, Alec realizes the fact they aren't together to celebrate signals that their pulling apart is accelerating. But deciding this isn't the day to probe, he contents himself with the usual holiday felicitations.

"When do you plan to get here?" his mother asks. "I certainly hope the lure of the gringo trail isn't going to capture you as it did a couple of years back?" she adds, allowing her skeptical tone to amplify her point.

"Be careful what you wish for, Mom," Alec replies with a laugh, "since in a couple of weeks I plan to be camping on your couch. But no worries because I'm already networking for a room in Brooklyn not Borneo."

"Music to my ears. Listen, I don't mean to invade your privacy, but since it's been ages since we've talked, I hope it's okay to ask whether the special young woman whose name begins with T is still in your plans?"

"Mom, you can ask anything you want, as long as you don't need an answer," Alec responds. Then, realizing from his mother's silence that his attempt at humor has landed with an impolite thud, he adds, "Mom, as you and Dad also seem to be learning, even when two people want to tango it's not always easy to stay in step. And then there's the fact that, after Tamiko's exciting adventure in Hollywood, I may no longer be at the top of her dance card."

After the rest of his calls are complete, Alec can no longer put off the question of whether to FaceTime Tamiko. But where is she? And, more to the point, who is she with? Probably still in L.A. finishing the film with Jed Streeter, he guesses. Then, after unsuccessfully trying to banish from his mind the image of Tamiko untangling herself from Streeter to answer his call, he decides to go for a long run on the beach.

. . . . .

On New Year's morning Tamiko awakes from an eerie dream in which she's being closely examined by a wall of lidless fish eyes to find Phoebe and Lily perched on the foot of her bed.

"You have six more minutes to sleep, that is, if you really need to," Phoebe exclaims, tapping her pink Mighty Munchkin watch.

"What do you think I should do?" Tamiko asks, glancing at the bedside clock to see that, indeed, it's 7:09 a.m.

"Maybe, get dressed pretty fast so you can tell us another story."

"Maybe there will be time for a short one if you two vamoose long enough for me to clean my teeth and get organized."

Entering the kitchen a few minutes later to the lush smell of dark roast coffee, Tamiko finds Amber putting bacon, eggs, toast and coffee on the table. "Lest you get used to this, on school days you get O.J., plus porridge with bananas, and maple syrup. Anything else is up to you."

"How about I do bacon and French toast with blueberries on weekends?" Tamiko suggests.

"Yay!" both girls yell, each vying to be loudest.

. . . . .

When Tamiko pushes through the door of LeFrak Gym five minutes early, the lights are already on and Coach Raines is shooting mid-range jump shots. "Where did you play?" Tamiko asks, as she sheds her long down overcoat and red Berkeley High sweatpants.

"Happy New Year to you as well," Coach Raines says with a laugh, before adding, "Kansas State. We were in no danger of making the Sweet Sixteen, but we had our moments. I started junior and senior years, which, looking back, were among my happiest. So, do you want to start 2019 by shooting on your own? Or do you prefer my putting a hand in your face?"

"How about you make me sweat for fifteen minutes—sprinting, calisthenics or whatever? Then, after I shoot a few, going one-on-one would be great. Since last night when you told me you want me to keep driving to the basket until I draw a double team, I've worried about finishing. It's like, if I don't actually put the ball in the hoop, no one is going to be intimidated by my quickness."

"All good. But I'm not in shape to go full out for long. I'll force you left and right and the rest will be on you."

When the Amherst players trickle in just before 9:30, Coach suggests that Tamiko catch her breath while the others do fifteen minutes of sprints. Knowing from experience that a new kid who is suspected of getting special treatment will never be accepted, Tamiko joins the others. Finally, all clumped together in the bleachers a few minutes later, Coach says, "Rosie's rehab is going well and we hope to have her back for the January twelfth game against Trinity, at least part-time. Until then I'm delighted that Tamiko Gashkin has generously said yes to my urgent request for help. I don't mean to underestimate any of our existing players, but as many of you know, Tamiko directed the offense for one of the best high school teams in California, so good that they would have given lots of college teams, including this one, a battle. Now, before I get down to strategy for Thursday night's game at Wesleyan, does anyone have anything to say?"

Given the team's desperate need for a floor manager, Tamiko expects a polite welcome, but is nevertheless pleased when Rachel Host, the small curly-haired girl at the end of the bench says, "Tamiko, just so you know, I'm the most grateful person here. If you hadn't agreed to play, the point guard responsibility would fall on me, and at this level I'm not ready for it."

Ball in hand, a few minutes later, Tamiko feels a burst of something approaching joy as she realizes that for the first time in over a month she knows exactly what to do. Moving the ball quickly around the court Tamiko sees that because the other four are competent shooters, even this basic spread offense can succeed. Reluctant to show up tiny Rachel Host, who is defending her, Tamiko finally responds to Coach Raines shouted commands to be more aggressive by switching her dribble to her left hand to explode past Rachel and pull up to swish a short jumper. After a stunned pause, Rachel, who may as well have been wearing iron boots for all the resistance she was able to mount, begins to clap and the others join in. When half an hour later Coach calls a break, Tamiko can't help but notice she now stands near the group's center, instead of at its fringe, as had been true an hour earlier.

Back in the gym a little before 3:00 p.m. for a second session, Tamiko watches the last few minutes of the men's team's practice. Derrick Fine, who she knows got back from Italy yesterday, scrimmages with the second team. Although Derrick's a half step slow and a hair awkward, his size and aggressive court savvy make him a tough defender. When the practice ends, Derrick catches her eye as he inclines his head toward the end of the court. After a quick hug, Tamiko asks, "So, how was the Bel Paese?"

"I'll tell you all about it when we have a minute. Are you free later?"

"Supper and story time with Dean Thomas's kids have me bound tight tonight," Tamiko replies, as she crosses her arms to clasp opposite shoulders.

"I have games both tomorrow night and Friday and I know you're playing Thursday and Saturday, so how about dinner Sunday?" Derrick asks.

"You're on."

"Great, and Tamiko, it's way cool that you're doing this for the team."

"And vice versa," Tamiko replies seriously. "After my bewildering month in L.A., it's a pleasure to stand on a simple wood floor with a ball in my hand and know what's expected of me."

. . . . .

Early Wednesday, January 2nd, Alec is in the blue-green water at the north end of Zicatela Beach looking forward to paddling into his first ride on its world famous tube-like waves.

Relaxing on his board while he respects the surfing etiquette giving precedence to locals, he waits until he receives a nod from a slim dude on a long green semi-gun board. Reading the next big wave Alec paddles hard until he feels the water begin to rise under him. Before he can register what's happening, the wave goes vertical and purely through reflex he pops to his feet as he drops down the fall line. Crouching now, he leans onto his toes before spinning the board toward the wave's foaming crest and gracefully riding it to the beach. After several more relaxed runs, Alec's feet begin to lose their chatter and he knows he's ready for something more aggressive. So, when he next pops up, he doesn't seek the wave's crest, but instead squats and shifts his weight back on the board to stall as close as possible to its fast rising vertical wall with the result that the turquoise water begins to curl over, and then around him. Enveloped, but untouched by the surging barrel of water, Alec finds himself in the remarkably peaceful place surfers call the Green Room. As he bombs southwest inside the tube at fifteen miles per hour, time seems to slow and his mind lights up with the realization that the only high that has ever rivaled this is holding Tamiko Gashkin.

Content after his close encounter with surfing nirvana, Alec enjoys a couple of relaxed runs before paddling to the beach and schlepping his board the few blocks back to his room. Twenty minutes later, as he collects his double-shot Americano at Brown Sugar on Boulevard Benito Juarez he is surprised to hear his name. Turning, he sees a tanned blonde girl wearing a white crop top over bright blue shorts, quick-stepping toward him. Sandra? Sara? Sasha?—he tries to recall, embarrassed that he remembers holding her toned, naked body, but not her name. It's only when she launches herself into his arms that it comes to him. "Hey Sam, it's been a while," he croaks as he tries to slide away from her enthusiastic lips as diplomatically as possible.

"Over two years since Chapadmalal, Argentina," the sun-drenched girl replies, still holding Alec tight. "And as I've told you on Facebook more than once, the eight days I spent surfing with you there were the best of my holiday—any holiday—really." Finally, stepping back as she pins Alec with her vivid blue eyes, she adds, "But, since at best I receive a three-sentence reply, I'm resigned to the fact that you weren't nearly as swept away as I was. But here we are together in Puerto and a girl can hope. So let me join you for a latte while we catch up."

As Alec sits at a tiny table waiting for Sam to add what looks to be a half pound of sugar to her bowl of milk-infused caffeine, he remembers their pleasant week together. It happened halfway through the gap year after he'd ditched both his Olympic hopes in the Modern Pentathlon and his junior year at U.C. Berkeley, to surf his way around the Southern Hemisphere. Perhaps, hanging out with this pretty, peppy young woman in Argentina had lacked the full measure of romantic pizzazz, but that didn't mean their time together wasn't special.

"My parents left for Chicago yesterday," Sam says as she perches on the edge of the mini-chair across from Alec. "UT doesn't start for a week so I decided to hang here for a few more days rather than freezing my tush in Austin. I've been surfing La Punta at the end of Playa Zicatela, but tomorrow the surf is supposed to drop a bit and I want to try the big boys at Zicatela. But, oh my god, Alec, it'd be so chill if you'll come out with me. It's not like I'm intimidated or anything, but, well, what can I say but that those tubes are pretty damn huge and so…. But, hey dude," Sam interrupts herself, "when did you get here? And were you out this morning when I heard there were ten-footers going? Also, where are you staying? I mean, I haven't seen you, so maybe you just dropped in. It's like I have a sweet room, so maybe…"

"Yowser Sam! When did you get to be such a motormouth?" Alec interrupts with a laugh.

"Sorry, but I'm psyched to see you. It's like when I realized who was standing in front of me I couldn't help thinking, here's that awesome dude. But like, I get it, if maybe you're not as into me? Sorry, I guess I'm still blabbering…"

"Sam, it will be my pleasure to do Zicatela with you *mañana* and hang whenever you want. Truly, it's great to see you and I too have fond memories of our time together. But, I have a girlfriend, or hope I do, anyway, since I spent the fall in Japan, where I also tumbled pretty hard for this Japanese girl. But now, I'm laser-focused on getting her back—the American, that is—which means I'm way off-limits as far as other romances go."

"So where are your two lucky girls now?" Sam asks, doing her best not to show her disappointment.

"Mayumi, the one I was with in Japan, is off traveling in Europe with a girlfriend. As for Tamiko, the American, I'm not sure what's up with her. She was in L.A. making a movie, but that may be wrapped by now."

"Really, Alec? Your girlfriend's an actress? Like a legit one?"

"Seriously! She's in the Ben Fine film that's shooting now. It turns out Tamiko is a college buddy of Fine's kids so he discovered her through them and cast her for a small part."

"Wait a second, are you talking about the movie about wife-swapping with Jed Streeter that was featured in *People* magazine last week?" Not giving Alec a chance to answer, Sam continues, "Oh my god, don't tell me she's the Eurasian one with all that fabulous thick, honey-colored hair and almond-shaped blue eyes who's standing next to Jed in a couple of the photos?"

"I missed the article, but Tamiko's part Japanese and part Russian and has thick light-colored hair, so it fits. But how come you're so interested?"

Staring at her latte as if it might otherwise run off, Sam finally looks up, her dusting of freckles standing out against her suddenly flushed face, "Just so you know, I never get crushes on film stars, but Jed Streeter is the exception. So the truth is I was envious when I saw him grinning at this girl who's more or less my age as if she was an ice cream sundae. Now that I discover that this Tamiko is also your sweet pea, I'm probably turning from pink to chartreuse. I mean, what are the odds of one girl stealing the two dudes I'm hot for?"

Not knowing how to diplomatically point out that Sam has never met Jed Streeter, and hasn't seen Alec for over two years, Alec is relieved when he spots the Mexican surfer coming through the door who had been so helpful to him out on the break. "*Hola amigo, puedo comprarte un cafe?*" Alec asks, springing to his feet and extending his hand.

"Thanks, Dude. Awesome out there today. And, sure, I could be down with a latte," the deeply tanned surfer replies in unaccented English as he grips Alec's hand and says, "Alejandro Perez." After introducing Sam, Alec joins the line at the coffee bar where he also orders a plate of conchas, the sweet Mexican bread whose irresistible sugary, buttery aroma permeates the cafe. When he returns five minutes later he sees, to his considerable relief, that not only is Alejandro talking animatedly to Sam, but that she's given up her tentative perch on the edge of her chair to lean back with an almost regal grace.

"I had you pegged as a Puerto dude, but you're obviously not from here," Alec says as he hands Alejandro his coffee.

"I was born in L.A., but my grandparents live just south of Puerto and I've visited often enough that on a good day I'm treated as a local. That's especially true this year since I'm doing my junior year in Mexico City and get down regularly."

When Alec explains that he and Sam surfed together in Argentina and that she knows her way around big waves, Alejandro agrees that tomorrow will be a great opportunity for her to give Zicatela a shot. "See you both on the beach at seven," Alec announces as he stands and says he needs to make a few calls. Glancing back to see Sam and Alejandro with heads close together, laughing, he wonders if he and Tamiko will ever again share such a carefree moment. But one thing is sure, Alec thinks, no matter where Tamiko is, what she's doing, and whom she's doing it with, we'll never have a future until I stop procrastinating and tell her I love her and want to re-up our committed relationship.

But, when Alec stops at an internet cafe to do just that, Tamiko's fourth La-La Land postcard, complete with her full-throated declaration of affection for Jed Streeter punches him in the gut. Just in case any doubt remains as to Tamiko and Jed's romantic status, the glowing photos she includes all but shout they're lovers. Not nearly as surprised, as he is dismayed, Alec slowly rereads Tamiko's message and feels only slightly better when he realizes she's back in Massachusetts to play basketball. Could this even mean that her romance with Jed is on hold? With no way to begin to answer this question, Alec asks himself how he should respond. Then, seeing he also has a Happy New Year message from Mayumi in Greece, the answer becomes clear. Since just two months ago he had at least implicitly asked Tamiko to accept Mayumi as his beloved friend, it's now his turn to suck it up. As with waiting for the right wave, Alec knows that patience rules.

. . . . .

For the next couple of days Sammy, Alejandro and Alec form a mini-star cluster with the new lovers bonded as tightly as bright binary suns and Alec, hanging on their periphery like a dim second cousin. Although the surf drops a bit each day, the waves are still big enough to unite the trio in the quasi religious experience of attempting to become one with the sea. When Sammy and Alejandro disappear to spend afternoons together, Alec stays in the water, which he has come to see as his best refuge from stewing over Tamiko and Jed. Several times he finds himself back in the internet cafe intending to send her one of the thousands of messages his mind endlessly invents. But it only takes another glance at Tamiko's fourth postcard for Alec to decide to hold his peace for another day. After all, he asks himself, if Tamiko is now open to my earlier proposals for us to get back together, isn't it her turn to give me a signal?

. . . . .

To keep the players fresh for that evening's game, practice on January 3rd is limited to an hour working on defensive strategy, with the focus on how and when Tamiko and Miki Nakamura, Amherst's other guard, should switch defensive assignments. Because Wesleyan runs a conventional offense primarily using screens and the pick and roll to free its outside shooters, Tamiko is familiar with everything Coach requests. True, since she and Miki haven't had time to develop the shared sixth sense as to where the other is about to move that long-term teammates take for granted, they're bound to botch a play now and then. However, when Coach assures Tamiko that against a middling opponent like Wesleyan, all will be well if they get their switches right three-quarters of the time, she relaxes and begins to have fun. At 11:00 a.m. Coach pulls the team off the court and into a chalk talk. "Assuming Tamiko shoots well enough to draw a double team," Coach emphasizes, "let's get the ball to either Margie or Leni, whoever is unguarded underneath the basket."

With a few hours to herself, Tamiko FaceTimes Amelia Jackson in L.A. Even before Tamiko can confess she hasn't had time to outline her ideas for the second episode of *Class of '24*, Amelia reports that since both she and her twins have heavy colds, she needs a couple of sick days. "Okay, then," Tamiko replies with relief, "why don't I give you until Monday before I hit you with my thoughts," even as she hopes by then she'll have a few.

· · · · ·

"Ready to go, Kidlet?" Tamiko asks when Lily returns from middle school. "I have a catcher lined up at four."

"Really, Tamiko? I mean, I know you have a game later and Mom said not to beg or bug, which she calls my double 'B' mode, which is just so mega-unfair because…"

"Do you want to pitch, or talk me out of it?" Tamiko interrupts with mock seriousness.

"Pitch for sure," Lily replies happily, already halfway up the stairs to change.

On the chilly infield behind LeFrak Gym a few minutes later, Tamiko finds Rachel Host shifting from foot to foot despite her industrial strength gray sweatshirt. Tossing Rachel a mitt as she introduces Lily, Tamiko says, "Big thanks for helping out. It's a lot easier to work on Lily's mechanics when I'm standing next to her, not squatting thirty-five feet away trying to catch the ball. And since we're already losing the light, we'll call it quits in half an hour."

"You play basketball too, don't you?" Lily asks shyly. When Rachel nods, Lily continues, "Tonight after the game, will you sign my program? I mean, Tamiko has already promised, but it would be great if…"

"How about I get everyone on the team to sign?" Rachel asks seriously.

"Super! That would be just so legit, but…"

"How about we work out the details later and get down to pitching," Tamiko says. "I'd like to see the drop ball you and your dad have been working on."

．．．．．

Because the campus is all but empty during winter break, barely a hundred people show up at 7:30 to see Amherst play Wesleyan. As each Amherst starter is introduced, the fans clap politely as they continue chatting with their neighbors. However, when the announcer intones, "And playing her first game with the Mammoths, Tamiko Gashkin, a five-ten first-year guard from Berkeley, California," everyone stops in mid-sentence to look up. A few know about Tamiko's history as an athlete, others that she's the first-year who got the movie contract, while most have never heard of her. But for everyone, the introduction of a varsity starter who has never previously donned the purple and white is a walloping surprise.

The game begins when Amherst's Josie Gold wins the center jump and tips the ball to Miki Nakamura, who flips it to Tamiko, who, as point guard, will direct the offense.

Dribbling with her right hand Tamiko moves to the top of the key tightly shadowed by a terrier-like defender in a black uniform with red highlights, who apparently believes Amherst's novice starter is ripe for the picking. Aggressively crowding Tamiko, the pink-faced Wesleyan guard positions herself slightly to Tamiko's right in order to block her expected lane to the basket. Feigning difficulty in controlling her dribble, Tamiko baits her defender into lunging for the ball. Then quickly switching her dribble to her left hand Tamiko accelerates untouched to convert an easy layup. As she runs back down the court to assume her defensive position, Tamiko grins when she hears the Wesleyan coach yell, "Number Nine, listen up, Amherst's new kid's a lefty."

When Wesleyan misses their first three-point attempt, Tamiko grabs the rebound and tosses a sixty-foot pass to Miki, who, having raced behind the napping defense, takes it in stride to score another easy deuce. A few seconds later, after Leni Silverstein blocks Wesleyan's next shot attempt, Tamiko brings the ball down the court dribbling with her left hand. Now positioning herself slightly to Tamiko's left, the still overconfident defender again stutter-steps too close as she reaches to try to steal the ball. Perhaps this will convince Terrier Girl she's not going to crowd me off the court, Tamiko thinks, as she easily switches the dribble to her right hand, and again steps unblocked past her astonished defender to put Amherst up 6-0.

After a Wesleyan timeout, a new defensive strategy is in evidence. Number Nine now hangs back a couple of steps so as to more easily cut Tamiko off should she again attempt to drive to the basket. Wesleyan, it seems, is betting that the surprisingly ambidextrous Amherst newbie doesn't have an outside shot. Hoping to prove them wrong, Tamiko slides to her favorite spot at four o'clock outside the three-point arc and is vastly relieved when her jump shot finds the bottom of the net. Jacked with the delicious feeling she's in the zone, Tamiko knocks down another three-pointer ninety seconds later. But this time as she turns to race down the court her brain conjures a voice from the past that rasps, "Beware the moment when you feel so invincible you believe you can do it all yourself." Grateful that wise old Mr. Swayze, her grade four coach, is still hanging out deep in her head to remind her that basketball is a team sport, Tamiko resolves to put a lid on her shooting. So the next time she brings the ball over the centerline, Tamiko whips a pass to Margie in the right corner, who tosses the ball to Josie, alone underneath the basket for an easy hoop, making the score 16-2. Not shooting again for the rest of the half, Tamiko continues to distribute the ball to her underguarded teammates. By the time the mid-game buzzer sounds, every Amherst starter has scored and the collective mood is fist-bumpingly high.

At the beginning of the fourth quarter with Amherst ahead by 24, Coach Raines replaces Tamiko with Rachel Host. Sensing an opening, the tall, black-clad Wesleyan coach discards her usual defensive strategy to instead order a full court press.

Wesleyan's goal now is clearly to steal the ball from the undersized Amherst guard before she can even initiate the offense. Rachel's quickness combined with a couple of fortunate down-court passes, means Amherst beats the press the first few times. But before long the much larger Wesleyan guards figure out how to either corner Rachel and grab the ball, or prevent her from advancing it across the mid-court line in the required ten seconds. When this happens a fourth time with the result that Wesleyan's extra shots cut Amherst's lead to 16, Coach Raines mutters, "Ms. Crow over there is too dumb to recognize that I've given her a present." Motioning for Tamiko to reenter, Coach Raines adds, "If she wants us to run up the score so be it." But, when the Wesleyan coach spots Tamiko crouching next to the scorer's table waiting for a break in the action, she scowlingly orders her team to retreat to their normal defensive positions, allowing Rachel to bring the ball across half-court unmolested. "Back in your seat Gashkin," Coach Raines says, "it turns out that my benighted colleague has belatedly glimpsed the fact that it's better to lose by a respectable margin than have you lead us to a blowout."

. . . . .

Friday morning Alec is hit by the smell of rotting garbage as he comes down the stairs from his second-floor room carrying his board. Not only has the wind died, and the temperature shot up ten degrees, there is no sound of pulsing surf, a combination that tells him he may as well go back to bed. Sure enough, when he arrives at Zicatela Beach, Sam, Alejandro and a knot of other surfers cluster disconsolately in the meager shade of an anorexic palm. When Alec joins them, he learns that today's depressingly flat water is predicted to last at least a week. To find reliably big waves he'll have to head a thousand miles north to Sayulita, or one of the other surfing meccas north of Puerto Vallarta. Before he can even consider his best course of action, Alejandro says, "Alec, since my classes start in a couple of days, Sam and I are flying to Mexico City this afternoon. Come with us and you can crash at my place tonight and hop a plane to the north coast tomorrow."

With a few hours to kill, Alec decides that, whether or not Jed Streeter is at, or near, the center of Tamiko's life, he needs to make contact. So, after a latte and a bowl of granola, he heads back to the turquoise house to call. Climbing the steps to see his shattered padlock lying in front of the open door, he knows his lousy morning isn't over. Touching the pockets of his shirt to confirm that his wallet and passport are safe, Alec feels more annoyed than worried as he enters his room to find nothing is missing except his iPhone and iPad. And since the phone is four models old and has a cracked face, and the iPad only works intermittently, he realizes he's lost little except the opportunity to call Tamiko.

A couple of hours later, having tossed his belongings into his duffel, and checked out of his room, Alec stops at the now-familiar internet cafe. Although he has half a dozen messages, there is still nothing from Tamiko. Clicking on a new email from Mayumi, he reads:

alec where r u? talk to me, my impossible love. yes, yes, i'm still kicking myself about the aki fiasco and its likely effect on sweet tamiko. but having read her last postcard from la-la land it's pretty clear she landed on her feet. jed streeter (movie star, notwithstanding) is a lucky dude—kinda like u, with me :). but whether jed is tamiko's big deal, little deal or no deal at all alec hold tight to the fact that u r the one she truly loves. so if u haven't already done so stop moping and reach out. and it's not only ur well being i have in mind since i know u won't forgive me until things r good with u and t.

so what's up with ur small japanese friend? i thought u'd never ask. in a nutshell, greece is so fascinating f & i will chill here 4 the rest of the month i wish i could report an exciting new romantic adventure but u seem to have spoiled me 4 anything but the best.

*and since neither u nor jed streeter is here (oops sorry i couldn't resist) i
haven't been tempted. but alec (and now i'm serious) no matter who i meet
whether it's tomorrow or far down the road i hope to keep u in my life and,
at least occasionally, inside me. so get used to it. and in the meantime f.c.o.l.
tell me what's going on with u.*

After doing just that, followed by sending quick travel updates to
Charlie, his mom, dad and a couple of friends in Berkeley, Alec can no
longer dodge the fact that Tamiko still hasn't answered his last email
telling her he plans to relocate to New York City. Is she still so mad at
him about Aki that getting in touch is the last thing on her mind? Or does
she somehow think that her fourth group-focused postcard means it's his
turn to communicate? Deciding to take Mayumi's advice and finally send
Tamiko the unequivocal declaration of love that's been overflowing his
heart, Alec is halfway through his third sentence when he feels a hand
grip his shoulder.

"Alec, I've been looking all over for you," Sam says. "A half a dozen
folks are heading to the airport now and to save a few bucks Alejandro
and I have gone in on their van and included you. But since a couple of
the dudes have an earlier plane we need to boogie, as in five minutes ago."

"Got it," Alec replies, grabbing his duffle and following Sammy out
of the store.

Telling Tamiko he loves her will have to wait until they reach Mexico
City.

. . . . .

After Friday morning practice, which again focuses on defense, Tamiko
trails Coach Raines into her small office. But before Tamiko can say
anything, Coach says, "Tamiko, what I just said to the team about your
stunning game last night—well, in case you are in any doubt, I meant every
word. In my three years here, and Ericka Williams notwithstanding, I've
never seen anyone dominate a game so completely. And to do it with only
a couple of days of practice is just plain amazing. But, I have a question.

What exactly went down with you after you drained your second three? I mean you were absolutely killing it, and then didn't shoot again until after the half."

"When I was a tyke I had a soccer coach, who would sit me whenever I got so full of myself that I forgot that our team had eleven players. Since I loved to score goals and hated to be off the field it took me half the season to get Coach Swayze's point. But eventually, it began to dawn on me that being the best player on the field isn't worth half as much as being a good player on the best team. Anyway, I try to keep Mr. Swayze in my head and hope he'll speak up when I'm in danger of going prima donna. Last night he arrived right on time. But, Coach, I have a favor to ask, which for lots of reasons may be impossible to grant, so I'll get it if you say no."

"I'll try, of course."

"Dean Thomas's twelve-year-old daughter Lily is a particular friend. She lives and breathes Amherst sports and it would be a huge deal for her if she could come with us on the team bus to Middlebury, assuming there's an extra seat. She could sleep on a cot in my room, which I gather I'm sharing with Rachel."

"Yes."

"Really?"

"If it's good with her mom, I'm fine with it. Even before you were in the picture that kid was cheering her heart out at all our home games. In fact, I even have an extra team jersey she can wear when she sits at the end of our bench."

"Seriously? The Middlebury coach will be down with that?"

"Why not, since she's got a couple of girls of her own."

. . . . .

On her walk back to Dean Thomas's to enjoy a few hours to herself before meeting with Professor Spurgeon to review obscure Greek verbs, Tamiko chews over the replies she's received from her fourth email. Although she hadn't meant it to be a declaration she'd slept with Jed, or at least hadn't thought she had, several of her friends took it that way, something she now worries may explain why she hasn't heard from Lec. Balling her chilly hands in her pockets as she again resolves to buy mittens, it hits her that Lec may even assume she intends Jed to be part of her romantic future. But, on the other hand, perhaps Lec's failure to respond to her email has nothing to do with any of this, but instead signals that he's hooked up with a surfer girl or three.

Deciding to clear the air, once and for all, Tamiko first makes herself a cup of strong black tea with two large dollops of honey. Then, sitting at the kitchen table with both feet firmly on the floor, she clears her throat and touches Lec's number. When her call goes straight to voicemail, she's not sure whether she's relieved or disappointed. Guessing that if Alec doesn't have phone service, he probably won't have an active internet connection either, Tamiko pushes back her chair. Then realizing an email will catch up with him eventually, she sits tight and enters:

Lec, assuming you read the fourth and last installment of my La-La Land Adventures, you'll know I'm delighted to be back at college (never mind the freezing weather and lack of gloves). And guess what? Your favorite Gashkin scored 18 points in her first game and the Amherst Mammoths (a name that must surely have been picked by men) blew Wesleyan off the court. It was way fun to be out there with a talented bunch who won the D3 National Championship last year. Tomorrow we have a longish trip to Middlebury way up in Vermont for what Coach says will be a tougher game.

Lec, during these past six weeks, yours and my timing around talking about our future has obviously been soap opera horrendous. But it's a new year and I hope a time for heartfelt resolutions to be acted on. Maybe you're having so much fun right now you're no longer thinking about our next steps, or maybe you're missing me as palpably as I miss you. Tried to call earlier with no success. In the meantime, hope the surf is up.

Love you, Tamiko

Even as she pushes send, Tamiko chides herself for stopping short of unequivocally declaring both her love and hope to fully restore last year's bond. *Did I hold back because somehow I feel my determination wavering?* Knowing, despite her head-spinning interlude with Jed, her heart still belongs 110% to Lec, she tries to confront what's really up. Concluding that at least some of her reticence stems from the fact that she's still hurt/jealous about Lec's Teri, Mayumi, Aki trifecta, Tamiko schools herself to stop rechewing stale gum.

. . . . .

Alec's stomach churns and sweat beads his face by the time the Aero Mexico plane taxies to the terminal in Mexico City. Barely scooting to the closest *baño* without embarrassing himself, he pokes his nose out only long enough to tell Sam and Alejandro he needs to hang right there until he empties out. "The *turista* strikes again," Sam says sympathetically. "And Alec, although I'm sorry it landed on you, I'm even more grateful that I'm not the one who needs to mainline Imodium."

Two hours later, feeling rotten and feverish, Alec crashes in a spare bed at Alejandro's dorm as he wonders if this lousy day will ever end. From past experience he knows it will likely be 48 hours before he feels well enough to fly north to Puerto Vallarta and from there grab a bus to Sayulita. Since his friends had promised to show up periodically with soup and ginger ale, he closes his eyes and waits for nature to take its course.

. . . . .

At 8:45 p.m. on Friday evening after Lily's and Phoebe's twice extended storytime, Tamiko calls her grandmother. "Even a forgetful old woman knows it's your turn with the Russian quote," Vera says, as she picks up.

"You never reach any truth without making fourteen mistakes and very likely a hundred and fourteen," Tamiko quotes.

"Why so easy on me? *Crime and Punishment*, of course."

"Because mistakes are what I want to talk about. I mean, Vera, I know you have to be way bored with my melodrama with Lec Burns, but it seems like since Lec and I began making mistakes with each other last summer, we haven't known how to stop."

"Ha! But *milaya moya*, even counting both of you, the important question is have you made all fourteen yet, or do you have a few more to go?" Vera asks with a chuckle.

"I'm guessing we're at least in the twenties," Tamiko replies seriously. "I'm just hoping we don't have to go all the way to one hundred and fourteen. I mean, I hate the thought of us loving each other to distraction, but continuing to mess up for years."

"*Lyubov moya*, despite what many Russians think, Dostoyevsky isn't God, or even Moses. I believe that no matter their number, people can both learn from their mistakes and mend them. But of course, this will only happen if you and Alec also believe this."

"For sure I'm doing my best to be a little wiser."

"Hmm. I wonder if that includes your sending pretty much everyone you know, including Alec, what amounts to a love letter to Jed Streeter, who incidentally looks like he could be Alec's older brother. Or maybe you took the sting out of your fourth La-La Land adventure by sending Alec a second, more personal message?"

"Oh my god, Vera. The trouble with mistakes is that once you start it's so easy to pile on. It's like I get now that I included Lec in that email because I still felt jealous, but it took me a few days to realize that rubbing his nose in Jed would likely push him further away. To try to mend things, I sent him a 'I hope to see you soon' message, but he's in Mexico surfing someplace and I don't know when he'll get it, or what he's doing in the meantime or with who, or is it whom?"

"I have three pieces of advice. Are you ready?"

"Definitely."

"First, never ask an old Russian about grammar. Second, you can't worry about everything. And, third and most important, leave your beautiful actor friend in the past. I'm not going to be a hypocrite and claim that in the years we were performing all over the world, often separately, Stepan and I never detoured into the occasional romantic interlude. But I can tell you that pretty quickly, and very fortunately, we both understood that if we wanted to stay at the center of each other's lives long-term, we had to act like it."

"Thanks Babushka, I'm going to do my very best to take that advice. I sure don't want to spend my life searching for a dude half as great as the one I let get away."

. . . . .

At her chalk talk Saturday morning, Coach Raines focuses on Amherst's need to rely on quick, crisp passes to break through Middlebury's smothering defense. And, when in turn Amherst is on defense, to tightly shadow Middlebury's two talented guards to deny them short jumpers. "If you make them shoot from behind the three-point line, their combined average completion rate is twenty-six percent," Coach continues. "But from inside fifteen feet it's more like sixty-five percent."

"But a three-point shot is worth fifty percent more than a two," Margie interjects.

"I hope math isn't your major," Coach Raines says dryly as several of the Mammoths chuckle.

"Psychology," Margie says, "but I don't…"

Turning to Lily, Coach asks, "If someone takes twenty shots from outside the three-point line and makes five, or twenty-five percent, how many points do they get?"

"Fifteen," Lily replies promptly.

"Correct. Now assume they take another twenty shots, but this time from closer to the basket where each one they make is worth two points."

"Got it," says Lily, seriously. "But to tell you how many points would be scored I also need to know how many they make out of the second twenty."

"As I said, sixty-five percent, which even at Kansas State in my day, came out to twelve and a half."

"So, from closer to the basket Middlebury would get twenty-five points instead of fifteen further out," Lily says, triumphantly.

"Which again means a big factor as to whether we win or lose will be how effective Miki and Tamiko are in denying Numbers eight and eleven short shots." Then, turning to make eye contact with both girls, she adds, "And it's also why it's no big deal if you two pick up a couple of fouls guarding them tightly."

A few minutes later, Lily slings her travel pack over her right shoulder just like the big girls, as they all head to their minibus. In the intermittent, sometimes heavy rain, it will take over four hours to reach Middlebury, Vermont, where they will have ninety minutes to stretch out and eat a light supper before the 7:00 p.m. game.

. . . . .

Saturday morning, Alec still has a low fever and even lower energy. Sam brings him toast and tea before Alejandro sweeps her off to the Frida Kahlo Museum. Feeling marginally better by the afternoon, Alec searches for a computer to check his email. But with Alejandro's door locked and no one else in sight, he decides he's still too wrecked to search the neighborhood for an internet cafe. Back in bed he worries about what's up with Tamiko and again reproaches himself for his part in letting their relationship jump its rails. Thinking back to the day in late July when he rejected Tamiko's unexpected request to accompany him to Japan, he finally admits to himself that it was as much about his desire to be on his own as it was about his insistence that she shouldn't miss out on college.

So, a key question he now realizes is, why after being bonded with Tamiko for the happiest year of his life, did he want to return to being single? True, until he met Tamiko that August morning seventeen months ago, he had never imagined settling down until he was well into his thirties. But, so what? That morning at Cal when they met, hadn't he instantly known she was his soulmate? So again, what had changed? A partial answer floats before his addled mind in the form of Mayumi's double-dimpled grin. As much as I love Tamiko, it would have been a shame to miss my adventure with Mayumi based on an early commitment to monogamy. But what about the others? For example, did my casual sex with Teri, no matter how much fun, justify disappointing Tamiko? And especially given how gut slammed I feel about Tamiko's relationship with Jed Streeter, was even Mayumi really worth it? Assuming my answer is still yes, would it change, if like Mayumi, Streeter proposed that he and I both stay in Tamiko's life? Suddenly too tired to try to sort out his train wreck of feelings, Alec rolls over and drifts into a fitful doze.

. . . . .

Just arrived at the Middlebury Inn late Saturday afternoon, Tamiko's heart skips a beat when she sees an email from Jed. Feeling exposed in front of Rachel and Lily she locks the door of the small bathroom before opening the message. The paragraphs pleasantly tick-tock between Jed's recounting of Allison's latest college thoughts, and his description of the last week's events on set. Then, Tamiko finds herself laughing at Jed's observation that Aphrodite and Mary Ann immediately cheered up when they realized that their beautiful young supporting actress had departed. But, even as she discounts this as typical Jed blarney, she is brought up short when she moves on to the last paragraph.

Given our discussion on our last night in L.A., possibly (make that probably) I'm out of bounds in making this proposal. But Tamiko, I'd like very much to see you again whenever and wherever. Tell me, please, how you feel.

. . . . .

The Middlebury coach who has obviously heard about Tamiko's head-turning performance against Wesleyan, deploys a screen defense overloaded to Tamiko's side designed to deny her easy runs to the basket. But whenever a defense concentrates on one player, others have to be open, so the moment Tamiko sees the second white-and-blue-clad Panther defender closing in, she flips the ball to Miki Nakamura on the periphery, or Josie Gold underneath. The result is that while Tamiko rarely shoots, her teammates get clear look, after clear look. On most nights this would result in a comfortable Amherst lead, but time after time Mammoth shots find ways not to fall.

During a timeout, Margie Prime swears that if her jump shot goes in, and pops back out one more time, she's going to go to confession for the first time since she was fourteen.

In the locker room at the half with Amherst down four, Coach Raines says, "B-plus on defense. But let's go for an A by pressing them even harder. On offense, I'm confident the lid will eventually come off the basket, but Tamiko, we absolutely need you to shoot more. Halfway through the second quarter the defenders forgot your rep from the Wesleyan game and began to drop back to clog the middle. It's past time for you to lure them back out by nailing a couple of jumpers and then to bust up the middle with some dribble drives. I'm guessing your goal tonight is to avoid being a prima donna, but you're way overdoing it. And just so you know, the one thing I can't stand on a basketball court is a nice girl."

Prodded by Coach's criticism, when Tamiko receives the toss to start the second half, she spins left around her surprised defender and sprints the length of the court for an uncontested layup. Pretending she's winded, Tamiko lags back when Middlebury inbounds the ball. With a flurry of quick steps she surprises the Panther's point guard into stopping her dribble. Then, when the flustered player attempts a long pass in an effort to advance the ball past mid-court in the required ten seconds, Tamiko leaps and bats it high in the air. Running down the loose ball, Tamiko continues for another easy score. Eleven seconds into the second half, the game is tied.

By the end of the third quarter thanks to several of Tamiko's three-pointers and the fact that Amherst's shots finally begin to find the bottom of the net, the Mammoths are up by ten. In the fourth quarter, with the clock now their enemy the Panthers pick up their pace. But Amherst tightens its defense resulting in a series of turnovers. With less than two minutes left and Amherst now ahead by fifteen, Coach Raines inserts the second team. A minute later with time running out on the thirty-second shot clock, Rachel Host tosses up a desperation twenty-five footer that somehow finds its mark.

Sitting next to Lily, Tamiko grabs her hand for fear the excited twelve-year-old will run onto the court to high-five Rachel.

A solid road victory over a scrappy, well-coached team leaves Amherst's players euphoric. But, because in winter small Vermont towns roll up the sidewalks before 9:00 p.m. there are few places to go to let off steam. So, after ordering half a dozen large takeout pizzas, everyone crowds into Coach Raines's motel room. If Coach hadn't been there, one of the older girls might have made a beer and wine run, but they are all so high on adrenaline that Coke and Sprite do fine. Tamiko, anxious to avoid thinking about Jed's proposal, is grateful the party lasts until someone in the next room bangs on the wall a few minutes before eleven. With Lily now asleep on a couch Tamiko grabs her arms, and Rachel her legs as they carry the twelve-year-old back to their room. Even though Lily is surely awake by now, she keeps her eyes tightly shut, delighted for the attention from her two heroes.

On the bus back to Amherst late Sunday morning Tamiko's head buzzes with things to communicate to Jed. Eventually she decides she'll send something like this when she reenters internet land.

Dearest Jed,

Back here at Amherst (where as you know I'm one of the youngest) I'm very clear that this is where I belong. L.A., 2+2 and, yes, even going more than a little nuts loving you, now seem as if they happened to someone else. OK, well, maybe not the you and me part which was so special it's tattooed on my soul forever. Just the same Jed, like Allison, I need to make my own way, not become an appendage of your meta-color life. So, although my heart did a happy somersault when I read your email, I must be transparently clear that the lovely moments you and I shared in L.A. must stay there.

Yet, when Tamiko gets back to her dorm room and opens her laptop a small voice whispers, why not hedge your bets by saying something more equivocal. After all, if Alec spends the entire winter on a tropical beach dripping with surfer girls, maybe, just maybe, one more meet-up with Jed would ease the hurt. Even as she knows in her heart that she can't simultaneously walk two paths, Tamiko decides to sleep on her answer. Especially if she sticks to her original intention to say *no mas*, Jed deserves to hear it via FaceTime, not through a kiss-off email. In the meantime, Tamiko sees she has a text from Derrick saying: *I'm thinking we have a dinner date? How about 6:30?*

I'm working on the diorama in Professor Spurgeon's office starting at 5:00, Tamiko replies, *but if you can curb your tummy until 7:00-ish we absolutely do.*

. . . . .

At 4:00 p.m. Tamiko again tries to call Lec only to get the now-familiar out-of-service message. Bursting with things to say, she decides to email him, only to see he still hasn't responded to her last message. Fuck you Lec, she thinks, how hard can it really be to find an internet connection? So letting her hot annoyance cancel the fond words she's been rehearsing, Tamiko enters: *Lec—If you haven't done so, check the sports page on the Amherst website. As you'll see, I'm having big fun being back here subbing for an injured player. Love you, of course. Me*

Pausing with a finger over the send button Tamiko searches for warmer words to add as a postscript. But still hurt by what increasingly feels like Lec's ghosting her, she gives up and hits send.

. . . . .

Alec is famished when he awakes Sunday morning, January 6th. Finally steady on his legs, he accompanies Sam and Alejandro for a plate of chilaquiles. And when the tortillas and salsa-draped eggs slide down without complaint, he goes with them to see the pre-Columbian collection at the National Anthropology Museum. On their way back midafternoon Alec asks Alejandro to help him buy a phone. But given that most of the stores are closed for Epiphany, or *Dia de Los Tres Reyes* as it is called in Mexico, the task is put off in favor of a much-needed nap.

Borrowing Alejandro's computer early Sunday evening, Alec checks his email for the first time in three days to see that he has a long list of messages from friends and family, including one from Charlie saying, *Call me when you can. I have an idea for a project when you eventually get to NYC. Hope the surf is huge and you knock yourself out having fun.*

There is also a Friday message from Tamiko, which Alec superstitiously saves until last as if this will somehow make it more positive. But he is disappointed when Tamiko does little but recount her return to Amherst and her success in the Wesleyan game. True, she says she misses him and hopes the two of them can do better in the new year, but this does little to convince him that Jed Streeter is out of the picture. Pausing to consider how best to reply with a declaration of his undimmed affection, Alec is surprised when a new email from Tamiko pops up, this one containing only a couple of short, impersonal lines about a second basketball game. "C'mon Alec, it's our last night together in the big city. Let's celebrate!" Sam yells from the hall. Not sure whether he's annoyed, or relieved, by the interruption, Alec decides it's a sign he should put off his reply.

· · · · ·

For the first time, working on the diorama of ancient Athens doesn't fully engage Tamiko. "Are you okay?" Professor Spurgeon asks, as he points to a fountain that she's put in the wrong place on the Acropolis.

"A little distracted by some personal stuff, I guess."

"Want to step into the other room and talk?"

"Thanks, I would, but I'm meeting a wise-ish friend at seven who already knows the back story so…"

"So, why not skip out on the world of Pericles for an evening and see if your friend is available half an hour early?"

"Thanks. And next time you can count on me to be one hundred and ten percent focused."

"I know I can."

. . . . .

On their walk from campus across the Amherst Common to Judie's, Tamiko waits for Derrick to unload first. When, instead, he shuffles along in companionable silence, she finally says, "C'mon dude, tell me what went down in Italy? I mean, like, are you feeling up, down or sideways?"

"Somewhere in the vicinity of sideways, I guess, but nothing a couple of Judie's popovers won't upgrade," Derrick replies with a chuckle that tells Tamiko he's come to terms with whatever transpired. Waiting for a tiny dog tied to a post in front of Arigato Sushi to stop yapping, he continues, "The short version is that Ericka and I had a couple of very sweet days together in Bologna where she's studying and then in Pisa where we went to celebrate Christmas."

"And that's it? The end of your mutual story, now and forever?" Tamiko asks after waiting in vain for Derrick to say more. "Are you actually telling me you two had a fabulous romantic adventure and then broke up?"

"Like I told you in October, from Ericka's point of view, the broken up part was a *fait accompli*. And, no doubt, the main reason she had space for me was that the Sicilian engineering student she's been hanging with had gone home to his very Catholic family in Palermo for the holidays."

"Obviously Ericka didn't go with him, so…"

"We're talking Southern Italy here. Not only is it *vietato* to bring an unengaged lover home for Christmas, but a half black Southern Baptist, c'mon. Leaving the prejudice issue aside, this was fine with Ericka, who is very definitely not in a 'meet the parents' frame of mind."

"So it's not just you she doesn't want to commit to…?" Tamiko asks. "Oops, sorry Derrick, that came out wrong."

"Not to worry. Although it took me way too long, I finally understand Ericka's point, which, in case you're wondering, makes me feel less rejected."

"And that is?" Tamiko asks, as soon as they thread their way through half a dozen high school students clumped in front of Antonio's.

"That in a world where many people will live until eighty-five or ninety, assuming of course, the world doesn't blow itself to bits, roast like a Christmas goose, or get wiped out by a rogue microbe, it's nuts to even think about mating long-term when you're twenty!"

"But doesn't that leave out the fact that when you're twenty you can think about little else?"

"Ha! The brain/pussy paradox as Ericka calls it."

"So what's her solution?"

"Spend the next ten years getting degrees, growing up and enjoying a tasting menu of lovers. Then think about commitment."

"And somehow you're okay with being yesterday's hors d'oeuvre?" Tamiko asks.

Then, as she realizes her cutting remark is likely driven by her own feeling of abandonment, quickly adds, "Sorry, Derrick, I seem to be channeling my bitchy side today."

"Actually, it's another good point. But, remember, as far as Italy was concerned, I essentially had a choice—a few fun days with Ericka, or start a fight I couldn't win before sloping off to nurse my grudges over a lonely Christmas. But here's Judie's, so let's nail a few popovers."

Sitting at the same table she, Clemmie and Derrick occupied the evening before she went to L.A., just six weeks, but seemingly a lifetime before, Tamiko orders a popover plus a cheeseburger. "So, you really were chill by the time you and Ericka split?"

"Chill is maybe an exaggeration, but like I said, by then it had begun to dawn on me that Ericka was telling me something I'd be wise to hear. Remember, I come from L.A. where as a result of the high divorce rate 'until death do us part' is often omitted from marriage ceremonies. There is also the fact that I have a couple of years of grad school plus figuring out a career to deal with. Anyway, the day after Christmas I took the train up to Cortina, one of those storybook ski towns in the Alps, which the Italians insist on calling the Dolomites. As you might expect, the place was full of college kids and twentysomethings so the clubs were bursting. On my first night I met Johanna, a cheerful German girl who downhill skis almost as badly as I do."

"But perhaps she's more skilled when horizontal," Tamiko says, not bothering to suppress a snort of delighted laughter.

"Perhaps," Derrick replies, deadpan. "Tamiko, it's your turn. I know the bones of what you've been up to from your four emails. And I confess to having extracted a few more details from Ben, Mary and Clemmie over the phone. But since you seem to have bewitched them all into seriously guarding your privacy, I still don't know half of what went down with you in L.A."

Tamiko begins with a disorganized, and often repetitive, rendition of her anxious first days on the set of *2+2*, before moving on to describe Mary's kindness in grooming her for Ben's big party. She's just starting to explain how much she's enjoyed working with the Golds when Derrick interrupts, "Tamiko, perhaps it's slipped your mind, but I'm the guy you climbed on top of a few months ago, not your spinster auntie in Omaha. So while all of this biographical stuff is fine, I'm kind of waiting for what went down with you and Jed Streeter. I mean, having a moment with the world's most desirable hunk should be worth a mention, right?"

"Oh my god, Derrick, you figured that out from my emails."

"More than half, anyway. And, c'mon, my sister couldn't exactly lie to me when I told her what I'd guessed. But, what about your old heartthrob, Alec, or Lec, if I remember right? Is he somehow out of the picture?"

"My picture? Or his picture?"

"Since you're the one who's my good buddy, let's start with how you feel."

"Okay then," Tamiko replies with a sigh. "It's true I surprised myself by pretty much flirting with Jed from the day we met. But, Derrick, nothing was going to happen until I got super-pissed at Lec for having a thing with this Japanese girl. And then, well…"

"The same girl you were daft enough to go meet in Boston?" Derrick interrupts.

"Not Mayumi. Like I tried to tell you at the time, she's so uniquely cool I kinda, sorta gave Lec a pass for her. No, this was a new one I only found out about when I called Lec to say I was about to hop on a plane to Tokyo to spend Christmas with him."

"Ah, the ups and downs of the jet-set diva," Derrick exclaims, as he raises two fingers to the waitress before pointing at their popover plates.

"Shut up, will you. Despite my admittedly poor precedent with Ericka, friends are supposed to empathize, not pile on."

"Point taken," Derrick replies, reaching out to touch Tamiko's hand. "So I gather instead of hopping over to Japan, you hopped, or is revenge-hopped the more accurate term, into Jed Streeter's bed?"

"Something like that. For sure, that first night when I pretty much seduced him I was on the bounce from feeling rejected by Lec. But Jed is…, well Derrick, you already know what a charismatic dude he is, so from the day we met it didn't take long for me to…"

"In case you haven't noticed," Derrick interrupts, "you're in danger of admitting that getting involved with Jed Streeter was something you wanted on its own."

"Subconsciously, maybe, or maybe even subconsciously, probably," Tamiko replies with a shrug. "Honestly Derrick, I'm beyond confused. But I guess the larger point is that whoever lit the first match, the time Jed and I spent together felt like I was in the middle of an…umm, a euphoric bonfire, I guess. I mean, I know that makes no sense, yet what can I say, if he wasn't older than my mom, and light-years out of my experience league, I might be totally cut up by wanting both him and Lec." When Derrick doesn't reply, Tamiko leans forward to add in a rush, "Derrick, for sure I didn't mean to imply that the time you and I spent together wasn't, well, very…"

"Pleasant is the word I think you're searching for," Derrick says with a laugh. "But, since I think we've both come to terms with what came down between us, let's stick to what happened to you in L.A., where I gather despite all Jed's heat and flame, he didn't quite push Lec off your personal volcano top."

"Not really. At least since my dad was killed, the year I spent with Lec was my most, hmm, I'm not even sure of the word—complete, fulfilled, contented I guess. This fall, suddenly being on my own and needing to make new friends, most especially you and Clemmie, I realized that I can cope with life on my own. And, in L.A., I kind of also proved to myself that I have game when it comes to romance. But, none of it really changes the fact that when I hang with Lec I feel like I'm wearing the world's most comfortable T-shirt. And when we have sex, I immediately blast so high I forget who I am. Maybe I'll be bored twenty years from now, but unlike Ericka, Mayumi and, I guess now you, I'm not into worrying about it."

"There's no shimmer like the Oxytocin Shimmer," Derrick responds with a chuckle. "But where is your magical dude now?"

"Surfing someplace in Mexico and for whatever reason out of touch. It's like, a few weeks ago when he was still in Japan, Lec said he was coming to New York City to work for his uncle and hoped we would get back together. Since then, *nada*, so have no idea what's up with him now. It's like a few years ago he took off surfing and didn't come back for eighteen months, so…"

"So why not reach out?" Derrick asks kindly.

"When my part in *2+2* was done all I could think of was to lose L.A. and get my head screwed back on straight. A couple of days ago when I did call, I only got his message, and today when I tried again, I was re-directed to an out-of-service kiss-off."

"He's traveling, so that could…"

"Jed just emailed that he wants to see me," Tamiko interrupts, her eyes firmly on her plate.

"Really." Then, as Derrick breaks off a big piece of his second popover and covers it in butter, he says, "I hope you know how you plan to respond?"

"Like I said, I know in my heart that no matter what comes down with Lec, it needs to be over with Jed," Tamiko replies, looking up to meet Derrick's gaze. Then tapping her forehead, she adds, "but then this little voice whispers, what if Lec disappears and…"

"Are you sure you've identified the correct body part? In my experience, when a person has magic sex, it's another area entirely that says *again, again, again*," Derrick replies, as he divides his last hunk of popover, sliding half to Tamiko, who has long since consumed hers.

"Ha! That's pretty much what Mom said eighteen months ago when she tried to warn me off from getting involved with Lec in the first place."

"Sounds like your mom knows a thing or two."

"No doubt, but Derrick, thanks for talking me through this. Whatever comes down with Lec, I really do need to put on my big girl pants and say *no mas* to Jed."

"A decision that will make Ben, Mary, Clemmie, your mom and everyone else who loves you, breathe a sigh of relief. But, if you don't mind me changing the subject, you've definitely made Coach Raines a happy camper and she's warbling your praises far and wide."

"It's a mutual admiration society since her reaching out to get me back on the court was exactly what I needed. But I also have a pile to do on my *Class of '24* workup before school starts in two weeks, so I'm happy Rosie Wilburn should be ready to play soon. And, with softball also starting February first, I'll have plenty to take my mind off mating."

"Good luck with that."

. . . . .

On Monday, January 7th, Alec is on an early plane to Puerto Vallarta where he catches a bus to the small coastal town of Sayulita, arriving at noon. Delighted to find that the surf is up, he meanders through narrow palm-lined streets strung with brightly colored *papel picado* banners. At the Quiverito Surf Shop on Calle Marlin he rents a board and arranges to leave his stuff for a few hours so he can have an immediate go at the roiling water. Three hours later, hungry and relaxed, Alec reclaims his bag, and heads to the Sayulita Central Hotel, just off the main plaza, only stopping at the OXXO store on Avenida Revolución to purchase a cheap phone.

Now weary from the residual effects of his illness, Alec naps for two hours. When he wakes, he texts both parents to reassure them he hasn't fallen off the earth and report that he expects to arrive in NYC in about a week. Then, after grabbing three shrimp tacos at El Itacate, he considers whether the time is finally right to call Tamiko.

. . . . .

Monday morning Tamiko is on the court with her team running through several new versions of the pick and roll play Coach Raines wants to use that evening in their non-league game against Springfield State. At the chalk talk that follows, Coach repeats for at least the sixth time that her goal for the game is to avoid anyone being injured. "Their number eight, Maggie something or other, is not only built like a tank on steroids, but she's out-and-out mean," Coach insists so angrily she has to pause to wipe a fleck of spit off her chin. "Most of you will remember that last year she deliberately knocked Ericka into the first row of spectators where she banged her head so hard we had to put her through the concussion protocol."

"And Maggie's not the only one to watch out for," Margie Prime adds. "Their tall forward with the carrot hair deliberately cut my legs out from under me when I jumped for a rebound. On rainy days it still hurts where I landed," she adds, massaging her right hip. "And the worst thing was, there was no whistle."

"Who won?" Tamiko asks.

"We did by four in overtime," Coach answers. "But like I've been saying, since winning a non-league game doesn't count, it's far more important we all survive."

"Is there video of last year's game?" Tamiko asks.

"Sure, but all you're going to see is a six-foot, one-hundred-and-eighty-pound pink-faced bully throwing her elbows at anyone who gets within range."

"At Berkeley High we faced our share of badasses, so much so that I became an ace bully baiter," Tamiko says seriously. "Let's see if I still have my mojo."

. . . . .

On her walk back to Dean Thomas's in midafternoon, Tamiko pulls on new red mittens accented by perky white snowflakes. With a leaden sky, and the temperature just below freezing, she raises them to the sky to encourage the heavens to give forth. In the week she's been back in Massachusetts there have been a couple of ten-minute flurries, but nothing a snow-deprived California girl can brag about to the home folks.

When Tamiko finally unlocks the black front door of Dean Thomas's white colonial-style house, she's met by a wall of silence. The girls, she remembers, have back-to-back dentist appointments, meaning Tamiko has a rare ninety minutes to herself before grabbing an early meal with the team and then on to the gym to warm up for the 7:00 o'clock tip-off. After a brief lie-down and a hot shower, Tamiko steps onto the mat as Adele begins singing "Rolling in the Deep." Muttering *Gospodi*, her grandmother Vera's favorite multipurpose expletive, Tamiko reaches for a towel with one hand and her phone with the other. Seeing it's Jed, she's tempted not to answer, having wanted to initiate the call making it clear she doesn't want to restart their relationship. But knowing that postponing a difficult conversation won't make it easier, she answers by saying, "Hey Cowboy, what's up?"

"I'd like to see you."

"Oh my god, Jed, I've been planning to FaceTime you after my game tonight to say that despite the great times we've had…"

"Before you finish that sentence," Jed interrupts, "you should probably know that I just checked into a hotel here in Amherst called the Inn on Boltwood."

"No way! You're kidding, right? It's like, you're telling me you're down the street…"

"Tamiko, I know I'm way out of order showing up unannounced. But, really, I'm not stalking you. Remember, I told you on our last night together that I had to be in New York for publicity appearances over this past weekend. Anyway, my PR person added an early TV show in Boston this morning, and so when Allison called a few minutes after it wrapped up with very positive college news, I took a chance and drove over."

With no clue how to respond, Tamiko says nothing. But Jed waits her out and so finally, when the silence threatens to shout louder than even the most off-putting words, she says, "Oh my god, Jed, no matter how much I loved our nights together in L.A., which you have to know were epic, I can't continue having sex with you. I just can't. It's like when you told me that despite having a good life you've always regretted losing Carol, it really hit home. I seriously don't want to look back with regret twenty years from now because I didn't try to put things back together with Lec when I had the chance—maybe my last chance."

"Can we at least talk? I hope you know I'll never try to pressure you into anything you don't want, but still, what we shared in L.A. was so…"

"Jed, I have a basketball game at seven and I'm heading out in ten minutes for a mandatory training table meal with my teammates before hitting the gym."

"Maybe I can pull a hat down over my face and catch your game."

"I hope that's a joke. School's not in session so there will probably be like ninety spectators tops, half of whom know each other. How many seconds do you think it will take for someone to ID you, and given the two of us acting in the same film, what conclusion do you think they'll reach three seconds later? And, with me still being seventeen…"

"Point taken," Jed interrupts. "But to reassure you, no one knows I'm here. My publicist used a phony name to make the reservation and arranged for me to come in through the Boltwood's deserted side entrance. So, please just take a breath and stop by for a minute on your way to basketball. I'm in room 232, which you can reach with no need to pass the front desk if you use the back entrance on Spring Street. Then, maybe after the game we can…"

"I'll be there in fifteen," Tamiko interrupts as she realizes she's perspiring despite standing naked in a chilly bathroom. "But, Jed, like I hope you heard me say, I'm not going to change my mind about our romantic moment being over."

The door is ajar when Tamiko arrives at room 232. Expelling a long breath she pushes it open to see Jed's lanky body stretched on the bed only a few feet away. "I'm gonna guess this is the smallest hotel room you've been in for at least the last fifteen years," Tamiko says with a chuckle, surprised at how pleased she is to see Jed's crooked grin.

Coming to his feet, arms open, Jed replies, "It's best not to occupy the bridal suite, if you want to fly under the media radar."

"Hugging, no kissing," Tamiko says, stepping forward.

"Got it," Jed says, tightly wrapping her in his long arms.

Feeling disconcertingly warm, safe and happy, Tamiko nevertheless pulls back as she says, "Like I told you, I'm supposed to be with my team right now. So, c'mon, tell me what's up with Allison?"

"Late yesterday afternoon she called the admissions people at Colorado State to ask if it was too late to add a video collage of steeplechase events to her application. The assistant director she talked to replied that it wasn't necessary since her application was already at the top of the admit pile. Of course that's not the same as a formal acceptance, but…"

"Still, Jed, that's wonderful news. I mean, from refusing to apply to any college six weeks ago, your girl has come a long way. Who knows how high she'll fly now that she's all in on a life plan," Tamiko adds, as she reflects that Jed had half a dozen easier ways to communicate this news than by driving an hour and a half from Boston.

As if reading her mind, Jed says, "Tamiko, since you had a key part in this I hoped we could celebrate, but the truth is I'd have come to see you anyway. But I know better than to try to make a romantic pitch when it's object is halfway out the door, so can we hang out after your game? Like I said, I won't try to pressure you into anything, just suggest possibilities for us if maybe you and Lec don't…"

"Especially if we win, the team will demand I hang with them after," Tamiko interrupts. "Since I only committed to play three games while the regular point guard is recovering from an injury, they'll be big into thanking me."

"Team bonding! Of course, I know how powerful a force that is. So, no worries about the time. Call me when you eventually pull free and we'll go from there."

"Sure, but Jed, like I've said over and over, talking is the only thing we're going to do."

"Got it, but Tamiko," Jed replies with his most beguiling grin, "when someone repeats something several times, I always wonder whom they are trying to convince."

. . . . .

Just short of the same side door she'd entered by, Tamiko makes a U-turn when she spots several women, probably hotel cleaners, smoking and chatting outside. Finding herself in the corridor leading to the lobby she picks up her pace. When the woman behind the desk says, "Good evening," Tamiko glances away as she almost sprints out the front door.

Outside on Boltwood Street, Tamiko begins to jog along the dark sidewalk, her long gray coat flapping wing-like behind. In two blocks she crosses College Street and enters the eerily empty world of a small New England college on winter recess. With only a few hundred yards to go, she picks up her pace, glad now that the snow has held off and the path is dry. All but flying through the door of the mostly empty Valentine Dining Hall, a full fifteen minutes late, Tamiko is greeted by relieved looks from her teammates and a hard glare from Coach Raines. With no good way to explain where she's been, Tamiko mumbles, "Sorry, my bad," as she grabs the empty chair next to Margie Prime.

The game is less than two minutes old when, after driving for a successful layup, Tamiko turns to see Leni Silverstein doubled over gasping for breath. With Maggie, the huge Springfield center turning away with a pleased smirk on her face, it's not hard to figure out what happened. With both refs concentrating on the action near the basket, Maggie had seized the opportunity to stick an elbow into Leni's gut.

A few minutes later, when Miki Nakamura tumbles awkwardly to the floor after a collision with Maggie, it's little consolation that this time the gloating Springfield player is called for a foul. Knowing that another hit like that could end Miki's season, Tamiko resolves to do whatever it takes to prevent it.

With the score now knotted at 8, Tamiko dribbles the ball just outside the three-point line. When Amherst center Josie Gold moves to the high post drawing her defender out from under the basket, Tamiko fakes right before crossing her dribble to her left hand, and bursting past the flat-footed Springfield defender. Anticipating Tamiko's lane to the basket, Maggie establishes a legal blocking position hoping to use her big body to punish Tamiko at the same time Tamiko draws the foul. But when Tamiko veers farther right, Maggie must either lunge in front of her, or allow Tamiko to put up an uncontested shot from the baseline. Taking Tamiko's bait, the red-faced Springfield player initiates a bruising collision just as Tamiko tosses up an off-balance left-handed shot. Two urgent whistles sound, almost before Tamiko crashes to the floor at the feet of the first row of spectators.

"That's a shooting foul plus a technical for aggressive contact," the taller of the two female refs shouts, as she points at Maggie. "The shooter gets two shots, plus Amherst gets an additional two for the technical, which anyone can take." Tamiko, who has an angry bruise on her left cheek where she banged the floor, but is otherwise unhurt, steps to the foul line and rattles in her first shot. Then, bouncing the ball a couple of times, she winks at Maggie before swishing her second. Now on the bench for a quick breather and an ice pack, Tamiko watches as Miki Nakamura makes one of the next two.

A few minutes later with the score again tied and Springfield inbounding the ball, Tamiko runs up the court next to Josie Gold and says, "Switch with me, I'll guard Maggie underneath."

"But Coach will hate me being on the perimeter, so I don't…" the tall, lean blonde starts to reply.

"Just do it," Tamiko interrupts as she shadows Maggie as the big girl lumbers into her usual offensive spot with her back to the basket. But instead of setting up between Maggie and the hoop, Tamiko positions herself in front of Maggie, in an effort to prevent her teammates from passing Maggie the ball. "Get out of my face, you slant-eyed bitch," the Springfield player mutters, as part of the continuous stream of mean-spirited chatter that has the unintended effect of allowing Tamiko to track Maggie's side-to-side movements without being able to see her. With their offense disrupted by Tamiko's unexpected defensive maneuver and the shot clock winding down, Springfield's point guard tosses up an off-balance shot that clangs high off the rim. Although Maggie is in perfect position to grab the rebound, Tamiko deftly slides to the big girl's right, and timing her jump perfectly, tips the ball to Leni in the right corner. The Amherst forward in turn fires it two-thirds the length of the court to Miki, who catches it several steps in front of her defender and continues to score an easy layup.

Back on defense, Tamiko again signals to Josie that she'll take Maggie. Now guarding the big center from her normal defensive position between Maggie and the basket, it's Tamiko who keeps up a steady stream of chatter, the point being that Maggie is too slow and clumsy to score. When a few seconds later a Springfield guard tosses the ball to Maggie, about seven feet from the basket, she aggressively swings her elbows back and forth in an effort to make Tamiko back off far enough so she can turn and get up a shot. But, instead of retreating, Tamiko holds her position alternately leaning back from the waist to avoid being flattened by a flying elbow, all the while daring Maggie to shoot.

Obviously frustrated, Maggie doubles down on her strategy by swinging her big shoulders wildly to the left. Anticipating what is sure to come next, Tamiko firmly plants her feet a step behind Maggie's right shoulder. So when, without looking, Maggie recklessly flings her big shoulders back to the right, her flying elbow catches Tamiko just below her left collar bone and sends her crashing to the floor. Even as the whoosh of the shocked spectators reverberates through the field house, whistles sound. "That's your second unsportsmanlike foul, lady—you're out of here," the short, gray-haired ref shouts, pointing at Maggie. For a moment the entire gym is silent as almost in disbelief the players and spectators absorb the fact that big, tough Maggie has just been ejected from the game. Only a few of the most perceptive understand how Tamiko engineered it.

Pink face aflame, Maggie raises a clenched fist as she steps toward Tamiko, who having grabbed Leni's hand, has regained her feet. But before the furious Springfield player can reach Tamiko, the tall ref steps between them. Extending her arm to Maggie she shouts, "One more step and this game is over." Apparently too furious to either hear, or care, Maggie leans toward the ref, only to be grabbed from behind by the Springfield coach, who with the help of two players pulls her to the bench.

With Maggie out of the game, Amherst goes on a 14-to-2 run with Tamiko, after a short breather on the bench, scoring 9. Eventually Springfield's stunned players begin to pull their game together, but even so, Amherst leads by 22 at the half. In the locker room during the break Tamiko holds ice bags to her cheek and upper chest as she listens to Coach Raines say, "As you know, my big fear was that number eight, or one of her running buddies would injure one of you. In all my years of playing and coaching I've never seen anyone take out a dangerous bully the way Tamiko just did. Tamiko, if you'd asked me in advance I'd never have approved of your doing half that. And if you were going to be with us long-term, I'd sit you for the rest of a game to be sure you knew who is in charge. But, in the circumstances, all I can say is, thank you."

With little Rachel Host and several other reserves starting the second half, Tamiko watches from the bench. For several minutes Rachel uses her quickness to get the ball up court and Amherst holds it's lead. But much as happened in the Wesleyan game, when Springfield adopts a full court press the diminutive guard is increasingly either stripped of the ball, or trapped in the backcourt. With two minutes left in the third quarter and Amherst's lead down to ten, a newly confident Springfield squad returns to their aggressively swaggering style. "Shoot without guilt, you deserve a big night," Coach Raines says to Tamiko as she reinserts the first team.

And Tamiko does just that, not so much by intent, but because her grateful teammates keep the ball in her hands. Even when Tamiko passes to a teammate with the shot clock winding down, the ball yo-yos back so that she is obliged to shoot to beat the thirty-second buzzer. With only ninety seconds left in the game and Amherst's lead now back to twenty, Tamiko runs up the floor in front of the Amherst bench pointing to Rachel. But Coach, who seems to have dropped something, is bending over to look under her chair. Shrugging, Tamiko receives a pass from Miki as she crosses mid-court and drives all the way to the basket to score. The next time on offense, and now with less than twenty seconds left on the game clock, Tamiko starts to dribble the ball in a circle not wanting to further run up the score, even against an opponent who so richly deserves it. But as she makes her second turn Coach Raines yells, "Number seven, shoot the damn ball. That's an order!" So with only a few seconds left, Tamiko takes a couple of steps toward the basket to toss up an off-balance thirty-foot jumper. Somehow, the awkward shot hits the backboard and rattles in a second before the game ending buzzer sounds.

As Tamiko and her teammates form the traditional line intending to slap hands with the still visibly pissed Springfield players, the gray-haired ref shouts, "Ladies, we'll skip tradition tonight and head directly to the locker rooms." When no one on either team moves, the refs step assertively between the two groups of players as they order the coaches to lead their players from the court. Then, as the small crowd stands and begins to disperse, the P.A. announcer says, "Ladies and gentlemen, before we depart, let's have a round of applause for Amherst guard Tamiko Gashkin, who with thirty-seven points has broken Amherst's single game scoring record of thirty-six points set by Ericka Williams last year."

. . . . .

In the locker room Tamiko is surrounded by her excited teammates. As soon as everyone changes, they all but carry her off to celebrate in Margie Prime's room.

Several times Tamiko looks for an opportunity to slip away from the hubbub to call Jed. Yet, enshrined at the center of this rollicking group, she can only manage a quick text: *Stuck for at least another 45—will call ASAP.* Then, turning back to her teammates, she realizes that a part of her wants the party to last as long as possible. Finally, at 10:00, knowing that kindness is the minimum she owes Jed, Tamiko pleads exhaustion to break away. Outside on the quad, where it's finally snowing heavily enough to blur the lines of the tall bare trees that unaccountably remind Tamiko of ranks of dead soldiers, she taps Jed's number.

"Hooray!" he says by way of answer. "I wish I could have been there to see you shatter the scoring record."

"Are the results online already?" Tamiko asks, even as she smiles at Jed's deft way of magnifying her one-point break of Ericka's record.

"An hour ago, at least."

"Jed, I'm truly sorry it's taken me so long to call, but I got scooped up in the celebration and since it was…"

"Don't beat yourself up. I know what it feels like to win a tough one and I also realize that my showing up out of the blue is awkward to say the least."

"I'm heading your way now."

"Maybe we should wait 'til *mañana*," Jed replies, his light tone suddenly gone. "To tell you the truth, that indigestion and heartburn I've been feeling lately are back and I should get some sleep. To do the Boston morning show I got up at five-thirty after maybe five hours of sleep. Add in jet lag and…"

"Jed, you've been feeling like crap on and off for two weeks," Tamiko insists. "I mean, I'm not trying to tell you what to do, but don't hotels have doctors on call?"

"Tamiko," Jed responds in the exaggeratedly patient voice Tamiko guesses he's honed over many years trying to manage Allison, "I know you mean well, but please stop acting like I have one foot in the grave. Also, unless memory fails, you're the one who wants to keep it a big secret that I'm here in Amherst." Then, apparently realizing he really is coming across like a pedantic parent, Jed puts a smile in his voice as he adds, "And I do have an appointment back home on Thursday for a nose-to-toes checkup. So how about I take a Nexium, sleep nine hours, and you come over for a room service breakfast at eight a.m.? I'll need to be on the road back to Boston by ten, but it will be great to have some time together. I may not be able to sell you on my proposal, but I'd like to have a chance to remind you about how head-spinning..."

"It's a date," Tamiko interrupts, determined to have their goodbye talk in person. "But will the side entrance to the hotel be open that early?"

"If it isn't, call and I'll come down. What do you want for breakfast?"

"Remember, I eat everything and about twice as much as you do."

"How about waffles and bacon with a chaser of pancakes and sausage?"

"Sounds perfect. I'm looking forward to it and to seeing you," Tamiko says with a laugh, relieved that both are true.

. . . . .

Alec is up at 5:30 a.m. and out on the Sayulita beach half an hour later. Delighted to see that the north swells are producing consistent six-footers he heads for the break on the far end of the beach. In the water in front of the campground, he takes his place at the end of the short line, nodding to a couple of surfers he met the day before. When an aggressive dude paddles in front of him, Alec backs off with a relaxed grin, knowing from experience that when the locals see him ride a couple of waves, they'll treat him with respect. Although kooks may push to the top in many fields, surfing isn't one of them.

. . . . .

Tamiko is up at 7:30. As she chats with the still excited Lily and Phoebe about last night's game Tamiko glances in the mirror. As her fingers fly up to touch the angry bruise under a vivid black eye, she realizes that even Joanie White, *2+2*'s skilled makeup artist, couldn't fully fix it. Dressed and downstairs a few minutes later, Tamiko reports she has a breakfast meeting and is out of the house before a surprised Amber can question her. Halfway to the inn Tamiko catches herself wondering if she's walking fast because she's cold? Or, if it's because she's excited about seeing Jed? A little of both she concludes as she turns left onto Spring Street, and continues for a block to the white brick hotel's deserted side door, which, to her relief, is unlocked. Pausing inside to kick snow off her boots and finger-comb her windblown hair, Tamiko climbs the steps to the second floor two at a time, even as she reminds herself that no matter what comes down with Lec, her answer to Jed's idea that they keep seeing each other, is, and must remain, N-O. A little surprised that the door to room 232 isn't ajar, Tamiko taps lightly.

After glancing at her watch to see she's a few minutes early, she knocks louder. When she thinks she hears a faint ringing sound, Tamiko puts her ear to the door. Sure enough, Jed's phone with its old-fashioned ringtone, is sounding. Pretty sure he wouldn't leave his room without his phone, Tamiko gives the door a couple of serious thumps. When a maid pokes her head out of a room down the hall to see what all the noise is about, Tamiko takes a step toward the slightly stooped, fiftyish woman as she says, "I'm supposed to meet my father for breakfast. Can you peek in to see if Dad is okay?" Extending her hands, palms up, the woman, whose name tag identifies her as Mavis Grady, starts to explain the hotel's privacy policy. Tamiko interrupts, "Please, Dad's been ill lately and I'm worried. Maybe he stepped out for some reason, but I have a date to meet him right now."

After a quick glance over her shoulder apparently to confirm that the hotel manager isn't stalking down the corridor, Mavis leads Tamiko back to room 232. Rapping the door twice as she calls, "Housekeeping," Mavis swipes her key card, not waiting for a reply.

Looking over Mavis's shoulder as she opens the door, Tamiko sees Jed sprawled awkwardly on the bed dressed in a blue T-shirt and loose black pants. Her gut already tightening, Tamiko pushes past the older woman. Even before she touches Jed's stiff, clammy arm, Tamiko registers that his eyes are rolled back in his head. Resisting the urge to try to shake or breathe life back into him Tamiko turns to ask Mavis if she knows CPR. But, seeing that the white-faced woman is leaning against the door frame looking like she's about to be sick, Tamiko fumbles out her phone and pushes 911. Resolving to stay calm so as to accurately report the situation, Tamiko nevertheless loses her patience with the operator's off-point questions and repeatedly shouts, *"Boltwood Inn, Room 232, emergency!"* Assured that the EMS crew at the firehouse just around the corner is already on the move, Tamiko tries to force open Jed's jaw in an attempt to breathe down his throat, only to quickly realize it's impossible.

Somehow spacing out the next minute or two, Tamiko is next aware of cold wind on her face as she waits for the medical techs outside the side door of the inn. Apparently, her stunned mind has worked out that a few seconds will be saved if she leads them up the stairs to Jed's room. But, almost immediately, Tamiko's ears tell her that the EMT vehicle, siren sounding, has arrived at the inn's front door. Even sprinting around the long building will take too long to be of help, Tamiko realizes, as she taps Dean Thomas's number on the phone tightly clutched in her right hand. "Amber, I need your help. Oh my god, so much help," Tamiko blurts as soon as her friend answers.

"Tamiko, is that you? What's up, dear? Calm down and tell me."

"You know how I told you that Jed Streeter was in *2+2*, and, like, we became friends when I helped his daughter…"

"I do, but Tamiko, please forget about L.A. for a minute and focus on what's got you so upset? For starters, tell me where you are?"

"Jed is dead, or I'm almost sure," Tamiko says in a breathless rush. "Seriously, Amber, I just found his body."

"What? You're kidding, surely?"

"No! I'm at his hotel, the Inn on Boltwood."

"Tamiko, are you seriously telling me Jed Streeter has somehow passed away here in Amherst while presumably visiting you?"

"Yes, and Amber, it's like I would have told you Jed was here, but he just showed up…"

"Tamiko, you were here in this house barely twenty minutes ago, so what could have happened?"

"Jed and I were going to have a room service breakfast, but when I got to his room and he didn't answer I talked a hotel cleaner into opening the door. Oh my god, Amber, Jed was lying on the bed, all stiff, and with his eyes…"

"But how can you be sure he's dead?" Dean Thomas interrupts. "You're obviously not an…"

"I'm almost positive. It's like, his skin was cold, gray and kinda rigid. I could tell Mrs. Grady, the cleaner who almost fainted, also thought he was dead. Anyway, I called 911 and then tried to meet the ambulance at the side door. But, they just went in through the main entrance, I'm all alone here on Spring Street."

"Did you give your name when you called 911?"

"I don't know. They kept asking me all these irrelevant questions, so I just kinda shouted 'Boltwood Inn, Room 232, hurry up, emergency' over and over."

"Tamiko, I need you to come back here now. Got it? Immediately. With the medical techs on site there is nothing you can do to be helpful. In the meantime I'll call Roger Barksdale, Amherst's police chief, to find out what's going on and whether Streeter has really passed. So, get a firm grip on yourself and walk straight back."

"Get a grip, get a firm grip," Tamiko repeats to herself as she almost frantically kicks through the four or five inches of fresh snow that paradoxically dress Spring Street as if for a morning wedding. Pausing to let a blue Nissan back out of a tight driveway, Tamiko realizes that, like a Sanskrit prayer at the beginning of yoga class, Amber's "get a grip" mantra is beginning to pull her back to the present. So, removing the mitten on her right hand, Tamiko scrolls through her contact list and taps Ben Fine's number. Immediately shunted to voicemail, Tamiko ends the call, unwilling to tell her macabre news to a machine. Again encountering a mechanical voice when she calls Mary McCarthy, Tamiko finally remembers it's only 5:15 on the West Coast, meaning no one is likely to pick up. So, after a moment's hesitation, she provides a bare-bones version of what she encountered at the Boltwood.

At the corner of Seelye and Spring Streets, Tamiko waits to cross behind a schoolgirl holding hands with her father. Slammed by a feeling of loneliness so intense she involuntarily reaches out her hand, momentarily forgetting her dad has been dead almost five years. When the traffic clears and the pair cross, Tamiko remains planted on the curb, still thinking of all her happy mornings walking to school with her dad. Then, unaccountably, her mind's eye conjures Lec Burns's smiling face with the only evident connection being how intensely she misses them both. Yet knowing all too well that Lec is almost as unreachable as her dad, Tamiko instead calls Lec's father, an attorney in White Plains, New York, whom she got to know and like the previous year.

"Tamiko Gashkin, is that really you?" Ted Burns answers on the first ring. "This is a pleasant surprise. But what do I owe the…"

"Not so pleasant on this end, I'm afraid," Tamiko interrupts, trying not to sob. "It seems like I'm in pretty big trouble, so much that I really need to talk to Lec, but he's not…"

"I spoke to Lec last night and he told me you're back in Amherst to play basketball," Ted interrupts.

"Oh my god, Ted, you actually talked to him? I mean, for the last week I've tried to call and email but…"

"Lec's phone and iPad were stolen last week in Puerto Escondido right before he got some kind of *turista* bug that knocked him out for a few days. He's on his feet now and just bought a new phone, but Tamiko, slow down and tell me why you are so upset. If it has legal implications, maybe I can help."

"It's like, Ted, I know I'm in trouble but I don't even know what kind, or how much."

"Start with the headlines while you save the background for later," Ted says, in the no-nonsense voice attorneys have honed to focus their clients.

"Do you know who the actor Jed Streeter is? I mean, probably Lec told you about my Hollywood film adventure, right?"

"I know who Streeter is, of course. And, yes, Lec did say you were in L.A. playing a college girl in a Ben Fine movie."

Lowering her voice to a whisper, even though the schoolbound dad and daughter are now half a block ahead, Tamiko says, "Ted, the headline is that a few minutes ago I found Jed Streeter dead in his hotel room, or at least I'm pretty sure."

"Tamiko, did I hear you right? Jed Streeter is deceased? Right there in Amherst? Or are you…"

"Yes, here in Amherst. And, yes, like I said, I'm almost sure Jed's dead."

"I'm guessing he must have been there to visit you," Ted says, matter-of-factly. "But, Tamiko, Streeter was barely middle-aged and certainly appeared robust in his films, so I don't understand what could have…"

"Jed showed up late yesterday afternoon," Tamiko interrupts in a rush. Then, pausing to catch her breath, she continues, "I had no idea he was coming and had a basketball game last night, so we only saw each other for maybe fifteen minutes. This morning—just now, I went to his hotel for breakfast and found him. Even though he was stiff and cold, I called 911 before I just kinda ran out of there."

"Tamiko, I'm sorry to have to invade your privacy, but time is short and since you're a minor, your truthful answer could make a big legal and practical difference. Did you stay with him last night?"

"No, no I didn't, really—I didn't," Tamiko answers, crossing the street to distance herself from a shaggy brown dog at a picket fence, woofing and breathing out little clouds of fog. Then, as if her words sound bogus, even to herself, she adds, "Honestly, Ted, I slept in my room where I'm staying with a friend, Amber Thomas, who is an Associate Dean here at Amherst. When Jed and I talked briefly by phone after my game he complained about chest pain, which he thought was heartburn."

"Tamiko, of course I believe you, but when people inevitably ask probing questions, can the Dean vouch for you? That you slept at her house, that is?"

"Last night Dean Thomas saw me go upstairs to bed before eleven. This morning we chatted briefly around seven-forty."

"Again, sorry to keep being invasive, but to help I need to ask you another tough question. Were drugs, alcohol, or anything else I should know about, possibly involved in Streeter's death?"

"If anything else means sex, there was none, either yesterday or today," Tamiko replies quickly, only belatedly realizing she's all but admitted she and Jed had previously been intimate. "As for drugs or alcohol, I doubt it, but I wasn't there so…"

"And I'm hoping that any romance that might have occurred in L.A. was discreet," Ted interrupts, picking up on her admission. "But Tamiko, given Streeter's international fame, coupled with the fact that he was in Amherst to see you, one thing is abundantly clear. You do need legal help and you need it pronto."

Having no doubt this is true, Tamiko says nothing.

"I'm four hours away, and not licensed to practice in Massachusetts, but fortunately a very able law school buddy, Adley Saperstein, practices law in Northampton and lives about fifteen minutes from Amherst. With your permission I'll call her now to see if she can drop everything and get over to wherever you are. But first, is there anything else essential I need to know?"

"I called Dean Thomas before I called you and she's getting in touch with the police chief to explain about me. I'm walking back to her house now, in fact, I'm only a block away."

"And her address is?"

"85 Lessey Street. And, Ted, oh my god, thank you."

"As soon as I reach Adley, one of us will get back to you. Also, I'm about to text you Lec's new number."

Before Tamiko can access the text with her nearly numb right fingers, on her ringtone Adele begins singing about the fire starting in her heart. Seeing it's Ben Fine, Tamiko switches her phone to her still-mittened left hand, as she asks, "Ben, did you talk to Mary?"

"Yes, she just relayed your message, or as much of it as she could understand. So, Tamiko, please tell me exactly what's going on."

With the benefit of having organized her thoughts for Ted Burns, Tamiko begins with the fact that she's just discovered Jed's apparently lifeless body, before adding enough background that hopefully Ben will grasp what went down. Then, catching herself starting to repeat, she stops mid-sentence.

"Tamiko, I don't mean to doubt you, but how do you know for sure that Jed's dead, not just asleep, or maybe unconscious?" Ben demands, as if refusing to accept what Tamiko has just said will somehow make it go away.

"Ben, really, I don't know anything for sure. All I can say is that Jed was a weird, pale bluish color, his body was stiff, and, his eyes were partially rolled back…" Tamiko trails off, beginning to sob.

Pausing for a moment, Ben says, "Tamiko, I'm so very sorry you're having to cope with this on your own, and starting now, I'll do everything I can to help. In the meantime, who can I call to confirm what's gone down without kicking off an instant media frenzy?"

"I called my friend Amber, that's Amherst College Associate Dean Amber Thomas, from outside Jed's hotel, just after the EMT's got there. She said she'd get in touch with the police chief on his private line. Amber's mobile number is (413) 610-0341. Ben, Amber's chill, so you can definitely trust her."

"Got it. I'll call now. In the meantime, are you okay?"

"As well as I can be, I guess. The campus is mostly closed for winter break so I'm staying with Dean Thomas and her family while I play basketball like I told you in L.A. Also, I just got a recommendation for a good local lawyer."

"Excellent! Assuming you're right about Jed, you're going to need experienced help to even hope to deal with what's sure to be a world-scale media circus."

. . . . .

Alec comes out of the water just before 8:00 intent on finding breakfast in the brightly hued seaside village that somehow manages to appear quaintly Mexican at the same time you can buy a latte and croissant on every second corner. Parking his board at the store where he rented it, Alec grabs an outside table under a cream-colored umbrella at Paninos, where he has been assured the French toast is *delicioso*. His order in, Alec checks his new phone to see that he has three calls from his dad, all in the last hour. Not bothering to try to access the unfamiliar voicemail, he calls back.

"'Lec," Ted Burns answers immediately, "sit down if you're not doing so already."

"Dad, you're scaring me. Is Mom okay? And what about Caitlin?"

"They're both fine, but Tamiko is in a tight spot. Not to sugar-coat it, Jed Streeter stopped by Amherst to see her yesterday afternoon and apparently died in his hotel room last night."

"Oh my god, was Tamiko with him?"

"Lec, under the circumstances that probably shouldn't be your first worry," Ted says after a pause.

"You're right, of course. Is Tamiko okay? And what the hell happened? I mean Streeter was barely forty, right? And where's Tamiko now? And is this all over the news?"

"Whoa! To answer your last question first, no. I only know about it because Tamiko called me half an hour ago, just a few minutes after she found the body. Being as smart as she is, she immediately understood she'd need expert help and she was also anxious to get in touch with you, something she says she's been trying to do for the last week."

"But Dad, you're in the New York suburbs, hours away," Alec says, as if focusing on this tangential detail will somehow restore his equilibrium.

"Which is exactly why I called a law school friend who practices in Northampton near Amherst. Adley Saperstein is already on her way to meet Tamiko."

"What can I do to help her, Dad?"

"What do you think?"

"Stop worrying about stuff I can't control and get there as fast as I can."

"Good answer and since I hoped that's how you'd feel, I made you a reservation on the ten-twenty Houston flight out of Puerto Vallarta with a connection to JFK arriving at six-forty this evening. Can you make it?"

"No problem," Alec replies, glancing at his watch. "And, of course, now that I finally have what passes for a phone, I'll call Tamiko."

. . . . .

Bundled in their heavy coats with backpacks in place, Lily and Phoebe stand by the front door as Tamiko almost runs in. "Mom's super-glued to the phone so Tessa's mom is taking us to school, which is great because we can tell her how we saw your new scoring record," Lily says excitedly, as the two girls skip down the snow-covered walk toward the white SUV that's rolling to a stop.

Finding Amber in the kitchen, phone indeed pressed to her ear, Tamiko pours herself a cup of coffee and wraps both hands around the mug.

"Worry not, Tamiko's just come in so she'll be here when you arrive," Amber says, before ending the call.

"That was Chief Barksdale. He's at the Boltwood where, sadly, he's confirmed that Jed Streeter is dead. As soon as the medical examiner arrives he, the Chief that is, will head over here."

"I called a lawyer," Tamiko blurts.

"Really?"

"I figured I may be in serious trouble. My boyfriend Lec, from last year—the one I told you about who's been in Japan—his dad is a lawyer in New York state. When I called Ted he said he'd get in touch with a law school buddy who lives near here to see if she can help me. As I came up the walk I got a text saying she'll be here by a quarter to nine and to absolutely wait for her before I talk to the police."

"Sorry to be cynical, Tamiko, but as part of my job I frequently deal with the small flock of local legal eagles who handle cases involving drunk, disorderly and otherwise miscreant students, to use my favorite nineteenth-century term. In short, I wouldn't expect a high flyer. But, tell me, who exactly is about to knock on my door?"

"Adley Saperstein."

"Tamiko, you never cease to amaze. In a couple of eye blinks you've found one of the few Hampshire County attorneys who might really help."

"You know Ms. Saperstein?"

"I read the newspapers about her high-profile cases and I'm on the Museum Board with her husband, Tom. When you strip out the students who pass through our five colleges, Hampshire County is a pretty small pond."

. . . . .

Adley Saperstein arrives at 8:44. A lean redhead in her early fifties, she's dressed in the well-worn blue parka with fluorescent yellow safety markings and sweatpants she had been wearing when Ted Burns interrupted her morning run. After a moment of small talk during which she and Amber agree on first names, the attorney gratefully accepts an oversized mug of coffee. Then turning to Tamiko she says, "My friend, let's you and I find a quiet nook while we let Amber get a start on her morning, which I'm guessing will involve promptly contacting the powers that be at Amherst College." When Dean Thomas appears reluctant to leave Tamiko, Saperstein adds, "Amber, as much as I'm sure your goal is to protect Tamiko's interests, there are two reasons I need to talk to my client alone. The first is attorney-client confidentiality, which I obviously have and you, just as obviously, don't. And, frankly, the other is that you necessarily owe loyalty to your college. While Amherst's and Tamiko's interests may turn out to be perfectly congruent, it's also possible that they…"

"Got it," Amber interrupts, "You two can use my husband's office behind the kitchen and I'll operate from the living room. But what happens when Roger Barksdale appears? As all the deans at our local colleges well know, Roger's a chameleon—chill when it comes to dealing with minor undergrad peccadilloes, but hotter than a tin stovetop when an issue like this threatens to affect his carefully cultivated media image as a law and order cop."

"Tell the good Chameleon we won't be long." Then, with a nod toward the bright plaid blanket that covers the end of the sofa, Adley adds with a grin, "It might be fun to seat him there."

. . . . .

Alec stuffs his belongings into his roller bag, grabs a coffee and pastry to go and quick steps toward Sayulita's main plaza, where taxis nest. On his way to Puerto Vallarta in a twenty-year-old VW Golf a few minutes later, he repeatedly tries to call Tamiko, only to find that her line is always busy.

. . . . .

When Tamiko finishes giving Adley Saperstein an outline of what's happened since Jed unexpectedly called her late the previous afternoon, the attorney takes a swig of coffee, steeples her long, very white fingers and says, "As I'm sure you know from watching legal dramas, the retainer agreement you just signed means you and I have a strict bond of confidentiality. That is, whatever you tell me, good, bad or indifferent, goes no further. And, perhaps you also know that one of the principal reasons for this rule is that I can't help you without all the facts, even potentially highly embarrassing ones, so…"

"I just told you everything…"

"Tamiko, since time is short, forgive me for proposing that you cut the bullshit. Do you expect me, or for that matter anyone, to believe that one of the world's hottest movie stars came all the way to our obscure little Pioneer Valley solely to tell a stunning young woman his daughter received encouraging news from a college? Or, put more directly, I need you to tell me everything that happened at the Boltwood Inn last night."

"Like I told you, after Jed's surprise call a few minutes before five p.m., I visited him briefly in his room before jogging to campus to have supper with my team. Then I played basketball, celebrated our win until ten-ish, talked to Jed by phone and slept upstairs. That's it, the whole story."

"No alcohol, drugs or boy-girl games with Jed Streeter? And remember, Tamiko, although people sometimes edit the truth, the sheets at the hotel won't lie."

"Huh?"

"If you had sex in Jed Streeter's room," Adley Saperstein says patiently, "Chief Barksdale already knows it, or soon will."

"How many times do I have to tell you there is nothing to know," Tamiko replies, as she begins to worry that despite Amber's endorsement, Ted Burns has sent her a dud lawyer.

"And in L.A.?" Saperstein asks.

"Okay then, it's like Jed and I did have a brief romance in L.A. while filming *2+2*. But nothing happened here and wasn't going to even if we'd connected in person later in the evening, which we didn't."

"And L.A. consisted of what exactly? Again, Tamiko, I really am on your side here. But we don't have much time and I need to know the whole story, warts and all."

"We spent a couple of nights together and that's pretty much it." Then, somehow thinking of the story of Apostle Peter attempting to save himself by denying Jesus, Tamiko adds, "Emotionally, it was a big deal for both of us, but in reality, Jed and I only got together romantically twice."

"Who knows about these trysts? For example, was your romantic relationship common knowledge on your movie set?"

"Not at all. Hardly anyone had a clue since the whole deal was over almost before it started and we never hung in public. Well, okay, Ben Fine, the director of the movie and his assistant Mary McCarthy did know what was happening. And then there are my buds Derrick and Clementine Fine, Ben's adopted kids who are also Amherst students, which is how I got involved in the film in the first place. And, oh, yes, Mary's niece and also Jed's landscape guy, Juan Gomez, drove me to Jed's place a couple of times, but he's like Jed's tight *amigo*—or I guess I should say 'was' now," Tamiko adds, as she wipes her eyes on her sleeve.

"I may not have learned a great deal in my twenty-eight years of practicing law, but there's one thing I can tell you for sure—six people never kept a secret. And Tamiko, more to the point now," Adley says gently, "Jed Streeter obviously did show up here with more on his mind than his daughter's education. So again, if you want to amend anything you've told me, please do it now."

"Nothing is different from what I've already said. However, a few days ago Jed emailed that he hoped to keep seeing me despite that we'd agreed our relationship was limited to L.A. I planned to FaceTime him to say no, but hadn't done it yet when he astonished me by calling from the Boltwood. So when I dropped by at five I reiterated that the romantic part of our friendship was over. I mean, underneath all the media hype Jed was a fabulous dude, really sweet and kind, as well as being Velcro attractive, but I'm only seventeen and I need to lead my own life. And just so you know, I did help Allison with her college decision and even edited her essay. I don't know if you have children, but when we met Jed was seriously worried that Allison, his only kid, wouldn't go to college at all, so it was a big deal that my ideas helped turn things around. But why is any of this important? I mean, Jed died of natural causes, right?"

"Let's get back to drugs and alcohol," Adley says kindly. "Tamiko, when you two got together in L.A. was Streeter, or for that matter, both of you, using anything illegal? Again, sorry to be blunt, but if the police are about to discover anything—coke, meth or whatever in that hotel room, I really do need to know."

"I've had two tokes of weed in my entire life, neither of them with Jed. One of the nights we spent together I had maybe half a glass of champagne, but that's it. At least with me, Jed barely drank, and definitely wasn't high on anything. Maybe it's hard to believe, but he was proud of those anti-drug TV spots he's famous for."

"Nice to know. But Tamiko, I'm not going to bet my house that Streeter died with nothing illegal in his system. After all, if he did he'd probably be the first youngish celebrity to do so this century and probably the one before as well. However, since I just heard the Chief's voice, it's time to face the music. Tamiko, your job is to tell him exactly what happened yesterday and today, but absolutely nothing about anything in L.A. beyond the fact that Jed Streeter was a helpful mentor during your film and in appreciation you helped his daughter with her college applications. Let me repeat, the nothing I'm talking about is spelled Z-E-R-O."

"My lips are zipped," Tamiko replies, drawing the tips of her thumb and index finger across her closed mouth for emphasis.

"Good. And you can trust me to intervene if Barksdale persists in asking about your personal relationship with Streeter. And since you are underage, I'll threaten to close down the interview if he doesn't back off. But let me greet the Chief first, while you call your mom. Fill her in briefly and tell her to look for an email form from my office authorizing me to represent you. To forestall any possible confidentiality issues, she should sign it and get it back. What's her full name and email?"

. . . . .

"Tamiko Gashkin, how can I help?" Tamiko asks, hand extended as she approaches the unusually tall, thick, fiftyish man wearing a dark blue uniform.

"By answering all of my questions as honestly and completely as you can," the Chief replies, ignoring Tamiko's hand.

"Before we start, I'd like to establish a few rules," Adley Saperstein says, from where she stands by the large front window next to Amber Thomas. Then, seeing Chief Barksdale's moonface begin to turn pink, the attorney adds, "Roger, like any public-spirited citizen, my client is happy to answer any questions pertaining to events of yesterday and today, but that's it. Ms. Gashkin is a minor who, as the facts will bear out, had absolutely no connection with Mr. Streeter's untimely death apparently from natural causes other than to discover his body in the company of a hotel cleaner. In other words, since you have absolutely no grounds to treat her as a suspect, I'm here to see that you don't."

"Hmph! Last time I checked, in the city of Amherst it's my job to decide who is, and isn't, a suspect," Chief Barksdale snaps. Then, with the habit large people in authority often develop, the Chief steps uncomfortably close to Tamiko. "If you're as innocent as Mother Mary, I don't see why the leading criminal defense lawyer in at least three counties is standing next to you barely an hour after you would have me believe you accidentally stumbled on Mr. Streeter's body."

"Roger, if you make another speech like that I'm going to break off this interview since you have neither warrant, nor probable cause, to arrest my client," Adley Saperstein says. "I just said Ms. Gashkin will answer any and all relevant questions about discovering Jed Streeter's body. There is no need to bully her."

Ignoring this, Chief Barksdale leans even closer to Tamiko as he says, "If you tell me the whole truth now young lady, everything will go easier for you. So, were you with Mr. Streeter when he died?"

"No," Tamiko replies simply, as she wonders if, with his huge shoulders and protruding eyes, Barksdale is somehow related to Maggie of the night before.

"That's it?" Chief Barksdale asks, after waiting in vain for Tamiko to continue. "That's all you have to say about the death of one of the world's most famous people, who obviously came all the way to western Massachusetts a few days after the two of you worked closely on what I gather is some kind of X-rated movie?"

Again, waiting in vain for Tamiko to elaborate, Barksdale eventually demands, "When was the last time you saw Jed Streeter alive? And when, and how, did you get that bruised face and black eye?"

Reasoning that whether a bully wears a basketball or police uniform, you are lost if you back down, Tamiko leans forward so that her face is only inches from Barksdale's as she replies pleasantly, "I last saw Jed Streeter alive yesterday about five p.m. for less than fifteen minutes. We also talked by phone briefly at a few minutes past ten last night. That's it, all of it, except that I'm very, very, sorry he died, especially that he died alone."

In apparent acknowledgment of Tamiko's refusal to give an inch, the Chief takes a step back as he asks, "When did you first know that Jed Streeter was coming to Amherst to see you for what I guess we can best describe as an assignation?"

Doing her best not to show how pleased she is that it's Barksdale who has retreated, Tamiko replies, "I learned that Jed had driven over from Boston to celebrate his daughter Allison's positive college news when he called me between four-thirty and five yesterday."

"And you were where?"

"Upstairs, getting ready to join my teammates for supper before a varsity basketball game."

"Now you're trying to have me believe you're on the Amherst women's team?" the Chief asks in what appears to be genuine disbelief. "Then, how come when I took my daughter to see a game in December you were nowhere to be seen?"

"Chief," Dean Thomas says, "At Coach Raines's request Tamiko returned from California to take the place of an injured player, Rosie Wilburn, for several games. I was at the Springfield State game last night with my daughters, the oldest of whom is a middle school classmate of your daughter Charlotte, and I can tell you that Tamiko not only started at point guard, she set an Amherst single game scoring record with thirty-seven points. In addition, she absorbed a couple of hard knocks resulting in her black eye."

Ignoring this, Barksdale persists, "So, when exactly did you last see Mr. Streeter—alive that is?"

"Perhaps you didn't notice, but my client already answered that question by saying a little after five p.m.," Adley Saperstein says.

"Unless, and until, Ms. Gashkin's answers begin to make more sense, I'm going to keep asking the same questions," Chief Barksdale growls. "And just in case you're in any doubt, Ms. Saperstein, when Jed Streeter's death is reported I don't think I'm the only one who will be skeptical that your client dreamt of sugarplums in her own bed last night."

Realizing the big policeman has finally made a valid point, the three women say nothing. Eventually, Tamiko breaks the silence by volunteering, "As I said before, when I got Jed's surprise call late yesterday afternoon, I stopped by the Boltwood for maybe ten or fifteen minutes. It was super smooth that Allison got good news from Colorado State, since it's her first choice. If I hadn't had a game, Jed and I would have had supper. But, since I was already late, I literally had to run over to Valentine to grab a bite with the team before heading to the gym."

"What exact time did you meet your teammates for supper?"

"Again, like I said, because I detoured to say hi to Jed, I was a few minutes late, probably arriving at Valentine a little before five-thirty. I remember Coach Raines looking at her watch so you can check with her."

"And after the game?"

"Jed and I planned on a late bite. But the game turned out to be a bear, both emotionally and physically," Tamiko replies, as she points to her black eye. "In addition, it was the last game I'd agreed to play before

Rosie Wilburn returns from her injury, so I was pretty much tugged along to the celebration party."

"And where was that?"

"At Margie Prime's room in Greenway B. If you want to check I can text you Margie's number."

Ignoring this the Chief continues, "And after that you went to the hotel to stay with Mr. Streeter?"

"Roger," Adley Saperstein says, "do you think it's possible to ask a question without supplying your preferred answer?"

Before the Chief can respond, Tamiko says, "And then I called Jed who reported he felt crappy as a result of a recurrence of what he thought was acid reflux and heartburn. Also, he'd gotten up at five-thirty a.m. to appear on a Boston drive time talk show so thought exhaustion was another reason why his body was rebelling. Anyway, we decided to meet for breakfast this morning, which, again, was why I went to Jed's room at eight a.m."

When Chief Barksdale's phone dings, he checks his texts. Pursing his lips he asks, "Young lady, if even half of what you just said is true, how come we have a reliable eyewitness who saw you exit the hotel after dark last night?"

Seeing the concern on Amber's face at the same time Adley Saperstein starts to object, Tamiko answers simply, "I'm guessing you talked to the receptionist who said 'good evening' when she saw me leave the hotel to join my teammates a few minutes after dark just as I said."

"After dark could just as well mean the middle of the night," Chief Barksdale replies.

"Roger, in case you're wondering, I can confirm that Tamiko got back here about ten-fifteen last night," Dean Thomas says. "We talked briefly about the game before she took a bath and went to bed before eleven. This morning I heard her in the bathroom about seven-fifteen a.m. and saw her in the kitchen a few minutes later."

"But since it's barely half a mile from here to the inn, Tamiko could easily have waited until you were asleep, snuck out for a few hours and tiptoed back," Barksdale insists.

"I was working on a report at the dining room table until at least eleven-forty-five, so it would have had to be after that. And doesn't the inn lock all its doors long before that except the front entrance where someone is at the desk all night?"

"Of course Tamiko could also have used a sheet rope to rappel out of her window before finding a ladder in the garage, and carrying it unseen to the hotel where she used it to climb into Jed Streeter's window," Adley Saperstein remarks, dryly.

Ignoring this, Chief Barksdale holds out his hand as he asks, "Tamiko, can I see your phone?"

"You don't need to show him…" the lawyer starts to say even as Tamiko hands the large officer her phone.

"Jed Streeter lives in L.A., so his area code is 424," Tamiko says helpfully when she observes the Chief nearsightedly squinting at the list of recent calls.

Registering that, indeed, Tamiko had called a Los Angeles number about 10:00 the previous evening, Chief Barksdale barks, "Absolutely none of this changes the fact that you were the last person to see Jed Streeter alive and the first one to find him dead."

"In the company of a hotel employee who opened the locked door," Adley Saperstein adds wearily. "More to the point, when will the autopsy be performed? I assume you'll expedite it so as to have something to report as soon as possible after the media learns of Streeter's death?"

"Late this morning I hope, which reminds me I need to take a break to check on that and a dozen other things. Ms. Gashkin, I need you to either accompany me to the station, or have both Dean Thomas and your legal representative here guarantee that you'll stay put until I say otherwise."

"You have zero legal right to require that," Adley Saperstein snaps.

"But I have every right to place two patrol cars out front and another at each end of the block, which I'm gonna guess will result in the media showing up ASAP."

"I don't need to go anyplace this morning," Tamiko says. "And if

Amber, that is, Dean Thomas, can stay here with me, everything should be chill, right?"

"Chill is not a word I'd use for what's going to happen in a few hours when the media finds out that Hollywood's hunkiest forty-year-old star died in a local hotel while visiting a seventeen-year-old starlet with whom he'd just made a raunchy movie," Chief Barksdale replies, as he heads for the door.

. . . . .

"Is everything as okay as it can be?" Ben Fine asks, when Tamiko picks up his call.

"I guess. I'm back at Dean Thomas's along with Adley Saperstein, the lawyer who is helping me. The seriously obnoxious Amherst police chief just left after trying to get me to admit that Jed died in the midst of what he fantasizes was our Fentanyl-fueled sexcapade. But, Ben, let me put you on speaker so Ms. Saperstein and Dean Thomas can hear."

"Hello to you both. I'm delighted Tamiko has help," Ben Fine says. "Amber, when we talked earlier Jed's death hadn't been officially confirmed, but I assume there's no doubt?"

"None. Jed passed last night," Dean Thomas says simply. "I'm very sorry, Tamiko told me you two were close."

"We were. But Tamiko, you and I will both have to put off mourning 'til another day while we concentrate on how best to navigate the next few hours. I'm guessing the powers that be will want to do an autopsy as quickly as possible?"

"Almost immediately, and they'll try to keep a lid on the fact of Streeter's death in the meantime," Adley Saperstein replies. "But with cops, EMS people, and even the hotel staff involved, someone has probably already shopped the story. Given the distance to Boston, I'm guessing it will be less than two hours before the national media arrives en masse in Amherst, and only a few minutes more before they pound on Dean Thomas's front door. In the meantime, Tamiko has agreed to stay put. In my view there is nothing to legally require this, but given the alternative of having Chief Barksdale take her to the station, it seemed like the best short-term compromise."

"Tamiko," Ben Fine says, "I just talked to Maddy Chilton, one of the top P.R. crisis people here in L.A. She agrees with me that it will be wise for you to prepare a graceful statement expressing your sadness concerning Jed's death, leave it with your lawyer, or Dean Thomas, and then get the hell out of town as soon as possible after the autopsy confirms that Jed died of natural causes."

"Seriously! Run away? Ben, you have to be kidding, right?"

"When does Amherst College open for the next semester?" Ben Fine asks in a tone that telegraphs he already knows the answer.

"Two weeks from today," Amber Thomas answers.

"Then, Tamiko, I can't see why your going about your business like any other student on break amounts to running anywhere. When classes start you can be back, ready to go."

"But shouldn't I stick around and answer all the media's questions as best I can? After all, I haven't done anything wrong and Jed died of…"

"Tamiko," Ben Fine interrupts, with the no-nonsense tone she'd gotten used to on set. "The fact that you were not remotely involved in Jed's death won't make a jot of difference as to how the media handles the story in the next few days. Or, put more bluntly, no matter the truth, and no matter what you say, a significant number of so-called objective reporters are about to join the paparazzi fringe in painting you as an underage sex kitten who somehow lured Jed to his death. And, sadly, they'll laugh in your face when you try to explain that this is total bullshit because you and Jed were somehow just tight buddies. But the good news is that given our twenty-four-hour internet-driven news cycle, even the most salacious stories don't last nearly as long as they used to, especially if it turns out that Jed died of a heart attack, or possibly a stroke."

"But still, Ben, since I really have nothing to hide shouldn't I at least…"

"Tamiko, you'll have the rest of your life to answer questions," Adley Saperstein says more kindly. "For now, and especially given your personal relationship with Jed Streeter in L.A., which experience tells me is bound to leak out, I agree it's best to make a written statement before immediately leaving."

"But if I head home to Berkeley won't the media circus follow me? I mean it's like it might even be worse on the West Coast."

"If you'll hear me out, Tamiko, I'm going to recommend that you simply drop out of sight for a week or two," Ben says.

"Truly! Is that even possible these days with electronic devices tracking me?"

"Mary is working to find a safe haven as we speak, possibly a vacation house in a remote area. And, no doubt you'll want to ditch your electronic devices and stay off the internet while you're there. But since your picture is only hours away from being front and center on at least two-thirds of the world's media platforms, Maddy Chilton also suggests a quick makeover."

"I may have the perfect place," Dean Thomas says. "My sister and her family are in Italy for the month and her condo on the upper West Side in New York City is empty. Isn't it a lot easier to disappear into a dense urban area than at someone's seasonal cottage in the country where everyone minds everyone else's business? I'm thinking that if we change Tamiko's appearance this morning, I can drive her down there before the reporters arrive, assuming, of course, we can get our local gendarmerie on board."

"Sounds like a plan," Ben Fine replies. "Which means, Tamiko, it's time to sacrifice your lovely long locks and dye whatever is left. Add glasses, a hat and some baggy clothes and hopefully your mom would have trouble recognizing you walking down Fifth Avenue."

"I've got a black eye and a puffy cheek from basketball last night so that's already a start," Tamiko replies with her first chuckle of the morning.

"To execute even a quick and dirty makeover we'll need at least ninety minutes, assuming I can rustle up a stylist," Dean Thomas says.

"Get started. And Tamiko, while you're being transformed, please compose the first draft of a media statement, which I'm hoping Adley can help with. And since Allison and her college plans are safe ground don't be shy about elaborating them since the more detail you provide, the more you divert attention from the other reasons why Jed may have visited Amherst. As soon as you get a preliminary draft, shoot it to Mary and we'll immediately weigh in before forwarding it to Maddy who is standing by."

"Okay, I guess, but didn't I just promise not to leave here without Chief Barksdale's permission?" Tamiko asks.

"In my experience, from the cop on the beat to the justices of the Supreme Court, the first job of law enforcement is to make themselves look good," Ben replies. "Fortunately, you have excellent people with you to help figure out a way for the good chief to accomplish this at the same time you're able to disappear."

. . . . .

When Alec reaches the Puerto Vallarta airport at 9:15 Central Time, he literally sweats his way through a seemingly endless security line with the result that his plane is almost finished boarding when he puffs up to the gate. Finally settled in the twenty-fourth row with his back to the bathroom, he again tries to call Tamiko, only to find that his cheap phone no longer has a signal. Half an hour later, when the plane still hasn't moved, the pilot announces that because an instrument panel light has failed, they are in the process of doing a manual check of the baggage compartment door latch. Now feeling so tense his jaw pops, Alec tries to call his dad, only to conclude that his phone really is as dead as Jed Streeter.

. . . . .

At 10:15, an ample woman with blond streaks in her dark hair appears at Dean Thomas's door, hefting a squarish black bag with both hands. "I'm guessing Bebe Rizzo's Portable Hair Salon should set up shop in the kitchen," she says with a grin, as Amber Thomas gives her a side hug, and thanks her profusely for coming.

"Your client awaits," Amber says, as she leads the stylist toward the back of the house and introduces Tamiko.

"Hold on a second, Amber," Bebe says as she deposits the bag on the kitchen table with a relieved *phew*. "When is it that you explain how I'm about to be part of the most explosive event in recent Amherst history? Seriously, if I don't have a good story for the two clients I just stood up, my goose is going to…"

"No worries, Bebe. I could just as well have said 'scandalous,' 'notorious,' and 'shocking' and all three would also be true. But, c'mon, time's a-wasting."

"That's hardly an explanation," Bebe protests, as she nevertheless tosses Tamiko a black smock and begins to empty the paraphernalia of her trade onto the table.

"Bebe," Amber Thomas asks from where she's sitting on the counter, "if we put you in the picture now, will you please cut while you listen and pinky-swear not to repeat a word until at least late this afternoon?"

· · · · ·

With Tamiko now sitting erect in a straight-backed kitchen chair, the stylist says, "My dear, cutting hair as beautiful as yours should be a felony, and dyeing it, a hanging offense. So how about I just take off a few inches and color it a few shades darker?"

"How about you take off everything but two inches," Tamiko replies with a laugh. "When I was ten I wanted to change my name to Bill and cut my hair like a boy's, but my mom went ballistic. Now's my chance."

"Very occasionally, moms know what they're talking about," Bebe replies in a long-suffering tone that all but announces she has a teenaged daughter. "But seriously, Tamiko, nothing short of surgery is going to make your body look even a little bit like a boy's, so I hope you have a double-X parka that hangs to your knees. After all, experienced paparazzi are sure to know it's easier to put on a hat, glasses and face covering scarf, than it is to hide a standout figure."

· · · · ·

"Brian, it's not like you to duck my calls unless you think I'm raising money for the hospital," Adley Saperstein says when she finally gets through to Hampshire County District Attorney Brian Carroll at 10:25.

"Apologies, Adley. After listening to Roger Barksdale rant about the unfairness of Jed Streeter choosing to die in Amherst, I had to talk to Traci Kim, the assistant medical examiner in Holyoke who will have to do the autopsy. Streeter is probably the most famous person to die in our little county since Calvin Coolidge passed away in Northampton in 1933, so, understandably she's up a tree."

"Just because you majored in history at Yale doesn't mean you need to flaunt it. But, come to that, Silent Cal and Jed Streeter do have one big thing in common—they both died of natural causes."

"Both for your client's sake and to make my job infinitely easier, I devoutly hope that turns out to be true. But in the meantime, my understanding is that Streeter came to Amherst to visit Ms. Gashkin and that she was both the last person to see him alive and the first person to see him dead."

"Assuming Streeter died by himself of natural causes, what does any of that have to do with the price of Dogecoin? And, c'mon Brian, when, after all these years, did you begin relying on Roger Barksdale's overheated judgment?"

"Adley, as you well know, at this stage what we don't know about how Streeter died is a lot more than what we do. And, Traci won't say a word until she cuts him open. I swear that woman watches too much *CSI*."

"When does she think he died?"

"Even Traci was willing to say that given how stiff the body was, death wasn't recent, probably between midnight and two o'clock."

"Given that my client talked by phone to Streeter about ten last evening when he was complaining about chest pains, isn't it obvious what happened?"

"Leaving aside the fact that we only have Ms. Gashkin's word for what was said, as well as her denial that she didn't somehow see him later, let me ask you two simple questions. First, when you hear an apparently healthy fortyish celebrity has died unexpectedly, what's the first thought that pops into your head? And, second, how often is that thought correct?"

"Since neither of us is supposed to be in the wild speculation business, let me ask you a far more pertinent question," Adley Saperstein replies. "Has Roger's team actually found any illegal substances at the scene?"

"So far, only a few Nexium, which you probably know is an over-the-counter acid reflux and heartburn remedy, and a couple of low-dose generic Ambien-type pills for sleep. But that doesn't mean Streeter couldn't have ingested all of the illegal substances he brought along, or, that your promiscuous seventeen-year-old client didn't make off with the evidence after he croaked in her arms."

"Brian, I call bullshit on steroids! And the worst part is you know it."

"We'll find out soon enough. Traci plans to start the autopsy in about an hour. Of course the tox report will take a lot longer, but one step at a time."

"By noon, if not sooner, Dean Thomas's house is sure to be surrounded by a good-sized army of reporters intent on harassing my client. So, since you don't have even a scintilla of evidence, I plan to escort her out of here."

"Adley, at my request Tabitha Marcus here in my office prepared a court order under Section one hundred and nineteen alleging that as a minor, Tamiko Gashkin is without proper adult guardianship and needs to be detained by the juvenile authorities for her own protection. I have Judge Carcetti literally standing by to sign it. In short, if you try to move Ms. Gashkin I'll have her carted off to juvie before she reaches the corner."

"For Christ's sake Brian, take a long look in the closest mirror to check whether you've gone mad. Tamiko Gashkin has A grades at one of the most selective colleges in the country, and is a nationally ranked athlete who, by the way, broke Amherst's single game scoring record just last night. And, oh yes, although she's still seventeen she's also a professional actress and screenwriter. In addition, she has a very competent mother, so capable in fact, that Amy Gashkin has hired me to protect her daughter from the likes of you and Roger. In short, when all the facts are on the table, no court will rule that she's an abused minor as defined in the Penal Code."

"Let me remind you, she's also a minor who was apparently involved in a sexual relationship with a forty-year-old film icon who apparently crossed state lines for an assignation at a local hotel. Perhaps you're right that after listening to your undoubted eloquence the juvenile judge will conclude there is no reason to pursue the matter. But by that time, your client will have spent most of the day cooling her heels at the detention center in Hadley, which, not so incidentally, will give Traci plenty of time to determine how Jed Streeter died."

"Brian, I very much doubt you'd risk frying your office's relationship with every college in the county, by pulling a stunt like that."

"Adley, I very much doubt you want to find out."

Softening her voice, as actors and attorneys can so easily do on command, Saperstein asks, "Short of my running against you in next year's election, how are we going to work out a compromise we can both live with?"

"Actually, I have an idea," Dean Thomas says from where she's been standing listening just inside the study door.

"Hold on a second, Brian, while I put you on speaker. Associate Dean Amber Thomas from Amherst College is here and very sensibly wants to get in on this."

"Hello, Brian. How are Judy and your two lovely daughters?" Dean Thomas asks. "If memory serves, your oldest, who is about Tamiko Gashkin's age, started at Dartmouth in September?"

"Good memory, Amber. And yes, Mindy is also a year ahead of schedule."

"So, Brian can I ask you, if Mindy was in this situation, what would you suggest?"

"That she fully cooperate with the authorities."

"Even if that meant she would be swarmed by an army of over-the-top paparazzi?"

"Amber, I hope I'm not as insensitive as Adley obviously thinks I am," the District Attorney replies. "Just the same, I can't and won't lose track of Ms. Gashkin until we have a cause of death. But if you have something to suggest, I'm listening."

"Here's my proposal. In about forty-five minutes, Tamiko and I leave here in my car, ultimately heading for New York City where she can hole up at an undisclosed location. But to keep you on board, we stop in the Costco parking lot in West Springfield, or any other similar place you designate, until you either say it's fine to continue, or, based on something potentially illegal you discover in the autopsy, you have good cause to require Tamiko to return."

"Are you making this offer personally, or on behalf of the college?"

"Both."

"I agree as long as you don't mind having a Springfield officer parked next to you at Costco."

"No problem, as long as they're in plainclothes in an unmarked car."

. . . . .

With his flight to Houston finally in the air, Alec pushes the cabin attendant button. When a pudgy young man in a too-snug blue uniform appears, Alec explains that he's responding to a family emergency and asks if he'll have enough time to make his connection to JFK.

"Given our ETA into Houston I'd say it's a medium maybe. As of now, you'll have twenty-two minutes from the time we open our door, but it's a schlep to the gate for the New York plane."

"Do you have a map of the airport?" Alec asks, hopefully.

"No, but the gate attendant will point you. However, your main problem will be waiting behind the one hundred and twenty people in front of you to get off this plane. Fortunately, I think I can help with that. Let me get back to you after we hand out drinks and snacks."

. . . . .

Dean Thomas's Mazda CX-9 pulls onto Highway 116 heading south for the forty-five-minute drive to Springfield, just north of the Connecticut border. Blowing out a long, slow breath, Tamiko calls her mom.

"Finally, here you are," Amy says, by way of answer. "I've talked to Amber Thomas, Ted Burns and Mary McCarthy in the last hour so I guess I'm more or less current with what's happening, but…"

"Mom," Tamiko interrupts, "I really am sorry I haven't gotten back to you since this morning, but things have been a blur. I mean, for one thing my hair is now three inches long and black with a purplish tint. It's actually pretty chill if you like the mohawk look. And, I'm dressed kinda like before I met Lec—you know, as if I've been shopping in a dumpster."

"Amber says that despite all that, plus your black eye and goggle-like glasses, you still manage to look cute. But, more to the point, where are you this minute? And how are you coping? Obviously, finding Jed must have been awful."

"It was all so fast. I mean, one second my tummy was turning happy somersaults at the prospect of French toast, and the next, there was Jed lying stiff on the bed. Mom, you met him so you know that despite all the media crap, Jed was a mega-sweet dude," Tamiko adds, now sniffling.

Waiting a moment to see if her daughter has more to say, Amy replies, "You're right, I absolutely did like Jed. It's a shame he didn't get to a doctor when he first started feeling bad."

"Mom, the horrible thing is that Jed came all the way to Amherst to see me and I had like almost zero time for him. And when we did see each other briefly, I was so busy trying to push him away that…"

"Sweetie, nothing you did or said, or didn't do or didn't say, had one iota to do with Jed's death, which sounds like some kind of vascular, or heart issue."

"When Jed was feeling crappy over Christmas, he called his ex-wife's doctor in Tucson who assured him it was unlikely to be serious. With all Jed's running and swimming and the fact he could have passed for thirty, no one, including Jed himself, thought he could have a heart problem. But, just the same, he died alone in a strange hotel when I could have…"

"Maybe try to think of it like this. What happened with you two in L.A. was one of life's miraculous little gifts—a moment of honest grace. But for so many reasons, it wasn't designed to last. The fact that you were wise enough to see that, doesn't make you a bad person and certainly isn't remotely connected with…"

"It was like I had no real choice," Tamiko interrupts, her mind chugging so fast she isn't able to listen. "I mean, Lec got into my soul first. For sure, getting a big crush on Jed was head-spinning, but every time I felt love for him begin to trickle into my heart, I'd think of Lec. I don't even know if Lec and I are going to put things back together, but Mom, I only have one heart and it's still his, well, most of it anyway. So when Jed sent me this sweet message a few days ago saying he hoped we could continue to see each other, I should have immediately FaceTimed him to say no. But, because of what went down with Lec and Aki and because I hadn't heard from Lec in a week, I guess a greedy, or maybe scared, part of me was tempted to keep Jed on the back burner. And then, oh my god, Mom, there he was a few blocks away."

"Sweetie, you're not the first woman who has hesitated to make an agonizing choice between two good men. While our bodies may be designed to be promiscuous, our hearts aren't, so the best you, or anyone in your situation can do, is make an honest decision. And, as for yesterday, remember it was Jed who showed up unannounced at a highly inconvenient moment. If he'd been wise enough to call first you'd have had the chance to reiterate what you both agreed to in L.A."

"I guess, and although nobody around here chooses to believe it, Jed's trip wasn't only about me. He was really excited about his daughter's good news from Colorado State. It's like Allison was the person he loved most in the world, so, at least he knew she was on a good path before he died."

"Happy news that wouldn't have been possible without you."

"Mom, I know when the publicity hits I'll probably be cast as the underage sex kitten and Jed will be the dirty old dude. Almost no one in the whole world will believe we honestly bonded at a deep level."

"I can't argue with that. But, Sweetie, here's the important thing, as long as you hold tight to your truth, none of the media lies need affect you. But, more to the point, right now I'm planning to fly to JFK this afternoon and hang out with you for a few days."

Tamiko starts to reply, only to find she's tongue-tied.

"Tamiko, are you still there?"

"Mom, I know this probably sounds borderline deranged, but I'm hoping that at some point Lec will show up in New York. I feared he was incommunicado in Mexico because he was pissed at me, or might even have fallen into some chill beach scene, but when I talked to Ted Burns this morning he explained Lec had been down with some kind of stomach virus and his phone and iPad were stolen."

"All the more reason why I should…"

"Mom, he got a new phone and called his dad last night to say he's fine."

"So you really think…"

"Mom, all I know is that if Lec was in bad trouble you couldn't keep me away. So how about this? In a few days if it turns out I'm wrong and I'm not coping, I won't hesitate to ask for help."

· · · · ·

"You good?" Amber asks. "I'll do my best to be a good listener if you want to talk about any part of what's been happening."

"Thanks," Tamiko replies. "I apologize for not telling you more about what's been going on with me. It was like I was so happy to be back in Amherst playing ball and hanging out with you and your girls, I wanted to keep the L.A. stuff behind me."

"I guessed part of it from your emails. Also, whenever you mentioned Jed Streeter your face lit up like the harvest moon in a cloudless sky."

"Amber, I'm guessing you're way too sensible to have ever fallen for two dudes at the same time so probably…"

"Ha!" Amber interrupts. "Then it will surprise you that I did just that. In truth, I still get tummy flutters when I remember what an emotional train wreck I got myself into."

"Really? So what happened?" Tamiko asks, so interested she momentarily forgets her own drama.

"Isn't this the day we talk about you?"

"It will be a relief to give my drama a rest while I maybe learn something from you. Of course, if you don't want…"

"Tamiko, as much as I like and respect you, even yesterday I'd never have believed I'd talk about any of this, especially not to a student. But, somehow what's happened with you today has blown me way past my discretion zone. The quick version is that my time of two-guy obsession, or torture may be the more accurate term, happened fifteen years ago when I was in my late twenties. Suddenly, after years of drifting from one imperfect guy to the next while wondering whether I'd ever find a good mate, I tumbled hard for Mr. Perfect—smart, compassionate, successful, and based on my experience up until then, a sweet romantic fit."

"Sounds sweet. You must have been…"

"Tamiko, hear me out," Amber continues. "On the very day I decided to say yes to his proposal, this other guy chatted me up on the coffee line at Peet's. He not only followed me into the parking lot, but somehow got me to say yes to lunch. Not only was this character, let's call him Mr. Rake, twice divorced and unapologetically trying to bed as many women as possible, he was over-the-top chick bait. When he walked into a room women actually glanced at each other to size up the competition. So it was beyond surprising that with all his choices Mr. Rake put his best moves on little old me."

"So, with a sweet, successful dude already in love with you, why was it a hard choice?"

"As it turned out, it wasn't. I chose the bad boy."

"Mr, Rake, really? But why, when you were already in love…"

"I was a medium-attractive twenty-eight-year-old grad student with a disappointing erotic resumé, in part because I hadn't been that excited about any of the relatively short list of experiences I'd had."

"But, didn't you just say Mr. Perfect was pretty chill, or maybe I should say hot, when it came to more, er, well, intimate pleasures, I guess?"

"No need to be circumspect, since in truth sex with Mr. Perfect really was more fulfilling than anything I'd experienced. But here's the point, while Mr. Perfect hit eight on my zero to ten pleasure scale, Mr. Rake turned me so thoroughly inside out that numbers no longer mattered. I know I'm oversharing, but I went from being a woman who rarely had an orgasm to going off like a string of firecrackers every time. The result was my body fell instantly in love with Mr. Rake, and truth be told, my heart promptly followed. Still, I hesitated, based on my head's gaggle of admonitions, remonstrances and warnings—this is lust, not love, among the milder. But, after a lifetime of being a sensible girl making sane decisions, I guess I just itched to make a huge, lusty, leap into the unknown."

"Can I ask what happened next? I know you're happily married to a sweet, reliable dude, so was it another major drama when somehow your husband Mark replaced Mr. ..."

"Mark is Mr. Rake and very fortunately nothing about his power has diminished."

"Yo! Seriously!" Tamiko exclaims, just as her phone sounds. Barely glancing at the unfamiliar number she decides Amber's story is too riveting to interrupt. But before she can let the call go to voicemail, Amber says, "With today's drama, best pick up."

"Tamiko, Adley Saperstein here. Are you two at Springfield yet?"

"Four miles out according to the sign we just passed."

"I got the press statement we drafted earlier back from L.A. and since they edited our version I want to read it to you. Also, you should know that twenty minutes ago Roger Barksdale issued a statement that said..."

"Hold on a second while I put you on speaker," Tamiko interrupts. "Amber's going to want to hear this."

"There's not a lot to hear, since all he said was that Jed Streeter had been found dead at eight a.m. at the Inn on Boltwood by a member of the hotel staff and a friend. And that an autopsy was being conducted, with preliminary results to be announced at a one-thirty p.m. press conference in Northampton. The only other facts he shared were that Jed apparently passed away in bed during the night and that there were no signs of violence."

"Was Tamiko's name mentioned?" Amber asks, apprehensively.

"Not by Roger. But several reporters who have made the *2+2* connection asked whether Streeter was in Amherst to see Tamiko

Gashkin. And if she was with him when he died."

"How did Roger reply?" Dean Thomas demands.

"*No comment*, which of course will be interpreted to mean that when Jed died Tamiko was in his arms, naked as a newborn. However, since we can't do anything about that, let me read the edited parts of Tamiko's statement."

"Go for it," Tamiko says, as she alternately clenches, and unclenches her fists.

STATEMENT OF TAMIKO GASHKIN: First let me express my profound sadness at the death of my colleague and friend, Jed Streeter. I know his daughter Allison, other family members and his many, many friends are also devastated by his untimely death and my heart reaches out to all of them.

Because, yesterday, by happenstance I was one of the last people to see Jed alive, and this morning, in the company of Boltwood Inn employee Mavis Grady, I discovered his body, it is appropriate that I share what little I know about his untimely death. But, first, a little background.

"Okay," Adley says. "In the interest of time, why don't I skip the next couple of paragraphs about how Jed mentored you on *2+2* and you helped Allison get her college plans together since they're largely unchanged. I'm picking up with paragraph four."

I'm telling you all this because once Allison's applications were submitted just before Christmas, I paid close attention to Jed's and Allison's trip to check out her first choice, Colorado State University. So, yesterday morning, when Allison was told her chances of being admitted were excellent, she, of course, relayed the news to her dad, who happened to be in Boston as part of a media tour for his new movie 1940—Fire in the Air. *Like any proud parent, Jed wished to share this exciting news so drove to Amherst to treat me to a celebration dinner. But, because Jed and I had been out of touch since I left L.A. ten days ago, he didn't realize I was scheduled to play a varsity basketball game last night, an activity that involved my being with the rest of the Amherst's women's team from our early supper at 5:15 p.m. until the game ended a little after 8:30. Unfortunately, this meant that by 4:45 p.m. when Jed called to tell me he was in Amherst, I barely had time to run by his hotel to say a quick hi before joining my team.*

At that point, Jed and I planned to check in with each other after the game in hopes of grabbing a late snack. Sadly, this never happened since after Amherst's emotional victory, I joined my teammates to celebrate, with the result that I didn't talk to Jed by phone until just before 10 o'clock. By then I was feeling the effects of a couple of hard knocks and Jed reported he was tired from his long day and also not feeling well as a result of a recurrence of what he thought was acid indigestion and heartburn. As a result, we rescheduled our celebration for breakfast this morning. However, because I knew Jed had had these same symptoms several times during the filming of 2+2, I suggested that he check with the hotel to see if they had a doctor on call. He replied that he'd just taken a couple of Nexium, was already feeling better and was sure he'd be fine until he got back to L.A. where he had already scheduled what he thought of as a routine physical.

"I'll skip the next paragraph," Adley says, "about when and how Tamiko discovers Jed's body since there were no significant changes. But since there are lots of edits in paragraph seven, please pay close attention."

Associate Dean Amber Thomas of Amherst College, with whom I have been staying, helped me focus on practical next steps. This included contacting Amherst Police Chief Roger Barksdale and notifying several trusted friends and mentors including Ben Fine, Jed's good friend and 2+2's director. At this point it became obvious to all that because of Jed Streeter's worldwide popularity, his untimely death would turn into a huge media event, and that even though my involvement was peripheral, I would inevitably be caught up in it. As perhaps you can imagine, I found this prospect to be intimidating. So, at the suggestion of a family friend, I contacted Northampton attorney Adley Saperstein to ask for help. Relying on Attorney Saperstein's suggestions I have written this detailed statement.

But since I have absolutely nothing to add I have also decided not to do any interviews at this time. Instead I'll spend the two weeks until Amherst College reopens later this month quietly with family and friends. Since I'm a seventeen-year-old full-time college student who loves Ancient Greek language and culture, creative writing and competitive sports, and am not a celebrity, I hope you'll respect my privacy.

Let me conclude by again emphasizing that I'm extremely distressed by the untimely death of my friend and mentor, Jed Streeter. As all his family and many friends know, he was a thoughtful, kind, generous man. Even though I had only a tiny part in the new film 2+2, it was my great pleasure to work with him, and I still find it difficult to believe he is no longer with us.

Sincerely, Tamiko Gashkin

When Adley Saperstein stops reading, Tamiko looks to Amber for her reaction. "I like it," Amber says. "But I wonder if it may come across as disingenuous for Tamiko to claim to be a naive young student when, in fact, she's just appeared in a high-profile movie about sexual shenanigans."

"My thought exactly," the attorney replies. "Tamiko, how about I eliminate the conclusory phrase about your not being a celebrity and punch up the part about how you unexpectedly got your small part in *2+2* through your friendship with Ben Fine's kids, hopefully encouraging the reader to arrive at the conclusion you are an accidental film personality? Can you give me a few more details as to how Ben Fine learned about you?"

As Tamiko explains the detailed chronology of how she got her part, Adley Saperstein interrupts. "Tamiko, I think I have the gist and since time is short, how about I rejigger a sentence or two and we go with that?"

"Thanks, Adley, I can't tell you how much it means to me not to have to appear before a room full of media types this afternoon."

"I'm afraid you're not home and dry yet. The moment the reporters realize that you intend to give them the slip they'll go into bloodhound mode, something they are very good at."

When Amber Thomas makes the left turn from Daggert Street into the Costco parking lot, the gray Ford Fusion perched next to the entrance follows them. After making a loop so as to pull into the adjoining space with her window facing Dean Thomas, the young woman driver holds up her badge. "I'm Officer Patricia Gomez," she says, "your license plate tallies with what I've been given, but do you mind showing me some ID?"

When this is accomplished, Officer Gomez says, "I'll move a couple of spaces over so it doesn't look like we're doing a drug deal."

"How about something to eat?" Dean Thomas asks. "Since I assume your instructions were to keep an eye on Tamiko Gashkin here, why don't I nip into the store and grab all of us some sandwiches?"

"Good idea," the officer says, reaching into her jacket pocket and pulling out a ten-dollar bill. "I could go for tuna on light rye with no mustard or onions."

Finally with a quiet moment to herself, Tamiko sighs as she slumps down in her seat, closes her eyes and sinks into an exhausted trance. Almost immediately her mind's eye fills with Lec's lanky form. But because he stands at the far end of a long football-like field facing away, Tamiko tries to shout, "I'm here, I'm here!" Yet barely able to croak she runs forward, only to see Lec stride away. Now overflowing with anguish, Tamiko is spared further torment when her daydream is interrupted by the sound of a motorcycle accelerating across the Costco parking lot. Somehow recalling that Springfield was once a motorcycle manufacturing center, she is grateful that this one has yanked her back to the here and now. Eyes open, chin up and no whining, she tells herself. Lec is either, still my soulmate, or he isn't, and I'll find out soon enough.

. . . . .

Eyes closed and fists balled, Alec is concentrating on keeping his turbulence-tossed jet from colliding with Texas, when he feels a hand on his shoulder. "Do you have luggage overhead?" the seemingly unfazed cabin attendant asks.

"One medium duffel."

"When the bouncing stops in about fifteen, come on up to one of the free seats in first class. From there you should easily nail your connection."

. . . . .

When Amber Thomas returns holding a paper bag, she invites Officer Gomez to move over to the back seat of her Mazda. As the comforting smell of mayonnaise and mustard fills the car, Amber says, "While I was waiting for the sandwiches I checked the news on my phone. As we already know, the Amherst P.D. has announced Jed's death, and so far that's it. But Tamiko, I'm afraid there's something else you need to hear. Jed Streeter, no surprise, is today's number one internet search request, but you're number two." Then seeing that Sergeant Gomez doesn't know what she's talking about, Amber Thomas adds, "Jed Streeter, the movie star, died last night at a hotel in Amherst."

"And you two are somehow connected to that?" the brown-eyed, round-faced officer asks in a voice that indicates she has just become a lot more interested in her babysitting assignment.

"By coincidence Tamiko happened to be the last person to see Jed Streeter alive yesterday and she also found his body this morning, which is why the powers that be want to keep an eye on her until the autopsy is completed, hopefully very soon."

"Seriously! Like, are you Jed Streeter's girlfriend?" Officer Gomez asks, as she leans forward to get a better look at Tamiko, "Oops, sorry, I guess I should say 'were' now, shouldn't I."

When Tamiko doesn't reply, Dean Thomas says, gently, "Patricia, perhaps you can guess we're in this parking lot precisely because Tamiko is trying to avoid questions like that."

"Sorry, I know it's not my job to bug you," Officer Gomez says to Tamiko, doing her best to sound contrite. "But I finally figured out who you are—the Amherst college student who landed the big part in the movie, right?"

"Not so big, the part, that is," Tamiko replies. "And just so you can relax, I was asleep eight blocks away last night when Jed died of what we're guessing was some kind of heart attack. As soon as the autopsy confirms this, I hope I'll be good to go."

"Tamiko, of course you don't have to answer, but do you mind if I ask how old you are?"

"Seventeen last September."

"I'm twenty-seven," the attractive, solidly-built woman replies, as she pushes her thick black bangs off her forehead. "And since I'm still living with my parents while I go to college at night, I'm guessing more exciting stuff has happened to you in the last few months than has happened to me in the last ten years."

"Be careful what you wish for," Tamiko says wryly. "For sure, I'm ready for a quiet decade."

. . . . .

At 12:47 Amber's phone rings, followed a few seconds later by Officer Gomez's.

Even before the Dean has said thank you and clicked off, Gomez has opened the back door and is climbing out. "The word from on high is that you're good to go," the policewoman says. "And, Tamiko," she adds with a wink, "I never saw you."

"Free at last," Tamiko murmurs, feeling the muscles of her jaw unclench. Then turning to Amber, she asks, "Is there anything else? Did you get details?"

"Nothing beyond the fact that three of the four arteries leading to Streeter's heart were blocked, resulting in a massive coronary. Tamiko, it's just so damn sad, since apparently, if he had gotten a scan when he first experienced symptoms they could have done a bypass, meaning he might have lived another forty years."

Starting to say something, but then knowing from the bitter experience of her dad's seemingly random death under the wheels of a truck, that there are no adequate words, Tamiko uses her sleeve to wipe her eyes. Then, after an extended silence both women experience as prayer, Tamiko asks, "Do you think this means the media will back off trying to chase me down?"

"I wouldn't count on it. Whether exaggerated, or not, I'm guessing that in many people's minds you'll always be tagged as Jed Streeter's last doomed love."

After a pause, Tamiko says in a soft voice, "I guess I sorta was."

"Even so, as we discussed earlier, I'd stick like a tick to the Allison story. But it's just occurred to me that we have another worry. When the press conference ends in Northampton, a gaggle of reporters is sure to flock to my office in Amherst since your statement says you've been staying with me. And if I'm not findable, someone may tumble to the fact that I'm helping you disappear and possibly even uncover my sister's condo."

"Makes sense. So how can I get to NYC on my own so you can get back to Amherst to fend them off?"

"My thought exactly. Let's rule out Bradley International, just over the border in Connecticut, since along with Logan in Boston, it's sure to be the airport they'll check, guessing you may head home to California. So, why don't you google the bus schedule from Springfield to New York, while I look at Amtrak?"

"There's a bus at two-forty that stops a bunch so doesn't arrive until six-thirty," Tamiko says, after a few seconds.

"I worry that gives the media posse way too much time to catch up. And I see here that the next Amtrak doesn't leave Springfield until four o'clock, which is even worse. But suppose you grab a bus west to Albany and then take the train along the Hudson River to New York from there. Of all the places to escape to in this world, Albany has to be near the bottom of most people's lists, so I doubt anyone will immediately suspect you'll head over there. And, to avoid any risk of being identified at Penn Station in New York, you could get off the train at the last stop before the city and Uber in from there.

"According to the schedule I just pulled up, there's an Albany bus in forty minutes. Why not ditch your roller bag and stick your toothbrush and a change of clothes in your book bag? Keep your glasses on, your ski cap pulled down and your coat buttoned and hopefully no one will glance at you twice." Then handing Tamiko an envelope, Amber adds, "The condo address and key are in here. I'll call Giuseppe del Bene, the doorman, so he'll know you're authorized to use it."

"But if he tumbles to who I am, mightn't he rat me out to the media for a few bucks?"

"The del Bene family have shared their very profitable job for decades precisely because, like most N.Y. doormen, they know the difference between seeing and telling."

. . . . .

With less than twenty minutes to cross the Houston Airport, Alec is grateful to follow a petite, quick teenage girl who has obviously made the New York connection before. Still, hoping to contact Tamiko, he asks the gate agent if he has time to use a nearby pay phone. "No problem," the small Black woman replies, tapping her watch, "as long as you can make your call and get back here in less than three minutes." Knowing this isn't going to happen, Alec trails the girl onto the plane.

. . . . .

Amber Thomas drops Tamiko in front of the Greyhound bus station on Springfield's Lyman Street at 1:05. With the collar of her plus-sized black coat pulled up, and her heavy black-rimmed glasses firmly in place, Tamiko wills herself to appear unremarkable as she buys her ticket and uses the bathroom. Choosing a deserted corner bench facing a wall, she calls Vera. The first ring barely sounds when her grandmother answers saying, "*What Russian does not love to drive fast. Which of us does not, at times, yearn to give his horses their head and to let them go and to cry, 'To the devil with the world.'*"

"Nikolai Gogol, from *Dead Souls*, of course," Tamiko says, with a chuckle. "And I assume your choice of quotes means you've heard about me being on the run? But Vera, Gogol notwithstanding, I hope you know my only goal is to drive my horses to a nice, safe barn, not off some angst-filled Russian cliff."

"Of course. And, I so very sorry that your good friend has died. But *Lastichka*, in addition to mourning, try to enjoy little bit of the excitement. I have no doubt, someday you will tell many grandkids about the day you were America's number-one runaway girl. But, where are you now? And, can Stepan and I help you?"

After outlining her plan to get to NYC via a bus to Albany and then Amtrak to the City, Tamiko is saying she's worried reporters may be waiting for her in New York when Vera interrupts, "Hold on while I tell computer to find map." Then, after a short pause, she continues, "I need to check with Stepan, but I think we have plenty of time to meet your train at Poughkeepsie at a little past six, which is maybe one hour north of the City. Then we can drive you rest of way. Oops, maybe I should not tell you this, but picture of you and Jed Streeter looking into each other's eyes, just flash on screen. One thing is sure, my dear, you'd better hide your beautiful hair or someone will be spotting you yesterday."

"What's left is black with purple streaks and short as your pinky," Tamiko replies. "And anyway, I'm wearing a green knit cap pulled down and thick rimmed glasses. And, oh yes, there's also the black eye I picked up at basketball last night. Put it all together, and I look like an escapee from juvenile prison."

"Sounds like good start, but still, keep eyes on shoes, since, I can tell you from long experience some people can recognize you under pillowcase. I text you in a few minutes to confirm Poughkeepsie."

. . . . .

Settled toward the rear of the half-empty Albany-bound Greyhound, Tamiko closes her eyes and begins the deep breathing exercises she learned to help cope with her anxiety attacks after her dad's death. Finally, after half a dozen repetitions, Tamiko feels her heart actually slow. But instead of drifting into a restorative catnap, her tears begin to flow. Not just an eye dampening, but fat wet drops that bead her cheeks and roll down her chin as her mind carries her back to Jed's small hotel room the previous evening.

And it's now that Tamiko realizes she's blubbering not only because of Jed's subsequent death, but from the conviction that she failed him in his moment of need. In December when she'd desperately reached out to Jed, he'd opened his arms despite his mountain of misgivings. But yesterday, when tired, needy, and as it turned out, seriously ill, Jed had appeared on her doorstep, she'd pushed him away. And the fact that she'd had a long list of good reasons for doing so does nothing to stanch her tears.

After a few more minutes of fierce sadness, Tamiko realizes that the grandmotherly woman across the aisle is staring at her with growing concern. Knowing she can't afford to call attention to herself, Tamiko buries her face in the oversized collar of the ratty black coat and reaches for her phone, surprised to see she has over two dozen texts and voicemails. Obviously the media has found her number since most messages are from reporters begging her to return their call. Can they somehow trace my location electronically, she wonders as she double-checks the list to see there's still nothing from Lec. Resolving to ditch the phone as soon as she exits the bus, Tamiko calls Ted Burns in the hope he has news about Lec. When Ted picks up she explains in a whisper that she can listen, but not really talk.

"I'll keep it short," Lec's dad replies. "I've talked to Amber and Adley in the last half hour, so, I gather things are proceeding as best they can. Did you somehow catch all or part of the press conference? Or do you want a quick update?"

"Yes, please."

"To his credit, and maybe to make up for treating you as first cousin to Jack the Ripper earlier, District Attorney Carroll repeatedly emphasized that because the autopsy showed Jed Streeter died from a massive heart attack, there were no ongoing inquiries. When a reporter asked about your involvement, Carroll repeated that since a natural death had been unequivocally established, no one was of interest to law enforcement. Then, after a particularly obnoxious woman persisted by asking if there would be an inquiry into Jed's having come from California to Massachusetts to have sex with a minor, the D.A. gathered his papers, looked at his watch and replied, 'In the ninety seconds since I last responded to that question, the answer hasn't changed.' Then, as Carroll headed for the door, Adley stood to say she represented you and that if anyone was interested she would read your statement. Needless to say, no one moved. When Adley finished there were dozens of shouted questions, most asking for details about your's and Jed's assumed romantic relationship."

"Oh my god, Ted, how did Adley respond?" Tamiko asks, forgetting to whisper.

"She smiled, extended her hands palms up, and said, 'Since that's all my client has to say, that's all I have to say.'"

"So, Ted, what do you think will happen next?" Tamiko whispers anxiously. "Based on the few highish-profile cases I've handled, my guess is that media hysteria around you won't peak for at least a few days. In the short term, your staying out of sight may fuel a *Where's Waldo*-type frenzy, but on balance I still believe it's wise. As the curve of media hysteria inevitably begins to flatten, your friends and colleagues will gradually be heard saying that you are a brainy young athlete trying to live a normal life, not a spoiled starlet who was out to steal Jed's fame and fortune."

Pressing her forehead into the window as she stares at a stubbly winter field, Tamiko whispers, "This is never going to really end, is it?"

"Sadly, I can't argue with that. No doubt, women in retirement facilities still talk about the actresses James Dean dated before his fatal Porsche crash over sixty-five years ago. But fortunately, Tamiko, you're a strong, centered young woman with a load of positive things you want to do in life. Hold on to that, my dear, and all will be well. And just in case you're wondering, after you called me this morning I talked briefly to Lec and put him in the picture."

"Really? I haven't heard from him," Tamiko croaks, her throat suddenly too choked to say more.

"Halfway through our conversation, the cheap phone he'd just bought began to cut out and I haven't been able to reach him since. But I know Lec, and I know how much he cares for you, so I'm betting he'll be in touch as soon as possible."

"Thanks, Ted. And thanks again for your help this morning. I don't know how I would have managed without Adley's help."

. . . . .

Tamiko arrives at the red brick two-story Albany-Rensselaer Amtrak station forty-five minutes before the Lakeshore Limited that originated in Chicago the previous evening is scheduled to arrive. Concerned about being recognized in the busy terminal, she heads out the front entrance. With so many things on her worry list she tosses her iPhone into a dumpster with hardly a pang. Despite the ponderous gray sky and dropping temperature, a fast walk works to blunt her anxiety. With heavy snow forecast she says a little prayer to Mother Nature that it will hold off until she's safely tucked into Dean Thomas's sister's condo.

Bags and coats literally spill from the overhead racks when Tamiko boards the overheated train car. Dismayed that virtually every seat is occupied, she is doubly alarmed when she sees that at least half of the open screens display the same image. But instead of Tom Brady or Aaron Rogers on Super Bowl Sunday, it's Jed Streeter and herself the passengers gawk at. Now almost frantic to get out of view, Tamiko nevertheless worries she'll only call attention to herself if she tries to awaken one of the several sleepers sprawled awkwardly across two seats. Importuning the elderly Black woman to move her pile of teetering luggage off the adjoining seat seems like an even worse plan.

Finally, two-thirds of the way along the car, Tamiko reaches a prim, stylishly dressed, forty-something woman attempting to guard her privacy by placing her designer bag on the empty aisle seat. Hoping to avoid a confrontation, Tamiko says "please" as she motions to the seat. But, when the woman only turns to stare out the window, a now fed-up Tamiko adds, "I'd hate to sit on Ms. Hermes, but you're giving me no alternative." Finally seated, with her book bag perched awkwardly on her lap, Tamiko again pulls her hat low, her coat collar high, and pretends to sleep. Then, remembering that, as a kidlet, her dad had told her the story of the doomed ostrich who tries to hide from a pack of lions by burying her head in the sand, Tamiko grits her teeth and prays for nearsighted lions.

After what Tamiko thinks must be well over an hour, she peeks at her watch and is relieved to see that the train is scheduled to reach Poughkeepsie in twelve minutes. It's only when she sees her own face staring back at her from her seatmate's iPad screen that she realizes just how long that can be. Worried that she may be outed in a matter of seconds, Tamiko twists her torso toward the aisle as she attempts to bury her face further into her black coat. Registering this movement, her sleek neighbor who apparently is now willing to overlook Tamiko's thrift store look says, "I just can't understand what someone like Jed Streeter could possibly see in this odd-looking teenager with giraffe legs, lion's mane hair and cat's eyes. I mean, she's not even attractive, right? And for Jed to go all the way to a tiny town in western Massachusetts to die in her arms is just so very disappointing. I always thought Streeter was a real man, not some kind of Lolita-obsessed sicko. Of course, everyone understood why he broke up with that witch ex-wife, but really, this girl is barely two years older than my daughter, who still wears braces! I can't be the only one who thinks she must be a world-class slut, right? So what do you think?" the woman asks as she turns forty-five degrees to face Tamiko.

Clueless as to how to respond, Tamiko stands and mumbles she doesn't really know who Jed Streeter is. Trying her best to keep her face averted, she then makes her way the short distance to the end of the car. As Tamiko pushes through the heavy door to enter the comparative privacy of the vestibule, her feeling of momentary relief is interrupted when a preppily-dressed young woman says, "Hi there." Politely sliding her roller bag complete with prominent Vassar sticker to one side, the coiffed blonde fixes her prominent blue eyes on Tamiko. Again, certain she's seconds from being busted, Tamiko removes her hat and glasses and points at her black eye as she says, "Sorry, I know I must look way scary. It's like my boyfriend got drunk and hit me last night, which is why I took off this morning when he went to meet with his probation officer. It's like, I'm trying to get to get to Kingston, where I hope I can stay with my sister who can also maybe lend me a few dollars."

"I'm so sorry," Ms. Vassar mumbles as she turns to the door, any notion she's discovered the celebrity runaway, replaced by her fear this battered girl will ask for money.

. . . . .

As if to prove his Russian sixth sense, Stepan stands within a few feet of the door when Tamiko steps down from the Lakeshore Limited at Poughkeepsie. "Let's hug for long moment to let the others hustle away," Stepan says as he wraps Tamiko in his long arms. "There is woman by stairs who looks a little curious, but I doubt she focus on elderly man greeting goth granddaughter. But, if she says something, keep walking. Vera is parked in handicapped space with engine turning. Nothing will make her happier than to be out of here *skoro*."

Safely in the Audi a few minutes later, Tamiko says, "Thank you both! Seriously, if I'd been on that train another five minutes I'd have been outed for sure. The only thing that saved me was that everyone was so intent on watching Jed and me on their screens, they barely looked up. But, oh my god, if the Spa Queen in the next seat is an accurate indicator of public sentiment, I'm in danger of being stoned."

"Probably like half women in country, she's had mad crush on Jed Streeter since *Moonscape*," Vera replies. "I know it make little sense, but I suspect she cover up sadness about his death by blaming young lover she see as poor substitute for herself. You would be surprised at how much anger and jealousy both Stepan and I collected in years when we perform."

"But I thought you two were everyone's favorite couple? I mean, I looked up a bunch of reviews and it seemed as if people adored you."

"On surface," Stepan says, as he points to the entrance to the interstate, which in the dusk Vera is in danger of speeding past. "But loads of men, and probably a fair number of women, would get mad crush on Vera and so dislike me, and I suppose it might sometimes also happen the other way."

"Ha! Now there be understatement of month," Vera says drily. "But listen, *milaya moya*, enough about things that don't matter. How are you this crazy day?"

When Tamiko doesn't immediately reply, her grandmother starts to say something.

Then, thinking better of it, she lets the silence rest.

"I'm not sure," Tamiko finally says in a small voice. "Out of, like, nowhere, I cried a small river on the bus. Then, in Albany, I took a fast walk and had a Coke and muffin and sorta got a grip. But still, I can't get past the feeling I somehow let Jed down."

"Nonsense," Stepan barks. "Medical report makes clear you had not one tiny bit to do with Streeter's death. To take responsibility for one's actions in this world is good thing, but to put self at center of made-up drama, is not. That he has heart attack can never be your fault."

Pausing for a moment to see if Tamiko will respond, Vera finally says, "*Lyubov moya*—as far as I can see, Jed Streeter had two main pleasures in last weeks before his death, seeing his daughter begin to grab hold of good future, and loving you. Since you made both possible, you should be proud of happiness you brought him. Beyond that, as Stepan say, nothing is your fault. But like any true Russian woman, it is also correct that when a lover dies you must pull out your hair, tear your clothes, and cry an ocean of tears."

"Thanks," Tamiko says simply. "Jed was just such a dear, dear man, but the weird truth is that even when I mourn for him I think of Lec and wish he was here to hold my hand."

. . . . .

After Alec comes through security in New York he eventually spots one of the few legacy pay phones, inserts his credit card and taps Tamiko's number. When the call goes to voicemail he hangs up and calls his dad. After receiving a typically efficient review of the day's events, which includes the address of the condo Tamiko is heading for, Alec asks if Tamiko knows he's coming.

"Because I wasn't absolutely sure myself," Ted Burns replies, "I told her only that I had talked to you."

Stepping outside a minute later wearing only his light windbreaker,

Alec is slugged by a wind so piercingly icy he considers heading back into the terminal to buy a sweatshirt. But since, even this minor detour seems like a betrayal of his determination to reach Tamiko as soon as possible, he hunches his shoulders as he heads toward the taxi stand to join the queue of wool- and down-draped citizens. Mercifully the cab has heat. But it also has a radio which the cabbie has turned at top volume to a Spanish-language news station that bellows excitedly about Jed Streeter's shocking death and the flight of his stunning young lover. Streeter, the announcer claims, was so completely hypnotized by seventeen-year-old Tamiko Gashkin, he followed her to a small town in Massachusetts even though he knew that without immediate medical help he would die. Then, as the broadcaster continues to pile fantasy on top of guesstimate, Alec asks the driver in Spanish to please switch to a music station.

"*Por supuesto*," the cabbie replies. Then almost shouting in fluent English over the inevitable mariachi band, he adds, "My wife and daughters loved Jed Streeter. They're never going to understand what he saw in this teenage girl. But one thing is sure, when I get home they will blame me for everything that's happened."

"Blame you?" Alec asks surprised.

"All men are so stupid, they will say, they always fall for bimbos with too much blondie hair and Barbie bodies. But for me, I think maybe this Tamiko is nice girl who feels so sad about what happened she wants to hide away from all those bullshit reporters. Of course, if I say this, I don't get my supper, so instead, will make silent prayer for her to be safe."

Sweet, Alec thinks as they exit the 59th Street Bridge into Manhattan and turn north to cut across Central Park at 76th Street. The snow, which a moment before had been barely a flurry, now begins to fall in earnest.

"Very cold outside, how come you have no coat?" the cabbie asks.

"I got a call about a family emergency when I was in Mexico," Alec replies, "and I haven't had a moment to spare."

"I hope everything will be all right."

"Me too," Alec says, loudly enough to be heard over the music. And then, more quietly to himself, repeats, "me too."

. . . . .

As Vera pilots the Audi across the Henry Hudson Bridge from the Bronx to Manhattan, the intermittent snow showers merge into a thin white curtain. "Barring heavy traffic, we about fifteen minutes out," Stepan says. "But, my phone tells me it's about to come down thick and hard."

"But what about you two?" Tamiko asks, as if suddenly realizing that she's not the only one with needs. "Oh my god, I hope you're not planning to drive back to Connecticut tonight in…"

"It's going to be a major storm, so we made reservation at the Carlyle for two nights," Vera interrupts.

"Was our favorite suite free?" Stepan asks.

"Not until Gabriela bribed current occupants with free dinner to move down the hall," Vera replies happily.

"You guys have a favorite suite in a favorite hotel?" Tamiko asks, admiringly.

"Romance, like wine, improves with age," Stepan says with a chuckle.

"As long as you don't fall asleep first," Vera adds with a grin so wide Tamiko is sure this isn't likely.

Turning onto West 85th Street, Vera strains to see the condo's address through what now is a nearly opaque wall of white. "I'm guessing it's next awning on right," Stepan says tentatively, as Vera guides the car to the curb behind a taxi whose back door has just popped open. When a tall guy in a light jacket holding a duffel climbs out, Tamiko's heart does an excited backflip. But, having so often been fooled in the last few months when her wishful imagination mistakenly conjured up Lec, she strains to be sure it's really him.

"Why that guy looks a lot like Alec," Stepan says, as he turns to face his granddaughter in the back seat. But, Tamiko, who is now sure this is true, is already out of the car.

"What now?" Stepan asks Vera. "Do we wait to see what happens?"

"Did you forget we have our own date," Vera responds, as with two toots of the horn she pulls away from the curb.

Tamiko quick-steps toward Alec, who having said "*Adios*" to the cabbie, turns in her direction. Suddenly slammed by her own shyness she stops. As the snow quickly blankets them both, she says, "If I had a book I'd drop it," recalling how they met eighteen months before when Lec had rescued her errant copy of *The Brothers Karamazov*.

"No need, since this time I'd catch it before it hit the ground and never give it back."

"Truly?"

"Truly."

"Just so you know, I got a haircut," Tamiko says, as she pulls off her cap.

"It goes beautifully with your black eye," Alec replies, as he steps forward, long arms extended.

Still rooted in place, Tamiko says, "Lec, I want to say something—two things actually."

"Out here in the cold. Really?" Alec asks as he lowers his arms.

"Since I've rehearsed a dozen times it won't take long."

"Okay, sure."

"First, you were right that each of us needed to learn how to live on our own. Even if it was a lesson that nearly killed me this fall. Second, no matter where, when or how, I plan to love and be bonded with you until I die."

"Do I get to respond?"

"They were statements, not questions," Tamiko replies, now stepping so close to Lec that the skinniest snowflake can't squeeze between.

"Then, how about I save my response until after I kiss you, bed you, and if memory serves, feed you enough for three."

"Sounds perfect, as long as you hang in when I push the repeat button," Tamiko says, as she presses her lips to his.

THE END

ACKNOWLEDGMENTS

Toni Ihara massaged every word of the *Lost in Transition* manuscript at least half-a-dozen times. Without her many positive suggestions, throat-clearings and straight-out admonitions, it would have to be renamed, *Lost with No Possibility of Transition*.

Ilene Gordon, a talented writer and friend, contributed much inspired line editing, and also let me know in no uncertain terms when she didn't approve of what a character was doing, or saying. Although I sometimes initially resisted her objections, when I eventually accepted the need for a rethink, the book got better.

I am also extremely grateful to my author friend Heather Merriam, who made a number of character and plot development suggestions as well as frequently challenging me to get deeper into my characters' psyches. *"Jake, clever dialogue isn't nearly enough if the reader doesn't know how the character feels."*

Ken Armistead was my expert on all things Japanese (except of course, any mistakes). Not only was Ken kind enough to walk me around key areas of Tokyo, he and his wife Mai Hagimoto helped orient me to what I can only inadequately describe as the Japanese sense of humor.

Toshi Ihara, surfer par excellence, made a number of valuable improvements to the Puerto Escondido and Sayulita sections. Growing up in the New York area I learned many practical things, but sadly how to ride a ten-foot wave wasn't one of them.

With the benefit of his long experience as a cardiologist, my friend Michael Gordon helped me with *Lost in Transition's* medical sections.

Irene Barnard, who proofread my flea-spotted manuscript, not only fixed much errant grammar and punctuation, caught an embarrassing number of mistakes, but also made many creative editorial suggestions.

Huge thanks to Susan Putney, who not only turned my manuscript pages into this hefty book, but also so brilliantly designed the arresting cover. Every time I pick up *Lost in Transition*, I give Susan a bow of gratitude.

Finally, Jaleh Doane always has my back on this and all my projects.

ABOUT THE AUTHOR

JAKE WARNER is the author of *Murder on the Air* and *Coming of Age in Berkeley* (with Toni Ihara) as well as a number of acclaimed children's stories including *Sheriff Daisy and Deputy Bud, The Tibbodnock Stories,* and *Clem, the Detective Dog.* He is also the cofounder of Nolo, America's leading source of consumer law information. Among his many nonfiction titles is the best-selling, *Get a Life: You Don't Need a Million to Retire Well.* Warner lives in Berkeley, CA with his wife Toni Ihara.

Made in the USA
Middletown, DE
28 November 2022

15870552R00265